"THIS IS A TRAP!"

"Yeah, I know," Lyons growled, slipping a hand inside his windbreaker to loosen the Colt Python in his shoulder holster. "I just spotted it a second ago."

The other men needed no further encouragement to get their own weapons ready for combat, and the van was filled with the soft metallic clicks of working arming bolts and safeties disengaging. Every car in the parking lot was dusty and badly needed to be washed, as if they had been there for days without moving. This was exactly the sort of detail that a street cop looked for to spot an abandoned vehicle parked along a busy downtown street. Now a grieving family might leave a car here for a few hours, or even overnight, but certainly no longer than that, and not ten of them. That was way beyond the limits of probability. These cars were merely window decorations to make the place look more inviting and less empty. Which meant the entire cemetery was a trap. But was it for them or somebody else? Did the enemy know Able Team had arrived, or were they still waiting for a target? Only one way to find out, and that was to go ask them, face-to-face.

The soft recon had just gone hard.

DON PENDLETON'S

STONY

AMERICA'S ULTRA-COVERT INTELLIGENCE AGENCY

MAN®

EXTREME INSTINCT

A GOLD EAGLE BOOK FROM

WORLDWIDE®

TORONTO • NEW YORK • LONDON
AMSTERDAM • PARIS • SYDNEY • HAMBURG
STOCKHOLM • ATHENS • TOKYO • MILAN
MADRID • WARSAW • BUDAPEST • AUCKLAND

Recycling programs
for this product may
not exist in your area.

First edition August 2010

ISBN-13: 978-0-373-61992-4

EXTREME INSTINCT

Special thanks and acknowledgment to
Nick Pollotta for his contribution to this work.

Printed in U.S.A.

EXTREME INSTINCT

PROLOGUE

Caucasus Mountains, Russia

A cold winter wind was blowing through the forest preserve, and the full moon illuminating the land with a clear silvery light made everything look as if it was cast in steel.

Rumbling steadily over the rough terrain, the BTR-70 "Battering Ram" armored personnel carrier plowed through a thick wall of shrubbery and came to a halt in a small clearing on the side of a hill. The dense stillness was only disturbed by the soft ticking of the massive diesel engines as they began to cool. Down in the valley below, the darkness twinkled with a million lights of the top-secret Russian army weapons facility code-named Mystery Mountain.

"Something is wrong here," muttered the master sergeant inside the APC, resting scarred hands on top of the steering yoke. The curved banks of twinkling controls illuminated his stern features.

In the rear of the vehicle, the troops angled around in their jumpseats to look out the numerous gunports. Several worked the arming bolts on their new AK-108 assault rifles.

"What is it, Sarge?" a stocky woman asked, squinting into the night. "Think we got some more TV reporters nosing about?"

"Don't know yet," the master sergeant replied slowly, trying to put into words a gut instinct honed in a thousand fights.

"Looks peaceful enough to me, Sarge," a private countered, craning his neck to glance outside.

The powerful halogen headlights of the BTR-70 banished the night, giving the recon platoon a clear view of the surrounding area. The forest was beautiful, old pine trees rising majestically into the starry sky and a thick blanket of laurel bushes covering the ground, the red winter berries glistening among the greenery like hidden jewels.

Somewhere nearby, an owl hooted and was answered by a lake loon. The master sergeant tensed slightly at that. Odd, we're nowhere near water...

"Sir! Radar reads clean, sir," a young recruit reported crisply, both hands working the compact monitoring station in the rear of the APC. The other soldiers merely grunted at the pronouncement and tried not to show their opinion of the young boot.

"Be sure to check the sonar," one of the older veterans muttered sarcastically.

The green recruit immediately started activating the underwater controls on the amphibian APC before he paused, then darkly scowled. "Blow it out your ass," he whispered out of the corner of his mouth.

Amused, the other soldiers openly grinned.

"Shut up, all of you," the master sergeant growled uneasily, reaching down to loosen the service automatic holstered at his side. "There is something wrong here. I can feel it."

The troops prepared to go EVA, pulling on insulated gloves and tightening the scratchy wool scarves around their throats. There was no snow on the ground, but the standing joke was that Russian winters killed more people than Stalin ever had. It was probably true, in spite of the best efforts of the bloodthirsty madman.

Just then the radio crackled. "Base to Wolf Nine, why are you not moving?" a voice demanded. "Confirm status, please."

Taking the hand mike, the master sergeant thumbed it alive. "Wolf Nine to Base, we…that is, I…." The master sergeant paused awkwardly, unwilling to tell the duty officer that he had stopped a security patrol because of a bad feeling. He did sense that something was out of place, but everything looked fine on the hillside.

"Wolf Nine, report!" the speaker demanded.

"All clear, Base," the master sergeant said, throwing the APC into gear and lurching into motion. "Nothing wrong here. We were just…using the bushes."

There came a friendly chuckle. "Can't blame you for that," said the voice over the speaker. "I'd also be guzzling coffee out in that bitter cold."

"Confirm, Base," the master sergeant replied, checking the rearview monitor one last time for anything suspicious in the clearing. "Wolf Nine back on patrol. Over and out."

AS THE SOUNDS of the APC rumbled off into the distance, the leafy ground cover stirred and five figures slowly rose like ghosts escaping from the grave.

Covered with frost and dirt, the Foxfire team was dressed in camouflage gillie suits, twigs and leaves deliberately attached to the material as additional disguise. Their faces were streaked with different colors of paint, and insulated hoods covered their heads to help keep them warm and also to hide their throat-mike radios.

Scanning the area with a pair of stolen Russian night-vision goggles, Andrew Lindquist checked for any guards, either human or mechanical. "The zone is clear," he announced, tucking the goggles away into a belt pouch. "Everybody okay?"

"No. Jimmy's dead," George Hannigan stated bluntly, looking down at the tread marks of the APC on the ground. Off to the side there was a slowly spreading dark patch in the soil, a bent human finger sticking out.

"The goddamn thing must have parked right on top of him," Sonia Johansen stormed, shifting her grip on an old AK-47 assault rifle. The cylindrical silencer attached to the end of the compact weapon gave it a futuristic appearance, and oddly, no moonlight reflected off the dull black metal. On this mission, every piece of equipment was either Russian made or legally purchased in the country. Even the military crossbows. Misdirection had always been the best friend of any mercenary.

"Same thing happened to me," John Barrowman said through clenched teeth, cradling his left arm. The limb was bent at an impossible angle, the sleeve of the gillie suit torn and spotty with blood.

"Let me give you a shot for the pain," Saul Kessler offered, swinging around a small Red Army medical kit.

"Can't." Barrowman grunted. "The drugs'll make me fuzzy. Gotta stay sharp. This is too important."

"Agreed," stated Lindquist, reaching inside his gillie suit to pull out a map. "Which is why you're going back to the escape vehicle to wait for us."

Barrowman frowned. "But, sir…"

"That was an order, mister," Lindquist said, tucking away the map once more.

Their employer had not raised his voice, but the mercenary reacted as if he had. Stiffening, Barrowman snapped a salute with his good arm and moved off into the forest, soon disappearing into the darkness and the shrubbery. The man had five miles to cover, and his left arm was useless.

"Think we'll see him again?" Kessler asked, rubbing his jaw with the back of a gloved hand.

"Let's go," Lindquist said, turning to proceed down the sloping hill.

Moving fast and low, the rest of the mercenaries skirted past the access road and the creek, keeping to the trees. Reaching the halfway point, they went motionless under a spreading oak as a Mi-28 Havoc helicopter gunship moved overhead, a blinding searchlight sweeping the roadway and creek.

"Damn, these guys are predictable," Hannigan subvocalized into a throat mike. The softly spoken words could not have been heard a foot away, but the rest of the Foxfire team heard them crystal-clear in their earbuds.

Clearly annoyed, Lindquist slashed a thumb across his throat for total silence. The burly mercenary nodded in understanding. The team was very close to Mystery Mountain, and God alone knew what kind of security the Russians had there.

The complex was rumored to be three times the size of NORAD high command at Cheyenne Mountain, which sounded very impressive but was also a great weakness. That much land could not be securely guarded without using so many troops that you gave away its location to enemy satellites.

As the Havoc gunship moved away, Hannigan pulled out a sonic probe and moved it around the sky and then along the roadway. When the passive sensor detected no other Russian troops or aircraft, he gave a thumbs-up to the others, and the team went on the move again. Only a few yards later Johansen detected a cluster of land mines on an EM scanner, and they skirted the area. Officially, land mines were banned in Russia, but here at Mystery Mountain, the military was free of most legal restrictions and did whatever it wanted.

Heading away from the clusters of bright lights that marked the military base, Lindquist and the mercenaries soon reached a cliff that overlooked a forlorn section of the valley. The landscape below was bare dirt and rock, the material churned and burned as if it had been strafed by a thousand heavy bombers. The only plant life was a few resilient weeds growing out of the bomb craters. Lindquist thought it resembled the dark side of the moon and was the most beautiful thing he had ever seen.

Down in the dried river, a full company of armed Russian soldiers walked alongside a BMW flatbed hauling a large cylinder of burnished steel. The object rested in a wooden cradle and was securely strapped into position with several heavy canvas belts.

Judging the cylinder against the height of the soldiers, Lindquist would guess it was just about the right size to fit snugly inside a SS-X-27 Topol missile. He had not expected anything so huge and immediately began to adjust his plans accordingly. This was going to be tricky....

Four armored scout cars flanked the procession, the drivers bulky with body armor, the young gunners standing behind the heavy machine guns alert and suspiciously watching the hillsides through infrared goggles.

Their breath fogging, several of the older technicians dressed in white lab coats fiddled with the controls set into the flat end of the cylinder. Their words were lost in the distance. One of them removed his glasses to make a suggestion. The others eagerly agreed, and more internal corrections were made. Suddenly a bank of lights changed colors and the technicians closed an access hatch, locking it into place with crescent wrenches.

At the sight, Lindquist felt his smile fade away. Son of a bitch! The soldiers were right on time, but the goddamn technicians were ahead of schedule. The T-bomb was live!

"Sir..." Kessler started to ask.

"This changes nothing!" Lindquist snapped, pulling a radio detonator from his belt. "We must have that bomb. End of discussion."

But even as he spoke the words, a gunner in one of the scout cars jerked his head in their direction and shouted something to the driver.

"They know we're here," Hannigan cursed, working the bolt on his silenced assault rifle.

"Too bad for them," Lindquist snarled, flipping back the cover and pressing a button as if thrusting a dagger into the heart of a hated enemy.

In the next microsecond the two weeks of work by the camouflaged mercenaries paid off as a series of explosions ripped along the riverbed. The fiery blasts threw the scout cars and pieces of the soldiers high into the cold night air. The flatbed rocked from the concussions, but did not flip.

The Foxfire team was amazed at the sight. The armored truck was completely undamaged. This crazy plan might just work after all!

Heads reeling from the ringing concussions of the detonations, the battered technicians barely had a chance to recover before a second explosion came from somewhere in the far distance. They flinched at the noise, then relaxed somewhat. However the new detonation kept building in volume and power, until the very ground itself shook.

Even as the truck driver turned off the engine of the flatbed, a strange and terrible light began to brighten the darkness until a fiery column rose above the craggy hills to form the classic mushroom cloud of a nuclear explosion. Instantly every light in the entire valley winked out and the earbuds of the team went dead. But that was part of the plan. The EMP blast of a tactical nuke permanently fried every piece of electronics within the blast radius. Until shielded equipment was brought out of storage, nobody at the military facility could call for help. This gave the mercenaries a window of several minutes. Hopefully, it would be enough.

Resting her AK-47 assault rifle on a shoulder, Johansen started to speak when unexpectedly something dropped out of the sky. A few seconds later there came the whine of a helicopter spinning out of control and the Havoc gunship crashed into the trees on the opposite side of the valley.

Down at the flatbed, the technicians were frantically shouting into radios for help. Except for one man with silver hair and thick glasses. Fumbling in his pockets, the scientist unearthed a keycard from his clothing. It was attached to his belt with a slim chain.

"That's him!" Lindquist stated.

Aiming their crossbows, Kessler and Johansen fired, the long quarrels slamming into the scientist. Gushing blood, he tumbled off the flatbed, and the mercenaries fired again, pinning him securely to a truck tire.

"Do it again," Lindquist snapped just as a hot wind blew along the valley, rustling every tree and sending flocks of startled birds streaming into the starry heavens.

"Too late!" Hannigan shouted.

Quickly, Lindquist and the mercenaries grabbed the nearest tree and held on tight. Somewhere a pistol shot rang out, closely followed by another, then several more that became a fusillade of rounds, the crackling rising in volume until it was a near deafening roar. The wind abruptly turned bitterly cold as a wave of blackness swelled from the distant mountains.

"Here it comes!" Kessler shouted, closing his eyes.

Rapidly growing in power, the tidal wave of escaping water from the nuked hydroelectric dam thundered along the dried riverbed. The deluge was filled with the countless bodies of Russian soldiers, civilians, motorcycles, cars and jetfighters.

Unstoppable, the Mystery Mountain lake poured over the flatbed, sweeping up the score of fresh corpses and the screaming technicians. For a chaotic minute, the valley was awash with turbulent waters, the foaming rush almost reaching the mercenary team. Then the rampaging cascade subsided, leaving the muddy ground covered with mounds of wreckage. All of the bodies were gone, washed completely away, except for the one scientist pinned to the tire of the armored flatbed. During the deluge, the vehicle had shifted position by a hundred yards, only to become trapped by the outcroppings of bedrock jutting up from the old riverbed.

Checking the radiation counter strapped to his wrist, Lindquist grunted in annoyance and dropped his backpack to retrieve a protective NBC environment suit. Stepping inside, he zipped it closed and quickly started down the slippery slope toward the flatbed lying sideways amid the assorted debris. The steel cylinder was clearly still strapped to the truck and, aside from dripping water, seemed completely undamaged. Excellent.

Donning their own protective suits, Hannigan and Johansen followed Lindquist, leaving Kessler alone on the hillside, thumbing a fat 30 mm round into the grenade launcher attached beneath the barrel of the AK-47.

Going to the sodden corpse pinned to the truck tire, Lindquist used a pair of bolt cutters to free the keycard. Climbing onto the flatbed, he fumbled to find the slot on the end of the T-bomb, then slipped the keycard inside. There was a soft beep, then the service panel disengaged and swung open wide. Knowing that all of the controls had been reversed as a security measure, Lindquist calmly pressed the detonation button on a small keypad. There was a brief buzzing, and he stopped breathing. But the internal lights dimmed and faded away completely.

"It's deactivated," Lindquist announced, tucking the precious card into a belt pouch, which he zipped shut. His hands were shaking from the adrenaline overload, and the man was glad the bulky NBC suit hid the fact from the combat veterans.

Suddenly machine gun fire erupted and a BTR-70 jounced out of the forest, a dozen weapons chattering from every gunport of the armored personnel carrier.

Caught in the glare of the halogen headlights, Lindquist stepped protectively in front of the T-bomb as Hannigan and

Johansen blindly fired back with their assault rifles. Both of the mercenaries knew full well that even if they managed to achieve a hit, the 7.62 mm rounds wouldn't even dent the heavy armor plating the military juggernaut. However, safely off to the side, Kessler had a clear view. Swinging up his AK-47, he aimed and fired the grenade launcher.

The yellow-tipped round slammed into the front of the APC, punched clean through and violently detonated inside.

Tendrils of flame extending from every vent and port, the APC raced past the flatbed. Kessler put another million-dollar round into the rear compartment. The depleted-uranium slug penetrated the armor plating as if it were cardboard, then the thermite charge violently exploded inside the working engine, filling the interior with a maelstrom of shrapnel.

Gushing fuel and blood, the decimated BTR-70 continued up the other side of the riverbed and rolled into the trees, careening off a boulder before vanishing into the night.

Returning to their work, the mercs diligently released the restraining straps, while Lindquist fired a flare into the air. With the radios dead, it was their only way to communicate over long distance. However the message was received, and soon Barrowman arrived in an old Soviet-era truck. The Cold War vehicle had been built long before the invention of electronic ignition and fuel injectors, and thus was completely immune to the neutralizing effects of a nuclear EMP blast.

"Think they'll ever figure out what really happened?" Hannigan chuckled, pulling out a crescent wrench from the tool belt around his NBC suit.

"Not until it's too late," Lindquist snarled hatefully, patting the keycard safe in the belt pouch. "Not until it's all over, and there is a new world order."

"Thought this was about protecting America?" Johansen asked sharply, beginning to work on a restraining bolt.

"Shut up, and work faster," Lindquist countered, walking over to the waiting Soviet Union truck, his face an iron mask.

CHAPTER ONE

Whitehead River, Colorado

Standing waist-deep in the chilly runoff, Harold Brognola found the morning Rocky Mountain air more than invigorating; it was damn near rejuvenating. With each passing hour, he could feel the pressures of his job at the Justice Department slipping away, muscles slowly relaxing. The top cop in America found himself involuntarily whistling.

Carefully keeping the split-cane fly rod in constant motion, Brognola let the line out, then the artificial fly touched the surface of the river. A large trout rose into view as it tried to reach the elusive food, then flipped back into the shadowy depths, slashing its tail in frustration.

"Better luck next time," Brognola chuckled, loosening the line to disengage a tangle. Fly-fishing was proving to be a lot like his regular line of work. There was a great deal of waiting and watching, then strike hard and kill when necessary.

Suddenly a dozen trout flashed past his waders heading upstream. Turning, the puzzled man watched them head for the pool below the waterfall. Okay, that was odd. Then the whistling stopped and his smile faded away as a dozen more trout flashed by in the same direction, closely followed by an entire school of sunfish and then several big-mouth bass.

Jerking his head downstream, Brognola saw nothing coming his way. Still he hurriedly sloshed through the river toward the nearby bank. Scrambling onto dry land, he shrugged off the suspenders and dropped the heavy waders, then sprinted for his car parked alongside the old gravel road.

Reaching the vehicle, Brognola yanked open the passenger door and reached under the seat to haul out a S&W .38 revolver and a brand-new Glock 18. The Smith & Wesson had been with the Justice man since his tour of duty in the old Mafia Wars, but middle age was taking its inevitable toll and the massive firepower of the deadly Glock machine pistol was a welcome addition. As Bolan liked to say, a man could never have too many friends or too much firepower. True words.

Working the slide on the 9 mm machine pistol, Brognola thumbed back the hammer on the police revolver and took a defensive position behind the car. It wasn't much, but some protection was better than nothing.

The sound of the approaching vehicle could be heard long before it appeared around a bend in the Whitehead River. Charging along the riverbed, the tires of a big Hummer threw out a wide spray, creating a traveling rainbow behind the speeding military transport. The soldiers wore the uniforms of Green Berets, and the men in the back openly carried M-16 assault rifles.

Vaguely, Brognola remembered there was a military base somewhere in the nearby mountains, but could not recall the exact name. However, if these were fake soldiers, the killers had done an excellent job. As far as he could tell, these were the real thing. He tightened his grip on both weapons. But a fool often dropped his guard for a friendly, smiling face. As the director of the Special Operations Group, Brognola had made a host of enemies over the years, and he had simply accepted it as part of the job that someday, somewhere, they would find him alone and extract a terrible revenge.

Barreling out of the river, the driver parked the Hummer on the sloped bank. A lieutenant stepped out and started to give a salute, but stopped himself just in time and changed the gesture into removing his cap.

Brognola grunted. So far, so good. Soldiers did not salute civilians. But he was still far from being convinced. "Morning," Brognola called, leveling both guns. "What can I do for you, Lieutenant?" The man's heart was pounding in his chest, but his palms were dry.

"Recognition code, Alpha Dog Bravo," the officer said crisply, then waited expectantly.

"Zulu Tango Romeo," Brognola replied, giving the countersign for the week and lowering the guns. "Okay, what the hell is going on here?"

"Sir, somebody needs to speak to you immediately. Your cell is out of range, so our CO sent us out on recon," the lieutenant explained, donning the soaked cap. "Since everybody knows about this fishing pool, we checked here first."

"Fair enough," Brognola said, tucking the Glock into his belt. The service revolver was slipped into a pocket of his jeans. "That somebody got a name?"

"Yes, sir. Eagle One."

Instantly all reticence was gone and Brognola walked over to the Hummer, holding out a hand. As he got close, the corporal in the back proffered a hand mike attached to a large transmitter situated between the seats.

Accepting the mike, Brognola impatiently waited while the soldiers moved away from the vehicle to give him some privacy. They might not be sure who he was, but they sure as hell knew the identity of Eagle One.

When the Green Berets were far enough away, Brognola thumbed the transmit switch and repeated his name, slow and clear. There was a brief pause as the signal was encoded and relayed across the continent via a series of military satellites.

Once NSA equipment on the other side analyzed his vocal patterns to ascertain it actually was him, a familiar voice crackled over the speaker.

"Sorry for the interruption, Hal," said the President without a preamble. "But I needed to talk to you immediately, and there was no time to fly you back to D.C. We have a problem in Russia."

"Is Striker in trouble?" Brognola asked.

Striker was one of the many code names for Mack Bolan.

"Not at the moment, Hal, no. This is something completely different," the President stated. "Just a few hours ago, a NATO courier delivered a coded report to the joint chiefs. One of their spy satellites detected a tactical nuclear explosion near Mystery Mountain."

"But that is not a nuclear facility," Brognola said, sitting inside the Hummer. The seat was damp from the rush up the river, but he paid it no mind. "The mountain mostly works on experimental weapons, plasma lasers, coil guns, orbiting kinetics, microwaves, robotics and such."

"Correct. And this was nothing new. Just an ordinary nuclear weapon." The President paused. "Except that the flash signature was Chinese."

The words were said quite simply, but Brognola exhaled as if punched in the stomach. China nuked Mystery Mountain? "Has that been confirmed?" he demanded brusquely.

"Triple checked from multiple sources." The President sighed. "There can be no mistake. The nuclear weapons of every nation are completely different, and the flash signature of the fireball cannot be faked to resemble another. This was a Chinese nuke."

"Son of a bitch," Brognola whispered. "How could a goddamn Chinese ICBM get that far inside Russia without being shot down?"

A scholarly man, the new President really did not approve of the crude language, but said nothing. Brognola had to be accepted on his terms, and thus was one of the very few people in the world who could address him this way. "It wasn't an ICBM," he corrected. "Just a tactical nuke. Barely a half-kiloton yield. Probably a suitcase model, very similar to our own man-portable charge."

"Well, that's something, then." Brognola sighed, looking across the river. "There could not have been that much damage. With any luck—"

"Hal, the base was obliterated. Utterly destroyed."

"With a tactical nuke?" Brognola scoffed. "That's not possible, sir, unless... Goddamn it, the Chinese nuked the dam and flooded the base."

There was an affirmative grunt. "As usual, Hal, you are correct. The death toll is in the thousands and the base will never fully recover. There is simply too much contamination."

"The Kremlin must be going insane."

"That's putting it mildly," the President agreed. "Their president has already contacted me to remind me of our mutual defense pact."

Which was the first step toward declaring open war, Brognola realized, shifting the Glock in his belt to a more comfortable position. A goddamn nuclear war. "Any response from China?"

"They say it is a Russian trick, and are massing troops along the border to repel a possible invasion."

"Which means Russia is doing the same thing to stop them from invading. Right?"

"Actually no," the President said, speaking slowly. "The Kremlin has authorized a full mobilization, land, sea and air, almost everything they have. However, all of it is heading toward Mystery Mountain. Not China."

"But why—?" Brognola inhaled sharply. "China had nothing to do with this—the nuke was a goddamn diversion."

The man ran stiff fingers through his hair. "Something was stolen from Mystery Mountain," he stated with conviction. "Something new, and big."

"Sadly, that is the same conclusion that my chief of staff, the national security adviser and I each arrived at about an hour ago," the President stated forcibly. "We have no idea what this new weapon could be, but the very fact that the thieves used a nuclear weapon to obtain the device clearly indicates it is more powerful. You don't use a rocket launcher to steal a handgun."

"Unless a rocket launcher is all you have," Brognola countered, momentarily lost in thought. "Could this have been done by some terrorist organization? Maybe Hamas, or the Warriors of God?" There was a brief surge of static and any response was lost.

"Sir? I missed that," Brognola said. "Please repeat."

"I said that terrorists doing this is most unlikely, but we should not rule out the possibility," the President acknowledged. "This might even be the work of some lone madman trying to bring back the glory days of communism."

God forbid. "What has been done so far, sir?"

There came the rustling of papers. "Homeland Security is trying to confirm if China is innocent or is working through some mercenary group. The CIA is concentrating on the larger terrorist organizations. Military Intelligence is looking into the radical splinter groups, while the FBI is tackling domestic terrorists, and the NSA is monitoring all cell phone traffic in western Europe and Asia for any reference to Mystery Mountain."

"Sounds good. What would you like for my people to do, sir?" Even over a scrambled transmission, Brognola could not bring himself to name the covert Stony Man teams. In spite of every conceivable security precaution, the Farm had been invaded once, and the man was grimly determined to never allow that to happen again.

"For the time being, merely to stay alert and watch for any unusual sales in the underworld," the President said. "If some new, experimental weapon has indeed been stolen, then most likely it will soon be offered for sale like those damnable Shklov rocket torpedoes a few years ago. Pay any price within reason—no, scratch that. Pay any price to get the whatever it is off the streets. We can decide what to do with it later."

"Rabbit stew," Brognola muttered.

The President snorted at that, obviously familiar with the military axiom. The recipe for rabbit stew was always—first and foremost—catch the rabbit.

"Confirmed, and what about the thieves?"

The President thought about that for a moment. How many people had been working at the dam when it blew? How many families, wives and children, had been living in the off-base facilities downriver? How many soldiers and scientists had drowned when the tidal wave arrived?

"Sir?" Brognola repeated. "What if we manage to capture the thieves alive?"

"Don't," the President declared gruffly, and hung up.

Staring at the radio for a long moment, Brognola returned the mike to a clip, then climbed out of the Hummer. "Lieutenant!" he bellowed. "Please have one of your men drive my car to the hotel where I'm staying. I'll have somebody pick it up later."

The soldiers walked closer. "And you will be coming back with us to the base," the officer said, not posing it as a question.

"And commandeering a jetfighter back to the east coast." Brognola nodded. "Eagle One wants me there ASAP."

"Going to the White House, sir?" a young soldier asked excitedly.

"Something like that," Brognola muttered evasively, climbing into the damp front seat and glancing at his watch. If he flew directly to Andrews Air Force Base, he could reach the

Farm in western Virginia by midnight. With any luck, the Russian army would have captured the thieves by then and the matter would be over. If not, then it would be time to activate the Stony Man teams.

Caucasus Mountains

As THE OLD Soviet Army truck raced along the mountain highway, Lindquist glanced in the side mirror and watched the river valley vanish behind them in the night. Good riddance.

Personally, there really was nothing in the world the man hated more than Russians, and Lindquist was extremely pleased that Foxfire had left the Russian weapons facility pounded flat, with large sections of the surrounding forest ablaze. The mushroom cloud of the nuclear explosion was long gone, but the hellish red glow of the growing conflagration was rapidly spreading across the hills. A forest fire had not been in the original plans, but it made a nice addition to their escape.

Give the bastards something else to worry about than trying to find us, Lindquist thought, smirking. Not that it would do them any good.

Now wearing civilian clothing, the man and his team were speeding away from the annihilated valley along an old logging road not on any civilian map. It was in surprisingly good condition. The pavement was smooth, the dividing lines freshly painted, and there were tiny plastic pyramids set into the material to reflect the headlights of a vehicle so that a driver could stay in the correct lane during even the worst possible winter storm. Obviously this road was reserved for use by visiting politicians and generals. But it would serve them well tonight, and in ways never dreamed of by the idiots in the Kremlin.

Keeping a hand on the wheel, Kessler shifted gears and glanced sideways. "What's that thing under the dashboard?" he asked with a frown. "Some sort of radar jammer?"

"Just an eight-track tape player," Lindquist replied, checking the map. Soon they should be nearing the tunnel where everything would happen.

"Yeah?" asked the puzzled man. "And what the fuck is that?"

Not in the mood to explain antiques to a child, Lindquist dismissed the question with a wave of his hand.

In the rear of the truck, Barrowman was practicing loading an assault rifle with just one hand, Johansen was wrapping an amazingly realistic-looking plastic baby in a soft pink blanket and Hannigan was hard at work on the last lock, sealing shut the huge cylinder recovered from the flatbed. A wooden box on the floor was filled with parts he had already removed, including a delicate Faraday Net, which protected the complex electronics of the weapon from the EMP blast of a nuclear bomb.

"How is it coming?" Lindquist asked impatiently.

"Almost there," Hannigan muttered, wiping his forehead with a sleeve and leaving a streak of grease behind. "Damn, these locks are intricate."

"It was not designed to ever be disassembled," Lindquist reminded him harshly.

"This I know," Hannigan rumbled, returning to the task.

Outside the truck, a car raced by, heading in the opposite direction, the headlights washing over them for only a moment before it was gone.

"Think that was the FSB?" Barrowman asked, bringing up the AK-47 assault rifle.

"Too soon," Lindquist stated. "The federal police will be the very last people the Kremlin lets know what actually occurred this night."

"Good."

Just then, Johansen jerked in surprise as the animatronic doll swaddled in her arms began to softly cry. With a scowl, she gently rocked the thing, and the noise stopped.

"Do I look like a fucking mother?" the mercenary angrily muttered under her breath, shifting uncomfortably in her plain woolen dress.

"More than the rest of us, yes," Barrowman said, clumsily working the arming bolt.

"Hmm, sounds like it's hungry. Why don't you whip out a tit and give it a drink?" Kessler called over a shoulder, both hands on the wheel.

"Why don't you jump up your own ass?" Johansen snarled, gesturing, and a knife dropped into her palm from a sleeve of her dress.

"Can't while I'm driving. Maybe later."

"I can wait."

"Got it," Hannigan cried, stepping back.

As he dropped a circuit board into the wooden box, there came the low hiss of working pneumatics and the middle section of the cylinder cycled up to reveal seven large spheres nestled inside the complex machinery, their smooth surfaces glistening with condensation. It took a moment before the mercs realized the white objects were not truly spheres, but some sort of decahedron, or more properly, a dodecahedron, the curved sides made of a smooth array of a hundred interlocking pyramids.

"Whew, so that's them, eh?" Barrowman said, scratching his arm inside the sling. "Kind of hard to imagine, isn't it?"

"Not really, no," Lindquist replied, feeling his heart quicken at the sight. The spy at Mystery Mountain had informed him that the Skyfire weapon system possessed multiple warheads, but he had expected to find two thermobaric bombs, not seven. This windfall once again changed his plans.

Shifting gears to take a hill, Kessler looked at the spheres in the rearview mirror. "What kind of a yield are we talking about here?"

"Close to the order of a kiloton of TNT," Lindquist answered absentmindedly, his thoughts elsewhere.

"Are you serious?" Kessler gasped. "But that Chinese nuke we used on the dam only had a quarter-kiloton yield."

"Then this would be more," Johansen said with a tolerant smile.

"Four times more powerful than a tactical nuke," Barrowman muttered. It was incredible. One of those spheres could flatten Manhattan. The cluster would burn all of New York City, from Brooklyn to the Bronx, clean off the map.

"Pity we're not selling them on the black market," he said impulsively. "We'd be millionaires overnight."

"Billionaires, more likely," Lindquist corrected.

The mercenaries exchanged glances, but said nothing.

"How much farther to the tunnel?" Johansen asked, licking her lips.

"We should be there any minute now," Lindquist answered.

"There she blows!" Kessler announced, taking a curve in the road.

Directly ahead of the truck was a wall of dark rock, impossible to climb or traverse. But smack in the middle was a small tunnel, the mouth just barely large enough for the huge Soviet truck to gain entry.

As they entered the tunnel, the truck headlights illuminated the interior for hundreds of feet. The pavement was old, but the smooth concrete walls were spotlessly clean, without any trace of diesel fumes or car exhaust, almost as if the tunnel was brand-new.

Or very rarely ever used, Lindquist mentally corrected himself. Only the top brass at the Kremlin ever used the secret tunnel, and not even the nosy Americans knew of its existence.

But almost instantly, Kessler downshifted and started to brake. "There's roadwork up ahead," he added in a suspicious voice.

Craning their necks to see through the windshield, the Fox-fire team scowled at the sight of a van parked in the middle of the roadway, the headlights beating to the rhythm of the idling engine. Surrounded by a ring of bright yellow cones, a team of workmen wearing bright orange safety jackets and carrying shovels seemed to be doing something to the pavement. There were several tanker trucks on the far side of the construction zone, the drivers standing outside their rigs smoking cigarettes.

Braking to a halt, Kessler pumped the gas pedal a few times to stop the engine dieseling. At first it did not seem to work, then the engine went still and a heavy silence blanketed the highway.

"Okay, we do this by the numbers," Lindquist said, pulling out a 9 mm automatic Tokarev and working the slide. "Everybody stay here, and I'll go see what's happening."

"We got your six, sir," Johansen stated, pulling the Carl Gustav launcher onto her lap.

Tucking the Soviet automatic into a pocket, Lindquist opened the side door and stepped down to the roadway. "Hello," he called, waving a hand. "What's the trouble?"

"Water main broken," a slim man shouted in a heavy accent, checking something on a clipboard.

"Can we get past?" Lindquist asked, walking over casually. Then he suddenly dived to the side.

Instantly the workers dropped their clipboards and shovels to bring up Red Army 30 mm grenade launchers and fire a salvo at the Soviet truck.

"What the… *It's a trap!*" Kessler bellowed, frantically trying to start the engine while the barrage of canisters impacted around the truck, gushing out thick volumes of a bilious green smoke.

"Gas attack," Johansen cursed, grabbing a gas mask from under a seat.

Everybody else did the same as the rising fumes seeped into the truck, swirling around their boots. Breathing deeply as they had been taught, the mercenaries now grabbed weapons, but a terrible wave of nausea overtook each of them. The strength flowed from their limbs like water down a drain. Their fingers turned numb, breathing became impossible, then they went blind. Foaming at the mouths, the Foxfire team dropped twitching to the floor, and went very still.

Staying safely where they were located, the workers waited for several minutes until the ventilation system of the tunnel cleared away the fumes of the deadly gas.

With a bang, the rear doors of the truck slammed open and out stepped a skeletal thin man wearing the crisp uniform of a Soviet Union admiral. There was a Tokarev automatic holstered at his stomach, the grip reversed for a left-handed man. A nylon cord connected the pistol to his belt in case it was dropped when at sea. He appeared to be much older than he actually was and his teeth were clearly false, but the bony man still possessed a full head of wavy hair and radiated authority the way a furnace does heat.

"Report please, Sergeant," commanded Brigadier General Ivan Alexander Novostk, both hands held behind his back. A smooth red scar crossed his throat from ear to ear where a Soviet Union paratrooper had tried to remove his head and failed at the cost of his own life. General "Iron Ivan" Novostk considered himself unkillable. His body was covered with scars from a hundred battles, hard fought and won. His long career in the Slovakian military was burned into living flesh, and most of the scars were a constant reminder of the brutality of the Kremlin and its monstrous lapdogs, the KGB, forever renewing his unquenchable hatred of the Communists.

"The air is reading clear, sir," Sergeant Petrova Melori announced in Slovakian, checking the monitor of a chemical sensor.

Rising to his feet, Lindquist dusted off his pants. "Two of you make sure they're dead," he directed in the same language. "The rest of you clear away these cones. The entire Russian army will soon be here, and we better be long gone."

"You heard the colonel!" a corporal bellowed, slinging the grenade launcher over a shoulder. "Kleinova, Louvsky, check the bodies and watch for traps. Everybody else, clear the way."

As the soldiers got busy, Lindquist walked over to the skinny man. "Good to see you again, sir," he said with a genuine smile.

"And you, Colonel," General Novostk replied, offering the man a hand. "How many T-bombs did we get?"

"Seven," Colonel Lindquist replied, drawing the Norinco automatic and tossing it away. "More than enough to get the job done."

"Excellent! I am more than pleased."

Damn well hope so. But the colonel said nothing out loud.

A sharp whistle came from the Soviet truck and a soldier waved. "They're dead, sir," he shouted through cupped hands.

"You sure?" Lindquist demanded, brushing back his hair.

There came the sound of four individual pistol shots.

"Yes, sir," the private replied. "We're sure."

Good enough. "Well done, Private."

After transferring the seven angular spheres to the van and strapping them down, the soldiers threw the box of spare parts across the tunnel and left.

"To enhance the appearance of an internal explosion," Colonel Lindquist said to the sergeant. If the general did not agree, he kept the matter to himself.

Satisfied for the moment, Lindquist drove away in the van, the soldiers easily running beside the slow-moving vehicle until it reached the other end of the tunnel. Idling there was a titanic Mi-6 Hook, the largest helicopter in the world.

The van was guided up the rear ramp into the Hook, where the soldiers lashed it securely into position. Then they took seats along the walls and put on their seat belts. This promised to be a bumpy ride. Lindquist and Melori went to the flight deck for their seats, and strapped in tight.

As they did, the pilot revved the power to full strength, and the nearly overloaded Mi-6 Hook lifted off.

As the tunnel dwindled below, Sergeant Melori waited until he was sure the cargo helicopter had reached a safe distance, then activated a small radio detonator and pressed the button.

The range was too great for them to feel the shock wave of the explosion. But from their great height, the two officers saw volcanoes of flame erupt from both ends of the tunnel. The fire raged unchecked until the steel support beams began to soften and the mouth of the tunnel melted shut.

"I wish them luck getting those open soon," Melori stated, tucking away the detonator.

"What did you use?" Lindquist asked, watching the white-hot flames recede until they were only a pair of bright points in the darkness, then only a single point, and then the natural contour of the landscape took them from sight.

"Rocket fuel," the sergeant replied.

Saying nothing, Lindquist tilted his head in disbelief.

"No, it's true, my friend." General Novostk chuckled. "Those tankers contained liquid oxygen and liquid hydrogen. We used the same mixture as the Americans do for their space shuttle. Two parts liquid oxygen and one part liquid hydrogen. Add some diesel fuel from the engines, and the mixture burns almost as hot as a thermobaric bomb."

"Almost. But not quite."

The general shrugged. "No, not quite. However, it should take them days to figure that out. And by then..." He grinned.

Colonel Lindquist understood. Soon enough, the whole world would have other things to worry about than the deaths of some thieves. Then he frowned.

"Were the tankers stolen?" the colonel demanded. From bitter experience, the man knew that hijacked trucks were easily traced, and this needed to resemble an accidental triggering of the Skyfire device, not a clever way of destroying any trace of forensic evidence.

"No, they were supplied by a dummy company owned by your employer in the Ukraine." General Novostk laughed. "On paper, they never existed, and thus cannot go missing, eh?" Then he pretended to punch the officer in the arm. "Do not worry, my American friend. Every detail has been considered and taken care of. We are quite safe. Nobody will ever know who we really are."

Angling away from the spreading umbrella of hard radiation tainting the clouds over the remote valley, the Soviet Union cargo helicopter moved low and fast over the rugged terrain, heading due south, out over the Black Sea.

CHAPTER TWO

Stony Man Farm, Virginia

"Just a few minutes ago, we caught another heat flash," Aaron "the Bear" Kurtzman said, turning his wheelchair away from his computer workstation to pour himself a cup of coffee. "At first we thought it was a second nuke, but this wasn't hot enough, and the chemical signature more resembled a space shuttle launch."

"Have the Russians put something into space?" Barbara Price demanded, her stomach tightening.

Without adding milk or sugar, Kurtzman took a long draft of the steaming coffee as if it was tap water. "No, we don't think so," the Stony Man computer genius replied carefully, setting the mug into a recess on the armrest of his chair. "If the blast had occurred out in the open, that might have been a possibility. This actually seemed to be two simultaneous explosions exactly where the CIA believes there is a hidden tunnel."

A tunnel? The Farm's mission controller frowned. "Okay, something exploded inside, and the blast came out the ends," Price rationalized, crossing her arms. "Could it have been the Red Army dealing with the thieves?"

"Or vice versa," Carmen Delahunt announced from her console. Perched on the edge of her chair, the redhead was focused on her computer screen. Dangling from the back of her chair an S&W Bulldog revolver was tucked into an FBI-style shoulder holster.

"Explain that," Price demanded.

"According to the NATO Watchdog satellite we hijacked, there were isotonic traces of diesel fuel in the chemical signature of the explosion," Delahunt said. "Along with similar amounts of vulcanized rubber."

"That sounds like a truck," Price said slowly, testing the words.

"Three trucks, by my calculations," Delahunt answered.

"Insulated trucks," added Akira Tokaido, removing his earbuds. "There was far too much cobalt in the signature to come from anything other than heat-resistant steel." Tokaido was of mixed Japanese-American ancestry. He seemed born to operate computers, code coming to him as easily as breathing to ordinary people.

"Maybe there was a tank, or an APC caught in the blast," Price offered hesitantly.

"I wish that was true, but no," Kurtzman countered, sliding his wheelchair under his console. "Russian military contains natural wood fibers to make the metal more elastic, and thus proof to most armor-piercing rounds."

Wood fiber in tank armor? "Are you positive?" Price scowled.

Tokaido gave a curt nod. "The spectrum analysis is conclusive. No military vehicles were involved in the blast. So unless whatever was stolen detonated while suspended in liquid boron, or something equally outrageously exotic like that…"

"Then the explosion was caused by insulated tanker trucks carrying liquid oxygen and liquid hydrogen. Clearly, it was a trick by the thieves to try to fake their own deaths," Huntington Wethers said, removing an old briar pipe from his mouth. "Unfortunately, it also tells us what was stolen."

Tall and distinguished-looking, Wethers seemed to be the epitome of a college professor with wings of silvery hair at his temples, a briar pipe and leather patches on the elbows of his tweed jacket. Although fully tenured at Berkeley University, the man had felt a strong need to serve his country, and left the world of academia to become one of the most feared cyberhunters in existence.

Thoughtfully, Price chewed a lip. An explosion powerful enough to be mistaken for a tactical nuke, but without any radiation. The only thing that came to mind was... Oh hell, not that. "What was the last weapon tested there?" Price demanded, trying to stay calm. If what she thought had just happened, the world was in for a long hard rain of blood and pain.

"Difficult to say," Delahunt answered. "The master computers of Mystery Mountain are not connected to the Internet, and the entire valley is covered with a camouflage net so that our Keyhole and Watchdog satellites can't see what was happening down there."

"However, the only logical extrapolation is that the thieves stole one of the new Russian thermobaric bombs," Tokaido interjected.

"Now, LOX and LOH don't quite burn as hot as one of those," Kurtzman stated, cracking his knuckles. "But pretty damn close."

Several decades ago, the Pentagon had started a program to create an arsenal of nonnuclear weapons, and the cream of the crop was the FAE bomb, or Fuel-Air Explosive, nicknamed Skyfire. The idea was simple, as all good ideas are. Imagine closing all of the doors and windows in a house, then turning on the gas oven but turning off the pilot. In only a few minutes, the house would be completely filled with highly explosive gas. Now stuff an ordinary fuse under the front door and light it. When the fuse reaches the interior, the house would thunderously detonate, obliterating the entire structure and quite often the homes alongside.

The FAE bomb did the same thing, but out in the open. A plane would drop the bomb and it would burst open, sending out a huge cloud of flammable gas, the exact composition of which was not known to even Stony Man. A split second later, the plummeting canister would explode, igniting the cloud, and a fiery implosion of unimaginable power would blanket the sky, uprooting forests, knocking over homes and office buildings and setting fire to everything within range. The one limiting factor was that a FAE bomb would not work if there were strong winds, or if it was raining, snowing, or even if there was heavy fog. It had to be a clear, calm day.

In spite of colossal efforts, no other nation had ever been able to duplicate the American trick of making a fuel-air explosion work. But a few months ago rumors had surfaced in the intelligence community that the Russians had not only figured out how to make an FAE but had also gone even further. They called their weapon a thermobaric bomb, and it worked exactly like an American FAE bomb, except it could function in high winds, rain, snow or fog. There were no operational limitations on a T-bomb, and if true, it was the most deadly weapon in existence. For all intents and purposes, it was a nuclear bomb that did not give off hard radiation—a clean nuke.

"Is there anything in space?" Price asked, walking closer to the wall screens, her hands clenched into tight fists. "Have the Russians created a new…I don't know, some sort of a new plasma weapon and it's running wild?"

"Space is clear," Delahunt intoned.

Damn. "Do we have any video from the valley? Security cameras or such?"

"Not after a nuclear explosion," Kurtzman scoffed, drinking from the old cracked mug. "The EMP blast of the nuke erased all of the electronic records."

Which was probably deliberately done by the thieves, Price realized dourly. It would be very hard for the FSB to track down the thieves if they knew absolutely nothing about them. The nuke destroyed the base, along with any video, then the tanker trucks in the tunnel faked the death of the thieves and vaporized any physical evidence. Whoever took the weapon was smart. Too damn smart, in her opinion.

Deep in thought, Price started to pace. Personally, she hoped that China had stolen the damn thing. At least with them, the United Nations could exert political and economic pressure to not use the weapon. If a terrorist group got their hands on a T-bomb they would immediately use it to destroy a major city—New York, London, Tokyo. The death toll would be in the millions.

"Okay, if somebody has stolen a T-bomb, then how do we track the thing?" Price demanded. "There must be remote telemetry or a lowjack on the thing."

"Which anybody with an EM scanner could find and remove," Tokaido stated, studying the monitor on his console. The screen was flashing through road maps of the Russian countryside. A flatbed had been seen by a NATO spy satellite amid the wreckage left by the tidal wave from the destroyed dam. If the bomb was particularly heavy, then it could only be hauled over specific roads. Unfortunately, most of the logging roads in the mountains connected with railroads, and those went everywhere in Russia.

Grudgingly, Price accepted that. "Okay, what about dogs or chemical sensors?" She rallied. "We can tune every one at every major airport to look for just T-bombs."

"Sorry, no can do," Kurtzman stated bluntly, placing aside his empty mug. "Hell, Barb, we don't even know what the damn thing looks like, much less how it works."

Chewing a lip, Price tried to find some way to approach the problem, but was coming up with nothing. The Russian superweapon was practically invisible. Nobody would know it had been smuggled into Washington until the Pentagon vanished in a fiery implosion that also ripped the White House from its very foundation.

"Okay, do we know of any operational limitations?" she demanded.

"Unfortunately, no," Wethers muttered around his pipe. Smoking was forbidden anywhere near the supercomputer, but the man found chewing on the stem oddly inducive to his creative concentration. "The Pentagon strongly believes that the T-bomb can be activated at extreme low levels, perhaps as little as five hundred feet."

Price stared hard at the professor. "Are you trying to tell me that it may not be necessary to drop the T-bomb from a plane?" she said slowly, absorbing the information. "Instead it could simply be rolled off the roof of a fifty-story building?"

"Sadly, yes."

"But no nation in the world can secure every office building over fifty stories tall. There must be hundreds, thousands, of them."

Deep in thought, Price poured herself a mug of coffee, adding a great deal of sugar and milk. Kurtzman liked the stuff strong enough to degrease tractor parts, but lesser humans preferred it at less lethal levels of corrosion.

Taking small sips, the woman finished the mug, then turned around with a new light in her eyes. "All right," she said forcibly. "If we can't track the weapon, then we go after the thieves."

"But we don't know who took it," Kurtzman tactfully reminded her.

Impatiently, Price waved the objection aside. "That doesn't matter. We know that they used a Chinese nuke. Start there. Send Phoenix Force to Milan to see if somebody purchased a black-market nuke recently. After that, they can try Paris and then Sudan. This whole thing might have been a trick by Russia for an excuse to attack their ancient enemy, China."

"You think the Kremlin nuked Mystery Mountain just to have a legitimate excuse to start a nuclear war?" Tokaido asked in disbelief, then frowned. It wouldn't be a nuclear war, but a Skyfire war. "On it," he announced, and bent over the console, his hands flying across the keyboard.

"The big question is, how did the thieves know about the test?" Kurtzman growled. "It wasn't exactly broadcast on the evening news."

"Which leaves two possibilities," Price continued. "Either there is a traitor, or somebody hacked into the computer system at Mystery Mountain."

"Not even we can do that," Delahunt stated in annoyance, curling her toes on the floor. "Their firewalls are just as good as those at the White House."

Kurtzman snorted. "So it's got to be a traitor."

"Or a spy," Price amended. "Carmen, check the first-class-passenger list at every major airport in the area, cross reference that to the personnel file we stole from the Kremlin last month. Find me somebody who went on vacation the day before the T-bomb was stolen."

"I'll also check with the health department to see if anybody recently got sick. Vacations can be cancelled by your boss, but nobody would interfere with a cancer treatment," Delahunt muttered.

Clenching her gloves, she closed the files she had been reading and activated the NSA communication protocols.

"Okay, if Russia and China were not behind the theft, this might have been done by mercenaries hired to do the bloody work," Price speculated. "Hunt, activate the Dirty Dozen, try to hire the top mercs and see who is not available."

"Already doing it, Barb," the professor muttered around his pipe.

Long ago, Mack Bolan had suggested the creation of some artificial buyers of weapon. In virtual reality, that was easy. But Kurtzman had decided to take the matter one step further. Together with his team, the Farm had created a dozen fake personalities in all of the major areas of crime, along with a team of black ops mercs called Blue Lightning.

The Dirty Dozen was a collection of artificial criminals invented by Kurtzman and his team long ago. Their entire lives were fake, forged out of nothing but the Stony Man hackers slipping data into files around the world. When a bank was robbed in Melbourne, the hackers started the rumors that it was financed by one of the Dozen. If a politician got assassinated in Norway, it was because he had crossed the path of another of the Dirty Dozen. Pirates attacked a cruise ship in the Caribbean, an Interpol agent was shot in Amsterdam, a plane crashed in the Andes—any unsolved crime was quickly attributed to these secretive masters of criminal underworld.

The names of the Dozen were constantly changed as they died in car accidents or were captured and executed—only to be immediately replaced by another Stony Man construct. The Dirty Dozen was a constant source of valuable information about international crime as people tried to sell them stolen goods. And whenever one of the Stony Man field teams needed to contact a terrorist group, a member of the Dirty Dozen was always available to vouch for them through e-mail or a phone call.

"Hunt, keep a watch for any secret arms sales," Kurtzman added. "If the T-bomb becomes available for sale, it is a safe bet that one of the Dozen will be invited to the auction. If so, pay any price to get it. Better to pay a billion dollars now than a hundred billion to rebuild Los Angeles."

"Agreed," the professor muttered, his hands busy. "However, it could be more than a billion."

"Don't care. Pay whatever is necessary. I'll have our Keyhole and Watchdog satellites initiate a planetary recon for any other gigantic explosions," Kurtzman declared brusquely. "The thieves may try to fake their own deaths again. Or worse, actually use the T-bomb on somebody."

"God forbid," Price muttered softly, glancing at the clock on the wall.

"Hold on…okay, I found him," Delahunt announced. "A janitor working at Mystery Mountain recently won a free vacation in an online contest and had to leave the day before the theft occurred or else he lost the prize."

A contest win, that was a good cover. She had used something similar once herself. "What's the name, and where did he go?"

"Stanislav Kominsky. Disney World, Orlando, Florida."

"The other side of the world," Kurtzman muttered. "Not very subtle."

"Okay, try this," Delahunt said. "He was killed in a car crash en route to his hotel room on the day he arrived. The body was taken to the Dade County morgue, and since Mr. Kominsky is Jewish, he had to be buried within twenty-four hours." She paused. "He was interred at Bonaventure Acres roughly six hours ago."

"Less than an hour before the theft took place."

"Yep."

"Ladies and gentlemen, we have a winner." Kurtzman's hands flew across the controls of his console with expert speed. "I'll have Jack Grimaldi warm up a C-130 Hercules, and Able Team can be there in a few hours to check the body."

"Why not have the local police or a CSI team do it?" Tokaido asked, tentatively glancing sideways.

"Because, with any luck, it could be a trap," Price stated with a humorless smile.

CHAPTER THREE

Balaklava Bay, Ukraine

The land around the secluded cove was rough and seemed almost half formed. Cold and deep, the Black Sea extended far beyond the shimmering horizon to the distant nations of Turkey, Bulgaria and Romania.

The small cove was protected from the worst of the storms by a natural breaker of glassy ballast. The barrier had been strongly reinforced under the Communist regime of the Soviet Union with huge concrete slabs. Abandoned pillboxes were secreted among the arcadia bushes along the barren shoreline.

Dominating the area was a crumbling lighthouse, the cupola only splintery framework, the glass long gone and the great stone blocks weathered to a dull sheen from the constant pounding of the waves. But only a hundred feet away rose a brand-new lighthouse, even taller than the ruins, the freshly painted sides glistening with the salty spray, the plastic cupola topped with radar and microwave receptors.

A town curved along the eastern side of the cove, the fishing shacks and drying huts converted into hotels and restaurants for visiting tourists. Under the indolent rule of the czar, Balaklava had been a thriving seaport, a bustling community of fishermen and sailors, plying their ancient trade. Then the Communists seized control and soldiers forced the people to leave their homes for reasons unknown. The few men foolish enough to ask were never heard from again. Then the Soviet Union fell, and the people of Balaklava returned to reclaim their ancestral homes, and to try to build a new life as a resort community. The fishing was excellent, the vodka cheap, and there were countless subterranean caves to be explored, along with the abandoned glory of a secret naval base. The massive fleet of submarines was long gone, but the dry docks remained, as well as the facilities to house and maintain a fighting force of over a thousand sailors.

Directly across from the seaside village was a wooden dock that led directly into a volcanic cave, the entrance to the underground redoubt. At one time, it had been a shooting offense to know the location of the cave. Now it was decorated with posters and photographs from the glory days of the Cold War, along with a stenciled placard announcing the days and times of each tour.

Standing on the other side of a woven yellow rope, a fat man in a loose white suit glared indignantly. His skin was pale from a life working under fluorescent lights. Mirrored sunglasses hid most of his face, and a large Nikon camera hung around his neck.

"What do you mean, closed?" the man demanded angrily.

"Closed. As in not open to the public anymore," the tour guide replied patiently. "The government is doing something here, and nobody is allowed inside until they're done. Okay?" The guide enjoyed using the strange American word. He had heard it often in movies.

"No, it is not okay!" the fat man bellowed. "I've come all the way from St. Petersburg to see this goddamn installation, and I want to see it right now. Fuck the government!"

"In the old days, that would have gotten you shot," the guide coldly reminded.

"But these are not the old days anymore, comrade," the tourist sneered. "We're a democracy now. Free men all. So fuck you, fuck the government and get the fuck out of my way, I want to see the submarine pens!"

"Fair enough," the guide replied, unclipping the rope and stepping aside.

Triumphantly, the tourist strode along the long wooden dock and into the volcanic cave. The man removed his sunglasses to see the interior better when the light vanished. Turning, he scowled at the sight of a thick black curtain hanging across the mouth of the cave.

"What the fuck is this?" the fat man demanded loudly, looking around for somebody to berate. Then he blanched at the sight of a dozen men coming out of a duty room. They were each dressed in combat fatigues and carried automatic weapons.

"Hey," the tourist mumbled only a split second before the mercenaries opened fire.

The silenced Kalashnikov assault rifles chugged softly, the 7.62 mm rounds tearing the fool apart. He hit the stone floor coughing and twitching, the white suit rapidly turning a deep crimson. The echoes of the muted gunfire repeated endlessly along the watery tunnel, disappearing into the distance.

Walking closer, Colonel Lindquist pulled out a Tokarev automatic and shot the civilian once more. Gurgling horribly, his head snapped back from the arrival of a steel-jacketed round, and then went still forever.

"Russians," Novostk sneered, stiffly walking into view. "The best way to make them do something is to tell them not to do it."

The skinny general had already changed out of the hated Soviet naval uniform, and now was back in his Slovakian uniform. It was plain and unadorned, with only the insignia on the collar showing his rank. An old Samopal Vzor assault rifle was slung across his back, and a web belt of ammo pouches encircled his skinny waist with a bulky Rex .357 Magnum revolver holstered on the hip.

"I knew we should have dismantled the dock," Colonel Lindquist said, holstering his pistol. "Mikhail, clean up the blood. Petrov, get rid of the body in one of the submarine pens. Zhale, put up a sign about falling rocks. That should keep away the fools until we're gone."

Quickly, the assigned men moved to obey. The rest stayed where they were, close to the general.

"Speaking of which, we're ready to leave," General Novostk said, shifting the Samopal Vzor assault rifle to a more comfortable position. The weapon was a Slovakian version of a Russian AK-47. Both the metal and wooden stock worn from years of use, but gleaming with fresh oil and polish.

"Already?" Lindquist asked in surprise. "Excellent. Has even the helicopter been dismantled?"

"Sealed off in a side tunnel," the general countered. "I did not know if you wanted to use the Hook again."

"Too risky, sir," Lindquist answered. "I'll use a boat for the next part."

The general arched an eyebrow at that but said nothing. The colonel was an amazing officer, in spite of being a mixture of American and Slovakian blood. Clearly, there was just a touch more Bratislava in his soul than Brooklyn.

"And how is your former employer taking the betrayal?" Novostk asked, heading deeper into the dim cavern.

"Fuck him," Lindquist snarled, clasping both hands behind his back. "He's part Slovak himself, but harbors no ill will toward the Soviets, in spite of everything they did to our nation."

"Then he is a fool."

"Agreed, sir. Which is why I had no trouble killing his mercenaries to turn Skyfire over to you."

"History will remember you as a true patriot, Colonel!"

Unimpressed, Lindquist shrugged in reply. As a soldier, it was his sworn duty to protect his homeland. The Soviet Union had plundered the natural resources of Slovakia, and that lunatic Stalin had sent millions of its citizens to the Siberian gulag work camps never to return. As a soldier, Lindquist would have much preferred a straight fight with the Russian army, but if this was the only way for Slovakia to strike back at Moscow, then so be it. Blood was blood, and terrorists were always heroes to the dead they avenged.

Turning at a corner, the officers paused at the sight of a bound man covered with chains. A soldier tried not to smile as he shoved the helpless prisoner forward. A muffled scream escaped his gag as the bound man toppled off the concrete apron, to land in the water with a large splash. He sank immediately into the depths, leaving behind a small trail of air bubbles.

"And who was that, Private?" Novostk asked casually. "Another fisherman who wandered in here by accident?"

"Smuggler, sir," the soldier replied, giving a crisp salute.

"Indeed," Lindquist muttered, glancing at the struggling man descending to the bottom of the pen. The water was over fifty feet deep, and soon there was only a trickle of escaping air bubbles visible in the underwater lights. "And what was he trying to sneak into Russia?"

"Heroin."

The general scowled, then spit into the water. "No loss, then. The fool only got what he deserved. We want the Russians dead, not enslaved to that filth."

"And what did you do with the drugs?" Lindquist asked sharply.

"Made him eat it, sir. A half kilo of Bulgarian black tar."

"And he lived?"

Suddenly the air bubbles stopped rising from the murky depths.

"No, sir, he did not." The soldier grinned savagely.

"Well, the fish should have a good time disposing of the carcass." Lindquist chuckled in dark amusement. "Very good, Private. Carry on with your duties."

"Yes, sir."

Proceeding along the tunnel, the officers headed toward an old Soviet Union submarine moored to the concrete dock. Purchased on the open market in Amsterdam, the borderline antique had been incredibly cheap, mostly because the submersible lacked any sort of modern convenience. It was slow and noisy, the air always smelled of diesel fumes, the toilet leaked, plus the torpedo tubes had been welded shut. The submarine was useless to anybody but ichthyologists and historians. In spite of that, a group of Iranians had outbid Lindquist's former employer, and the first assignment of the Foxfire team had been to convince the Iranians to give them the sub, in exchange for a few ounces of subsonic lead.

"How is the work of the bombs progressing?" General Novostk inquired.

"Poorly. So far, we are having no luck opening one of the T-bombs," Lindquist admitted unhappily. "They are well sealed, and our sensors indicated numerous traps. They're designed to never be accessed." He paused. "We may need some special help."

"Just make sure he is good," the general snapped, kicking a stone out of his way. "Our contact in Mystery Mountain had said there was only a slim possibility that the weapon being tested today would contain multiple warheads, and here we are with seven of the bombs. Seven!" He shook a bony fist. "This changes everything. Four will be assigned targets, and we need to keep one for analysis—that is a given—and yet another will be reserved for an emergency. But the remaining bomb should be used immediately."

"As a diversion."

"Exactly. And to let the world know what kind of a horror is now loose among them." The general sneered, touching the scar on his neck. "That will buy us enough time to complete the analysis."

"In my experience, people fear the unknown, sir," Lindquist offered hesitantly.

"No, that is only true of the individual," the general countered. "Nations are only frightened of demonstrable threats. The United Nations and NATO must see the weapon in operation! Then they will panic." The old man glanced sideways. "Have you chosen a target yet?"

"Of course, sir," Lindquist replied. "Something highly visible that the entire world will hear about."

"And blame the Russians?"

"And blame the Russians, yes, sir."

"Excellent. And what about the spy?"

In reply, Lindquist only gave a hard smile. The general nodded in approval. Traitors always reaped the whirlwind.

Nearing the end of the dock, the two officers paused in front of a heavy wooden table covered with electronic equipment. Sergeant Melori was bent over the devices, adjusting the controls with a fingertip. Behind the slim man stood a massive lieutenant, a borderline giant, his Herculean frame almost bursting out of the largest Slovakian military uniform the quartermaster had been able to obtain. A smoked-beef stick stuck out of his mouth as if it was a cigar, and he chewed steadily.

Only a few yards beyond were a pair of old wooden planks extending to the conning tower of a submerged submarine. The emblem of the Soviet navy had been covered with black paint and replaced with the flag of the Republic of the Ukraine, fellow victims of the savage Communists. Just a tad more confusion to any possible witnesses.

"Anything on the radar?" Lindquist asked, studying the small glowing screen.

"No, sir," Melori replied, standing and saluting.

"At ease," General Novostk commanded impatiently. "Give me a report on the outside world. Do we have any more uninvited guests today? We seem to have taken refuge in the main train station of Bratislava." All of the other soldiers chuckled at the joke.

Not exactly sure why they were doing that, the colossal Lieutenant Gregor Vladislav merely grinned to be polite. Most people said things that he did not fully comprehend. But that was okay. His expertise was with weapons, killing came as easily to him as flying did to a bird. It was only people that he could not really understand. As a child, his father had wisely taught Vladislav that there was always somebody smarter than you in the world. Intelligence was rather like the martial arts; no matter how good you were, there was always somebody a little bit faster or a little bit stronger. The trick was to not attract attention to yourself, and then strike from behind.

"The outer perimeter is clear, sir," Melori reported, fondly touching the delicate sensors. What his friend Vladislav did with a knife, he could do with electronics. Together, they were an unstoppable team. "Both radar and sonar show no unusual activity in our vicinity."

"And what is the usual activity?"

"Schools of fish to the west, fishing boats to the east, a commercial jetliner to the far north, some oil tankers to the far south."

"Very good, Sergeant," the general said with a nod. "Let us know if anything approaches very fast. That will probably be the FSB."

"Closely followed by the entire Russian army," Lindquist added in a snarl.

"We can stop them, sir," Vladislav stated in a voice of stone. "The missiles are live and ready to fire."

The other soldiers stoically said nothing, but Melori seemed slightly embarrassed by the outburst.

"Yes, I'm sure the fight would be glorious, but in the end, a thousand will beat fifty every time," General Novostk said tolerantly. "So until we're safely back home, I would prefer to avoid the enemy."

"Yes, sir, of course," the lieutenant growled. "Pull back in a feint, then strike from behind."

Patting the giant on the arm, Novostk smiled. "Something like that, old friend."

Leaving the men to their work, the two officers shuffled carefully along the planks over the dark water.

"Why are we keeping that idiot alive?" Lindquist muttered.

"I have my reasons," Novostk replied curtly. "And they are none of your concern."

Stepping onto the conning tower, the officers found the watertight hatch already open. A clatter of noise was coming from inside the submarine, the command deck below a hive of activity.

As Lindquist stepped aside to let the general climb down first, Novostk touched his arm. "Are the scuttling charges ready?" he asked in a low whisper.

The colonel maintained a neutral expression in case somebody was watching them. "Absolutely, sir. Just give the word."

"Hopefully, we will not have to," General Novostk stated, rubbing the scar on his throat. "But it is always best to be prepared for the worst."

Without further comment, the two Slovakians clambered into the old submarine and began the final preparations for their departure, and the beginning of World War III.

Boca Raton, Florida

SWOOPING GRACEFULLY out of the clear blue sky, the huge C-130 Hercules landed on a private airstrip on Miami/Dade Airport and taxied straight into a private hangar at the extreme end of the field.

As the massive aircraft came to a stop, the rear ramp cycled to the ground and out rolled a small cargo van, the windows tinted darkly. The unmarked van seemed perfectly ordinary enough, but it contained more armor than an APC, along with a small arsenal of military weaponry tucked inside hidden ceiling compartments.

Dressed in loose civilian clothing, the men of Able Team were planning on making this mission a soft recon, low and easy. But just in case of trouble, they also brought along some heavy iron.

Suddenly the radio speaker built into the ceiling crackled alive. "Sky King to the Senator," the voice of Jack Grimaldi said over the background static. "Sky King to the Senator, ten-four?"

"Ten-two, Sky King," Rosario Blancanales said into a hand mike from the passenger seat. "This is the Senator. Is something wrong?" Glancing into the side mirror, Blancanales watched the door to the hangar close as the building itself dwindled into the distance.

"Negative," the pilot replied. "Just wanted you to know that I should have the Hercules refueled and ready to eat clouds in an hour, just in case we have to leave in a hurry."

"Roger, Sky King. Much appreciated," Blancanales said with a wan smile. "We'll give a holler if things get exciting."

"You do that. Tails high, brother! Ten-two."

"Over and out," Blancanales replied, returning the mike to its clip.

"'Tails high'?" Schwarz asked from the rear of the van, stuffing tools into his belt pouch from a small worktable bolted to the wall.

"Hermann, not even I understand the humor of pilots," Blancanales sighed, opening a ceiling compartment to take down an M-16 M-203 assault rifle combo.

Broad and powerful, the man radiated charm the way a furnace does heat, only the salt-and-pepper hair suggesting his true age. A master of psychological warfare, Blancanales had talked his way out of more hot spots than could be easily counted, and had earned his nickname of "the Politician," a thousand times over.

"I think the thin air makes them crazy," said Carl "Ironman" Lyons from behind the wheel, shifting gears to accelerate the van. The Able Team leader was a stocky man with short blond hair and cool blue eyes. "Or rather, it makes them even more crazy," Lyons amended, turning onto an access ramp. "All pilots are odd to begin with."

Schwarz was busy tucking a U.S. Army laptop into a black shoulder bag. Even though the battlefield laptop was sheathed in bullet-resistant titanium, the bag was a ballistic cloth resistant to fire, knives and most small-caliber rounds. If anything, Schwarz believed that planning for a disaster was the best way to achieve success.

A stocky man with short brown hair and full mustache, Schwarz had a friendly, smiling face and bright, intelligent eyes. An expert in electronic warfare and countersurveillance, "Gadgets" Schwarz designed most of the communications equipment for the Farm. Barbara Price had been known to joke that Schwarz could chew a toaster and spit out a cell phone. The man could make, repair or alter anything that used advanced electronics, including high-explosive booby traps.

Chuckling in agreement, Blancanales closed the grenade launcher, then eased a clip of 5.56 mm hardball ammunition into the receiver of the assault rifle. Before Able Team left for the mission, John "Cowboy" Kissinger had tried to persuade Blancanales to take along one of the XM-8 assault rifles that would soon be replacing the old M-16 as the standard weapon for the entire United States military. But Blancanales had declined, at least until the Pentagon removed the "experimental" prefix from the sleek weapon. The XM-8 looked great on the gun range, but the difference between that and actual combat was often measured in the length of a dying soldier's prayer.

Still sitting at his small workbench, Schwarz began to whistle as he opened a wall compartment and removed an XM-8 assault rifle. The new weapon gleamed with oil and polish. Working the arming lever, Schwarz inserted a plastic clip. The 5.56 mm HEAT rounds inside were clearly visible through a clear plastic window.

"Had a little talk with Cowboy, did you?" Blancanales asked mockingly.

"Why not? We've got to field-test these things sometime," Schwarz stated, checking the 40 mm grenade launcher attached to the side of the XM-8 assault rifle.

So far, he approved of the new weapon. The XM-8 had excellent balance, an oversize ejector port to reduce jams, ambidextrous safety and was a good two pounds lighter than an M-16. That didn't sound like much, but after a twenty mile run through the jungle, that measly two pounds could feel like half a ton. Two pounds lighter, yet it had greater range and was significantly quieter.

"Five miles to the cemetery," Lyons announced, checking the navigation unit clipped to the dashboard. "Better get those out of sight." Near his sneakers was a long box marked with the name of a local florist. It was tied with a ribbon and smelled slightly of gun oil.

"Anything on the radar?" Blancanales asked, working the slide on his Colt .380 automatic. The weapon was equipped with a bulbous acoustical silencer. That made it harder to draw fast, but the acoustical silencer would last forever, unlike a conventional silencer, which only worked for a few rounds.

"Passive is clear," Schwarz reported, checking the machines. "We had a ping before, but it was just a traffic cop checking our speed."

"Are you sure?" Lyons demanded, signaling to change lanes.

"Hell yes, I'm sure," Schwarz snorted, crossing his arms defiantly. "The day I can't tell the damn difference between traffic radar and a missile getting target acquisition, please shoot me."

The other men accepted that, and settled in for the long ride. There were small airports a lot closer to the Bonaventure Cemetery that the commercial one they had used, but none of them were quite large enough to accommodate a C-130.

Only a few minutes later, they reached Boca Raton. The cemetery was located outside town, safely behind some tree-covered hills, and thus out of the sight of the most-elderly townspeople so as to not impolitely remind them of their own mortality.

Sculptured hedges divided the different sections, and an artificial waterfall splashed down from a central hillock to form a shallow stream that meandered through the lush greenery. The sprawling cemetery was a rich green, the perfect condition of the smooth expanse almost resembling a golf course. On the crest was a stand of oak trees with a tiered fountain splashing playfully inside the cool shade. Only the neat rows of orderly headstones marred the sylvan expanse. Only a few monuments stood amid the others, along with a row of garish mausoleums.

A high stone wall completely encircled the cemetery, and the front gates were simple affairs of wrought iron, thick enough to stop a Mack truck.

"Very impressive," Blancanales muttered as they drove through. "I'll bet they have very little trouble with grave robbers here."

"This is Boca, you idiot, not Transylvania!" Schwarz snorted in amusement.

"No, Politician is right. Lots of rich folks live around here," Lyons agreed, driving along the curved roadway. "And most of them want to be buried wearing their favorite gold watch or diamond jewelry. A fast man with a shovel could make a small fortune if he struck right after the funeral of a millionaire."

Disgusted, Schwarz frowned. "When I die, just drop me into the sea with my dog tags and a rock for ballast. You can keep everything else."

"And the way you play poker," Blancanales added, "that's all there will be—tags and a rock."

"Bitch, bitch, bitch, that inside straight paid for your new plasma screen, didn't it?"

"For which I thank you, in high definition and Dolby stereo."

"You're welcome, old buddy." Schwarz chuckled, patting the other man on the shoulder, then his face tightened. "Oh, shit, this is a trap."

"Yeah, I know," Lyons growled, slipping a hand inside his windbreaker to loosen the Colt Python in his shoulder holster. "I just spotted it a second ago."

The other men needed no further encouragement to ready their weapons for combat. The van was filled with the soft metallic clicks of working arming bolts and safeties disengaging. Every car in the parking lot was dusty, and badly needed to be washed, as if they had been there for days without moving. This was exactly the sort of detail that a street cop looked for to spot an abandoned vehicle parked along a busy downtown street. Now, a grieving family might leave a car here for a few hours, or even overnight, but certainly no longer than that, and not ten of them. That was way beyond the limits of probability. These cars were merely window decorations to make the place look more inviting and less empty. Which meant the entire cemetery was a trap. But was it for them or somebody else? Did the enemy know Able Team had arrived, or were they still waiting for a target? Only one way to find out, and that was to go ask them, face-to-face.

The loose gravel of the parking lot crunched under the tires of the cargo van as Lyons casually headed into the far corner and stopped well away from the other cars.

"Get hard, people," Lyons said, pretending to adjust his collar to activate the throat mike hidden underneath. "If this is not for us, they will not want to damage the van and give away the show. Whoever this is, they'll wait until we step outside and then take us down hard."

"Blood on the gravel being a lot easier to disguise than a burning car wreck," Blancanales added, adjusting the flesh-colored radio bud in his ear. Unless the entire cemetery was mined to blow, any snipers would have to wait for the Stony Man operatives to reveal themselves to become targets. The soft recon had just gone hard.

"Especially this one," Lyons said, brushing away the top of the flower box to extract a massive Atchisson autoshotgun.

"Confirmed," Schwarz stated, looking through a scope of the new XM-8 rifle. "We're already painted with a UV laser from somebody in those trees on top of the hill. I can see it sweeping back and forth, waiting for us to step outside and say welcome."

Tugging on a dark baseball cap to cover his blond hair, Lyons started to reach for the hand mike, but stopped just in time. Even if the sniper was scanning the EM bands, he'd never be able to decipher the encoded transmission, but the mere fact that there had been a transmission would tell him far too much. The last thing they could do was call for help, because it would literally be the last thing they ever did. Their pilot, Jack Grimaldi, was on his own.

"The numbers are falling, brothers," Blancanales stated, draping a bandolier of clips and shells around his neck. "If we take too much longer, the sniper will know we're wise, and then all hell breaks loose."

"For him," Lyons whispered menacingly, easing open the driver's side door and slipping quietly outside.

Crawling on their bellies into the flowering shrubbery, the three men snaked along the wood chips covering the dark soil. The smells of nature surrounded them, but their focus was on the copse of oak trees on top of the distant hill.

Entering a thick growth of laurel, Schwarz swung up the XM-8 and looked through the built-in telescopic sights to try to find the source of the UV laser. The beam entered the shadows in the crown of the tree and vanished. He knew where the sniper was located, but could not get a clear view.

"This could be a friendly," Schwarz whispered, shifting position in the greenery. "The Feds or even Homeland."

"Unlikely," Lyons began as a flash of light came from within the oaks and a fiery dart raced down the hill to violently explode on the side of the van.

The strident concussion seemed to shake the world, it was so loud, and the car alarms on the other vehicles in the parking lot began hooting, whooping and blaring.

Swirling around, a thick cloud of smoke masked the van as a soft rain of shrapnel sprinkled the gravel. But as the dark fumes cleared, the cargo van was still there. A side panel had been burned completely clean from the explosion, and the bare armor underneath now exposed.

"Well, he knows who we are now. Go, go, go!" Lyons commanded.

The Stony Man operatives broke cover to charge across the open field of gravel and dive for safety behind some granite headstones.

Almost instantly, there came the hard chatter of a powerful machine gun, and the headstone shook from the arrival of hot lead, sharp chips flying off from the hammering impacts.

Recognizing the sound of a FN Mini-Mi, called a M-249 SAW by U.S. troops, the Stony Man team waited until the 200-round belt cycled empty, then they moved again, fast and in different directions. Only a suicide gave an opponent a group target.

As the SAW lurched back into operation, Blancanales and Schwarz took refuge behind a tall hedge, only to recoil from a pungent reek. Looking around, they spotted the tattered body of an old man in work clothes next to a lawn mower, his dried blood splattered over the machine. The hedge had hidden the corpse from them in the parking lot. Filled with a cold certainty, the Stony Man operatives knew in their guts there would be more corpses scattered around the beautiful cemetery.

Carefully aiming between the body of an angel and her outstretched wings, Lyons cut loose with a long burst from the Atchisson, the sustained discharge briefly sounding louder than the rocket attack. The leaves in the copse of trees shook wildly from the arrival of the steel buckshot, but there was no answering cry of pain or spray of blood.

Chattering away once more, the SAW probed the hedges randomly, and Lyons responded with another barrage, letting Blancanales and Schwarz jump ahead several rows. Racing behind a hedge, they fired short bursts from their own weapons into the air. Both of the grenade launchers could reach the trees by now, but the team wanted the man alive. This mission was still basically a recon, and hard intel was the goal, not revenge.

Slapping in a clip of rubber-tipped stun bullets, Schwarz angled a long burst at another obelisk near the top of the hill, and he managed to get some of them to ricochet into the trees. The SAW stopped firing, but only for a moment. Blancanales tried the same tactic from a different direction, but the results were sadly the same.

"Hollywood to Sky King," Lyons subvocalized into his throat mike, firing a short burst into the trees. "We have a guests at the party. Repeat—" A strident squeal erupted in his earbuds, and the man bit back a curse as he turned down the volume. The radio signal was being jammed.

As if focusing on the brief transmission, the SAW rattled the headstones around the man, the 5.56 mm rounds annihilating more flowers and bushes. Blancanales and Schwarz answered on full automatic as Lyons sprinted for the protection of a granite bench. He made it just in time, a single round plowing through his shirt to glance off the body armor underneath.

Once more the M-249 roared into life, spent brass tumbling from the crown of the tree like hot autumn leaves. The billiard-table-smooth field of grass churned from the arrival of the hollowpoint rounds, and several headstones were knocked over, leaving a large gap in the neatly trimmed hedges.

Sending back a full drum of cartridges in reply, Lyons cursed at the realization that the sniper was creating a shatterzone, an open space that Able Team would not enter without getting torn into pieces. Smart. Too damn smart.

A grenade came sailing out of the trees, arching high into the clear blue sky. Quickly jerking up the Atchisson, Lyons emptied an entire drum of 12-gauge cartridges, and the grenade detonated harmlessly over a reflection pool, the halo of shrapnel hissing into the water.

Crouching behind a marble statue of Venus, Blancanales sharply whistled to catch the attention of the other men, then he raised a fist, splayed his fingers and flashed two. Silently, Lyons and Schwarz nodded in agreement.

As the other men opened fired with their weapons, Blancanales stepped to the left, then spun around and sprinted to the right. His heart pounded savagely in his chest, and he almost tripped at the startling discovery of a young woman lying dead in the grass. Jumping over the body, Blancanales did a shoulder roll and took cover behind a wide obelisk. Forcing himself to ignore the deceased civilian, the soldier concentrated the M-203 on the distant trees.

Running low behind the hedges, Schwarz discovered more bodies, a family this time, including a swaddled infant.

Snarling, the soldier stood and fired the grenade launcher. The 40 mm shell sailed up the hill to arc between the oaks and slam into the tiered fountain, blowing debris in every direction. Softly, somebody cursed in pain, and a large machine gun tumbled out of the branches to smack onto the sodden ground. It looked like an M-249 SAW.

Suspecting a trick, the three Stony Man operatives patiently waited, reloading their weapons. A moment later there was a powerful boom from within the trees and a headstone violently exploded, throwing out a corona of broken granite. When the smoke cleared, the headstone was gone.

That had been a Barrett 25 mm rifle! Blancanales realized, blood trickling down his face from a cut on his temple. Bolt-action, 5-round clip and way too accurate for this short a range. We'll have to do something about that double-quick.

Another headstone detonated, closely followed by a statue of Jesus, and Schwarz grunted from an impact on his body armor as he fired the XM-8 assault rifle. However, there was no feeling of a spreading warmth, which meant there had been no penetration. Level Five ballistic cloth was a foot soldier's very best friend. Tomorrow his bruises would hurt like hell, but right now his job was to keep low, move fast and stay alive.

With the stink of propellant and old blood in his nostrils, Lyons spit the foul taste from his mouth, and eased in his last ammo drum from the Atchisson. After this, he would be down to the Colt Python. Even worse, these last cartridges were all fléchette rounds, stainless-steel razor blades would mince a grown man into hamburger in a split second. Not exactly what he would have chosen to capture an opponent. However, that gave him pause. Fair enough.

Drawing the massive handcannon, Lyons dashed sideways, triggering both weapons. The sniper attempted to aim the Barrett just ahead of the running man, and make him run into the deadly blast, but Lyons constantly changed direction until he reached the temporary safety of a headstone, only to roll into the shallow runoff from the waterfall. Half a heartbeat later, the headstone detonated like a bomb.

Thumbing in a fat HE shell, Schwarz launched it high into the sky and it hit on the far side of the hill, the roiling blast achieving zero results.

Taking a moment to catch his breath, Blancanales spun around the granite slab to fire his own grenade launcher. The 40 mm stun bag disappeared into the trees yielding no effect. But a large swatch of leaves was gone, leaving a deadly gap in the protective cover of the lush greenery.

Understanding what the man was doing, the other Stony Man operatives now attempted to do the same, their stun bags ripping away the leafy boughs until something metallic was seen nestled amid the thinning foliage.

Thumbing in a loose cartridge, Lyons scowled at the sight. Son of a bitch, that was an Auto-Sentry! With the knowledge that there was no living opponent in the tree, he unleashed the full might of the Atchisson. Leaves exploded into the air in a whirlwind of destruction, and something man-size fell to the ruins of the fountain.

Giving the fallen machine a wide berth, the Stony Man operatives warily checked for any other Auto-Sentries in the trees and bushes on the hillock. When satisfied that they were alone, the men approached the Sentry. They scowled in open disapproval at the sophisticated device. The video camera was still attempting to aim the lethal Barrett toward them, a LAW rocket launcher clicking futilely. The antenna was gone, so the deadly machine was merely attempting to perform the last command it had received.

"Whoever installed this here was watching through the camera until activating the jammer," Schwarz said, swinging around his laptop. "They waited until those poor folks back there were in the proper position, and then killed each one, making sure the bodies fell behind cover to not warn anybody pulling into the parking lot."

"Ruthless," Blancanales muttered in open disgust.

"Monstrous," Lyons amended, resting the hot barrel of the Atchisson on a broad shoulder. "They were watching the cemetery through that video camera, until we arrived. Then they put the Sentry on automatic, and activated the radio jammers."

"And burned out the transponder," Schwarz added glumly, lifting a piece of melted electronics. "There's no way we can track them through this."

"Wait a second. Those are blocks of C-4 inside the Sentry," Blancanales said with a frown. "If this thing was designed to explode and destroy any possible evidence if somebody captured it, then why didn't it?" Slowly he smiled. "Oh, right."

"Exactly," Schwarz agreed, patting the laptop. "They were jamming us, but we were also jamming them."

Lyons almost smiled. "You're a devious man, Gadgets."

Blancanales snorted. "Never saw an Auto-Sentry equipped with multiple weapon systems before. That also something new, Gadgets?"

Attaching some wires to an exposed circuit board, the man shrugged. "Nothing I ever heard about. Must be a modification they did. Clever idea, though."

"Yeah, clever as hell," Blancanales muttered, glancing back at the dead people sprawled in the ruined shrubbery. From this angle, he could see that the team had missed several corpses scattered around the hillock.

Typing some commands into the laptop, Schwarz grinned in satisfaction. Reaching past the twitching Barrett, the man yanked out some wiring, and the Sentry went dark and still. Instantly, the jamming field went off the air.

"Sky King to Rock Hounds. ETA, four minutes." Grimaldi's voice blared in their earbuds. "Repeat, ETA three minutes."

"Sky King, this is Hollywood," Lyons said quickly into his throat mike. "The party is over. Return to base. We'll—" He glanced down at the van in the gravel parking lot. The chassis was dented, but still serviceable. Even the Lexan plastic windows were intact. However, all four of the tires were flat. "We'll grab a cab, and be there soon."

"What happened to your roller skate?"

Lyons grimaced. "Somebody brought a firecracker to the party."

"Ah, understood, Hollywood," Grimaldi continued smoothly. "I'll have Bear call off the local cops, and send a couple of blacksuits to recover what's left of the van."

"Much appreciated," Lyons said, listening to the howl of sirens growing steadily louder.

"All a part of the service, Hollywood." Grimaldi chuckled. "This is Sky King, returning to blacktop. See you soon. Out."

"Over and out," Lyons said, brushing back his blond hair.

The three men waited expectantly for a few minutes until the police sirens abruptly stopped. In the ringing silence, the decimation of the cemetery somehow seemed even worse than before.

Loosening the clips and wires, Schwarz returned the laptop to his shoulder bag, then began ripping out the circuit boards from the Sentry.

"All right, anybody feel like checking the grave of the Russian janitor?" Lyons asked, clicking the safety on the Atchisson.

"I'll do it," Blancanales snorted, swinging up the M-16 assault rifle. Sweeping the rows of headstones, he found a fresh mound of dirt, checked the name on the headstone and then fired a single round. Instantly the grave exploded, blowing a geyser of dirt and rocks toward the clouds.

"Yeah, thought so," the man muttered, lowering the assault rifle. "You would have to be a fool to booby trap an entire cemetery, but not the main reason we came here."

"And whatever else these people are, they're not fools," Lyons agreed dourly, bending to recover one of the empty 25 mm rounds for the big Barrett.

Inspecting the bottom, the man was not surprised to see there was no lot number on the brass. There was no way to trace the ammunition. The Stony Man team used something similar in their weapons, as did the CIA, Navy SEALs, Homeland Security, British MI-5, the Mossad, a lot of folks who wanted to keep their involvement in clandestine operations out of the public scrutiny.

"Then again, maybe they are," Schwarz muttered in a measured tone, extracting a tiny microprocessor from the morass of wiring and holding it triumphantly to the noon sunlight.

FIVE MILES AWAY in nearby Boca Raton, an armed man on the roof of the tallest downtown building released the telescope. When the transponder signal of the Auto-Sentry stopped broadcasting, that meant the jammer was in operation, which meant the balloon had gone up at the Bonaventure Cemetery. However, he was safe. No matter what sort of advanced military optics the invaders might have with them, there was no way for anybody to find him this far away without astronomical-grade equipment, the kind that could not be transported without a hundred men and a fleet of trucks.

Pulling a PDA from his belt, the man thumbed in a coded text message, then sent it out over the Internet as a microsecond T-burst. The message was simple and concise. "Package delivered, goods en route."

Tucking away the device, the man wiped his prints off the big telescope and headed for the elevator. Time to go home. Briefly, the mercenary wondered if the three men were with the FBI, CIA, NSA or more of those triple-damn Homeland

Security agents. Those were very hard boys, and mighty hard to stop. Then again, it really didn't make a difference. Once Westmore had them strapped down to a surgical table and then began to remove pieces of their internal anatomy, they'd talk.

Everybody always did.

CHAPTER FOUR

Podbanske Base, Slovakia

When the Communist government fell, the Russian soldiers assigned to the Czechoslovakian missile base simply turned off the equipment and went home. Naturally, they took along everything they could in lieu of pay, but all of the big machinery stayed intact and fully operational—including a mainframe computer and all of the big thermonuclear weapons. Only the tactical nukes had been carried away, which was why General Novostk had been forced to trade a Euro-Russian hydrogen bomb for a Chinese tactical nuke. That trade was the key to get the much more useful T-bombs.

In every way possible, the Soviet missile base was superior to the old headquarters of Saris Castle in the badlands of the Carpathian Mountains where even the goats found nothing to eat. Easily half of the crumbling ruins were inhabitable during the winter, with the water pipes freezing solid, the toilets backing up and the electricity fading away for no apparent reason. Then the soldiers had been forced to become extremely proficient with their handguns to eliminate the staggering rat population. One section of the cellar they had declared a demilitarized zone, and simply nailed the door shut in surrender.

But here at Missile Base Nine, the Slovakians had lights, heat, food, weapons, vehicles, everything needed to wage war on the hated Russians. Of course, the general had known about the base for decades, but even when it had been abandoned, there was no way to get past the massive armored door at the entrance. Then, like a gift from God, some crazy American billionaire had hired them to steal a T-bomb, and offered full technical support, including an American criminal who was an expert at opening bank vaults. Once the Slovakians got past the door, the general discovered the nuclear weapons in storage, and a bold new plan was made, with Lindquist eagerly on board from the very beginning.

Prompted by a blast of the Russian truck's horn, a dozen soldiers rushed out of a tinted-glass office on the loading dock to assist with the unloading of the T-bomb.

Masking his impatience, General Novostk waited for the unloading to commence. On their way to Slovakia, Colonel Lindquist and Lieutenant Vladislav had been dropped off at a small island in the Black Sea to proceed on their individual assignments, recruitment and misdirection. This would allow the general to concentrate on the real mission: revenge and mass destruction.

"Good to have you back, sir," a corporal shouted to Novostk, giving a stiff salute. "May I take it that the mission went well?"

"More than well. We have acquired seven of the weapons," Novostk replied, returning the salute. Normally, soldiers did not salute a superior officer while inside a building, but the entire Red Army base was underground, and so technically inside, so he accepted one if offered, but did not push the matter. These were patriots, ready to die to serve their nation. Novostk would not begrudge them some minor blurring of the rules of military etiquette.

"Seven," the corporal gasped. The word was repeated several times by the unloading crew. "That's grand news, sir. We'll smash the Russians for sure now."

Did that mean he had harbored doubts before? Novostk wondered privately. That was disquieting, but then soldiers always grumbled, even patriots.

Just then, an electric crane rumbled into life, the arm swinging out over the truck, heavy chains jingling as they descended. The soldiers were scurrying to attach the chains to the precious T-bomb.

"Handle them carefully, gentlemen!" the general bellowed in his best parade-ground voice. "If you set one off, I will be most displeased."

That made the soldiers crack smiles, and they redoubled the work efforts, the previous tension massively eased.

"I'm always impressed how you do that, sir," the corporal said in clear envy, resting a hand on the Rex pistol holster at his side. "I'll never make much of an officer until I learn how."

"You will learn in time," General Novostk said, walking out of the way of the busy workers. "Now, is there anything to report on your end? How is the house cleaning progressing?"

The corporal flashed a toothy grin. "Complete victory, sir. We got rid of all the bats by using a flamethrower and roasting the little bastards alive."

Slowly, the general raised an eloquent eyebrow. The hull of an ICBM was just strong enough to withstand launch, and keep the fuel tanks attached to the engines long enough to reach the target halfway around the world. There had been ten missiles snug in their silos. All of them had been damaged in some way from sheer neglect, but by cannibalizing parts for one to fix another, he had hoped to get three, maybe four of them, into working order.

"Son, did you just tell me," the general asked in a measure voice, "that you used a flamethrower to clean out the colony of bats inside the launch tube of a thermonuclear ICBM?"

That caught the corporal off guard. "Why...yes sir. I mean, no, sir. I mean..."

With a gentle thump, the first decahedron was placed on the loading dock, and men swarmed to remove the chains to go for the next.

"Were the missiles damaged in any way?" Novostk demanded, every trace of humor and patience gone from his demeanor. Suddenly the friendly old man in a uniform was gone, replaced with "Iron Ivan," the terror of the Carpathian Mountains.

"No, sir," the corporal replied hastily, giving another fast salute. "Well, a little, but during the course of fighting the blaze we found a sealed tunnel that led to a cave on the surface. It holds ten SS-25 Sickle missile trucks, sir. Each of them in prime condition, with no work needed at all to make them ready for combat. Well, aside from charging the truck batteries."

The general squinted. "Ten of them?"

"Yes, sir, ten."

The second bomb was placed alongside the first.

"Indeed," the general murmured, deep in thought.

The quartermaster records had only listed one such truck on the premises, and the soldiers had never been able to find the vehicle. The natural assumption was that it had been stolen along with so much other equipment when the staff departed. But now the general could see that report had meant one wing of the deadly missiles. True, they had nowhere near the range of the monster ICBMs in the silos, but those needed a lot of work to get working once more, while the SS-25 Sickles were ready to go. As the old saying went, a copper in your hand was better than a bag of gold in your dreams.

Ten missiles and seven bombs, with one of those held back as a reserve and Colonel Lindquist using another to divert the world's attention. If the technicians could not crack the defenses of the weapons, he would launch all ten missiles, one live and a dummy toward every target. That would double the chances of the T-bomb getting through the air defenses of each city chosen: Beijing, Paris, London, New Delhi and Washington. Millions would die in the volley, quite possibly a lot more. Which would guarantee the start of World War III, and the end of Russia. The war might spread to other nations, but the Slovakians would be fine, and that was all that mattered.

"That is excellent news, Corporal," Novostk said, repeating the man's rank to let him know he could keep it, for now. "Make me a list of every major city they can reach, along with flight times."

"Here you are, sir," the corporal said, thrusting out an envelope. "Population numbers, size of military, any known antimissile defenses, distance in kilometers and miles and estimated flight times. Once we install the bombs in the warheads we can launch in five minutes."

Waving the fellow away, Novostk read the report while the rest of the bombs were laid down as gently as Christmas eggs.

"Sir, the six bombs are unloaded," Sergeant Melori reported with a casual salute. "I already have some men hauling one down to the basement to be attached to the self-destruct circuits." He knew there used to be a big hydrogen bomb hardwired there, but they had traded it at Milan in exchange for the NBC suits, the VX nerve gas and many miscellaneous items needed to bring the base back to a full war status, including several tons of food. Trading bombs for corned beef—the technician wasn't quite sure who got the better of that deal.

"Very good," the general said, folding the report to tuck it away inside his jacket. "Now, I fear that I must speak to you on a most delicate matter." He paused. "A private matter."

"Of course, sir," Melori replied, wondering what his oafish friend Vladislav had done now. Killed someone or broken another piece of irreplaceable equipment? Soon the general would decide the man was a menace to the mission, and ask to have a quiet word with him somewhere in private. Just the two of them, on the end of the cliff, and a gun containing a single bullet.

Joining the general at the end of the loading dock, the sergeant warily kept his back to the wall.

Noticing the surreptitious maneuver, Novostk smiled. "No, Sergeant, I am not here to deliver some gun-barrel justice. Instead, I need to ask you a very personal question."

"Sir?" Sergeant Melori asked, also not liking the direction this new line was heading.

Clearly unsure of how to proceed, the general fumbled for the correct words, not wishing to insult the man he needed for an important favor.

"I think I know what you're trying to ask, sir," Sergeant Melori whispered softly. "And I would admit this to nobody else, but the answer is yes, I do not care for the intimate company of women." Even as the man said the words, his stomach tightened. Back in the hill country, such a declaration would get you killed. But Melori had taken a solemn oath to die for the general, so at the very least he should tell the man the plain, unvarnished truth.

"Thank God." General Novostk exhaled in relief. "Sergeant, I need you to return to our headquarters at Saris Castle and oversee the safety of a prisoner. The professor will most likely be…uncooperative…and may need to be forced to do as we wish, and unlock the secrets of the T-bombs. She is also supposed to be a very beautiful woman, and I do not want the men at the castle to, shall we say, lose sight of our real goal. We need her to remove the antipersonnel hardware defending the bombs, not set one off early to end her unbearable sexual torture."

"Or to replace the traps with new ones of her own," Melori finished in sudden understanding. "And with my knowledge of electronics, I'll also be able to stop her from doing any unwanted augmentation of the weapons." He blinked. "This is why you're having her work at the castle, and not here. Just in case."

The general was pleased to see his choice had been the correct one. "Exactly. Our work is too important to risk being derailed by a madwoman defending her honor."

"Yes, sir. I'll take ten men as an escort, have them load a T-bomb into a half-track and leave immediately."

"Make it fifty, and bring along some motorcycles, and the Soviet tank. It is a hard journey through rough country, and nothing must get in your way. I want you there long before Lieutenant Vladislav arrives."

So let the men have time to get used to me being in charge. Smart. The old man didn't miss a trick. Then an unpleasant thought occurred. "Sir, what if…what if she cannot be convinced to help us?"

"She must," the general said flatly, turning away. "There is no other option."

Slowly comprehension dawned and the sergeant nodded in grim understanding. They would attempt to do this honorably, but as the hated KGB had taught the entire nation, the end always justified the means. The prisoner would be made to comply, end of discussion. And may God have mercy on our souls.

Milan, Italy

A GLOSSY BLACK Hummer drove slowly along the street as it meandered through a series of low hills. At a fork, the vehicle waited as liveried guards swung an ornate iron gate aside. Rolling through the barrier, the people inside the Hummer saw the gate close behind them. The gate meant nothing; it was merely a social courtesy to deter outsiders from taking this particular road. However, it also served as a line of disembarkation, clearly showing the local police where their jurisdiction ended. Technically the land beyond the flimsy fence was still Italy, but in reality it was a world as unreachable as Mars. The mansion and surrounding grounds were privately owned by the Norel Corporation, the biggest arms dealers in the world.

Carefully moving along the private street, the driver of the Hummer stopped for a security check at a brick kiosk where the guards carried holstered pistols. Everything was in order, and the Hummer proceeded up a steeply sloping road into the rugged mountains. On the beautiful azure sea below, sailboats moved in the far distance, along with an unusually high concentration of yachts, and a couple of cargo carriers flying the flag of either the politically neutral Switzerland or Luxembourg.

Privately owned helicopters flitted back and forth from the vessels, steadily conveying passengers to the heliport of the mansion sprawled on top of the craggy mountain. All of the vessels were moored just past the twelve-mile mark from the coast, and thus were in international waters and safe from any unwanted intrusion by the federal police, the Italian navy or even NATO.

Once more, the driver of the black Hummer stopped at a kiosk for a security check. This deep into Norel territory, the kiosk more resembled a concrete pillbox. The guards were carrying AK-105 assault rifles, each one equipped with a 30 mm grenade launcher. Off to the side was a sandbag nest where guards were manning several of the new MANPAD rocket launchers, powerful enough to blow a hole through even a U.S. Army Abrams M-1 tank or an Apache gunship.

The security guards found the people in the Hummer acceptable and waved them through. Sheikh Abdul Ben Hassan was a regular customer here, although he always seemed to send different representatives. But that was the prerogative of a customer; the only person a man could trust was himself, and the only safe place on Earth was the grave.

Following the road to the crest of the mountain, the driver of the Hummer stopped the vehicle in a spacious parking lot nearly filled with luxury vehicles.

"You can almost taste the money," David McCarter muttered, running a finger along his stiff collar. He was wearing a designer suit, a blue cravat of raw silk held in place by a gold stickpin. His shoes were Italian loafers and a Rolex Supreme glinted on his wrist. As a former member of the elite British SAS, the lanky man felt about as uncomfortable as a nun in a whorehouse on coupon night.

"Smell the blood money, you mean," muttered T. J. Hawkins, maintaining a neutral demeanor as he set the brake. Born Thomas Jefferson Hawkins, the combat veteran was called T.J. by his family, and Hawk by his fellow soldiers. A sleek Beretta machine pistol was holstered at his side, spare clips thrusting up from an ammo pouch like ancient Japanese samurai swords.

Stepping out of the Hummer, the two men coolly studied the high stone wall separating the parking lot from the Norel estate on the other side. There were no coils of concertina wire, electrical wires or even video cameras edging the defenses of the mountaintop mansion. But the former member of Delta Force knew that the plain-looking wall was jammed full of reactive tank armor, antipersonnel mines, EM scanners and more proximity sensors than the west wing of the White House. There was nothing crude or slapdash about the Norel operations, but then the international weapons merchants were richer than most small nations. Every weekend, the Norel exposition was open for business, and as old saying goes, business was good.

As with many aspects of life in Italy, the operators had an understanding with the law, along with an uneasy truce. No deaths occurred here, and no weapons were sold to anybody who lived within a hundred miles. If the federal police or the military ever did arrive, they could arrest many of the customers, but the next day Milan, Rome and Venice would be flooded with advanced weaponry sold at discount prices, the Norel cartel practically giving the guns away as revenge.

Both of the Stony Man operatives knew that there were no actual weapons at the exposition. Only brochures and smiling salesmen. A customer perused the merchandise, made selections and paid a hefty deposit, with the rest of the money upon delivery, which was always very far away from Milan. It was a genuine den of thieves that operated on the honor system.

After a moment McCarter snapped his fingers and the remaining three members of Phoenix Force climbed from the Hummer as if they had been waiting for permission. They were all well dressed, freshly scrubbed, yet carried the unmistakable aura of controlled violence, the calling card of every mercenary alive.

"Man, I hate doing this naked," Gary Manning muttered. The burly Canadian brushed a callused hand over his slicked-down hair. He felt like a damn fool in the tailored clothing, with a small diamond clipped to his left earlobe. There was a bulky Desert Eagle automatic holstered under his jacket, two spare clips attached to the straps. An expert sniper, his preferred weapon was a Barrett .50 rifle, but that had to be left behind for this particular mission.

"At least you have that popgun," Rafael Encizo countered, adjusting his glasses. "I only have my winning smile."

The eyewear was fake, merely sheets of clear glass, but they served as a vital part of his disguise as the money. The Stony Man operative was wearing a dark business suit of only moderate price range, but the attaché case handcuffed to his wrist was sheathed in the finest Moroccan leather. The lock was a biometric sensor plate, and the hinges glistened like solid gold. The stocky Puerto Rican had a quick smile, and even faster hands, and was considered one of the best underwater demolitions experts in the world.

"No guns allowed, brother," Calvin James said in a thick Chicago accent. The former U.S. Navy SEAL was wearing a yachting outfit, including white deck shoes and a jaunty cap. He was also armed with a Desert Eagle .357 Magnum, the big-bore automatic carefully fired a dozen times to take the clean sheen off the brand-new weapon.

"Rather ironic for a weapons market, don't you think?" Encizo asked out of the corner of his mouth.

"I don't think they know what the word means," McCarter replied, striding for the front gate.

Leaving the Hummer unlocked, the other men followed close behind as befitting their place as his staff. At the gate, the Stony Man operatives showed their identification once more to the guards. These men were wearing Level Five body armor, the so-called Dragonskin, and carrying MP-5 submachine guns slung on their shoulders. Grudgingly, McCarter approved of the choice of weapons. The Heckler & Koch MP-5 was what his team regularly used on combat missions, and in his opinion was the best all-purpose weapon in existence.

"Welcome to Norel, gentlemen," a bald guard said, waving a hand toward the plastic arch of a weapon scanner. "Step this way, please."

As McCarter stepped through the arch, a soft beep was audible.

"No guns," the second guard stated in halting English. "Leave it with us."

"But this is a gun show," McCarter stated in mock outrage.

Laying a hand on the MP-5, the guard stiffened. "No guns."

"Excuse my partner, sir," the first guard said smoothly. "The Norel weapons policy is for your own protection. There are far too many—shall we say—old friends who meet here, and in the heat of the moment... well..." The guard smiled tolerantly, spreading his hands in a classic Italian gesture.

Pretending to be annoyed, the members of Phoenix Force passed over their never-before-used weapons, and McCarter incredibly received a claim chit in return, as if they had just stored their coats at a restaurant.

"And how is the sheikh these days, sir?" a guard asked out of the blue.

"Still deceased," McCarter replied, then added a smile that said the exact opposite was true.

The two armed men laughed and bowed slightly as they waved him forward.

One at a time, the Stony Man operatives walked through the weapon scanner. There was a brief moment of concern about the locked attaché case carried by Encizo, so he reluctantly opened it to display a double row of small bars of gold bullion. The guards probed for a false bottom, but found nothing and finally allowed Encizo through to join the other members of Phoenix Force.

It was clear that the guards were suspicious of that much rare metal being used as a payment, as diamonds were much more prevalent. They were lighter, smaller, easier to transport and could be smuggled inside a human mule if necessary. However, there was nothing forbidden about using precious metals; only narcotics were not acceptable as payment for the goods. Not for any ethical reasons, but purely because the quality of drugs was often too difficult for even a professional to properly ascertain.

Strolling casually, McCarter led the way into the weapons market, the team effortlessly joining the milling throng of international criminals, terrorists and warlords. Waiters moved through the crowd carrying silver trays of snacks or glasses of champagne, and everybody seemed to be smoking.

More guards stood in cupolas on top of the mansion, watching the crowd intently, their hands full of bolt-action Remington rifles, the barrels tipped with bulbous silencers. On top of the cupolas, tiny radar dishes spun around, endlessly sweeping the sky for any conceivable danger.

A colossal stripped tent large enough for a circus completely covered the grounds, masking any activities from the prying cameras of spy satellites. The sun was shining brightly over the outdoor exposition, and everything inside the camouflage-colored canvas was cast with dappled shadows. Humbugs and radio jamming units were everywhere, protecting the buyers from being overhead or recorded. With this much electronic trash being broadcast, not even the brute force signal of a primitive spark coil could reach more than even a few feet, and a cell phone, digital recorder or conventional transponder was utterly useless.

Having come to a similar opinion, McCarter grunted at the observation. These Italian bastards truly were the merchants of disaster.

The booths under the tent were elaborate, sometimes garish, edged with neon or flashing lights. The first booth displayed cell phones that could fire .22 bullets but still function as regular phones. The next offered the new Neostead shotgun, computer monitors showing live demonstrations on the wide variety of 12-gauge shells the double magazines could carry, stun bags and fléchette rounds that could, and did, literally cut a bound man in two. There was fresh sawdust on the grass for the more squeamish patrons.

Another booth decked out in metallic silver was selling Samsung Auto-Sentries, the next offered Heckler & Koch G-12 caseless rifles, and the following booth was jammed full of people buying HEAT rounds in a variety of calibers. Clearly, the High Explosive Armor-piercing Tracer bullets were a very hot commodity.

"A flea market from Hell," James muttered.

Trying not to scowl, Manning nodded agreement. "Except the bite of these fleas will fucking kill you."

Near the center of the tent, an oversize booth was offering a wide variety of Armored Personnel Carriers, including some extremely inexpensive Bradley Fighting Vehicles.

"Aren't…aren't those the original models with the aluminum armor?" Hawkins asked in surprise.

"Damn straight," Encizo snarled. "One hit with a LAW and that thing will burst into flames, and give off toxic fumes that'll kill everything for a hundred yards, including the crew."

"No wonder they're so cheap," McCarter muttered, continuing onward. The next generation of Bradley was fine, a lot of the mistakes fixed, but this early model was a deathtrap, plain and simple. "Bloody hell, a man has got to really stay on his toes here."

"*Caveat emptor,* baby," Manning replied with the brutal wisdom of a combat veteran.

The next booth was selling the same type of body armor as that worn by the guards, and business was brisk.

"Dragonskin by Pinnacle Industries," the salesman boasted proudly. "The best body armor in existence. The only way to kill you while wearing this would be with a rocket."

"Or a rock between the eyes," Hawkins drawled unimpressed. A trained soldier was always more dangerous than the weapons he carried. Only civilians thought otherwise.

The next couple of booths promoted an assortment of performance-enhancement drugs, then came knives in every size and shape, and then a long booth filled with photographs of smart bombs, an easel showing how the canister carried a hundred smaller bomblets of different functions: high explosive, caltrops to stop vehicles or even listening devices to find a hidden enemy. Grinning customers placed orders, payment was arranged and deliveries scheduled around the world. The transactions were completed in only a few moments.

"Very efficient," Manning noted, hands clasped behind his back. "Like sheep getting shorn."

"Only not as smart," Encizo muttered, shifting his grip on the attaché case. "Their security sucks. They didn't weigh this gold to see if it was kosher."

"And if they had?" James asked, broadcasting a dazzling smile at a passing waitress. She dimpled in reply, then hurried off, terrified of the handsome killer. Everybody here was a mass murderer several times over, or else they would not have gotten an invitation to the Norel market. People who simply showed up unannounced at the door promptly disappeared through a chute in the kiosk that fed directly to the edge of the cliff overlooking the sea. The rocks caught them at the bottom, and the crabs had a feeding frenzy.

"If they had checked the gold, I would have broken their necks and taken their place at the gate," Encizo replied coolly.

"Glad to hear it," McCarter growled, sliding on a pair of mirrored sunglasses. "There are far too many people in this place who would love to—"

"You!" a voice bellowed, and several customers were rudely shoved aside to reveal an enormous man with a full beard and a single gold tooth.

"Adolfo Mendoza," McCarter growled in unhappy recognition. "Now, I thought you died when I blew up that bridge, but I guess shit floats, eh?"

"Kill you, I will!" Mendoza bellowed, waddling closer. "Like dog in street!" The words were heavily accented with Portuguese, almost comically so, but the expression on the fat man's face was in deadly earnest.

Since they were in the middle of a crowd, the rest of Phoenix Force unwillingly melted back, leaving McCarter alone to handle the matter. They would have to pretend this was a private concern and nothing to do with them. That way if McCarter was expelled or killed, they could continue the mission.

As Mendoza got closer, McCarter dropped low and spun around fast, sweeping a stiff leg across the ground. The Portuguese crime lord went tumbling to the grass hard, momentarily knocking the breath from his lungs. However, there was clearly a lot of muscle under the layers of fat, and Mendoza surged to his feet in unexpected grace to swing a haymaker at McCarter that would have taken off his head if it had connected.

As the pudgy fist sailed past, McCarter stepped in close to slam a stiff palm into the side of his neck, momentarily crushing the carotid artery. Staggering backward, Mendoza recovered, and surprisingly lashed out a martial-arts kick, the toe of his black shoe just missing McCarter's nose, the killing blow only scoring along his cheek.

Rushing forward with both hands, McCarter grabbed the foot and heaved upward. But the trick failed as Mendoza went along with the move and spun around with astonishing grace for somebody his size and buried a fist in McCarter's stomach.

He recoiled from the blow and was shocked to see a piece of fabric sticking to the fat man's hand. Glancing downward for only a split second, McCarter saw a ragged piece of his shirt gone, the ballistic cloth of his body armor underneath deeply scored. That was when he saw the glitter of steel on the other man's hand.

Dodging, McCarter grimaced. So the son of a bitch had a rosette ring, eh? Well, the concealed razor blade wouldn't help him today. Time for the fat man to die.

Deciding that diplomacy was over, McCarter dived forward, coming up in a roll and slamming an elbow behind him directly into the exposed throat of the overweight behemoth. Hacking for air, Mendoza moved away, but McCarter pressed the attack, chopping his flat hand at the side of left side of his neck, and then the other. The crime lord blocked a strike with his forearm, showing that he had some training at the martial arts, but then McCarter grabbed the hand, twisted hard and doubled over. There came the audible sound of a bone break, and the crime lord howled in agony.

The crowd had formed a circle around the combatants, and wages were being laid in a dozen different languages among the bystanders. So far, the odds were equal.

Channeling the pain into rage, Mendoza lashed out with amazing speed and kicked McCarter in the groin. His body armor took the brunt of the attack, but as McCarter backed away, the crime lord pulled a large fountain pen from a pocket with a satisfied jerk. But as Mendoza raised it high, there came a powerful report of a rifle and the pen went flying. Sailing end over end, the pen hit the side of a booth and promptly exploded, spraying out an oily fluid that immediately started smoking and eating deeply into the polished wood.

A squad of guards in matching uniforms marched out of the excited crowd and moved between the combatants.

Bending to pick up the pen, a lieutenant delicately sniffed at the broken reservoir. "Acid," the guard sneered. "Do we have this on tape?"

"Yes, sir," another guard confirmed, working the arming bolt of the deadly MP-5 submachine gun.

"That is not mine," Mendoza started, but a single look from the chief sentry shot down the lie. Sluggishly, reluctantly, the crime lord raised both hands above his head in surrender.

"Mr. Mendoza, you have violated the rules of the exposition," the guard accused harshly, casting away the trick pen. "Please leave the exposition. You are hereby banned for ten years."

"Ten years!" Mendoza cried, spittle on the side of his mouth. "Nonsense. Do you know who this man is?"

"Not in the least," the guard replied. "Is he Interpol or CIA? Perhaps MI-5 or the Mossad?"

"Not recently," said McCarter, calmly lighting a Player's cigarette.

"Yes, he is," Mendoza shouted, then relented. "No, he is not. But he's with Blue Lightning. They killed my brother and—"

"So he is not a policeman or a law-enforcement officer working undercover?"

"Well...no, he is not."

"Pity, there is a very large reward for revealing such an operative," the lieutenant stated, tapping something into a BlackBerry. "But perhaps the sun is clearly too hot today, eh? I would suggest leaving immediately, Mr. Mendoza, sir."

"But I—"

"Immediately." The change in tone was obvious.

Radiating fury, the crime lord started to speak, then reconsidered and turned to walk toward the front gate, his good arm carefully cradling the damaged wrist.

"And why is Blue Lightning here at our little market?" the lieutenant asked coolly. He had heard about the mercenary group before. They were very expensive, and always got the job done no matter the opposition. Once they had successfully assassinated a billionaire at the world famous Dubai Hotel even though he had been protected by a hundred armed men.

"Just making some purchases for Sheikh Hassan," McCarter replied, brushing some dirt off his sleeves.

"Nothing more?"

"Nothing."

"The sheikh is an old and valued customer, so I will accept your word that there will be no more unpleasantness."

"You have it."

"Fair enough. Sorry for the inconvenience, Mr. Tower," the lieutenant said as the humming BlackBerry printed out a small slip of paper. He passed it over. "There will be an extra five percent discount on your first purchase over a million euros as remuneration."

Tucking the paper into a pocket, McCarter watched the guard walk away, the other men falling into a tight formation close behind.

"Anything damaged?" James asked, looking the other man over.

"Only my pride," McCarter answered gruffly, massaging his stomach. "I had no idea the fat bastard was studying Double-H."

"That was not Portuguese military hand-to-hand combat, but kung fu," James corrected. "And he was pretty good at it, too, for a guy the size of Montana."

Smiling in spite of himself, McCarter started walking again. "Come on, let's find Weeks."

In the extreme far corner of the main tent, the team found a small booth without any markings or signs. Inside there was a wooden desk, a blackboard covered with numbers and a folding metal chair. Nothing else. The unspoken message was quite clear. If you did not know what they sold here, then you were not important enough to buy one.

As the rest of the team formed a wall across the doorway, McCarter took the chair and puffed away on his cigarette, tapping the ash onto the neatly trimmed grass until the back curtain parted and a woman stepped into view.

She was dressed in a simple black business suit, with a pink silk blouse, only a hint of black nylons visible between her shoes and the bottom of her trousers. She wore little jewelry, aside from an emerald pendant that hung around her neck on a silver chain and drew attention to her impressive cleavage. Her hair was long, with soft highlights of silver, and she was clearly on the far side of middle age, but still more than attractive enough to catch the attention of any man.

"Good afternoon, Mr. Towers," she said in a soft contralto. "I'm Rebbeca Weeks. What may I do for Sheikh Hassan today?"

Dropping the cigarette to the grass and grinding it under a shoe, McCarter tried not to show his annoyance over the fact that he had clearly been under observation since he'd entered the market. Good thing Kurtzman and his people kept the sheikh in good standing with most of the criminal underworld.

"My employer has a problem, and needs your assistance," McCarter said without any preamble. "An item of his was misplaced—stolen, actually—and we have only recently learned that it was used very recently in Russia." He paused. "Near Mystery Mountain."

Placing her hands in her lap, Weeks raised a single eyebrow but said nothing.

Without waiting for a cue, Encizo stepped forward and laid the attaché case on the desk. Swiping a thumb across the sensor pads, he released the locks, and the lid rose to display the bars of gold.

"Now, it would be very bad for your business if the word was spread that you purchase stolen weapons, only to then sell them to another customer," McCarter said, pulling a fresh cigarette from the pack and tapping the end on his hand to compact the tip. "The sheikh is a very forgiving man, and does not wish to cause any trouble. The item is gone, so it cannot be reclaimed." He paused to light the cigarette, drag in the dark smoke and let it out very slowly. "However, the name of the person, or persons, involved would be of inestimable value." He smiled. "And the generosity of Sheikh Hassan is famous."

"As is his revenge," Weeks observed, reaching out to stroke the leather case with a fingertip. "And this is…?"

"A down payment," McCarter stated.

Her nails were bright red, the same color as her lipstick. They were also very short, more fitting for a soldier than a salesman or business executive. Suddenly, McCarter had the strong feeling that Weeks did more than buy and sell nuclear weapons.

"Unfortunately, Norel is not in the habit of releasing such information," Weeks said, lifting a gold bar and weighing it in her palm. "Not even for such a valuable customer as the sheikh…" Her voice trailed off. "This bar is light." It was not a question.

"No, it's hollow," McCarter said, crushing out the cigarette on his Rolex. There immediately came a hard click, and the fake bar broke apart, a bluish fluid gushing out to cover her hand.

Dropping the gold, Weeks yanked a handkerchief from a pocket and tried to wipe the foaming chemical off her skin. But that only made it seep in faster, and turned her entire hand a deep, rich blue.

"W-what is this?" she whispered in a hoarse voice.

"It's called Nightfire," McCarter said, pitching the dead cigarette away. "We stole it from North Korea several years ago, and it kills in five minutes. We've taken the antidote already, but you now have five minutes before you die."

Horrified, the woman stared at the bubbling goo, unable to speak.

"Four minutes, and counting," McCarter said, glancing at the Rolex and stifling a yawn.

"Yes, I remember him," Weeks said, licking dry lips. "Skinny man, bony. Said he was a colonel, but acted more like a general. You know, expecting things to be done for him instantly."

"I know the type," McCarter said honestly.

She smiled hopefully, but it faded at his stern visage. Clearly, more was needed. "Strange fellow, odd accent," Weeks continued, struggling to recall anything important. "It reminded me of that actor, played a vampire..."

"Tom Cruise?" Manning asked incredulously.

"Lugosi," she snapped impatiently. "Bela Lugosi."

"So, he was Hungarian?"

"Romanian, Czech, Slovakian...I don't know, but from that region," Weeks replied, her voice rising in pitch. "He was a new customer, no credit, no references, but it was a good trade. Two Soviet Union thermonuclear bombs for a Chinese tactical nuke."

The Stony Man team went still at that pronouncement.

"The general did what?" McCarter demanded, suddenly alert.

"He traded two big nukes for one small nuke. We assumed he wanted to use it to break into someplace or to kill somebody without leveling the countryside. Thermonuclear weapons are terror weapons—their strength is that they are so devastating nobody wants to use them. Tactical nukes, however, can be utilized in a host of different ways, if you don't care about the fallout." She grinned at the pun.

Crossing his arms, McCarter did not share her amusement. "More."

"There is no more!" Weeks told him, holding out her bubbling hand. The stain was past her wrist, her back was drenched in sweat and she seemed to have trouble breathing. "Please, that is all I have for you."

Picking up the middle gold bar, James twisted it hard with both hands. The thin veneer of pure gold snapped off and a foam block dropped out. Ripping off the foam exposed a small metal box, and inside that was an ampoule of clear fluid and a syringe. Deftly the Phoenix pro loaded the syringe, tapped out an air bubble, then pulled the woman's arm closer and pressed a thumb on her wrist to bring out the veins.

She started to smile, and that was when he stopped, the needle hovering above her skin.

"How were the thermonuclear devices delivered?" McCarter asked quietly, not even looking her way.

"A Soviet Union Mi-6 Hook cargo helicopter, with two Hind gunships as escort," Weeks answered quickly, the words tumbling out in a rush. "His troops were armed with Kalashnikov 47s, the old models, original issue, no laser sights. All of their equipment was old but in excellent condition."

"Anybody have a name?" James asked, easing in the needle and depressing the plunger. "Or something unique? Butterfly tattoo, eyepatch, missing limb?"

Inhaling through her nose, Weeks said nothing for a moment, unable to take her vision off the slowly lowering level of the antidote as it coursed into her veins. Already her heart was slowing and breathing was becoming less of a chore.

"Nobody wore any insignia," she whispered, suddenly very tired. "But the s-skinny general accidentally called a large man 'lieutenant' once, and every…body else seemed to be taking their orders from h-him."

A general and a lieutenant? That was an odd pairing. Sounded like war buddies. "Where are the big thermo-nukes now?" McCarter demanded, leaning in closer. But the only response was a soft snoring from the unconscious woman.

"I told you this would work," James said.

"Damn straight it did," Encizo said with a hard smile. "What was that anyway?"

"Peanut oil. According to Bear, she has a terrible allergy to the stuff, and it would raise welts in only a few seconds." James smiled. "Sure did look like a neurotoxin, didn't it?"

"Close enough," McCarter agreed, sliding a hand into the dress of the woman and fumbling about to unearth the pendant. Placing it on the table, he smashed it with one of the solid gold bars, and then lifted a small key from the sparkling residue. There were no teeth on the key but the smooth sides were freckled with tiny microdots, identification codes for a computerized lock.

"All right, if there's anything more to learn it will be in the master files," McCarter said, tucking the key into a pocket and buttoning it closed. "Those will be somewhere inside the mansion—"

"Hold it," Hawkins advised, raising a hand. "Something's wrong."

"Guards?" Encizo asked.

"Don't know for sure," Hawkins muttered, looking skyward. "But I think we just ran out of time."

Pausing, the other men listened intently. A soft thumping could be heard over the steady chatter of the crowd around the booth. It was muffled and low, like the beating of a human heart. But the noise steadily increased in strength and volume until it overpowered the hundreds of confused voices and seemed to buffet the canvas walls.

"Okay, that's trouble," Manning snarled, a hand reaching for his hip but finding only cloth. "Helicopters aren't allowed this close to the market. Not when it's open."

"Well, it can't be one of the stolen T-bombs," James observed bluntly. "Or we would already be dead."

Suddenly there was the strident howling of an alarm, closely followed by the roar of a 40 mm Gatling gun, and then the rushing exhalation of a launching missile. There was no way of knowing if it reached the target, but it seemed to explode far too soon. Instantly there came a barrage from the sky, machine guns, the whoosh of missiles and the hiss of rockets.

"That's not a helicopter, but a gunship," McCarter cursed, grabbing the arms dealer by the collar and starting to drag her under the table. But before he could, the top of the booth exploded into splinters and a rain of bullets chewed a path of destruction through the booth, sweeping across the Stony Man operatives and their unconscious captive.

CHAPTER FIVE

Bosporus Straits, Istanbul

A thin fog covered the Black Sea, masking the cold water and rocky landscape. Located on a small isthmus, the powerful white beam of a lighthouse swept around in a stately procession, and somewhere a horn sounded, warning the ship away from dangerous rocks and shallows.

Although only a few miles wide, the Bosporus Strait was a vital passageway from the Black Sea to the vast Atlantic Ocean, and was always alive with maritime traffic. Fishing villages dotted the pebbled beaches, slowly growing in size until becoming the legendary city of Istanbul. The sprawling metropolis was a marvel of contradictions, ancient stone mosques standing alongside towering glass skyscrapers. The air was a mixture of diesel fumes and perfume. Minarets and clusters of microwave dishes all pointed upward, their goals oddly similar, sending messages toward the distant heavens. The winding cobblestone streets and graceful steel bridges were full of horse-drawn carts, limousines, bicycles, cars and endless swarms of busy people of every possible description.

The rising sun was slowly burning off the fog as a small wooden boat chugged over the horizon heading directly for the wide mouth of the strait. Scarcely more than a dingy, the craft was old but in good shape, the engine operating at a gentle purr. Two men in heavy overcoats sat in the dingy.

In the rear section was a single, large object covered with a moth-eaten blanket that still bore the hammer and sickle emblem of the Soviet Union. A silver antenna was sticking out, thin and almost invisible in the morning mist.

On a nearby hill, a man and a woman were finishing off the last of their wine, preparing to turn a special evening into an even more special day. Unlike so many other women, this one had actually seemed to enjoy having a picnic dinner on his speedboat, *Constantine,* a sleek British-made two-seater with an oversize engine that roared like morning thunder. He worked on a trawler and lived on a houseboat; the sea was in his veins, and until only a few hours ago the *Constantine* had been the love of his life. Now, however, its status was rapidly on the decline.

"Another, my dear?" the burly fisherman suggested, proffering the warm bottle. His clothing was worn but clean, his old boots polished to within an inch of their lives.

"Yes, please." She smiled, accepting a refill. His hands were covered with scars, his arms with tattoos, and he looked like a monster from a French horror film. But his eyes were gentle, and his smile made her tingle inside and think of raising children. He was not a perfect man, but he was perfect for her, and soon she would show him that in ways he could never before imagine. Deftly she remove the scarf from around her throat, exposing a wealth of cleavage. Instantly, his eyes flickered in that direction, then he looked away, trying to behave like a gentleman. She felt herself grow moist at the courtesy. Yes, he will do nicely.

Finishing off the bottle, the blushing man laid it aside and clinked glasses with her before taking a sip. The summer wine was sweet, but nowhere near as sweet as her kisses. He had held off asking her out on a date because she was a gypsy, considered by some to be unclean. But his heart overcame the ancient prejudice, and now he knew it was the smartest decision of his life. Incredibly, the life-long bachelor found himself thinking about how amazing their children would be with her mind and his strength.

Summoning the courage to ask her a question, the man suddenly found his arms full of the woman, her lips pressed against his in an ardent embrace. The touch was electric, overwhelming the wine in their blood, and soon eager hands roamed across warming bodies, removing articles of clothing to reach the secret flesh underneath. Touching, tasting, savoring, the banquet of intimacy quickened to a frenzied pace, and soon they were as one, moving underneath the thick blanket.

"Ahoy," a voice called from the shore.

They ignored the interruption, but there came the sound of a boat scraping onto the pebble beach, and then footsteps.

"Sorry to interrupt," Lindquist said to the couple. "But is that speedboat for rent?"

It took the fisherman a moment to reorient himself, and he sat up, draping the blanket over his future wife. "Who the holy fuck are you?" he demanded, his eyes no longer loving or gentle in the extreme. "Go away, fool."

Under the blanket, the woman was scrambling, then a slim hand darted into view for a moment to grab a loose item of intimate clothing off the wicker basket and snatch it away.

"I asked, is that boat for rent?" Colonel Lindquist asked, resting a boot on the rocky dock. Some work had been done to level the natural outcropping and turn it into a proper dock. Boards had been laid over the stones and spiked into place, a wooden pylon thick as a telephone pole jutted from the shallow waters and old car tires dangled off the sides to offer protection from the arrival of less skilled pilots than the Slovakian soldier.

"My boat?" the big man asked incredulously, clenching the loose trousers around his waist with a fist the size of Gibraltar. Buckling his belt, he was confused, embarrassed and furious at the same time. "You…you interrupt a man and woman to ask that?" Inhaling deeply, he sneered at the foreigner. "No, it is not for rent or sale. Not for a billion euros."

"Go away, tourist!" the woman shouted angrily, poking her head into view. "The show is over." Her raven hair was a wild corona, and her breasts were very large, the crescent top of a dark nipple peeking from a tiny hole in the blanket.

The colonel smiled at the sight, and the soldier in the boat openly chuckled. Both of the men would have liked to spend some private time with the fat whore, but day was almost upon them, which would mean a new shift starting at the NATO base across the strait from the city, and that danger should be avoided at any cost.

"So be it," Lindquist sighed, and fired a revolver twice from inside his heavy coat.

The fabric puffed out from the passage of the subsonic rounds, and the woman flipped backward with most of her throat blown away, red blood splashing across the magnificent breasts. Clutching his belly, the huge fisherman staggered backward, crimson gushing from between his fingers. Then the man incredibly straightened and pulled a curved knife from a sheath at his side to charge at the two strangers. He had no idea who they were, but he knew what a bullet in the belly meant, and if this was his day to die, he would take the murdering son of a bitch with him into Hell.

Spinning easily out of the way of the clumsy attack, Colonel Lindquist fired twice more into the back of the fisherman. Shuddering, he raised the knife to throw it, and Lindquist shot him twice in the heart. With a low groan, the fisherman collapsed onto the ground and went still, the knife clattering down the rocky slope to splash into the Black Sea.

"A brave man," Lindquist said, reloading his weapon.

"Just a stupid ass civilian," the Slovakian soldier snarled in disgust, holstering his own automatic. "He could have made some money and gone back to fucking the woman. But no, he had to be rude. Bah, some people were just too stupid to be allowed to live."

"Get the keys for the boat," Lindquist commanded, holstering the revolver under his coat. Then he paused at an unexpected flash of light from the top of the nearby cliff.

Silhouetted against the morning sky was a lone figure holding a camera with a telephoto lens. Some tourist had also been enjoying the show on the beach.

"Take him," Lindquist said softly, waving a friendly hand in greeting.

Hesitantly the man on the cliff waved back, suddenly not sure of what exactly had happened only moments before.

Brushing back his overcoat, the soldier swung up an AK-47 carbine. Placing a finger on the trigger activated a small laser clipped to the underside of the barrel, and a thin red beam lanced out to jump along the edge of the cliff until finding the tourist. Instantly, the soldier fired a short burst.

Five hundred feet above, the startled tourist recoiled as the camera exploded, the 7.62 mm hardball rounds driving the shards of plastic and glass into his face and out the back of his skull. Reeling blindly, the tourist reached out for help and went straight over the cliff to violently impact on a boulder only a few yards off the shore.

"You stand guard, I'll get the keys," Lindquist growled in annoyance as the echoes of the gunfire faded into the distance.

Getting the keys from the blood-soaked pants of the fisherman, the colonel got inspired, and dragged the huge corpse over to the Soviet dingy and buckled him into position behind the wheel. Then he hauled over the woman, and put her in the passenger seat, then tipped her over to rest her head in his lap.

"You're sick." The soldier chuckled. "It looks like she's thanking him for the picnic."

"That is the point. A couple having sex will confuse any-body who notices anything odd about the dingy," Lindquist answered, flipping back her skirt to expose the well-rounded backside.

Lashing the wheel of the dingy into position, Lindquist and the soldier pushed the craft into the water, then started the engine and guided it toward the center of the strait where a dozen other vessels were moving in ragged procession toward Istanbul.

Claiming the new speedboat, Lindquist took the wheel and together the men raced away at top speed.

"Civilians die this time," the colonel said in a hard voice. "This is where we cross the line from freedom fighters into terrorists."

"You care?" the soldiers asked in surprise.

"No, just wanted to see if you did." Lindquist smiled, re-moving his hand from the revolver inside his coat.

STANDING AT THE BOW of the Egyptian supertanker *Imhotep,* the sailor flicked a match alive with a thumbnail and let the sulfur burn off before applying the flame to the tip of the Cuban cigar. A cloth cap kept his hair in place, and a heavy pair of binoculars hung about his neck.

It was almost the end of his shift, and he was already thinking about hot food and an even hotter shower. One of the many benefits of working on a vessel this huge was that the crew had all of the amenities, there was even a small movie theater to keep them entertained during the long sea voyages.

Dragging in the dark smoke, the middle-aged sailor held it for a moment, then exhaled slowly. Ah, magnificent. A very long time ago, his father had told him the secret to a happy life: Cuban cigars, Swiss banks, Scotch whiskey, German cars and Japanese women. As a child, the information had meant nothing. But as an adult, his respect for the wisdom of the old man went up every day.

"Why do you let the match burn for a moment before lighting the cigar?" a younger sailor asked, standing nearby. A rifle was slung across his shoulders as protection from possible trouble from pirates.

"You have to burn off the sulfur," the older sailor commented, watching Istanbul flow by along the bank of the strait. "Or else the smoke tastes..."

"Tastes like what?" the younger man asked eagerly, his interest piqued.

Silently, the smoking man pointed down to the port side.

Leaning much farther over the gunwale than was advisable, the young sailor squinted into the distance, then smiled broadly. By the blood of the prophet! Only a stone's throw away from the supertanker was a tiny wooden dingy, a man and woman inside having sex.

Swinging up the rifle, the man worked the focus on the telescopic sights and soon brought the loving couple into sharp focus.

"They're not..." He started, then tried again. "Sir. Those people are dead."

"What are you babbling about?" the other man demanded, allowing the fragrant smoke to trickle out his nose. "Dead tired? Dead sexy, as the British like to say, or—"

"Dead as in not alive. They've been shot!"

Scowling in disbelief, the smoking man took a look through the binoculars to see for himself. Sure enough, the couple was actually thoroughly dead, shot several times.

"Alert the captain," he said around the cigar. "This may be some sort of a diversion for pirates."

Nodding assent, the younger man raced off, pulling a cell phone from his pants and shouting for the bridge.

Sweeping the Black Sea for anything coming toward the *Imhotep,* the old sailor saw only the usual assortment of cruise liners, cargo freighters and fishing trawlers, and a small gunboat flying the blue-and-white flag of Greece. No dangers there.

Returning his attention to the dingy, the sailor briefly wondered if some local crime boss had dispatched a cheating wife and her lover, when something in the back compartment of the vessel caught his attention. Partially covered by a ratty old blanket was some sort of a large globe. He looked again. No, that was a decahedron, made of hundreds of tiny pyramids. Bizarrely, some of them were glowing bright cherry-red, while others seemed to be covered with ice and frost.

A split second later the decahedron burst apart, the sections sailing away, trailing a green exhaust. The thinning mist hovering over the choppy sea was sliced into sections by the radiant pieces, the green fumes merging with the fog until it was completely replaced. Expanding with lightning speed, the green fumes hit the supertanker and flowed around the hull to engulf every other ship and actually reach the rocky shore and dockyards. In under a heartbeat the entire strait was blanketed with the pulsating emerald gas. The action happened so fast, the startled sailor could not really be sure it had actually occurred. Then his world exploded.

A wave of heat hammered the sailor, driving him back from the gunwale, a death scream cooked from his lungs as the atmosphere disappeared, horribly replaced with searing pain—and then eternal blackness.

For over a mile, every ship and boat in the strait became lost in the rampaging firestorm. People were blown off the decks, sails burst into flames and anything made of wood simply flashed out of existence.

Reaching the dockyards, the tempest flowed into every doorway and window. Cars exploded like firecrackers in the streets and people turned into shrieking torches as the roiling flames flooded the cobblestone streets like a maelstrom from the deepest pits of Hell. Smashing into the hills and cliffs, the force of the blast was repelled and doubled back upon itself, massively increasing the near-nuclear temperatures. Pavement boiled, water towers erupted into steam and dozens of gas stations thundered into gushing fireballs.

With nobody left alive at the helm, a dozen of the larger ships continued along their original course, randomly smashing into the rocky shorelines and spreading the halo of destruction into the suburbs and decimated NATO base. Completely out of control, a Syrian freighter slammed into a burning warehouse, and a few moments later its cargo of illicit munitions cooked off from the amassed heat. The blast annihilated the entire village to the nearby hills.

Hundreds of charred bodies were flung far out to the sea as the roofs were ripped off burned homes, stores and mosques. Heavy manhole covers sailed free, bridges crumbled, then the entire side of a skyscraper momentarily bulged before shattering in a stentorian crash of thousand windows. A tidal wave of tumbling glass shards rushed across the metropolis, annihilating the few staggering survivors.

The sea appeared to boil from the rain of loose debris, and every vessel in the strait was bombarded by the shotgun blast, their hulls punctured again and again. Most of the smaller boats were already sinking, the passenger liners tilting badly, the crew and passengers already dead from the heat, shock wave and lack of oxygen caused by the blast.

Gushing streams of oil, a dozen supertankers moved through the turbulent waters, two of them crashing into each other and ripping open the already weakened hulls. A black torrent cascaded into the sea. Then a spark from the grinding hulls ignited the horrific welling of crude oil and a new firestorm washed across the strait, swamping every other vessel, coating the shoreline and pouring into the damaged city, setting everything ablaze.

Soon enough, a swirling column of dark smoke rose into the tumultuous sky, spreading rapidly outward in a hellish death shroud that was clearly visible from far away.

Vilnius, Lithuania

DAWN WAS JUST STARTING to lighten the sky above the bustling metropolis, but the cobblestone streets were alive with cars, vans and pedestrians of all sorts. Most of the vans were for neighborhood stores, the few long-distance trucks already off on their daily journeys to the more lucrative markets of Poland and Germany.

A small group of big men stood on the corner of the busy street, trying to appear casual. They smiled at the people passing by, stepped out of the way of an old woman using a cane and occasionally winked at the pretty teenage girls.

However, none of the locals was fooled by the transparent deception. The strangers were unknown in this part of the city, which was bad enough. But they also wore clean business suits that were badly rumpled, and identical shoes. Their hair was short, too short to be grabbed in a fight, and their eyes were hard and empty as gun barrels. After so many years of Soviet oppression, there was no doubt in the minds of the local people that these were secret police, and within minutes the street was deserted.

The Moscow unit noticed the events, but gave no reaction that they had been identified. Back in Russia, they wore windbreakers with FSB written across the back in neon yellow letters to let everybody know that the Federal Security Bureau had arrived. However, here in Lithuania, they had no jurisdiction, and thus were forced to be a bit more discreet.

After the fall of communism, the first act of the newly created FSB had been to capture as many former KGB agents as possible and bring them in for questioning, then swift trials, followed by an even swifter execution. But few members of the secret police had ever been found, and none of them surrendered alive.

"Yes, yes, I understand, but when will…are you sure?" the leader of the FSB unit said hurriedly into his cell phone. The reception in the isolated village was terrible, the bars flickering in and out of existence like teasing ghosts. But the landlines were from the days of Stalin and operated even worse. The standing joke was that the best way to call a friend in Lithuania was through an open window.

"Repeat that, please?" the man stressed loudly. Then he smiled broadly, crinkling the long, jagged scar that bisected his face. "We have permission from the Lithuanian parliament to proceed," he stated, snapping shut the phone.

"About goddamn time," a burly man growled, and went to a nearby car and popped the truck.

Quickly passing out body armor, the agents dressed for combat, then armed themselves with brand-new AK-105 assault rifles equipped with 30 mm grenade launchers. Stuffing their pockets with spare clips, the federal agents then did something they had seen their American FBI counterparts do in the movies. The men tucked their identification booklets into the cummerbund of their bodyarmor, so that the Great Seal of Russia was clearly visible. They proudly wanted the entire world to know that they were the duly authorized police, not the politically motivated secret police.

Working the arming bolts on their Kalashnikov assault rifles, the FSB unit went around the corner, aimed and fired their weapons at an old warehouse. The 30 mm grenade launchers banged softly, the fat canisters arcing high to smash through the second-story windows. Almost instantly, there appeared roiling clouds of thick green smoke from the military ordnance.

Inside the warehouse, a fire alarm began to clatter as the FSB unit raced across the street reloading their weapons.

Separating into teams, four of the men headed around the warehouse for the dockyard, while the rest plowed straight for the front door. Kneeling at the curb, they fired the grenade launchers once more, but this time the 30 mm rounds thundered a maelstrom of fléchette rounds, blowing the wooden door into splinters. As the smoke cleared, there was revealed only a second door of riveted steel completely untouched by the barrage.

Passing off his AK-105, a small man with a mustache swung around a black leather bag and extracted a bulky pressurized canister. Moving quickly, he went to the door and sprayed a bubbling line of gray material in a fast circle, then stepped back, barely getting out of the way before the oxygen in the air ignited the military compound. Blazing hotter than a blast furnace, the thermite ate through the resilient steel, rivulets of molten metal flowing down to crack the sidewalk.

"Windows!" the leader commanded, and a second barrage of smoke canisters was fired into the second floor.

At the first whiff of the vomit gas, the agents started inhaling through their noses, the filters stuffed inside allowing them to breath freely without any adverse effects. But anybody inside would soon be forced to the ground level or collapse from endlessly retching.

"By the mother of God, I wish we could gas the bastards here and now," one agent snarled, thumbing in a fresh round.

"Now, I have found it very difficult to question a corpse, my friend," another agent retorted, adding a canister of tear gas to the noxious brew swirling inside the warehouse. "But if you figure out how, then I'm all for it."

"Be fun to try," a third man snarled, watching the roof for any suspicious movements.

Suddenly a man appeared over the ledge, working the bolt on an old-fashioned AK-47. The FSB agents burped off a short barrage, and the man tumbled backward, literally torn into pieces.

With a sound like shattering glass, the circle of steel dropped to the sidewalk, and the FSB unit rushed forward to fire all of their weapons through the white-hot opening. There was no chance of innocent civilians being present in the KGB safehouse. Everybody inside was a legitimate target.

Startled cries of men and women came from the other side of the metallic door, then automatic weapons shot back. But the FSB agents responded with a hail of 30 mm grenades, a mixture of vomit gas and buckshot. The defensive firing ceased as the KGB operatives backed away, and an FSB agent dropped his assault rifle to race forward to insanely dive through the red-hot opening.

Hitting the concrete floor, he rolled into a crouch and brought out a pair of 9 mm Tokarev automatic pistols. The interior of the warehouse was dark, the shadows misty with the military gas and thick with furtive movements as men wearing gas masks dragged their retching companions to safety. Remembering to breathe only through his nose, the FSB agent tracked the dimly seen figures, firing steadily. He only had to hold the breech clear for a few seconds before—

An AK-105 came sailing through the opening, closely followed by an FSB agent. As the man stood, somebody in the rafters fired a shotgun and he was blown backward against the steel door, blood spraying out from his ruined face and neck.

Emptying both of his booming pistols toward the ceiling, the FSB agent kept the sniper at bay as the other members of his team scrambled through the rapidly cooling doors and reclaimed their weapons. Now all of the FSB agents trained their assault rifles upward. The chattering barrage of 5.45 mm hardball rounds ricocheted wildly off the steel beams, and a man cried out in pain as he dropped into sight. The fall of sixty feet took only a few seconds, and he hit the concrete floor with grisly results. A moment later his shotgun clattered alongside, the wooden stock marked with the infamous symbol of the KGB.

A score of weapons chattered from the darkness, and the FSB agents responded in kind, the muzzle-flashes brightening the dim warehouse. This mission was what they had been training for their entire professional career. It was more than simple revenge; it was justice. Hot lead was flying everywhere, spent brass covering the floor like golden offerings to a pagan god. From amid the chaos, a man screamed, another vehemently cursed and a shotgun boomed.

"FSB!" the leader of the team bellowed, slapping a fresh clip into the Kalashnikov. "Come out with your hands raised!"

"Hail Stalin!" a voice boomed in reply over a loudspeaker, and a truck lurched into motion at the far end of the warehouse. Charging past the stacks of crates and barrels, the big BMW ground gears as it attempted to accelerate as fast as possible.

Expecting something like this, the FSB agents dived to the sides as the agent outside filled the breach, leveling the wide tube of a Carl Gustav rocket launcher. The agent aimed and fired in a single smooth motion. The fat 84 mm rocket streaked past the other FSB agents and barely had enough distance to arm before slamming into the grille of the charging truck.

Trapped within the confines of the warehouse, the blast sounded louder than doomsday as the front end of the truck was ripped apart and the cab of the vehicle exploded into flames.

Grabbing the ruin of his face, the burning driver shrieked as the truck sharply angled away from the door and crashed into a stack of wooden crates. The splintering containers burst apart and a deluge of shiny gold bars tumbled to the cold floor, each one stamped with the hammer-and-sickle of the Soviet Union.

Completely ignoring the cascade of stolen wealth, the FSB agents maintained steady suppression fire as they darted from packing crate to packing crate, covering each other as they forced the KGB operatives farther back into the gloomy warehouse. The chatter of their AK-47 assault rifles was soon peppered with the sputter of Uzi machine guns and then shotguns.

Without warning, a snarling mastiff lunged into view. Caught off guard, an FSB agent swung his weapon fast and clipped the huge dog in the side of the head with the wooden stock. The animal went down hard, then scrambled back up and advanced at him sideways, snarling in rage. With no other choice, the agent fired the grenade launcher. The range was too short to arm the warhead of the 30 mm round, but it still slammed into the mastiff with brutal force, breaking bones and sending it skittering across the floor into a grease pit. Weakly, the wounded dog tried to scramble back onto the floor but failed.

As if taking that as a signal of some kind, the mob of KGB operatives broke from cover and raced toward the rear of the warehouse. Warily, the FSB stayed close behind, shooting constantly.

Passing by a glass-walled office, the team scowled at the huge red flag of the Soviet Union framing a portrait of Stalin. Snarling in disgust, an FSB agent fired at the picture.

"No, don't," the leader of the unit shouted, but it was too late.

As the glass shattered, the explosive charge buried into the wall detonated, and the surprised man was blown in two by a deadly hail of shrapnel.

Before the team could recover, the writhing orange lance of a flamethrower extended from the shadows, setting fire to everything it touched. The office was a trap.

Scattering fast, the FSB agents tried to reach cover, but one man was a heartbeat slow and became engulfed by the burning wash. Covered in flames, he shrieked wildly. Knowing he was already dead, the other FSB agents gunned him down on the spot, then rained a fusillade of 30 mm rounds at the KGB operative carrying the flamethrower. Expecting to die from a barrage of antipersonnel buckshot, the operative was startled when he was instead brutally pounded by stun bags. The wand of the flamethrower was smashed from his breaking hands, his ribs audibly cracked and then his gas mask went flying. Unable to stop himself from inhaling, the badly wounded operative doubled over, gagging and shuddering.

Streaming past the fallen man, the FSB agents tagged him with a taser and continued on to a flight of metal stairs leading down into the basement. Pausing for a precious moment, the leader of the FSB unit pulled an empty clip from his pocket and tossed it down the stairs. As the item bounced off the first step, there immediately came the buzzing roar of a chain gun. The stairs visibly shook from the onslaught, and holes appeared in the distant ceiling admitting hundreds of streams of foggy daylight.

Pulling the pins on sleep-gas grenades, the FSB unit rolled them over the edge, and kept it up until the chain gun stopped firing. Then they proceed swiftly down the dented stairs, half expecting to die with every step.

Reaching the basement level, the team unexpectedly found a score of men sprawled on the floor, their hands full of assault rifles, the old WWII issue gas masks still tightly secured around their faces. Nearby, a man lay across a chain gun, the belt of linked ammunition tangled around his arm.

"What a bunch of idiots!" a man snarled in disgust. "Did they really think these antiques would protect them?"

"The KGB never did place a premium on intelligence," the leader muttered, kicking a Neostead shotgun from the limp hands of a snoring man.

A utility door slammed open and a man in a Soviet Army uniform shuffled into view, his empty hands raised high. "I surrender!" he shouted through the gas mask, his eyes bright with fear. "Don't kill me!"

Not believing anything said by the KGB, the federal agents tore the man apart with concentrated gunfire, driving him back into the room. A split second later the explosive charge strapped to his back detonated, spraying out a hellstorm of fléchettes. The death cloud hissed through the air, and two of the FSB agents staggered from multiple impacts. But then they slowly stood, their body armor shiny with the embedded metal, but there was no sign of blood.

"All right, I want a full sweep of the premises," the leader commanded, dropping a partially used clip from the assault rifle and inserting a full one. "Check every room, closet, crawl space and cabinet. Try to capture anybody you find alive, but I want no more deaths on our side. Understood?"

A chorus of agreement answered the directive, and half the team left at a run, their weapons at the ready.

"Let's get this over with," the leader muttered, slinging the assault rifle over a shoulder and lifting a shotgun off the floor. A small part of him did not want to do this, but the nation was in peril, and there was no other choice. The Kremlin needed answers fast, and these fools were the most logical place to begin.

Checking the load inside the shotgun, the leader of the FSB team pointed it at a KGB operative wearing the collar bars of a major. "We'll start with him," he declared grimly.

Arranging a line of chairs, the FSB agents securely tied the unconscious KGB operatives in place, then administrated the antidote for the sleep gas. Sluggishly, the operatives struggled awake, then stiffened at the sight of the stern men facing them with assault rifles.

"So, why are we still alive, pigs?" a bald man snarled, struggling against his bonds.

A grim FSB agent pulled some soft tubing from a pouch on his belt and began tying it around the leg of the bound man, just below the knee.

"What the hell are you doing?" the KGB operative demanded in confusion.

"What needs to be done." The leader of the team sighed and aimed the shotgun.

The operative barely had time to gasp before the weapon roared and his boot vanished in a cloud of buckshot and smoke.

Reeling from the incredible pain, the officer shrieked and began throwing himself around in the chair, savagely struggling to get free. "You motherless bastards!" he roared, spittle flying from his mouth. "If I ever get you in this chair—"

"You already did," the leader muttered, stepping closer and pointing to the scar on his face. "You used pliers on my brother and scissors on me."

"Good," the mutilated man snarled, blood dribbling from the ragged end of his leg. "I remember how your brother squealed for mercy and—"

Raising the shotgun, the FSB agent fired again, ending the conversation forever.

"That was a foolish lie. Petrov died before making a sound," the agent whispered, working the pump on the shotgun to chamber another round. Then he faced the next man in line.

"Look, I don't know you," the KGB agent sputtered. "Ask me whatever you wish. I'll talk!"

"Good. Where is Skyfire?" the FSB agent asked, pulling out another length of soft tubing.

"Where is what?" the prisoner asked, staring at the tubing in abject horror. "I don't know what that is."

"Wrong answer," the agent snarled, and began tightening the tubing around the leg of the prisoner.

"Please, in the name of God, I do not know what you are talking about," the operative wailed, his mind flashing memories of a thousand other helpless men and women telling him exactly the same thing before he slowly took them apart, inch by inch.

Something must have shown on the face of the operative, because the leader of the FSB team did not ask the question again. He simply fired the shotgun directly into the belly of the man. The strident blast tipped over the chair, and the operative hit the floor gurgling horribly as his intestines slithered out like oiled ropes.

At the sight, the other prisoners went wild, but the tubing was strong, and their efforts achieved nothing.

"Where is Skyfire?" the man asked, sliding a fresh round into the breech of the hot weapon.

The old KGB operative had trouble getting out the words. "I...that is...please! I only—"

Solemnly, the other agent knelt and began applying a fresh length of tubing.

The shotgun was aimed. "Where is Skyfire?"

"I don't know."

"Last chance."

"Please. I swear to God."

"Commies don't believe in a God!"

The weapon roared once more, and the FSB agents moved to the next enemy of the state. Any crimes committed by the KGB agents in the past were soon paid for in full, but that was only the beginning, and the screaming lasted long into the afternoon....

CHAPTER SIX

Cheyenne Mountain

Since its creation, the War Room of NORAD had always been noisy, full of people coming and going, talking, joking, delivering reports and drinking coffee. But that was considered a good sign. Noise meant nonimportant conversations, chitchat and idle gossip. The louder the War Room was, the more peaceful and secure was the nation.

At the moment the War Room of Cheyenne Mountain was dead silent. Scores of technicians from every branch of the military sat hunched over consoles correlating and confirming the deluge of information pouring out of Europe.

Directly in front of them was a colossal triptych of screens. The left showed Europe. The middle screen, the North American continent. The right was filled with a real-time view of Istanbul. Although very little of the city could be seen through the dense clouds of swirling black smoke.

In a loud crash, the double doors to the War Room slammed aside and a four-star general strode through with his entourage close behind.

"All right, what the hell happened at Istanbul!" he bellowed.

"Sir, unknown, sir," a young major replied, crisply tucking a clipboard under her arm in lieu of a salute. "Reports are still coming in from the few survivors of the NATO base located just outside the city, and a handful of civilians who were lucky enough to be working in the underground sewers at the time." She paused. "Nobody above the ground is alive."

"Nobody?"

"Not on this side of the mountains."

Grudgingly, the general accepted that. If only half of what he had heard was true about the disaster, then he was astonished that anybody at all had managed to live through the holocaust. "Any idea on the number of people dead?" he demanded, accepting a cup of coffee from a young lieutenant.

"No, sir, no accurate numbers. The Turkish army and navy are still fighting the fires. However, a guesstimate on the breakage—" The major abruptly stopped at the dark scowl forming on the face of the general. "A guesstimate on the death toll," she smoothly amended, "would be somewhere around the hundred-thousand mark, although it could easily climb to double that. Perhaps more."

Having seen more than his fair share of death, the general let nothing show on his face, but his heart went cold at the sheer size of the number. Dear God, roughly a quarter of a million civilians dead in only a few minutes?

"How sure are we that this was not a nuclear blast?" he demanded, taking a sip of the scalding brew.

"That has been confirmed by several Keyhole and Watchdog satellites, sir, and the built-in ground sensors of the NATO base," the major replied without bothering to check the clipboard. These data she knew by heart. "There is absolutely no unusual amount of radiation present."

Damn, then it had not been a nuke. "What was the weather like? Any strong winds?" he asked, rising to walk closer to the railing that separated the gallery from the rows of busy consoles. Nobody was allowed to disturb the technicians at their work, not even the President. Even a minor distraction could make them miss something vital.

"Yes, sir. South-by-southeast, nine miles per hour, gusting to twenty."

Damn it, then this was not done by an FAE device. But what did that leave aside from... Oh hell, hadn't there just been a nuclear accident at Mystery Mountain? "Any word on what type of aircraft dropped the bomb...bombs...whatever?" he asked, setting the mug aside.

"None, sir. It must have been a stealth plane."

"Unless it actually was a T-bomb and the bastards simply rolled it off a tall cliff," he muttered, thoughtfully cracking his knuckles.

"Sir?"

"Nothing of importance, Major."

Suddenly a wall monitor changed to a satellite view of the Bosporus Strait. The air was murky with fumes, but he could still see a score of burning vessels, several of them clearly supertankers, and a monstrously large patch of crude oil slowly spreading outward in every direction. The toll on sea life and the fishing industry would be devastating. Istanbul, the unbreakable city, might finally have fallen.

Could Russia have bombed Turkey? the general wondered. But that made no sense whatsoever. Moscow was dependent upon the flow of crude oil from the Middle East. Of course, Siberia had more than ten times the oil reservoirs of the Middle East, but the Russians were saving that for when the Middle East ran dry, and then they could have heating oil and gasoline for their cars, aviation fuel for their MiGs, while the rest of the world went hungry. The politics of survival were an ugly thing indeed.

Regretfully, the general turned his back on the monitors. There was nothing the navy could do about the oil spills, so he concentrated on something else. "How are rescue operations proceeding?"

"Sir, the United States, Canada, Britain, France, Greece and several other nations already have dozens of fire-fighting planes en route to help try to control the ground fires. There are several major pipelines that travel through Turkey from the Middle East, and if the fire reaches them, the results would be catastrophic."

Like they weren't now? the general fumed internally.

The major continued. "Plus, the United Nations is preparing several hundred cargo planes to deliver medical supplies, water and food. NATO has a battalion of replacement troops en route to handle any looting that might occur. ETA one hour." The major frowned. "Although what there is left to steal…" She finished with a shrug.

"The food and medical supplies," the general answered brusquely. "The NATO troops are being sent in to guard the medicine and food from being hijacked by the warlords from the outer provinces. Turkey is the drug-processing capital of the world, and those bastards in the hills will have a field day over this unless we stop them cold."

The major did not speak, but her face spoke volumes about her opinion on people who stole food and medicine from the victims of any disaster.

"All right, send in a wing of F-22 Raptors to bomb the pipelines somewhere safely outside the city," the general directed, massaging an old bullet wound. "If we can't stop the blaze, then we can at least divert it to somewhere with far less people."

Briefly, the major spoke into a VOX microphone attached to her collar like the silver antenna of an insect. "Done, sir. What next?"

"Prayer would be good," the general growled. "But we'll start with those NSA satellites."

Milan, Italy

GRUNTING HARD from the fusillade of rounds punching through the walls of the booth, the men of Phoenix Force staggered but grimly stayed on their feet, knowing that to dive for cover would put the unarmored sections of the body into the deadly path of the hail of bullets. But as the barrage stopped, they dropped flat onto the grass, their fingers twitching for weapons that were not there.

The side of the booth was in tatters, penetrated by a thousand tiny holes, which now offered a kaleidoscope view of the frightened and screaming people. The crowd was already running in blind panic, the warlords and crime bosses clearly not used to being on the receiving end of what they purchased.

Just then, there came the familiar chatter of an MP-5 machine gun from a guard, and the beat of the gunship increased, accompanied by the hard chatter of an electric Gatling gun, closely followed by more yelling and cursing.

"Anybody hurt?" James demanded, patting a pocket. As the field medic for the team, he had come prepared for a fight with several bleached handkerchiefs for minor damage, shoe laces for tourniquets and tampons for deep bullet wounds. It wasn't much, but better than nothing. The guards had considered the items odd, but nothing more.

"No red showing," Manning answered, glancing over the other men.

"Also no bullet holes," Hawkins said, running a hand over his shirt. "What the hell did we just get hit with?"

Overhead there came the thump-thump of the gunship moving low and fast over the main tent, the flutter of the canvas from the wash of turbo blades an audible rumble, sounding almost like distant thunder. Another rocket streaked over the tent, and the Gatling briefly spoke, the sound of the rocket ending in a loud explosion. Nobody had to tell the Stony Man operatives that one heck of a fight was happening in the clear blue sky above Milan.

"Take a look at this," Encizo said, reaching out to pick up a black round from the manicured grass. It was undamaged, not even bent, and the surface yielded slightly under the pressure of his fingernail.

Suddenly, there came a lower throb as a second helicopter joined the first. But whether it was reinforcements or the Norel security guards finally responding to the attack, there was absolutely no way of knowing.

"Rubber bullets?" James snorted. "This isn't an attack, but a kidnapping. Somebody must have had the same idea as us and wants Weeks alive."

"That may be moot," McCarter stormed, pressing a finger against the bloody throat of the woman. There was no detectable pulse. Lifting a fist, he pounded on her chest, paused, then did it again.

Sliding closer, James pinched her nose shut and started breathing into her mouth.

"She died from rubber bullets?" Hawkins demanded incredulously. Then he noticed the line of splintery holes stitched across the desk. "That wasn't done by any 7.62 mm rubber bullet," he stated. "But hot lead, and a mighty large caliber. Maybe a 12.7 mm."

"A very popular size for a gunship," Encizo said. "So the goddamn market is being attacked by two different groups at the same time?"

"That's either very bad timing," Manning noted sagely. "Or else one of the invaders has a traitor in the midst."

Something violently exploded in the distance, the frightened cries of the crowd getting noticeably louder.

"Bad for them, good for us," Encizo muttered, hauling down the attaché case. Busting open the second row of gold bars, the man extracted five metallic objects.

The other men flipped the handles apart, releasing the blades, and then closed the handles again. Now each of them was armed with a six-inch blade. The knives were Delta Force issue, and the metal was a dead black for night work, and sharper than original sin.

Swelling quickly, the beat of the gunship returned, and the sides of the booth shook as bullets punched through again, the lead rounds sweeping over the sprawled Stony Man operatives and shattering a blackboard covered with the conversion rates for different currencies. Cries of pain sounded from outside the booth, along with a great deal of cursing. Almost immediately, the second helicopter fired its own weapons, then the airships moved off again, their aerial battle continuing dimly in the distance.

"Well, this can't be the T-bomb people," Hawkins said, testing the balance of the knife. "Or else the entire market would already have been burned out of existence."

"Unless the bomb isn't here yet," Manning retorted, thumbing the lock on the blade firmly into place. "However, if we've got two groups with opposite goals—"

"Then we play them against each other and make Weeks our key to those files. If we carry her in plain sight, then one of the invaders will have to try to protect her from the others, instantly cutting our opposition in two."

"Yeah, if only she was still—"

With a shuddering gasp, Weeks opened her eyes wide and began heaving for breath.

"Easy now, you've been shot," McCarter said soothingly, brushing the loose hair off her face. "We're taking you to the hospital. Okay, the hospital?"

Weakly she nodded, then went still.

"Just unconscious," James answered the unasked question, emptying the meager medical supplies from his pockets. "Buy me some time, guys."

"How much do you need?"

"Ten minutes."

"You got five," McCarter countered, cracking his knuckles. "Rafe and Gary, get her some body armor. Hawk, with me."

Trained professionals, the men surged into action. As James got to work, Encizo and Manning shimmied out of the booth under the left wall, while McCarter and Hawkins crawled to the front opening and looked over the streaming mob. Pandemonium ruled the market. Apparently a lot of people had smuggled in knives, and there were a dozen bodies sprawled on the grass in plain sight. Several booths were on fire, the flames licking up at the riddled canvas roof. The barking staccato of handguns had joined the fray, and everybody seemed to be running for their lives.

Billowing clouds of smoke filled the air, making it difficult to breathe and even harder to see. Everywhere, people were coughing, and some had removed their shirts to bind them around their heads as crude masks. But that only seemed to make them targets for others.

Leveling a hand, Hawkins pointed. A security guard lay nearby, a horrible bubbling coming from tattered clothing. A sucking chest wound, which was one of the worst injuries that could happen to any soldier. The guard was only muscle for the Italian arms dealers, but Hawkins still felt a momentary flash of sympathy for the dying man. It was a bad way to go, not that there were any good ones, the soldier mentally amended.

Preparing to move, McCarter stopped and pointed. Dashing past the security guard, a bald man in a ripped three-piece suit abruptly paused. Frantically looking both ways, he then dropped, sending a bent knee into the throat of the guard. There came the crack of bones, and the guard went terribly still.

Snatching away the subgun, the bald man was searching the warm corpse for spare ammunition clips when McCarter and Hawkins both tackled him. The bald man went down hard, the MP-5 briefly chattering at the canvas roof, the 9 mm rounds adding a dozen new holes into the tattered acreage. McCarter yanked away the weapon, while Hawkins stabbed down with his knife. The bald man blocked the attack with a jerk of his wrist, then stabbed his fingers at the belly of Hawkins in a killing martial-arts blow.

The bones shattered against the Level Five body armor, and the bald man drew back a crippled hand just as McCarter rammed the stock of the MP-5 into the back of the man's head, ending his pain.

"Son of a bitch was pretty damn fast," Hawkins muttered in annoyance, retrieving the dropped ammunition clips.

"Now, he's just damned," McCarter countered, working the arming bolt to clear a jam from the ejector port.

Stepping out of a cloud of smoke, another security guard frowned at the sight, then quickly swung his own gun off a shoulder to work the arming bolt. Before he finished the motion, Hawkins jerked his hand forward and the knife thudded into the man's left eye. Shrieking in pain, he dropped the MP-5 and McCarter fired a short burst, ending the matter forever.

Returning to the booth, the two men arrived just as James stepped into view, Weeks cradled in his arms, the white handkerchiefs tied around her throat and left wrist. The woman was asleep.

"What now?" James asked as Encizo and Manning charged around the booth. Each of them was carrying an MP-5 subgun. Manning had a bloody nose, and Encizo a bad cut across his cheek. However, he also had a spare set of body armor draped over a shoulder. Quickly, it was laid across Weeks and strapped tightly into place.

"Dragonskin?" James asked, impressed.

"Level Five. Nothing but the best." Encizo smiled.

"Okay, head for the mansion," McCarter commanded, taking off at a brisk run.

That caught the others by surprise, then they understood and followed at double-time. The Hummer was full of weapons, assault rifles and heavy ordnance that would be more than capable of taking down any gunship. But with most of the terrified buyers heading that way, it would be next to impossible to reach the vehicle and keep Weeks alive. Even worse, the nearby cliff was much too high for a dive, even if the wounded woman could have taken the brutal impact of the fall. They didn't have any parachutes, and there were no helicopters at the heliopad. Which left the team only one way out of the weapons market—straight through the center.

Overhead the battle between the gunships raged unabated, and twice the men of Phoenix Force had to scatter to avoid a burst of rounds coming down through the tent, first lead, then the rubber bullets, followed by more lead. A score of booths was ablaze by now, and the crowd was fighting for any available weapons.

A trio of large men made a unified charge at Manning, and he ruthlessly hosed them with the MP-5, moving the barrel in a sideways figure eight to maximize the kill potential. They toppled over, spraying out their life onto an empty booth that had been full of body armor only minute ago.

Lurching out of the smoke, a bald man made a try for the body armor covering Weeks. Turning away to protect the woman, James kicked backward, burying his shoe into the man's groin. Doubling over from the pain, the bald man started to gag and then noisily retch.

Passing the deserted APC booth, Phoenix Force saw a howling mob of men and women at the gate in the stone fence that led to the parking lot, and a fist fight was raging out of control. Then somebody appeared with a fire ax and started wildly chopping, fingers and hands flying from the gore-drenched blade.

"Dear God, they're going insane," Encizo snarled, dropping a spent clip and slapping in his last.

"That isn't half of it." Manning spit, firing single rounds to conserve his dwindling supply of ammunition.

Situated on top of the majestic hill, the stately Norel mansion was in flames, smoke pouring from the busted windows, and the roof had collapsed inside. Hawkins scowled at the sight. Anything recoverable in the mansion was long gone.

"Frag the files, time to leave!" McCarter barked, running toward the tiered water fountain. Then he stopped.

Coming out of the swirling banks of smoke was Mendoza, a bandage wrapped around his wrist, but still carrying a bulky Stoner Weapons System, a glittering belt of ammunition dangling from the port.

"Hey, Blue Lightning," Mendoza yelled, squinting into the billowing fumes. "Blue Lightning." He waited expectantly, and when there was no reply, the man randomly sprayed the booths and tent screaming incoherently. People dropped, gushing torrents of blood.

Taking aim, McCarter fired the MP-5 once.

Jerking back, Mendoza touched the bullet hole in his chest, the hand coming away covered with red. Sagging to his knees, the dying crime lord tried to speak, failed, and died. But even before he dropped, a dozen people swarmed over the Stoner, fighting for control of the weapon.

Putting his back to the animalistic feeding frenzy, McCarter continued, warily approaching the edge of the bedraggled main tent to scan the sky for any sign of the gunships. He found them easily enough, about a half klick off the cliff, moving quickly around and around each other, machine guns and rockets firing nonstop. One was a huge Egyptian Chinook, and the other was a sleek German Tiger-class Eurocopter. It was a classic David versus Goliath fight, yet somehow, McCarter strongly doubted that either was being flown by representatives of those particular nations.

Near the ruins of the mansion, several security guards in dirty uniforms were firing a massive .50-caliber machine gun at the darting gunships, and constantly scoring hits. But the heavy rounds only threw off bright sparks and never achieved penetration. Stepping out from a kiosk, a young guard carrying a flamethrower tried for the helicopters, but the burning lance never even made it halfway.

"God, I hate amateurs," James muttered in annoyance. "Bet you a sawbuck I could take one out with a LAW."

"Find one, and I'll take ten of that," Encizo said, triggering a short burst from his subgun to clear the pathway ahead of them from a group of men holding broken glass bottles and knives. Three bolted and two fell to never rise again.

Reaching the garage, the Stony Man operatives found a dozen of the guards throwing boxes into the back of a LAV-25, a U.S. Army APC that was harder to stop than a Congressional pay raise.

Gunning them down without hesitation, the Phoenix Force crew seized all of the ammunition clips for the MP-5s, then tucked Weeks in the APC. Cracking a wall locker, James found a full medical kit and wrapped the woman in some blankets before feeding her some plasma. After only a minute, some color returned to her cheeks, and he allowed a small chuckle of victory.

"She'll live," he announced.

"Good. Keep her that way," McCarter shouted, going to the front of the craft. Taking the driver's seat, he started the engine, slammed on the gas and crashed through the garage doors.

"Why the rush?" Encizo demanded, bemused. "Think the exit will be gone by the time we get there?"

"No, because sooner or later," McCarter replied, steering with both hands, "somebody is going to figure out what we've done and—"

Behind them, something streaked across the sky to arch downward and slam into the garage. The building disappeared in a thunderous blast, flaming chunks of cars and men flying out to the sea. A rain of debris peppered the APC as it crashed through some decorative shrubbery, and knocked aside a marble statue of Ares, the god of war, ending his reign over the flower garden forever.

"Jesus, that was close," James muttered, holding on to a ceiling stanchion. "David, you're a genius. Okay, what's the plan?"

"Paranoia," McCarter shouted back, fishtailing the bulky machine as if it was a stock car. "There is no way through the big stone fence without killing people, some of whom may be innocent bystanders."

"Doubtful." Manning scoffed, wedged in tight between a pile of cardboard file boxes and equipment trunks.

"But possible," McCarter noted, ramming through a burning booth and swerving to smash a radio jammer, then again to avoid crushing a man cringing on the ground. "However, these people sell weapons. So I'm betting that anybody who has an APC stashed away as their bleeding escape vehicle would also be smart enough to have on board at least a couple of—"

"Oh, yes," Hawkins cried, lifting a Carl Gustav multipurpose rocket launcher into view. "Now we're in business."

Unexpectedly, there came the sound of incoming rounds hammering the roof of the speeding APC. The men tensed for a moment, but there was no penetration. However, they all knew that both of the gunships were also armed with 35 mm rockets and Sidewinder missiles. They had briefly seen them. And against one of those deathdealers, the mighty LAV-25 might as well have been a Toyota Corolla with a sunroof.

"Belly hatch," Encizo snarled, throwing aside the boxes to reveal an armored hatch set into the floor.

Something violently exploded alongside the APC, the concussion rocking it hard and sending all of the loose items sailing. With a curse, Hawkins lost his grip on the Carl Gustav but James caught it and tossed the weapon right back.

As McCarter drove like a madman, veering wildly in random directions to try to throw off the aim of the gunship pilot, Encizo frantically struggled to get the thick metal plate free, Hawkins prepared the launcher and Manning stuffed spare rockets into his vest.

Meanwhile, James strapped Weeks into a jumpseat set along the wall, tightening the safety harness as much as he dared. The seats were hardpoints, extra protection for the soldiers inside the APC, and right now, she needed all of the protection he could give her against any shrapnel that might blast inside. Unfortunately, her wounds were starting to bleed again from all the violent gyrations, and there was nothing the determined field medic could do about that aside from applying pressure with his bare hands and hope this ended fast. If not, the team would lose their only chance at finding the seller of the Chinese nuke.

"On my mark," McCarter shouted, swerving around the swimming pool, destroying another radio jammer and careening past a rose-covered cabana. "Get set...and...go!"

Bracing himself against the wall, James hugged the woman tight as McCarter slammed on the brakes. Before the LAV-25 had even stopped rocking back and forth, Hawkins and Manning were out the hatch and running. Throwing the APC back into motion, McCarter roared off, narrowly missing a woman kneeling on a bench and clearly praying for divine assistance.

"God helps those who help themselves," he muttered under his breath, pouring on the speed for a brief moment, the big Detroit engines roaring with power. Crushing another radio jammer, he braked and turned sharply. Half a heartbeat later, the grass erupted from a rocket strike exactly where the APC would have been.

McCarter cursed at the sight of the second gunship as something large came streaking out of the billowing clouds. For one eternal moment, the two drivers were face to face, their machines charging directly toward each other, then they both swerved, and the gunship cut loose with its 30 mm nose cannon cutting an oak tree in two, chunks of wood slapping against the APC.

McCarter cursed as a spray of splinters came through a tiny gunport and stabbed into his left arm, sticking out like tiny spears. Then Encizo was behind the man, one hand on the steering yoke, the other held flat over the gunport.

"Got your six, brother," he breathed, a trickle of blood flowing down from a cut on his temple.

Suddenly, James jerked as his cell phone rang. Hot damn, they'd busted enough of the jamming units to clear the airwaves. "This is Chicago," he barked as identification.

"This is Texas and we're ready to shoot the moon," Hawkins said brusquely. "Just tell us when."

"They're ready," James shouted to the men at the front of the speeding APC.

Immediately, McCarter slammed on the brakes and downshifted to bring the LAV-25 to an abrupt halt.

The beat of the gunship got noticeably louder over the purring Detroit engines, and the 30 mm nose cannon spoke again just as there came the telltale rush of a rocket launch. Then the entire world seemed to exploded into fire and chaos....

CHAPTER SEVEN

Prague, Czech Republic

The ancient city spread out bright and alive and almost too perfect to believe. There seemed to be equal numbers of churches, bridges, skyscrapers and bronze statues.

The Czech Technical University dominated the Latin Quarter of the city, so named because Latin was considered the language of scholars, and anybody who wanted to attend the university had to be fluent in Latin. It vastly amused the students that quite a few American tourists went there in search of Mexican food.

Flanking the stone steps of the main library were two huge stone lions, guardians of the treasure inside, the only true wealth there was in this chaotic world: knowledge. Streams of teachers and students walked by at various speeds, some strolling along chatting nonstop, while others rushed by in silence, grimly intent upon reaching a class before they were officially declared late.

Loose skirts swirling around strong thighs, teenage girls freshly blooming into womanhood put a very serious strain on their tight sweaters, and none of the male population ever complained. A few of the young women were dressed all in black, their young faces serious and somber. They were radicals who rallied against conformity by dressing exactly the same as if it was a uniform of rebellion. Other students dressed in expensive fashion, but were covered with garish tattoos, their faces glinting from numerous piercings. They were the so-called New Savages, primitives of the twenty-first century. Prague was a bizarre mixture of the very ancient and the cutting edge of new, a vibrant dichotomy that generated a steady flow of art and invention.

Folding a stick of gum into his mouth, Lieutenant Vladislav started chewing as he walked through the boisterous university. The man thought the children looked silly, but then, that was what children did best, play games. He had done the same when young. However, then the Communists arrived and children became adults overnight in a fierce struggle to survive that had lasted for endless decades.

As the big lieutenant strolled along, several of the younger people passing by frowned openly at the action, thinking he was smoking, but most of the older students ignored the big man in the dirty jumpsuit of a maintenance worker. The iron heel of the Soviet Union was long gone, and social status had returned with a vengeance to Czech. Money was the great equalizer now.

Reaching an island of bushes and trees, Vladislav set down a folding yellow sign bearing an international warning sign. Prague was a truly international metropolis, and more languages were spoken here than anywhere else in the world. It was the new Babylon. That odd fact gave the soldier a small kick of pleasure. Although Slovakia and Czech were no longer a forced political conglomerate, the friendship of the neighboring nations was legendary. Vladislav briefly considered his mission for today, and decided there was no conflict. He was not here to kill anybody, that is, unless it was absolutely necessary.

Checking his hard hat, the man extracted a wrench from his toolbelt, then knelt amid the sculptured greenery to release the bolts on a manhole cover. The bolts were painted over, and resisted, but the big Slovakian put his shoulders into the task and with a screech of metal on metal they suddenly came loose and turned freely. Tossing away each bolt, he finally swung the cover aside and clambered down the long ladder into the steamy darkness.

Reaching the bottom, Vladislav clicked on the light attached to his hard hat to study the walls of the old steam tunnel. The area was surprisingly clean; the bricks had only the ghost of ancient graffiti remaining, most of it in Czech, some in Russian, and all of it vulgar. The concrete floor was clean of waste, rat droppings or even cigarette butts. Although there were a few tiny glass vials. The sight saddened him greatly. Back in the Middle Ages the Black Plague had killed millions of people across Europe before it finally burned out. Now in the twenty-first century, the new plague was crack, rock cocaine, and so far there did not seem to be any cure for the terrible social ailment aside from the Draconian solution of attrition.

Following the tunnel through a maze of twists and turns, Vladislav had extracted every ounce of flavor from the gum but was still chewing when he finally exited into the subbasement of the university. Humming a tune, a janitor was sitting at a workbench tinkering with a thermostat for a clothes dryer. Silently easing behind the man, Vladislav pulled out a knife and slit his throat before even consciously considering the matter. As the janitor fell gurgling to the floor, the lieutenant cursed his military training. Then he shrugged in resignation and moved on to the furnace. Nobody had to know about his slip. After all, with so many people about to die, what did one more matter?

It was unseasonably warm today, and the three big furnaces were cold. But that was not a problem. Smashing open the plastic box around the controls, Vladislav raised the setting higher and higher until the furnaces rumbled info life. Good enough.

Stuffing a pair of fibrous cones into his nostrils, Vladislav practiced breathing through them for a minute. They tickled, and made him want to sneeze, but seemed to work fine. Satisfied, the lieutenant removed a small cylinder from his belt. The man carefully attached a slim rubber hose and used the knife to stab a hole into the aluminum air ducts. Stuffing the tube into the breach, he sealed it tight with the chewing gum, and then turned the handle on the cylinder. With a soft hiss, the pressurized contents flowed into the stream of hot air rising to fill the entire building.

When the cylinder was empty, Vladislav removed it from the duct, and wiped off any possible trace of fingerprints, then proceeded directly to the elevator banks. If there were no open windows, then everybody in the entire building should now be asleep and would remain so for the next few hours. He had no idea how the military gas worked, but the general was never wrong about such things.

Dimly the big lieutenant remembered fighting against somebody with the general, when a sniper attacked them from the trees. Vladislav had thrown himself in front of his friend, and there was a great pain between his eyes. Sometime much later, he awoke in a hospital, and now found many things confusing or difficult to fathom. But the general always treated him with reverence and found him work that was suitable to his talents. Math and science, his favorite subjects in school, were now alien languages, but weapons moved in his hands like eager young lovers. He did not want to kill, did not like it at all, but if that was what the general needed, so be it.

Reaching the elevators, Vladislav pressed the call button and soon the doors opened to reveal a pile of bodies, three young women toppled in a heap. He chuckled at the sight, and immediately began to feel woozy. Cold adrenaline flooded his stomach and Vladislav violently exhaled, emptying his lungs before hesitantly drawing in a breath through the filters. It took a few minutes before the dizziness passed and he felt able to continue. That had been close, too damn close.

Riding the elevator, Vladislav kept his back to the sleeping students to not be tempted again. Many women were attracted by his size, but when he spoke, their fascination vanished just as quickly. Whores were nice, but there was nothing to discuss with them afterward, and one had given him a terrible sickness. After he was better, Vladislav killed her, and after that had turned to rape. It was much cheaper than dating, and infinitely safer than using the dirty whores of Budapest.

As the doors opened on the thirty-ninth floor, Vladislav was startled to see a young man shuffling along the corridor with a damp sponge held to his face.

"Help me," he mumbled frantically. "There's been a gas leak. Everybody is dead."

"No, just you," Vladislav mumbled, pulling a silenced Tokarev pistol from within his shirt and firing twice. The student flailed backward with most of his face gone. He hit the brick wall alongside an open window and slid down to the carpeting, leaving a gory trail along the rough material.

Patiently, Vladislav waited for any reactions to the muffled gunshot, then went over and closed the window. Just bad luck.

Sweeping down a long corridor, the lieutenant checked inside room after room, finding a score of unconscious students sprawled in their beds, crumpled on the floor, playing video games or naked in the showers. Thankfully, none of them was awake, and no further killing was necessary.

However, turning a corner, he quickly jerked back at the sight of a security camera set into the ceiling. Breathing hard through his nose, Vladislav stepped into the room to find a towel. Unfortunately, the place was a sty with empty food wrappers covering the floor, and ashtrays piled high with old butts, and empty beer cans were everywhere, almost as if they were breeding. Slumped over a computer in the corner was a teenage girl with pink hair, wearing only matching panties. Her face was lying on the keyboard and sending an endless stream of random letters into an online chatroom to the obvious annoyance of the other people. Vladislav was amazed he could actually see them in a series of tiny windows, mostly young men wearing no pants, and—

Jerking up his head, the lieutenant stared hard at the unblinking eye of the Web cam sitting on top of the monitor. Snarling a curse, he slapped the camera aside and it smashed into the wall with a crash of plastic and glass. Furious over the breach of security, Vladislav turned off the computer and glared down at the sleeping whore. Terrible feelings welled within the man, and he gently stroked her throat with the dull edge of his knife. She should die—all whores should—but the pink girl was so pretty, the lieutenant decided against it and simply cleaned his blade on her arm, leaving the janitor's blood in wide crimson streaks. There was a lesson there for her to learn.

Returning to the door, Vladislav eased the blade around the jamb to watch the range of the security camera, and as it moved away he stepped into the corridor and fired the Tokarev once. The camera exploded into sparking trash.

Past the dead camera, Vladislav found a plain door marked with the word Resident. Eagerly he went inside, the pistol at the ready. Unlike the other accommodations, this more resembled a proper apartment with a living room, dining room and even a small kitchen. There was Chinese food on the table delivered from a local restaurant. In spite of his dislike of the Chinese, the lieutenant loved their food. However, his military filters removed any trace of wonderful aromas.

A man and woman were asleep on the sofa, a bottle of wine on the coffee table and two broken glasses on the floor. A movie was playing on the television. The language sounded French, and a drunken man in a striped swimsuit seemed to be caught inside a broken rowboat. Blinking in confusion at the comedy, Vladislav shot the screen on impulse to make the images go away. As silence returned, he smiled. There, much better.

Pushing the snoring man aside, the lieutenant rolled the woman over and checked her face. She looked right, but just to be sure, he pulled out his wallet and checked the small picture taped inside that the American mercenary called Lindquist had downloaded from the Internet. Yes, this was Tanya Zemina Karlov.

Vladislav paused. Or was it? Her clothing was in disarray, skirt hitched up high, showing a tattoo of a blue lotus under her stockings, and her blouse was open, a breast fully exposed with a tiny gold ring through the rosy nipple. He checked the picture again, and there was no doubt. The whore was his goal. Fair enough. If the general wanted her, then that was all he needed to know.

Cupping the breast, Vladislav fondled the warm flesh for a moment. The ring tickled his palm. Feeling a rush of lust, the man quickly released the woman and wiped his hand on the sofa. What was he doing? The instructions had been clear. Do not harm the Czech woman in any way.

Looking around nervously, Vladislav debated going back to the pink girl and using her briefly, but decided that would take too much time. The people on the computer had seen him, and the university police might already be on the way. They were not a threat to Vladislav, but the city police would be right behind them, and those were former soldiers. Real trouble. Besides, the general would not be pleased about the momentary diversion.

Going into the kitchen, Vladislav got a dish towel and wrapped it around his hand before stuffing the breast back where it belonged and then buttoning her blouse shut. When he was done, the lieutenant was drenched in sweat, his heart pounding wildly, and he turned to shoot the sleeping man several times as punishment for being a silent witness to his weakness.

Feeling much better, Vladislav moved aside the coffee table and rolled the professor into the rug. Then the soldier slung her over a shoulder and started back for the basement. Mission accomplished, and no breakage. Well, not really. Soon enough, the steam tunnels would take him to the river and freedom. Within only a few hours, Vladislav would be safely back in Slovakia with the slumbering woman. Professor Tanya Karlov, nowadays a Czech teacher of advanced electronics, was also a former Czechoslovakian technician who had worked at Mystery Mountain on a special project code-named Skyfire.

Ponca, Arkansas

BRAKES SQUEALING, the old man slammed his car to a halt in the middle of the dirt road. "Well, I'll be a ring-tail baboon," he whispered, shaking his head slightly as if trying to clear his vision. "Emily, you seeing this, too?"

Along the berm was an open field of alfalfa stretching to the Ozark Plateau Mountains. But across the road was a rolling expanse of smooth green grass, automatic sprinklers creating a dozen rainbows as they systematically watered the sylvan glen. There were wrought-iron benches located underneath spreading oak trees, and neatly trimmed flower beds larger than most homesteads. But that was nothing in comparison to what was on top of a low hillock dominating the entire lush vista.

"You bet I see it, Bob," his wife replied slowly. "That's the goddamn White House."

"Ten miles outside of Ponca?"

Reaching out a hand, Emily turned off the navigational unit glued to the dashboard. "I told you these things were crap," she announced with absolute certainty.

Ignoring that, Bob started rummaging through the glove box. "Gotta get a picture of this," he muttered eagerly.

Just then, a state police car came around the bend and eased to a stop along the parked sedan, window to window.

"Something wrong folks?" the sergeant asked politely, one arm draped across the steering wheel, the other out of sight.

"You tell me, Officer," Bob remarked. "We still in Arkansas?"

Tolerantly, the sergeant smiled, having heard that question a million times before. "Yes, this is still Arkansas." He laughed. "That's just the home of a local millionaire. Well, some say billionaire, not that I can tell the difference. The name is Duvall, Brandon Duvall, and he built himself an exact duplicate to live in."

"Nice fellow?"

"Quiet man. Mostly keeps to himself."

"Fair enough." Bob's attention was now focused on a sleek, black helicopter that circled once around the stately mansion as if getting its bearings before angling away toward the south and the distant city of Fayetteville.

"That his?" Bob asked. "He owns a helicopter?"

"I said he was a millionaire," the sergeant answered.

Emily gave a low whistle.

"A private helicopter, Lord alive, that Duvall guy must be double rich," Bob said, a touch of envy in his words. His own work clothes were clean, but worn, the patches expertly done by his wife while they watched television. Suddenly he felt embarrassed by the dirt on his car, and knew that he would never drive along this road again without washing and waxing it first.

"Gotta be a true patriot, too," Emily added, feeling an unusual swell of pride over the notion. "You don't live in a goddamn copy of the White House and not fiercely be a real American."

Or plumb crazy, the sergeant thought privately. But he wisely kept that opinion to himself. A smart man did not bad-mouth Brandon Duvall on his own property. Unless you had mighty fierce urge to taste dirt.

"Well, better move along and give the man his privacy," the sergeant said, slipping effortlessly into his official voice. "This is Arkansas, ya know, not Manhattan."

Laughing, Bob slipped the car into gear and drove off slowly, unaware that men on the roof of the mansion were closely watching his every move through the scope of a high-powered sniper rifle. Another man held the remote control to activate the land mines buried under the road and the automatic mortars hidden in the hills.

SITUATED IN THE MIDDLE of the duplicate Rose Garden, protected from every direction by the tall Jefferson Mounds, a handsome middle-aged man sat at a small table reading tomorrow's newspaper. The billionaire had an expert hacker who hijacked the roughs from the major papers around the world and cobbled together a crude edition to try to keep him a full twenty-four hours ahead of everybody else.

With the advent of the Internet news services, that number had been reduced to only four hours, but that edge was still enough for Duvall to move his stocks around and steadily increase his net worth until he no longer cared about the numbers. After the first billion, it was all just a bunch of zeroes. Uninteresting and unimportant. There was always enough money to do anything he wanted. Including change the world.

Or at least to try, Duvall added grumpily.

Although in his late fifties, Brandon Duvall claimed to merely be in his forties, which fooled nobody. Duvall was a devilishly handsome man, tall, with broad shoulders and a narrow waist, the type of physique that most women found very attractive and other men found intimidating. Rigorous exercise kept the billionaire in peak physical shape, and his skin was deeply tanned, almost a bronze in color. His coal-black hair was natural, as were the wings of silver at his temples. He wore no jewelry of any kind, not even a watch, but there was a miniature cell phone of a very advanced design tucked into his left ear. He was rarely seen without it, even when taking a shower or having sex.

Because of a facial scar received in childhood from a botched Fourth of July fireworks display, Duvall always seemed to be faintly smiling, which proved to be extremely unnerving to his enemies, both in the financial world and law enforcement.

Dressed in only pajama bottoms, slippers and a bathrobe, Duvall was pouring himself another cup of the wretched herbal tea, and wishing to God it was strong black coffee, when the double doors of the rotunda opened and a butler stepped into view.

"I just received a confirmation from the guards, sir," the man said, closing the doors behind him. "The tourists have finally departed. We ran a trace of the plates, and they were a Robert and Emily Townsend, farmers from Dogpatch. That's a small town just to the north of here, sir."

"Yes, Harrison, I know where it is," Duvall said sipping the herbal muck without looking up. "I was born there."

Having no response to that surprising revelation, Harrison gave a half bow and returned inside the mansion. It would appear that his employer was in a bad mood today. Truthfully that was nothing new. The billionaire seemed to be permanently annoyed these days, although it was difficult to tell because of the damn scar.

Setting aside the cup, Duvall tried once more to read about the stock market, but his mind kept slipping away to the disaster in Russia. How could it all have gone wrong so fast? He had worked out every possible detail with Colonel Lindquist, and there were a hundred contingency plans in case something unexpected happened. And yet, in spite of the thousands of hours spent planning, and the millions of dollars spent, to obtain one of the new superweapons from Russia, the entire Foxfire team was dead, vaporized along with Lindquist when the thermobaric bomb detonated inside a tunnel.

At least my son wasn't with them, Duvall mentally added, for once thankful that the boy preferred pushing papers to throwing lead. There was nothing wrong with paperwork. Even in Foxfire, it took five clerks to support each soldier in the field. Maybe it wasn't glorious, but then many patriots, such as Thomas Paine and John Adams, hadn't fought in the American Revolution. They had been the men behind the man behind the gun. Besides, just being around real men should teach the boy some control. His love of violence had cost Duvall a fortune over the years in hush money, and once a lot more than that when he was forced to purchase a building with the remains of one of his son's rampages buried in the basement.

Setting aside the paper, Duvall banished the dark thoughts and rose to walk to the edge of the garden and gaze at the construction site for his duplicate of the Washington Monument. The foundation was completed, and the first ten feet of the great obelisk was slowly rising from the ground. The reflecting pool connecting the monument and the house had been finished long ago, but unlike the original in the District of Columbia, this one was a full yard deep and well stocked with rainbow trout and small-mouth bass. Duvall saw no sense in having a private lake, unless he could sneak in some fishing from time to time. Mansions, private jets and sex with young movie starlets, were all well and good, but the little things truly made life worth living; a cold beer after a hard day's work, the smell of a new car, killing an enemy and protecting the nation he loved so much.

In his heart, Duvall knew that the United States of America was the hope of the world, and she must be strong. But without the secret of the thermobaric bomb, America was hobbled into being on equal footing with the Russians again. That was an intolerable situation. His father had spent billions artfully arranging to bankrupt the Soviet Union, only to have goddamn Russia rise up even stronger for him to face, with the Chinese right behind them. Stealing the T-bomb and arranging for a private war between the two rival nations was the perfect solution to the problem. America would be made strong, while her enemies tore each other apart. A win-win situation. But now...

With a sigh, Duvall returned to the table and tried to take another sip of the herbal brew, but could not get it down. "Harrison," he said, touching the earbud. "Bring me a pot of Jamaican Blue, and no lectures on how it's bad for my heart."

"At once, sir," the butler replied. "However, Mr. Russell asked if you could come down and see him as soon as possible. He gave no details, sir, but I have a feeling it's not good news."

"Fine, bring it to his lab."

Leaving the garden, Duvall nodded in greeting to the armed guards standing in the vestibule. They gave a salute in return as he turned into the west wing and rode an elevator down to the subbasement.

Getting off at the bottom level, Duvall approached a burnished steel door and rolled up his sleeve. With some marked trepidation, the man put his bare arm into a hole in the wall. Soft clamps closed on his forearm while the scanners checked the microchips buried under his skin. This procedure always made the man a little nervous. If there was anything wrong with the implanted chips, the arm would be removed, the antechamber would be flooded with VX nerve gas and then Claymore mines in the floor would detonate. No unauthorized personnel would ever get inside the private lab of Sir Greg Russell.

After an interminable wait, the box gave a low beep and his arm was thankfully released. Massaging the undamaged skin, Duvall took down a fur parka from a row of pegs and slipped it on while the steel slab that served as a door slid aside. Zipping the parka, Duvall entered the chilly room and the door closed immediately in his wake. Only a single person at a time could enter the lab. Any more than that would result in a great deal of mopping and dry cleaning.

A soft hum filled the air and dozens of servo-units stood like soldiers on review along both walls, ending at the hulking mound of an IBM Blue/Gene supercomputer. As he drew near, sensors detected the new source of heat, and the big tanks of liquid nitrogen hissed softly to maintain the perfect operational temperature for the delicate machine.

Surrounded by a curved wall of flashing monitors, a pale man was reclining in an orthopedic chair, a VR visor wrapped around his head, while one gloved hand manipulated the air and the other typed steadily on a small keyboard. A small British flag hung off the back of the chair, almost touching the floor.

Sir Gregory Hanover Russell was a short man with a wild crop of platinum hair, interrupted by a tiny streak of black on one side where he had received a massive head injury in a car crash. Duvall smiled at that. Russell was a genius, but like most of those, he was also a little crazy. The man and cars simply did not get along. After his fifth crash, and both legs broken for a second time, Duvall hired the hacker a driver and took away his license. Greg Russell was a genius with electronics, but anything mechanical almost seemed to frighten the man.

In spite of the cold, the hacker was dressed in only blue jeans, sneakers and a dark turtlenecked sweater. An open thermos of steaming coffee was clipped to the chair, the smell a tantalizing delight, and the partially eaten sandwich on a nearby table looked as if it had been there since before the arrival of Columbus.

"How can you do two different things at the same time?" Duvall demanded, stopping a few feet away. He knew better than to jostle the hacker's elbow during work.

"Years of training at Oxford," Russell replied with a strong accent. Stopping the typing, he slid off the VR glove and massaged the fingers, then slipped off the VR visor and set it aside, shaking his head to loosen the sweat-dampened curls.

"Okay, bad news, I'm afraid," Russell said. "I just stole a report from NATO to the Pentagon which confirmed that the lightning strike at the Bosporus Strait was actually caused by a thermobaric bomb."

Duvall frowned. "What? But that is impossible, unless..."

"Yes, sir, I think Lindquist killed his team and sold the bomb to some second party."

The words rang in his mind, building tempo and strength, until the billionaire thought his head would explode. "Then he's alive? Lindquist is alive?"

Russell gave a curt nod. "That would be the most logical explanation, yes, sir."

For several minutes Duvall could not speak, his anger was so great. Betray. He had been betrayed! A red fog filled his mind, and his every thought was of a violent act of insane mayhem.

"How should we proceed, sir?" Russell asked, placing a hand on the miniature keyboard. As small as the gesture was, it made the sleeve ride up to reveal the scars on his wrist from the steel manacles the former bank robber had worn for ten long years at La Santé, the infamous French prison that delivered harsh justice with chains and whips. Not even his sex partners saw the hacker with his shirt off, so embarrassed was he from the layers of overlapping scars.

"We shall proceed with swift revenge," Duvall muttered, his handsome face a feral mask of rage. "I want his mutilated body sent to me in little pieces! I want his balls in a Mason jar. I want…"

With a supreme effort of will, the billionaire regained his composure. "Forget that." He forced his hands to unclench. "The man is not to be harmed until I say so. First and foremost, I want that bomb. Contact Foxfire. They should be very eager to become reacquainted with the traitor who killed their fellow mercenaries."

"Find the man, find the bomb," Russell said, thoughtfully tilting his head to consider the idea. "They'll like that. Revenge and money are a powerful combination."

"Especially once I agree to pay triple their standard fee," Duvall added savagely.

The hacker barked a laugh. "For that much money, they'd assassinate the queen. But they'll need some local help, a native guide, so to speak."

"Got anybody in mind?"

"Yes, sir. A man named Novostk. He's quite old, but his crew is not. Some of them used to do wet work for the KGB, and their reputation is stellar."

"Good. Hire them, pay any price," Duvall growled. "Get me that bomb, then have Novostk slowly tear Lindquist apart. But the primary mission is to get that bomb."

"What if there was only the one?"

"My intelligence says the weapon being tested at Mystery Mountain was a multiple warhead unit, a sort of MIRV," Duvall stated, stumbling over the foreign word. "So there should be at least one more of the damn things. Get it or get a new job!" With that, the billionaire turned and stormed from the cold room.

"Whatever you say, sir," Russell muttered in Slovakian, slipping back on the VR visor and returning to his real job.

There would be an auction soon, and it promised to be incredibly lucrative.

Even if it was a fake.

CHAPTER EIGHT

Saris Castle, Slovakia

Sluggishly, the woman struggled awake through the warm curtain of sleep. She and a friend had been watching the classic French comedy *Mr. Hulot's Holiday,* then everything became oddly blurry and chaotic.

Dimly she remembered seeing Emile slump over, and then came vague sensations of having a breast fondled, then of flying through a steamy tunnel. For a very brief instant, a cold breeze that carried the smell of the river revived her from the warm cocoon, then something soft pressed against her face and the world went away again. After that there were only disjointed memories of boats and planes and cars. There had been a long winding staircase, cold stones, flaming torches, iron doors. Then once more she was floating past a window filled with infinite blackness that expanded to fill the universe....

Jerking awake, Professor Tanya Karlov tried to grab her aching head, and was startled to discover that her arms would not move, not at all! Panic flooded the woman at the sight of gray duct tape wrapped around her wrists and forearms, holding them tight to the wooden arms of a chair. Attempting to stand, she was not overly shocked to find that her ankles were also bound to the chair. The use of the tape was fiendishly clever. There were no ropes to stretch or knots to chew through. She was pinned, utterly helpless, like a laboratory specimen on an examination board, ready for dissection.

Trying to look around for her purse, the professor abruptly realized that there was something around her throat, a band of cold pinning it in place. Inhaling to scream, she started coughing, her chest unable to expand enough.

Stay calm, Karlov mentally commanded herself. Stay calm, goddamn it! I'm not dead. So this is either rape or a kidnapping. But either way, life meant hope.

Taking shallow breaths, the bound woman looked around the room. Stone block walls and floors said this was an older building, eighteenth century or earlier. Perhaps a fort or castle. Nearby was a recessed door, showing granite walls at least two feet thick. That made the place sixteenth century or so. There were no windows that she could see, nor any sounds of the outside world, no wind or traffic or airplanes. Crude iron rings were attached directly to the walls, and heavy chains dangled from them ending with manacles. There were no locks on those; they were the kind that a blacksmith would hammer closed, sealing the prisoner in them permanently until cut loose. More and more, this was starting to resemble a sixteenth century castle, or to be more precise, the dungeon of such a castle.

I'm a prisoner in a dungeon. A shiver ran down her spine at the thought. Only recently, she had heard on the cable TV news shows that the Sardinians and the Albanians were kidnapping young women again for their sex slave market. The concept was ghastly beyond belief. Whoever bought her would find that he had made a very poor choice. Death was far preferable than eternal servitude in a stinking brothel serving the drunken, diseased dregs of humanity.

Slowly, Karlov became aware of a low humming noise, and managed to twist her neck just enough to see a large kerosene heater in the corner of the room. It radiated delicious heat.

Having experienced bitter cold as a kid, she was thankful for the heater, then wondered if it was there to keep her health or for the comfort of her captors. The glow of the heater was the only source of light in the room—the jail cell, she corrected— and it made the stonework seem to be cast of solid gold.

From somewhere there came the report of a cracking whip, closely followed by the tormented howl of a man in mortal agony. The noise shook her resolve, and the professor tried not to shudder, which only made it happen more powerfully. Casting back to her childhood for the words, the professor prayed to God for deliverance, apologizing for her sins and promising to start life anew, if she could be allowed to leave the room alive.

Suddenly there came the sound of boots in the outside corridor. They stopped at the door, and there was the clatter of heavy keys. The lock turned and the door swung open to admit a group of men in military fatigues. They were big men, much larger than her, and heavy with muscles. There were no weapons on their belts, guns or knives, nothing she could grab to defend herself. Worse, one of the men had a rolled-up exercise mat tucked under an arm, the kind she often used at the university gymnasium. Under the circumstances, the sight of it made her blood run cold.

As one of the soldiers closed and locked the door, another man walked closer until she could smell his unwashed body.

"Ah, you're awake at last." He grinned. "Excellent."

"Look, I—" Karlov started when he lashed out a palm, slapping her against the side of the head. For a split second the woman thought her eye would explode from its socket, the pain was so great.

Grabbing a fistful of her hair, the man forced her to look at him. The angle cut the tape into her flesh, and she fought to bring in enough air. Panting for air, she felt her nose become stuffy, and something warm trickled down her cheek.

"My name is Mr. Yes," the soldier said in a flat, conversational tone. "And every time I ask you a question, that is what you will reply, with a yes. Do you understand?"

"Yes," she croaked, and he released her hair.

Gulping down air, Karlov simply breathed for several minutes while the other men circled around her.

"I'm rich—" Karlov tried, but was instantly interrupted by another vicious slap.

"Stupid Czech whore." He sighed, slapping her with every word. "Do not speak again until spoken to. Do you understand?"

"Yes!" she screamed, the pain threatening to overwhelm her sanity. "Yes, I do. Please. Oh God, yes."

"Better, much better." He smiled, then reached down to grab a fistful of the silk blouse and violently pulled.

Almost bodily yanked from the chair, Karlov heard the flimsy material rip more than she felt it. The tape around her throat made her gag once more. Time passed while she fought for air, but she could feel the warm air now on her bare stomach and breasts. Shame burned her cheeks at the realization that she was clad only in a lacy bra, designed to inflame the sexual passion of Emile. Now it was her key to the pits of Hell.

Hooking a finger between the cups, the soldier tugged on the bra. A breast came free, the tiny nipple ring glistening in the yellow light of the gas heater.

"Nice," another soldier muttered in appreciation, and reached out a hand.

She flinched from the expected contact, but the guard stopped less than an inch from her flesh. His hand was rough and coarse, covered with a fine network of scars, new ones over older scars, and there was a crude prison tattoo peeking out from inside the sleeve.

Frantically trying to think of something to do, or say, she went stiff as a third soldier knelt before her and slipped off her shoes to cast them into the corner. They landed with a clatter, and Karlov tried not to scream as the guard slipped a hand up her leg, the black nylons snagging from his many calluses.

"Don't tell him anything, little one," the man whispered in a hoarse voice, easing his fingers under her trembling thigh to brush her panties. "Do nothing. Don't cooperate, then you and I can become friends." He rose suddenly and leaned over the woman, his breath hot on her ear. "Close friends, you know, eh?" Then he described some of the more intimate details.

"I see that she has courage, or is it desperation?" a new voice said from the direction of the door.

The newcomer closed the door behind him and slowly walked closer. He was a slim man with an intelligent face, neatly combed hair and the slim hands of a surgeon, or a fellow scientist. He wore a green military uniform, neatly pressed, but devoid of any insignia showing the nationality or even his rank. Unlike the other men, the slim man had a large revolver holster at the small of his back. He was also carrying a folding metal chair.

"You have two choices, Professor Karlov," Sergeant Melori said, setting the chair a few inches away and sitting in it backward, arms placed across the top. "You can help us with a technical problem, and sleep alone, and unharmed, in your cell every night. Or you can choose not to help us with our technical problem, and return every night to the barracks of my troops, where you will not be alone, or unharmed, and I doubt highly that any sleep will be involved on your part."

Panting hard, her heart pounding in her chest, Karlov said nothing.

"It is your choice, Tanya," the sergeant said, pulling a handkerchief out of his shirt pocket. "So choose wisely." Turning the cloth upside down, he dropped the contents into her lap.

At the contact, Professor Karlov felt the universe shrink to a tight focus at the sight of two eyes and a human tongue lying on her skirt, the freshly severed end still oozing droplets of red blood. A wild scream boiled into her throat, and this time she cut loose, madness threatening to shatter her mind as the woman threw herself against the binding tape, the heavy chair not moving an inch from the frantic efforts.

Lighting cigarettes, the soldiers did nothing, waiting patiently until sheer exhaustion made her stop, her throat raw and painful.

"She would not cooperate," Melori said. "And so we recruited you as a replacement."

Hot tears came unbidden, and the professor hung her head. "Whatever you want, yes, I will do it," she burbled, weeping uncontrollably. "Yes, I'll fix it, make it work. Yes. Whatever you want."

Melori stood. "You're too tired to talk at the moment. Get some sleep, and we'll discuss the project in the morning."

Confused, the professor watched the soldiers march out of the cell and close the door. In only seconds, she was alone. A wave of relief filled the woman, until her attention snapped back to the grisly objects still in her lap. Shaking and wiggling, Karlov managed to dislodge the eyes, but she was bound too tight to remove the tongue, and all she could do was make it jiggle with a hideous mockery of life.

"Please, come back and take it away," Karlov shouted at the top of her lungs. "In the name of God, take it away. Take it away!"

THE SOLDIERS LISTENED to her wails of terror dwindle behind as they continued down the main stairwell to the barracks. In the morning, the scientist would do whatever they wished, meekly as a whipped dog. She would be their slave, body and soul. When forced to work for the Communists, they had done this sort of thing before many times.

Standing at the bottom of the stairs was Lieutenant Vladislav, his arms crossed, his face impassive. "Is she willing to help us?" he asked.

"Of course, my friend," Sergeant Melori cried, patting the giant on the back. "Was there ever any doubt?"

"Whose tongue was that anyway?" the lieutenant inquired.

"Just a whore from a local village," Melori replied with a shrug. "A nobody that we picked up to keep the troops happy."

"I see." The lieutenant stood tall at that. "Then her family must be proud that she gave the last, full measure of duty to Slovakia."

The soldiers openly laughed at the remark.

"When she is done defusing the bomb, can we have her as usual?" a man asked eagerly.

"If you wish," Sergeant Melori replied with a shrug. "But only a few times, then shoot her in the head."

That news pleased the rest of the soldiers. Only Lieutenant Vladislav did not join in the crude humor. His personal opinion on the matter was kept private behind a clumsy tongue and a foolish belief in justice.

Fox, Arkansas

SCAMPERING ALONG, a small dog holding a Frisbee was chased by a howling group of children across the parkland, dodging trees and laurel bushes with the complete disregard for their own safety that only comes with extreme youth.

"Ten bucks on the dog," Schwarz said, typing away at his laptop perched on top of a redwood picnic table.

"I'll take five of that," Blancanales replied, using a pocketknife to remove the cap of a beer bottle.

Moving out from the mob, a little girl with pigtails and freckles never paused as she whipped out a slingshot and fired. The Frisbee was knocked free, but it only bounced once before the dog had it again and the chase continued, even louder than before.

"Good shot," Lyons acknowledged, lifting his bottle in salute to the underage marksman. Hitting a moving target while on the run was more than good luck; that was gut instinct. Give the kid twenty years, and some proper training, and she could give Manning a run for his money.

Charging into the tall weeds, the dog and the kids vanished from sight, but their cries could still be heard as they circled the parkland, skirting along the parking lot, then the river, then back across the grass in an endless loop.

It was a beautiful Southern afternoon, but Able Team was not at the park down the road from Foxfire HQ just to enjoy the scenery.

The laptop gave a soft chime.

"Okay, we're in," Schwarz said eagerly, rubbing his hands together.

Gathering close, the three men studied the aerial pictures of the Foxfire complex. It had been relatively easy for Kurtzman and his team to track down the sale of the computer chips in the Auto-Sentry that Able Team had recovered in Florida. Ultimately the weapon had been traced back to Foxfire Incorporated, Fox, Arkansas.

Both Barbara Price and Hal Brognola had been familiar with the reputation of the mercenaries, and thought they were only interested in corporate security and industrial espionage, with a little sabotage on the side. Just some muscle for Wall Street, nothing more. But apparently the "ghosts of Arkansas" had recently expanded their repertoire to include more covert activities. Such as kidnapping, murder and possibly the theft of a Russian superweapon.

"Okay, I'm impressed," Schwarz grudgingly admitted, reaching out for his beer. But the man changed his mind and pushed the bottle away.

Unfortunately, Lyons and Blancanales agreed with the assessment. The headquarters for Foxfire was a formidable hardsite, to say the least.

Relayed via the Farm, the satellite photographs of the base revealed a lot, and none of it was good. Listed as a training facility, most of the base was out of sight beneath military-grade camouflage netting, and even when Kurtzman switched to infrared, little more was revealed by the NSA satellite as every building seemed to be located inside a Quonset hut, the curved sheet of corrugated steel arching over the smaller buildings to completely hide any pertinent details.

Surrounding the base was a granite block wall thick enough to stop a LAW rocket, and precisely six feet tall, the legal maximum for a solid barrier. However, a ten-foot-tall iron fence was on top of the granite wall, with a dense grove of evergreen trees right alongside. From the ground, or in space, there was absolutely no way to see what was happening inside the base. On top of which, the stone wall was edged with electrified wiring, the iron fence with multiple video cameras and small domes that looked suspiciously like proximity sensors.

Located nearby was a small airfield with a single landing strip and an odd collection of aircraft, including an old Bell & Howell bubble copter, a brand-new Blackhawk, a classic DC-3 Gooneybird, a state-of-the-art C-130 Hercules, a Cessna Skywagon and even an old F-101 Delta Dagger jetfighter. All of the armament was clearly gone, but the aircraft still looked fully capable of reaching Mach speed. The fuel dump was surrounded by water towers, so that blowing it would achieve a lot of noise, but little else.

The three men scowled at the spy pictures. Whatever else was true about the mercs, they were certainly well financed.

The land around the base and airfield was smooth and flat for nearly a mile, which was quite a feat of engineering in a hilly state like Arkansas. There wasn't a rock, or a tree stump, in sight. Absolutely nothing that could be used to sneak in close. There was a culvert along the access road, but it appeared to contain more barbed wire and video cameras than the main wall.

"Is all of this legal?" Blancanales asked, rotating the beer bottle between his palms.

"Sure, why not? Everybody is entitled to some privacy, even paramilitary assholes."

"Nobody said they were stupid," Lyons admitted honestly, draining the beer and then drying his hands on a paper napkin. "We could try to enlist. They must always need trained personnel, and there is nobody better trained than us."

"Useless, I'm afraid," Schwarz sighed. "The company Web site says they're not hiring right now. Even if they were, there's a waiting list, and then a ten-month training course in New Mexico before you get on the other side of that wall." He tapped the plasma screen with a finger, making the picture swell and zoom in with every touch.

"Sounds like they're afraid of undercover FBI agents," Blancanales said thoughtfully, twirling the bottle around on the table.

"Damn well should be," Lyons answered, crossing his arms. "Show me the front gate again."

"The only gate," Schwarz corrected, stroking the mouse pad with a thumb. The picture flipped to a tight shot of the only breach in the thick wall.

The gate was actually a box and just as thick as the wall itself. It extended out from the wall fifteen feet in both directions, and was equipped with a score of lights and video cameras. A guard kiosk was on either end, each containing ten or so armed men, and something large covered with a tarpaulin. Obviously an additional defense weapon, probably a heavy machine gun, but it could be a small howitzer.

There was a metal gate located at both ends of the box, with a third in the middle, making the idea of ramming through pointless. The middle gate would not even open until the first was closed and locked, as was the case with the third.

"Notice how they left the camouflage netting off the gate?" Blancanales said. "They want people to know how tough it is to get inside."

"We could get a warrant," Schwarz, said, glancing at the van parked only a score of yards away. The printer in the back could produce exact duplicates of over a thousand U.S. government documents, everything from arrest warrants to notices of eviction, whatever was necessary for the team to get the job done. However, this time the documents would not work.

"Useless," Blancanales stated gruffly. "They have to know by now that we've identified the bodies in Russia as their people, and have sealed the base tighter than a crab's ass. So unless we parachute in at midnight—"

"Which would only get our heads blown off," Schwarz chimed in.

"Which would get our heads blown off," Blancanales agreed. "Then, brothers, we are not getting inside."

"Sure, we are," Lyons said softly, the warm breeze ruffling his short blond hair. "That part is easy. The big question is, how do we get out again?"

Nobody spoke for a minute, then Schwarz gave a half smile and changed the screen to the local Yellow Pages, found what he wanted and got directions.

"Is that really going to work?" Blancanales asked skeptically. "A cable TV dish?"

"Watch and see." Schwarz grinned.

"Of course, you know what this will also entail," Lyons added poignantly.

With a sigh, Schwarz stroked his mustache. "Yeah, I do. But what the hell, it's for a good cause."

AFTER GETTING the new supplies and installing the satellite dish in the tree line outside the flatlands around the base, Able Team changed into the classic dark blue suit and sunglasses of the FBI, strapped on government-issue S&W automatics and mentally crossed their fingers. They'd only get one shot at this, and if anything went wrong they would be in a world of pain before the sweet release of death. But that was the job.

"If this tanks, Gadgets, no hard feelings," Blancanales said, checking the clip in his weapon. "It was a damn good idea."

"Same here, Pol." The man grinned, using a remote control to activate the self-destruct function on his laptop.

"It has been an honor, gentlemen," Lyons added, turning on the engine. "But let's try really hard not to screw this up."

Schwarz jerked a thumb. "See? Positive thinking. That's why he gets the big money."

"But I don't get paid anything," Blancanales said, pretending to be shocked.

"Well, I make double that," Lyons said with a half smile.

"He is in charge," Schwarz reminded.

Circling the Foxfire encampment, the team approached from the far side with blue lights flashing behind the grille of their cargo van. By the time they reached the front gate, there was a contingent of twenty burly guards blocking the entrance, their hands full of M-4 assault rifles, along with a frowning man wearing a crisp, clean uniform. The tabs on his collar marked the man's rank as that of a brevet general, his boots shone with fresh polish and his shirt carried more military decorations than the combined Joint Chiefs of Staff.

"Wow, I didn't know that Blackjack Persing and Napoleon Bonaparte had a kid," Schwarz muttered, smoothing down his hair. "Think he's happy to see us?"

"The way glass does a flying brick," Lyons replied out of the corner of his mouth.

From their position, the Stony Man operatives could see that the American flag decorated almost everything in sight, video cameras, the kiosk windows and belt buckles, but it was always accompanied by the company logo of a fox made entirely out of fire sprinting through the stars. The mixture made Able Team more than apprehensive. This sort of patriotism carried the hollow sincerity of a whore talking about love. It could be true, but a wise man would proceed with care and keep a hand on his wallet.

Braking to a gentle halt several yards from the kiosk, Lyons let the dust settle before the team climbed out of the van. This close to the guards, the team could see that they were wearing Dragonskin body armor, the expensive stuff proof to anything under a .44 Magnum. The 9 mm S&W automatics in their hands would have been about as dangerous as snowballs.

"Good morning," Lyons said with a broad smile, a hand easing slowly inside his jacket.

"Hold it right there!" the general shouted, raising a palm. Instantly the row of guards worked the arming bolts on their M-4 rifles, the clatter most impressive. "You are on private property, sir. I need to see some identification right now."

The forced courtesy was a nice touch, but Lyons felt sure it was added purely in case the encounter was being recorded.

"Of course." The former L.A. cop smiled, producing an FBI commission booklet and flipping it open to show the photo ID inside. "I'm Special Agent Mann, and this is Special Agent Pohl and Getts." He paused. "And you are…?"

"Brigadier General Daniel Smith," the officer replied, snapping off a salute. "I'm the CO here. What do you want, Officers?"

The team clearly heard that he had not said "What can I do for you?" More often than not, the subtle difference between those two sentences often ended in a gun battle.

"There is a matter of national security that needs to be addressed," Lyons said, slipping the commission booklet into the breast pocket of his suit so that it stayed on constant display. "If we could step inside the compound for a moment…" He smiled but didn't finish the sentence.

"Sorry, but we have a recent outbreak of cholera," Smith said smoothly, without even a pause. "Nobody is allowed to enter, or leave, for the sake of public safety."

"Then, by law, we need to make an immediate health inspection," Lyons replied. "As per our original 1925 charter." Actually, the guidelines of the FBI said no such thing, but it sure sounded good.

As if knowing it was bullshit, the guards grew noticeably hostile, tightened their grip on the assault rifles.

"Sorry, but I must refuse for your own good," General Smith replied with a strained tone in his voice.

"Then I have to serve you with this search warrant," Blancanales said, producing the document. "Now you will comply with this, or have you seceded from the nation and started your own little empire?"

"Shut your mouth, commie," a guard snarled, leveling the M-4 rifle.

"At ease, soldier!" General Smith snapped, without turning around. "Let's not offend our brothers in blue. May I see the search warrant, Special Agent?"

Wordlessly, Blancanales passed it over, and everybody waited while the officer gave it a cursory inspection. "It gives no particular reason for the search," he said, turning a page.

"Under the Patriotic Act, none is needed," Schwarz answered.

"So it would seem. It also seems that I now have little choice in the matter," Smith said, tucking the document away. "Open the gates and let them through, Corporal."

"Sir?" the guard asked, a hand instinctively going to the Glock at his hip.

"You heard me!" the general barked. "Let 'em through."

Going inside the kiosk, the guard lifted a receiver and briefly talked. As he hung up a few seconds later, the massive steel gate rumbled aside to the sound of working hydraulics.

"This way," the general said, turning and walking through.

Returning to the van, the men of Able Team silently exchanged fast looks and forced their hands to stay away from the arsenal of weapons hidden all around them in the war wagon.

Now we come to the tricky part, Lyons thought, rolling down his window. In one minute the team would either be dead or inside the base. Engaging the gears, Lyons drove toward the line of guards, and they reluctantly parted, clearly unhappy about letting outsiders into their little world.

The middle gate was already open, and the general was striding through. But as the van entered the box, the gate slammed shut behind the man just as the front gate also slammed shut. Trying to appear frightened, Lyons grabbed the hand mike on the dashboard and thumbed the transmit button, but before he could speak a strident howl came from the ceiling speakers, as every channel was jammed with oscillating hash.

"Here we go," Schwarz whispered, then loudly shouted, "Holy crap, it's a trap."

Even as the team pulled out weapons, white gas hissed from hidden vents set into the four walls. With their windows open, the men were bombarded directly in the face by the thick fumes, and the world spun crazily until they slumped in their seats, the guns falling away. As Lyons's twitching foot slipped off the brake, the airtight van lurched forward to loudly crash into the middle set of gates, smashing a headlight and sending the unconscious men tumbling to the floor....

CHAPTER NINE

Rimpfischhorn, Switzerland

"Hold on, comrades, we're almost there!" Captain Daniel Lee shouted over a shoulder, both hands on the joystick of the huge Chinook helicopter.

The bandaged copilot slumped in the navigator seat said nothing in reply, nor was there any response from the normally chatty crew of Red Star operatives sitting strapped into the jumpseats along the walls. With a sinking feeling, the Chinese pilot was starting to think that he was talking to the dead.

Fighting to maintain control against a savage and tricky crosswind, Captain Lee could not spare a second of his attention to glance at the control panels. They were flying too low and too fast, and that goddamn Eurocopter Tiger had shot the ever-loving shit out of them with that 30 mm nose cannon. The rear engine was overheating, the hydraulic pressure was virtually nonexistent, the fuel was nearly gone and most of his crew was dead.

Dodging tall pine trees while trying to stay below radar both civilian and military, Lee shouted in joy at the sight of the Rimpfischhorn Bridge, located just below the equally famous granite peak. Once they were past that, the Chinook would be legally back in Switzerland, safe from any attempt by the Italian army to capture them for a very public trial and private execution. Switzerland did not have an extradition treaty with any country, so once the battered Chinook touched soil, he was home free.

Lee briefly tried once more to rouse his comrades, but to no avail. The pilot of that triple-damn German Euro Tiger had been exceptional, the gunner even better, augmented by the fact that their guns had been loaded with live ammunition, not rubber stun bullets. In short order, the fight gone badly against the Red Star agents, when Private Shen-Wa decide to try something not in the operations manual and launched an Armbrust rocket while still inside the cargo helicopter. The other operatives had tried to stop the act of insanity, but it had proved to be too little, too late.

The backwash of frozen nitrogen snow that exploded from the aft port of the stealth rocket launcher filled the Chinook like a winter avalanche, throwing the other men hard against the hull and knocking one of them unconscious. In a split second it was impossible to see through the swirling flakes, and it became so bitterly cold that the fuel lines froze, the radar crashed and the fire alarms went off. The chilling effect was only temporary, and by the time everything returned to normal, the Tiger was splashed, the ocean rippling with oil-slick waves.

Captain Lee loved that sight. However, his Chinook had been helpless for more than a minute. If the desperate gamble had failed, the Tiger would have removed the Red Star agents from this plane of existence like wiping a blackboard clean. But they survived. Unfortunately, the woman they had wanted to kidnap was also gone, taken by a group of big men whose description sounded suspiciously like the rather infamous Blue Lightning mercenaries.

Suddenly the forest stopped and the land below became rolling hills of green pastureland dotted with small herds of dairy cows. A small farmhouse sat astride a creek, smoke rising from the stone chimney. The driveway was made of crushed white stones. There were some bricks in the driveway arranged in the form of a star, a red star, the symbol only visible from the air.

Buffeted by a strong wind from the northern valley, Captain Lee cut the electrical power, then cut the fuel to both engines and braced for the crash. The colossal aircraft descended the last fifty feet with the overhead blades spinning from sheer inertia and it slammed into the ground like the fist of God. A powerful shudder shook the entire helicopter, as the windshield shattered and there came the terrible sound of bending metal and popping welds. The unconscious people flailed, one of the men slamming his head into a stanchion.

Slapping the release button on his safety harness, Lee got free and stumbled for the open hatchway, ducking under a cluster of loose wiring. The deck was uneven, and his footing was precarious, but the captain still paused to check the condition of the man who had hit the stanchion. There was a deep gash across his face, but no sign of blood. Sadly, Lee turned away from his friend. Clearly the operative had been dead for quite some time before receiving the disfiguring wound.

Clambering to the open hatch, he jumped to the ground and walked quickly away from the ruined helicopter. There was a strong smell of fuel in the air, and even though he turned off the power to the electronics, if there was even a single spark…

The explosion sounded louder than doomsday, and the heat wave cooked Lee to the bone before the man found himself flying through the air. Disjointed visions of the farmhouse and the parked cars filling his sight for only a crazy moment before blackness ruled the universe.

"LEE? Captain Lee!"

Wearily opening his eyes, the pilot looked around to see five people in dark suits standing around his bed. Four of them were men, and one woman, but she was so inherently masculine it was hard for Lee to tell for sure without asking.

The brick walls were covered with paintings of pastoral scenes, flowers mostly, and there was a dresser covered with unwrapped boxes of medical supplies. That was when he noticed the IV of something clear dripping into his arm, and there was a strong smell of cooked pork in the air. Lee found that odd for a hospital, until the pilot realized the smell was coming from his cooked flesh.

"Captain Lee!" a man bellowed again.

"Sir?" the pilot asked, and tried to salute, but his right arm was in a cast. Then he noticed that both of his legs were also in casts, the plaster still shiny it was so new.

"Report please, comrade," the woman asked tolerantly.

"We...the mission failed, sir," Captain Lee said, the words tumbling freely from his mouth. Whatever painkillers were in the IV had him feeling warm and loose. Almost carefree. Get a grip, act like a professional. "Sir, we got ambushed by some assholes in a Tiger that shot the ever-loving shit out of my Chinook with a 30 mm chin cannon."

Impatiently, one of the men waved that aside. "Yes, comrade, we have seen the pictures of your wrecked vehicle. Very sad. But what about the woman who sold nuclear weapons? Weeks, Rebecca Weeks. Is she alive or dead?"

"My crew is dead," Lee said, the words tasting funny in his mouth. "All dead from shrapnel. Bad way to go."

"Comrade! What about Rebecca Weeks?"

"Alive," Lee said, forcing his mind to focus. "Taken by Blue Lightning." Then he added, "My crew is dead. All dead from shrapnel. Bad way to die, that."

Wordlessly, the other men looked at the pilot for a long moment, then turned and walked from the makeshift hospital room.

"Bah, he is too far gone to be of any use to us," one of the men growled, closing the door. "You should not have given him so much painkiller."

"Any less and his injuries might have killed him," another man declared. "This way, at least we learn something about what happened in Milan."

"His statements are not reliable."

"Comrade, his best friend and entire crew just died. I think we can safely assume that he wants the people responsible killed."

"The television news—"

"Is controlled by the state. The broadcasts will contain nothing of any use, or interest, to us."

"Blue Lightning," one of the older Chinese men muttered, walking to the window of the farmhouse and looking across the pastureland to the smoldering ruins of the Chinook. "I know of these people. They are supposedly freelance, but always seem to be working for Sheikh Abdul Benny Hassan."

"The word is *ben,* not *Benny,*" another man said with a sniff. "In Arabic, it means 'son of—'"

"Shut up, fool. His middle name is Benjamin, and never correct me again."

"We are getting off the point," a fat man said, tucking his hands into his pockets. "Somebody has hired mercenaries to kidnap Weeks and find out who used the nuclear device to steal a T-bomb from Mystery Mountain. After what just happened at Istanbul, this much is obvious."

"Agreed. Comrades, we must recover that stolen bomb! Communism is the natural order for humanity, and slowly the world will see it is their destiny to join us in brotherhood. But until then, China must be protected, the way a father does his child."

Everybody nodded at the wise statement. True, no Communist nation in the history of the world had ever been able to produce enough crops to feed their own people, but eventually that minor problem would be solved.

"If our enemies get control of this superweapon, they would be free to attack China at any time they wish, without fear of significant reprisal. Oh, some of our nuclear missiles will manage to reach their targets, New York, London, Moscow and such. But China will be annihilated, and most of them will survive. Which means they win, and humanity is doomed to a maddening freedom that in the end will kill our entire race!"

"This we know, comrade," a man sighed. "It seems that we have no choice. Our only hope is to have this new weapon under our control."

"What do you suggest, that we kill the sheikh?"

"No, that would weaken our relationships with those fat fools in the Middle East. Instead, we only hire somebody to kill him. That would force Hassan to send Blue Lightning to remove them."

"And we capture the mercenaries to discover the true whereabouts of the T-bomb? Comrade, that is brilliant."

The man gave a polite nod of thanks.

"And what if our agents fail?" a man asked dourly.

"Sadly, if it appears that the weapon will fall out of our reach, then we attack the area with a thermonuclear warhead. It would be infinitely better for China for nobody to control such a weapon, than to have it fall into the hands of the United States."

"On that we agree."

"Comrade, such a strike would invoke massive retaliation from NATO."

"Not if it was done by a radical splinter group with no connections to Beijing whatsoever. Insane fundamentalists with no regard to human life."

"You mean us."

"Under some new name, yes, I do."

There was deep silence in the farmhouse for a very long time as the upper echelon of Red Star considered the matter from every possible angle.

"So be it, comrades," their leader sighed. "Red Star will do whatever is necessary to save the world from itself."

"Sometimes that is the price of freedom," another man agreed solemnly.

"Wait, why incriminate ourselves?" the woman asked, smiling slowly. "Do we not have a tactical nuclear artillery shell from America at our disposal?"

Blame the United States? That took a moment, then everybody smiled and pulled out their cell phones to start making fast calls.

Balaklava Submarine Base

"GET HARD, PEOPLE," McCarter ordered, working the charging lever on an MP-5 subgun. "There will be traps inside waiting for us."

"The same as last time," Hawkins attested, studying the rocky shoreline of the volcanic bay.

"Wrong, brother," James countered. "The last time we hoped there were traps. This time we hope to get out alive."

After a moment Hawkins grudgingly accepted the subtle difference.

A million twinkling stars filled the heavens above the Stony Man operatives as they rowed a small inflatable craft across the choppy bay. Their C-130 Hercules was parked just over a low hill on the only smooth ground in the area for miles. The landing had been exciting to say the least, and bets were laid that if this was the base of the thieves, then they must have used a helicopter to escape from Russia.

Across the bay, the old fishing village of Balaklava had settled in for the night, the bars closed, the street lights dimmed. The only illumination was from the moon in the sky and the sweeping searchlight of the lighthouse on a tall cliff overlooking the rough Black Sea. There were a few ships moving along the horizon, their hulls dotted with tiny running lights, ebony ghosts seeming to float between the inky sea and black sky.

Nearing the jagged shore, Manning and Encizo hopped out to help pull the rubber craft farther onto dry land. Checking their weapons and equipment one last time, the members of Phoenix Force assumed a combat formation and started toward the abandoned Soviet Union submarine base. Warily the team stayed in the shallows where the slapping waves and seagulls would mask the sound of their boots, and the countless schools of fish would confuse any sonar under the water. Hopefully.

"Stay alert," McCarter whispered into his throat mike. "It was a bold move to seize control of a tourist attraction as their base. Which makes them fanatics or loonies."

"Same thing in my book," James noted, checking the compass attached to the barrel of his submachine gun.

With so much ambient noise from the waves lapping on the rocks, if there were booby traps set in the base then they were probably triggered with proximity field sensors. If the team members tried an active EM scan that would only trigger the bombs. So they were reduced to the primitive level of a passive scan using a compass. If there were any proximity sensors, then the compass needle would react strongly, swinging away from north to point directly toward the traps.

Keeping clear of the dock, the team proceeded through the shallows, noting the presence of spent brass shells glittering among the lumpy rocks and countless black mussels. Pausing for only a moment, McCarter plunged his bare hand into the turgid water and extracted several of the casings, tucking them into a pocket for later analysis.

"Rifle rounds, 7.62 mm?" Hawkins noted into his throat mike, giving the brass a glance. "The brass looks old. I wonder if they're using stores from the base."

"Makes sense," James subvocalized. "The Soviets left a ton of weapons and equipment behind when things fell apart."

"Even some nuclear weapons," Encizo stated.

Proceeding between the old concrete dock and the natural rock wall of the lava cave, McCarter gave the possibility of abandoned nukes some hard consideration. That certainly would explain why they traded two big thermonuclear weapons for a small tactical nuke, and then exchanged another for ammunition and supplies.

"I don't care what Ironman and his boys found in Arkansas," Manning observed, pressing flat against the wall to get past some dangling chains. "This is sounding less and less like Foxfire. The mercs are very well financed from their corporate clients, and don't need to barter nukes for SPAM and toilet tissue."

After reviving, Rebecca Weeks had been very cooperative, and gave the team as detailed a list of items wanted by the thieves as she could remember. Most of it was standard supplies: boots, blankets, bullets and beef stew. A lot of canned beef stew. But there were also some oddball items, such as military crossbows, NBC suits, VX nerve gas grenades and depleted-uranium rounds for a 30 mm grenade launcher. That was clearly for an AK-47 assault rifle, and was something the team would have to watch out for. Their body armor was rated Level Five, the best in the world, and would stop a .357 Magnum round at point-blank range. But a DU round would punch through their Dragonskin vests as if the stuff was made of cotton candy and good wishes.

Entering the cave, McCarter found the darkness ahead seemed to become impenetrable, and he flipped down his visor to activate the IR function. However he still couldn't see anything past a few yards. Suspicious, he switched to

UV, and under the invisible glow of the ultraviolet light, the Phoenix Force leader now saw that a curtain of heavy cloth hung across the entrance, completely blocking the way. Slowing to a crawl, he kept a close watch on the compass. But the needle never even flickered as McCarter lifted the curtain with the stubby barrel of the MP-5 and slipped underneath.

Half expecting to be immediately attacked, McCarter stood there for a moment, studying the huge cavern on the other side. Everything was brightly illuminated by the UV visor, although colored green and white. The dockyard was impressive, with cranes attached to the rocky ceiling to facilitate moving supplies, and oversize slips that would have been more than capable of holding a Cold War submarine. There were even racks for holding torpedoes to arm the sub, but upon closer inspection those were streaked with rust, while the other equipment had been thoroughly cleaned and oiled. Okay, no nuclear torpedoes in their future. That was good news.

"Report," a concerned voice said in his earbud.

"All clear," McCarter whispered, touching his throat, and then proceeded farther into the cavern to make room for the rest of the team.

As they slid under the curtain, McCarter switched to IR to check for any heat sources, but the massive submarine base registered cold. Even if there had been men hiding in those NBC suits, there was always some thermal leakage to betray their presence, especially if any of their weapons had been discharged.

There were offices carved into the living rock along the main dock, and the work area was filled with assorted machinery, forklifts, stacks of wooden boxes and old-fashioned steel drums. These days the containers were made of high-impact plastic that was tougher than steel and far less likely to leak or corrode. McCarter found it odd that everything they encountered on this mission seemed to be old or out of date. That was when he noticed the body under the dock.

Going back to UV, McCarter saw that the corpse was in very poor shape, the flesh having been feasted upon by fish. The clothing and smashed Nikon camera around his neck proclaimed the fat man to be a tourist, but the tight grouping of bullet holes in his chest spoke of professional soldiers. Civilians and amateurs wasted ammunition, but trained soldiers put three rounds in your chest and moved on. Most of the bullet holes were in groups of three.

Looking around, McCarter found some empty brass in the rocks and pocketed a couple more spent shells, along with a slimy piece of yellow plastic that was the wrapper for a commercial brand of salted beef stick. It was not the sort of item that the Milan exposition would sell in exchange for nukes. More than likely it came from the dead man, but it never hurt to check.

"This curtain is made out of ballistic cloth," James noted in his earbud. "Smart. Very smart. If they had to shoot an intruder, any rounds that missed wouldn't keep going to hit the village across the bay."

"I can confirm that," McCarter said. "I've got a DB over here, shot in groups of three."

"Pros," Hawkins muttered. "Well, Foxfire is supposed to be some of the second best shots in the world."

"Yeah? Then who's the best?" Encizo asked, a smile in his voice.

"That would be us," Manning answered.

"Oh yeah, right. Sorry, I forgot."

Back in formation, Phoenix Force continued along the edge of the water until reaching a short flight of steps up to the dock proper. With no other choice, they very slowly walked out of the sea, trying their best to keep the noise to a dead minimum.

"Hawk and I will check the first office," McCarter whispered, watching the gloom for any suspicious movements. But nothing stirred in the underground darkness. "James and Rafe do the second. Manning is god."

"Got your six, brother," the man replied, going behind a stack of wooden crates. Sliding a waterproof bag off his shoulder, he withdrew a massive Barrett .50 sniper rifle. For this probe, the usual Starlite scope had been replaced with a Nighthunter version that allowed him to illuminate a target with UV.

Advancing in a standard two-on-two formation, the Stony Man operatives moved forward while Manning eased in a clip of ten rounds and worked the arming bolt with a muted click-clack. Resting the huge weapon on top of the crates, Manning watched the other men through the crosshairs as they slipped into the first office, only to return in a few minutes.

"Anything useful?" Encizo asked hopefully.

"Nothing," McCarter answered.

James and Encizo did the next office, and then McCarter and Hawkins checked the storeroom. With Manning staying close behind, the two groups of men rotated their way along the dock and down a main access corridor until reaching a wide set of double doors.

Approaching them, McCarter saw the compass on his gun barrel jerk, and instantly flung himself backward. "Proximity sensor!" the man subvocalized, then grunted as he hit the concrete hard and rolled for the safety of a wooden crate.

A few seconds passed with the team braced for an explosion or the sound of running boots. But nothing happened, and after a minute they started to relax, when there came a hard sniff over their earbuds.

"Why am I smelling rancid horseradish?" Manning demanded then bitterly cursed. "Oh, fucking hell, it's mustard gas!"

Spinning around, the team saw a dense yellow cloud expanding from the front of the cavern, billowing ever closer. The swirling fumes filled the entire front of the cavern like a yellow tidal wave, and there was no way past. The telltale reek hadn't hit them yet, but the Stony Man operatives knew the color, and every team member slapped at his belt pouch to yank out a protective gas mask. But even as they exhaled deeply to clear out their lungs, then slipped on the masks, they each knew the masks would only buy them some time. Mustard gas was hellishly corrosive and also worked on skin contact. So unless they were in airtight NBC suits or under water...

"Head for the pens," Hawkins said, stepping toward the water in the submarine pens, only to come to an abrupt halt. Where the waves lapped against the mooring chains, there were bright sparks.

"Son of a bitch, the water is electrified," Encizo snarled, crouched over with his MP-5 held in both hands. "The current must have come on as the gas was released."

Backing away from the oncoming fumes, McCarter raged internally. Goddamn it, the team had walked into another trap. Somebody on the other side really knew their stuff. Stand still and the gas would kill them. Dive into the water and they'd be electrocuted. Or go through those double doors and face God alone knew what.

Just then a bat fell from the hidden recesses of the ceiling. Squeaking in torment, it flopped around on the concrete, bloody foam bubbling from its tiny gasping mouth. Then another bat fell, closely followed by a dozen more.

Firing a burst from his MP-5, McCarter put the poor creatures out of their misery. "Manning, open the door!" he shouted, running close along the rock wall.

Swinging up the Barrett, Manning fired twice, the titanic 750-grain rounds slamming into each door and knocking them off the hinges. The dented doors hit the floor in a strident crash, and tumbled away as the Claymore mines attached to the walls violently exploded, spraying out death clouds of steel ball bearings at chest level. The antipersonnel barrage hit the opposite walls and ricocheted off to then hit the first wall again.

The men of Phoenix Force had to admire the ruthless simplicity of the trap. Anybody caught in that hellstorm would have been torn into mincemeat. Not even Level Five armor protected every inch of your body. It would have been like being thrown naked into a wood chipper.

Now spraying the walls and floor with their machine guns in an effort to trip any further booby traps, the team raced through the ragged opening and down a long corridor that ended in a smooth concrete wall.

"Bullshit, that's new!" Hawkins snarled, spraying the seamless expanse with a full clip of hardball 9 mm rounds.

The rest of the team was only heartbeats behind the Texan, and under the combined assault the concrete cracked off in big chunks to reveal another set of double doors. Quickly Manning fired the Barrett twice more, removing the doors and tripping the expected set of Claymore mines, the shrapnel humming through the air as it zigged back and forth.

Glancing down the corridor McCarter saw the mustard gas billowing ever closer, and on impulse pulled a willie peter grenade from his web belt, yanked the pin and rolled it down the passageway. It came to a stop just in front of the toxic fumes and flared into incandescent brilliance, the charge of white phosphorous filling the corridor with a sizzling chemical flame.

Momentarily trapped between the fire and the shrapnel, the team reloaded their weapons. If nothing else, they would turn the gun upon themselves rather than slowly die coughing out bloody chunks of their dissolving lungs. Mustard gas was banned by every nation on earth. All of them, even the insane military dictatorships of Africa and South America.

Where had the thieves gotten their hands on the stuff? Not even Milan carried the forbidden compound anymore. More antiquarian leftovers from the Soviet Union?

As the blazing white phosphorous began to fade, the ricochets eased, and the Stony Man operatives rushed into another cavern. The rough floor had been smoothed by machinery, along with the walls, but were still natural stone and rose straight up, sleek as a gun barrel, to reach open sky, the twinkling stars only partially obscured by camouflage netting. But much more importantly, sitting in the middle of the floor was a Mi-6 Hook helicopter bearing the hammer and sickle of the Soviet Union.

"This is their escape route!" McCarter cursed, knowing that nobody left their back door unguarded.

"Yeah, but have we tripped the defenses," James snarled, priming another willie peter grenade, "or are we being herded into a killzone?" Yanking the pin, he flipped off the spoon and tossed the canister through the ruined doorway. The military charge flared into lambent coronas, and the mustard gas receded a little, building pressure, trying to seep past the thermal barrier along the corners of the ceiling.

"Only one way to find out," Encizo stated, swinging up his MP-5 and grabbing the handle of the side hatch for the cargo helicopter. "On my mark...go!"

Yanking the door aside, the men fired blindly into the aircraft just as the horde of dogs lunged for freedom. Five of the animals slapped onto the floor dead, but the rest raced past Phoenix Force, biting at their hands and groins. The dogs were big, pitbulls mixed with something else, but they were skinny, their eyes wild and fur ratty, looking ill kept and even diseased.

Jerking back to protect their vulnerable points, the men hammered the beasts with short burst of 9 mm rounds, the ricochets throwing off sparks from the hard stone flooring.

"On me, by the numbers," McCarter shouted, his voice relayed through the throat mike to echo in their earbuds.

Converging on the man, the team laid down tight suppression fire, driving the dogs away as they backed inside the helicopter and slammed shut the hatch.

The interior was a mess, reeking of feces and rancid food, a dozen empty cans of military beef stew lying open on the deck. Off to the side lay the partially eaten corpse of a dog. With the canned food gone, the starving animals had finally turned on their own pack.

"Get this thing airborne, brother," Manning muttered, drawing his pistol and firing a fast five shots through a gunport. None of the dogs was hit.

"That's the plan." Thankful that he was wearing combat boots with nonslip soles, McCarter tried not to slip in the filthy deck and half fell into the pilot's seat, only thinking that it might have been rigged to blow a split second after the fact.

Flipping a row of switches on the overhead controls, McCarter brought the cockpit alive and checked the gauges. Power good, oil good, hydraulics good...

Just then something heavy hit the cargo hatch trying to get through, and a dog yipped in pain. A split second later another pitbull clawed at the Plexiglas view port in the nose, barking savagely at the man sitting only inches away. Busy with a preflight check, McCarter could do nothing, but the rest of the team shoved their machine guns into gun ports and rattled off long bursts. At first, the dogs scampered away in terror. But then they returned, running around the big aircraft, hitting it with their bodies, trying to find a way inside once more to reach the living meat.

"Alert, the grenade is almost out," Hawkins said in forced calm, looking out an observation port. A hand was resting on his web belt, only an inch away from a grenade, but the gun ports were designed for automatic weapons, not grenades.

The only way to use the military charge would be to open the door, inviting the dogs to charge back inside, and in close quarters the dogs would have all of the advantages.

Shoving the barrel of his MP-5 through a port, Encizo cut loose with a long spray, rotating the weapon. He was rewarded with a yip from a wounded dog, but it did not carry the sound of a kill. James tried the same tactic on the other side with a similar lack of success.

"Kill the lights," McCarter snarled, pulling out his service pistol to smash the overhead panel. "Kill everything. There's no fuel in the bloody gas tanks. Not a fucking drop."

It took the men a full second to follow that chain of reasoning before they began to bust apart anything powered by electricity: radio, navigation, radar, radar jammer, internal lights, external search light, PS system. All of it had been left on, but with the current turned off by the former owners. Just another deadly link in the chain tightening around their throats like a steel noose.

As the grenade in the corridor began to sputter out, McCarter had no choice. He set a row of dials, then flipped a switch and pressed a button hard, his primordial will to live putting a lot more feeling into the simple action than he would have believed possible.

There was a low whine from the rear and top of the huge aircraft as the overhead blades began to move sluggishly, slowly building in speed and force until they were chugging along steadily, creating a strong downdraft.

The entire helicopter was vibrating from the electric starter, and the circling dogs outside howled in fear at the unnatural noise. Filling the crude heliport, the wash drove the animals behind the Hook and forced back the yellow cloud of mustard gas filling the doorway.

"Can't reach them at this angle," Hawkins raged, firing single shots at the dogs behind them. "Any gun ports in the aft?"

"Not on this early model," McCarter snapped in reply, his hands busily ripping out wiring under the control panel. Whole sections of the panel went dark, but the power gauge continued to slowly creep toward the zero mark. At that point, the blades would stop and the gas would flood into the heliport, killing man and dog alike.

"Anybody got a bright idea, now would be the time," Manning said in artificial calm, sliding a fresh clip into his .357 Magnum Desert Eagle automatic.

"Yeah, I do," Encizo muttered, yanking open a tool locker and grabbing a large wrench. "I seriously do not think that we need both of these turbo engines."

"One will do," McCarter agreed from the cockpit, smashing glowing indicators with the butt of his pistol.

The Stony Man operatives made their choice and started ripping out wires with their hands, bright sparks snapping and crackling over their bare skin.

With a ratcheting groan, the rear turboprops slowed and then unexpectedly locked into place. The jar threw the helicopter off balance and it began to tilt when Phoenix Force dived to the opposite side and hung on to anything they could. For a long moment the craft was precariously off balance, then it slowly eased back down onto the rock floor, and the forward blades returned to their previous steady rhythm. But it was noticeably slower now, and regularly decreasing. Nobody needed an advance degree in flight engineering to know that it would stop soon, and that would be it for the team. Death would swiftly follow.

"No choice then, brothers," Hawkins stated, returning to the main deck. Standing at the side hatch, the solder grimly leveled his MP-5 and Beretta. "We're going EVA."

Gathering at the hatch, the men of Phoenix Force prepared their weapons, then kicked back the emergency release handle. The heavy door slid aside smoothly and they opened fire.

Driven insane by hunger, the dogs charged the chattering guns, getting hit several times before burying their fangs into legs and arms.

Shoving his Beretta into the ear of a dog, James blew out its brain, and the animal released McCarter. Another grabbed Manning between the legs, and he rammed down the barrel of his Desert Eagle, thanking whoever that Level Five body armor covered that part of his anatomy.

Releasing its grip, the dog tried for his throat, and he desperately threw up an arm. The teeth sank into his flesh, the pain blinding him for a heartbeat, and he swung the animal bodily around to crash into the side of the open hatch. Ribs audibly broke and the dog dropped free. Hawkins put a burst into its belly, blowing out the internal organs.

The fight had become too close for guns, and knives were drawn, the men falling back into the tiny engine room hacking and slashing. Meanwhile, the overhead blades slowed to a complete stop and the billowing cloud of war gas once more flowed relentlessly into the heliport.

As the last animal fell bloody to the deck, McCarter grunted in relief, trying not to move his wounded shoulder. He could see the swirling yellow fumes on the other side of the observation port. The Briton bitterly cursed, then paused at the sight of an unattached battery sitting in a recharge socket. If there was any juice at all in that thing...

Dropping his weapons, he grabbed the battery and yanked it free from the nest of wiring, then flipped it over and pressed the terminals hard against the exhausted battery for the forward blades. For a second, nothing happened. There came a low, sluggish whir from the electric starter, and the casing of the battery began to grow uncomfortably hot. Miraculously the blades began to slowly move again, and the mist receded slightly.

Rushing outside, the rest of Phoenix Force literally held their breath until the noxious war gas had moved into the corridor, then they rolled in their last grenades, one at a time, willie peter first, then thermite and finally the stun grenades, the flash-bangs actually forcing the war gas away better than anything else. All they had left were the high-explosive antipersonnel grenades, which would be useless against a cloud.

A few minutes later the blades slowed to a stop again, the last stun grenade detonated, the boom rumbling along the corridor and up the exit shaft of the heliport.

"Been nice knowing you, brothers," Manning said, holding the bite on his forearm. His clothing was soaked with blood, most of it his.

"Not dead yet," Hawkins snarled, grabbing the Barrett and flopping down into the bloody rock.

Working the lever, he tried to find the curtain of ballistic cloth blocking the entrance to the cavern. The man did not know if a couple of bullet holes in the material would slow the advance of the mustard gas, but it was worth a try. Unfortunately a gentle curve in the corridor and dockyard put the curtain out of sight, and he lowered the sniper rifle in frustration.

"What's the antidote for mustard gas?" Encizo demanded, hefting his Walther PPK .38 automatic.

"Aside from lead in the head? Nothing I have available," James replied, then he stood taller. Wait a second, that was wrong.

Clawing for the AP grenade on his web harness, he primed the sphere and pitched it as hard as possible down the corridor. It bounced off the walls and clattered past the second set of broken doors to splash into an open submarine pen. The grenade instantly detonated upon touching the electrified water, throwing up a huge gout of brine that rained across the yellow gas, making a wide portion of it disappear.

"Mustard gas dissolves in water," James shouted, throwing a second grenade.

The rest of the team followed suit, and the barrage of thundering detonations shook the entire subterranean base for several minutes.

When they finally ran out of explosives, the exhausted men stood waiting for the unstoppable return of the yellow cloud, but nothing happened. There were only some lingering golden fumes in the darkness, and those were visibly thinning from the gentle salty breeze coming around the curve.

Hefting a spare clip in his palm, Encizo threw it down the corridor and it splashed into the pen without the expected crackle of voltage.

"Guess that last gren must have killed the power," Manning said, tying a field dressing around his wound. "Anybody feel like a hundred-foot dash through poison gas?"

"Not a problem," Hawkins said with a hard expression, removing his mask to pour the contents of his canteen onto the fibrous material. When it was soaked, he put the mask back on and sprinted along the corridor, with his eyes closed. He collided with the second doorway, and almost fell, but managed to keep going and fell more than dived into the sea water.

The rest of the team waited an anxious few moments, then heard the crackle of static over their ear buds.

"Made it," Hawk said, exhaling the word. Then there came a splash and only chaotic noise.

Soaking their own masks, the Stony Man operatives charged down the misty corridor, every inch of exposed skin stinging as if it was on fire. Then there was only open air beneath their boots before sweet water covered them completely, taking away the searing pain and bringing the promise of life.

CHAPTER TEN

Stony Man Farm, Virginia

Huntington Wethers was watching the wall monitor that showed a vector graphic of Earth and all of the military satellites in orbit above the planet.

Russia seemed to have shifted all of their hunter-killer satellites into an attack posture along their border with China. Naturally China was responding, and that section of space was rapidly becoming jammed full of satellites, massively increasing the possibility of a nervous technician making a small mistake with very big results.

"How is the Pentagon responding?" Wethers asked.

"How do you think?" Kurtzman snapped, shaking his head. "They get hard, we get harder. The UN Security Council is having a donnybrook at the moment. Half the nations are demanding to know what a thermobaric bomb is, and the others are demanding that the technology be shared."

"For what possible use?" Wethers asked.

"Oh, they have a lot of uses." Leaning back in his wheelchair, Kurtzman ran stiff fingers through his hair. "Everything from national defense to clearing out unwanted forests. Although with Great Britain added, they make a wonderful fireworks display for Guy Fawkes Day."

The professor smiled at the famous dry wit of the British. "What's the Russian ambassador saying?"

"Nothing, he stayed at home today with a fever."

Wethers had encountered such an illness before, back when he taught at Berkeley. It was called yellow fever, or more colorfully, a coward's cold. "Anything new on the attack at Istanbul?"

"All radar records from the Istanbul airport and the nearby NATO base show clean," Carmen Delahunt reported crisply. "There were no unauthorized planes above the city." A few hours ago Price had brought the woman a change of clothing and now she was in gray sweatpants and a turtlenecked sweater bearing the slogan I Am Not A Member Of A Secret Government Agency.

"Which only means that it was dropped by an unauthorized plane," Kurtzman scoffed, rubbing his chin to the sound of sandpaper on rock. "Or maybe they used a goddamn weather balloon or rolled it off a cliff."

"Anything is possible, chief."

"From the patterns on the ships, the initial burn spread outward across the Black Sea, then it hit the cliffs and re-bounded back upon itself," Wethers added. He started to type with both hands. "See? Look there. That was the confusing factor. But this was not exploded in the sky."

"Damn, I thought it had to be detonated above the target," Kurtzman started, then corrected himself. Obviously that was wrong because Istanbul had just gotten its ass kicked. The T-bomb must have been in a boat with a timer or they'd used a suicide bomber.

This was unsettling news. The weapon could be fired on the ground with diminished effect, yet the results were still quite impressive. Half a million people dead, and billions in damage. Great, it had been hard enough to patrol the skies of the world, now add in the land and sea, and their job just became damn near impossible.

"Anything on the brass that Phoenix Force recovered?" Kurtzman asked.

"Sorry, no," Wethers replied, sounding annoyed. "It was too old. However, the beef-stick wrapper came from a small farm that cures their own meat. They're located in the southern region of Slovakia."

Kurtzman frowned. Foxfire was working for the Slovakian government? Hmm, that would explain the host of old technology. The Russians left behind entire military bases when the Soviet Union collapsed, and Slovakia had been treated worse than slaves under Stalin. Suddenly a lot of things were beginning to make sense.

"Get me a list of Slovakian—no, a list of Czechoslovakian military personnel who were born anywhere near that farm," Kurtzman directed, his eyes narrowed in thought. "Cross reference it with Interpol, the CIA and NATO for any connections to organized crime or terrorism."

"Already processing," Wethers replied.

"Good man," Kurtzman returned, accessing the Homeland Security database. The multiple firewalls, false leads and intrusion countermeasures were formidable, the best in the world, but easily breached by the Stony Man computer genius.

"I've got more good news," Akira Tokaido said out of the blue. "The FSB seems to be running amuck. They've already conducted raids on suspected KGB safehouses, the headquarters of the Russian Communist Party, the *mafiya*—everybody and damn near anybody you can think of who would have the muscle or the lack of common sense to attack Mystery Mountain."

"Any results?" Kurtzman asked.

"Eight dead FSB agents, and an estimated hundred civilians and bystanders," Tokaido said, pushing back his chair to stand and stretch. His joints popped and cracked audibly. "That's what I meant by running amuck. These guys are cops, but they don't seem to give a damn about right or wrong anymore. They're out to find those bombs and God help anybody who gets in their way. Innocent or not." Sitting again, Tokaido lifted a ceramic mug to take a drink, only to discover it was empty.

"Yeah, that sounded like the FSB," Kurtzman agreed, thumping a fist on the arm of his wheelchair.

"Anything from our Quisling?" Wethers asked. On his console, a submonitor was scrolling theoretical ways to find a thermobaric device passing through customs at an airport. Apparently it was impossible.

Working steadily, Kurtzman snorted at the allusion. The professor knew his history. "Our guy is asking around," he said. "But in his circles that was generally a good way to get your throat cut, so it may take him some time."

"Our man being Mr. Zero?"

"Who else?"

Benny Zero was their contact criminal in the underworld of the Middle East. He worked both sides of the fence, Israeli and Palestinian, the Mossad and the Hamas. But he owed his life to Stony Man, and was always willing to sell them information. It was previously thought that he had died in the Skyhammer war, but it turned out that the little thief was a lot more resilient than previously thought possible. He had ridden out the attack by taking refuge in the sewers of Palestine, where he lived for a week waist deep. Death would be preferable.

"Damn, there goes another T-burst," Delahunt rumbled. "There has been a lot of those in the last few hours."

"Any luck?" Tokaido asked, going to get a fresh cup of coffee.

"No, it was too fast," she said. Relatively new, a T-burst was the Internet version of a radio blip transmission, a huge amount of information condensed into a microsecond pulse. Unless you were listening at exactly the right place, at precisely the right time, they were almost impossible to catch, much less stop.

"A major weapon systems has been stolen, and now we have a hundred T-bursts going over the Net," Tokaido said, getting a clean mug and filling it from a steaming percolator. "Sounds like an auction is going down."

Incredibly, the brew smelled delicious, and faintly of hazelnuts. At the first sip, Tokaido knew that Kurtzman had not made this pot. His coffee was banned by the Geneva Convention, while this batch could be safely consumed by carbon-based life forms despite being much stronger than anything served at the so-called coffee shops. The poor clerks who worked there visibly flinched when Kurtzman wheeled in through the door. If they saw his van arrive in the parking lot, the staff often locked the doors and pretended to be closed.

"An auction makes sense," Kurtzman concluded. "I have the Dirty Dozen up and running, ready to be invited, but in this sort of a scenario, we can't ask to attend. The buyers have to contact us."

"Any way we can encourage them to do just that?" Tokaido asked, reclaiming his console. Then he coughed twice.

Looking up at the signal, Delahunt and Wethers rushed over to the kitchenette to get some coffee.

"Nothing comes to mind, but I'm open to suggestions," Kurtzman said, pretending not to notice. He had made this batch of coffee, but purely as an experiment.

Slipping back under her console, Delahunt took a long swallow with obvious satisfaction. Instantly she sat bolt upright. "Alert," she said in a tense voice. "Somebody is trying to buy a hit on Sheikh Abdul Ben Hassan. They say he had an affair with their wife, and they want revenge."

"But the sheikh is artificial," Kurtzman stated, looking up in confusion. "So how could he have… Oh, it's a trap. Somebody in Milan must have recognized McCarter, and they think Blue Lightning is behind the stolen superweapon."

"So they hire mercs to kill Hassan, knowing that Blue Lightning will go to his rescue, delivering McCarter directly into their grasp," Wethers rationalized coolly, setting his mug aside. "Deuced clever, I must admit. Where did the signal originate?"

"Unknown. Hell, if I knew that, I'd send in the Marines."

Good point. "Okay, where is Phoenix Force at the moment?"

"Balaklava, little fishing village on the Black Sea, hot on the trail of the Chinese nuke."

"Then do nothing. Let them try to kill Hassan. Since he does not exist, they're in for a long hunt to find the man."

"Or better yet, let them succeed," Tokaido said slowly, a sly grin forming. "Have another member of the Dirty Dozen accept the commission, then proclaim they killed Hassan and have McCarter alive. Then they arrange to deliver the captive to their employer."

"Use an artificial personality to kill another artificial personality, so that we can find the real person who hired them?" Kurtzman muttered thoughtfully. The idea sounded like an episode of *The Twilight Zone*. However, it also sounded like the plan might just work. At the worst, it would give McCarter somewhere to check if Balaklava turned up empty.

"Where is Hassan at the moment?"

"On his yacht, *Raincloud,* somewhere near Spain."

"Good enough. Have Emile Salvatore, the Brooklyn crime lord, accept the commission, then report the yacht sunk and McCarter captured alive."

"And then?"

Still typing, Kurtzman checked the wall screens as Britain and Australia activated their own hunter-killer satellites. "Then we see who comes to collect him to be tortured."

Fox, Arkansas

SLOWLY COMING AWAKE, Lyons held back a groan of pain. His head was pounding, his arms felt incredibly heavy, and every inch of him felt as tender as a raw wound. The man had never been on the receiving end of sleep gas, and now wondered why the Pentagon considered it a humane replacement for rubber bullets. Having been shot by those once, Lyons considered that race a tie.

Barely opening his eyes, the man glanced around to see if the ploy had worked. At the moment he was lying on the bare wood floor of a log cabin. The ceiling was thick wood beams that supported sheet steel, the sight of which gave him a momentary flashback to fortified buildings of the Farm. Concrete pillars stood at every corner, and the front door was also metal, with an iron grille in front, like a jail. But then, that was most likely where he was, in the Foxfire brig, or whatever they called it.

Also lying on the floor, Blancanales and Schwarz were only a few feet away, with steel chains attached to their wrists, the ends bolted to the wall. Surreptitiously checking, Lyons found he was similarly bound. The team was still wearing their blue suits, but everything was now rumpled, showing that they had been searched to the skin. It didn't take much for the man to tell everything he had been carrying was gone, even the wedding ring for his failed marriage. That was when he noticed that each of the members of Able Team was only wearing one shoe. That sent a surge of adrenaline through the man. It was damn near impossible to charge somebody when you were off balance that way. It meant one of these men was trained in interrogation techniques and possibly torture. Escaping from this cabin might be a little harder than he had originally estimated.

Across the cabin were five men in Foxfire military uniforms, going through a collection of items on top of a heavy wooden table. Each of them was armed with a holstered pistol, tear gas and a rib-spread baton, a prison tool designed to cause maximum pain with minimum damage. Although, in trained hands, the baton could smash in the skull of a prisoner as easily as an empty beer can.

"Told y'all they weren't no feebs," a private boasted, both thumbs hooked proudly into his canvas gunbelt. "They'll be a drivin' Buicks and such, not va-ans."

Continuing to lie still, Lyon tried not scowl. The mercenary's accent was so comically thick that it had to be fake. This was the twenty-first century, and the Old South was long gone, television shows and satellite radio flattening the regional differences of the entire nation into a smooth, homogenous whole. A bland new America. Lyons knew Texans who sounded like they came from Back Bay, Boston, and these days everybody seemed to have just a touch of Brooklyn in their speech from the idiotic cable show about the family life of gangsters.

Personally, the former cop considered the show vile. Who gave a damn if a mad dog felt guilty about eating you, especially if he was just going to eat somebody else tomorrow? The main characters were thieves, murderers and worse, so in his opinion the only entertainment would have come from them being arrested and sent to jail for life.

Or shot in the back of the head, Lyons amended privately. Nothing wrong with a little street justice.

Just then Schwarz shifted slightly, showing that he was also coming around.

"Shut up, Connor," a sergeant growled, checking a cell phone. "Nothing, it's been wiped clean."

"Well, whoever they are, these guys are very well financed," a corporal said, inspecting the bullets in one of the service automatics. "These nines have no serial numbers or product code on the bottom. That's CIA-level shit. Nobody can buy that kind of ammo for love or money."

"And the warrant was fake as a stripper's new tits," another private stated, hoisting a leg and resting a thigh on the corner of the table. "It looked good, but Russell checked and it wasn't registered anywhere in the state. And faking one of those is a freaking federal offense."

"Are we in the van yet?" a bald man asked, brushing back a heavy curtain to look out a window. "Last I heard, the goddamn thing was venting tear gas at anybody who got behind the steering wheel or tried to open any of those trick panels."

How in hell did they know about those? Lyons wondered. Unless some of the panels had popped open from the crash.

"Nah, itsa c'ackling wid 'lectricity. Who-ee, sure as sheet knocked the gineral on he ast," Connor drawled almost incomprehensibly.

"Private Connor, we all know that you're from fucking downtown Atlanta, Georgia," the corporal snapped. "So talk normal. You're about as Deep South as deep-dish pizza."

Snapping off a salute, Connor smiled. "Sir, fuck you, sir," he said clearly.

The bald man sighed. "If you weren't the best sniper in the whole damn company…"

Impulsively, Lyons glanced at Schwarz. He guessed there was a joker like him on every team, in every military, in the whole world. Somewhere in the wilds of the outer Yucatan, a sergeant was rolling his eyes over the latest nonsense from a grinning private, who was just a touch too good at his work to either hang or kick out of the service.

"But, O'Malley, did you see that shit that came tumbling out of the ceiling?" a burly private asked, stroking his mustache. "M-203 rifles, Colt Python, SPAS 12-gauge, grenades, garrotes and all kinds of crazy stuff."

"Didn't recognize half of it," Corporal O'Malley admitted honestly.

Another man laughed. "Who the fuck do they think they are, Mack Bolan?"

"If I was, you would all be dead by now."

Pivoting around fast, the mercenaries grabbed their side arms at the sight of Lyons sitting up, resting his back against the wall.

"Playing possum, eh?" O'Malley growled, advancing while working the slide on a .357 Magnum pistol. "Okay, who are you people? FBI or the CIA?"

"Library police. You're all under arrest for overdue books," Lyons said calmly. "No, wait, I forgot, apes can't read."

"Shut up, asshole, and answer me!" the corporal snarled, whipping the pistol across his face.

Expecting that, Lyons moved with the blow, taking away most of the force of the strike. But as he looked up, there was the taste of blood in his mouth. "You gotta get to the gym more," he said in a conciliatory manner. "Work on those biceps. Your mom hits harder than that to let me know she's ready to flip over for another go."

His face tightening in fury, the corporal aimed the big-bore automatic at Lyons's head.

"Stand down, O'Malley," the sergeant ordered in a stern voice. "I said, stand down, mister!"

Reluctantly the corporal did as commanded, but his eyes promised a return match real soon.

"Anytime, punk," Lyons whispered in a voice of stone.

"All right, we're all very impressed," the sergeant said, crossing his arms. "You don't scare worth a damn, and from the scars I saw under your body armor, which by the way is mine now, you've seen more combat than hot meals. My guess would be Navy SEALs or maybe Delta Force."

"You forget the Junior Birdmen and Salvation Army," Blancanales said, getting up from the floor.

"Now, I prefer the Girl Scouts myself," Schwarz chimed in, rolling into a sitting position. "Gotta love those cookies."

Private Connor snorted a laugh, but the rest of the men looked ready to start dealing lead.

"Cut the shit, pal," the sergeant said in a soothing tone. "We understand, you're tougher than boiled iron and born to die. Fair enough. But we are, too. So let's talk straight. Soldier to soldier." Going over to a desk, he got a chair and sat backward, his holstered pistol far outside the reach of the chained prisoners.

"I'm Sergeant Pitman," he said, jerking a thumb at his chest. "The jolly fellow over there is Corporal O'Malley, and those are Privates Connor, Genovese and Lyons."

That caught Carl Lyons totally by surprise, and his face must have shown something, for the sergeant grinned slightly as if winning a small victory.

"Your name, too, eh? Small world, isn't it." Pitman laughed, pulling out a pack of cigarettes. "Smoke?"

"Now it's good cop, bad cop," Lyons snarled, wiping the blood off his mouth with a sleeve. "Do we look that green?"

"You'd be surprised how often it works." Pitman tucked a cigarette into the corner of his mouth and lit it with a match. "By the way, take off that shoe, old man, and I blow off your head."

Sitting on top of his feet, Blancanales froze in the act of easing off the loafer. "Can't blame a man for trying," he sighed.

"Sure, I can," Pitman said around the smoke. "You're the guys who tried to sneak into our base, not the other way around." He puffed for a few minutes, then added, "What puzzles me is that you must have known, or at least guessed, that we have hackers on staff. We ran your plates before that van reached the kiosk, and knew they were fake. Your FBI identification is also top-notch, and would probably fool most people, even some cops."

The men of Able Team said nothing.

Thoughtfully Sergeant Pitman exhaled deeply. "But none of them are registered with either the regional or head office." He tossed the booklet away, and it sailed across the cabin to hit the wall and bounce directly down into a wire trash can.

"You knew that we'd figure out you weren't FBI," Pitman said around the cigarette. "Or state cops or CNN or..." The man made a vague circular gesture with a hand. "Which raises the question of who you are."

Still alive, Blancanales thought. Nobody kills an intruder until they are identified. They might be your own people doing a security check. As long as we're a mystery, we're safe.

Suddenly the front door was jerked open and a busty mercenary slammed aside the grille, her fist full of crumpled papers.

"They're mercs!" the private raged, shaking the documents. "I ran the fingerprints we found on the engine block. Nobody ever thinks of cleaning that. These men work for Blackwater."

Instantly the tension in the room intensified.

"Blackwater," Corporal O'Malley sneered in open hatred. "Then let's shoot them in the belly and bury them alive. We got more important things to do than to waste time talking to these wannabes."

"Agreed," Sergeant Pitman said, dropping the cigarette and crushing it under a boot. "Sorry, boys, time to die."

"We know about the Russia thing," Lyons said, deliberately keeping the details vague. "And we want in on the deal."

"The deal," Pitman repeated as if never hearing the words before. "The deal? The deal is about protecting America. We're not doing this for profit, you money-worshipping freak."

"Want me to find out what they know, sir?" Connor offered without any trace of an accent, pulling out a skinning knife, the edge flashing in the fluorescent lights.

"He's good, too," Pitman said encouragingly. "But I have a better idea." Pulling out a small can of liquid butane, the kind used to recharge old-fashioned lighters, the mercenary squirted a small puddle on the hardwood floor, then dropped in the cigarette. The flammable liquid whoofed into blue flames that rose over a yard high, then dwindled away just as fast and were gone.

Then before the men of Able Team could react, Pitman squirted the butane over them, making sure it got into the hair and soaked deeply into the clothing of the chained men. When the can became empty, the sergeant tossed it away and struck another match to light a new cigarette. He puffed for a few moments to get the end cherry-red, then took it out of his mouth and held it over the slowly expanding puddle of fuel on the floor.

"Tell me why you're really here," Pitman said in a grave-yard voice. "Tell me everything."

Moving fast, Lyon lashed out a leg, and his shoe came off to streak across the cabin and hit the window. The glass loudly shattered, and the shoe rebounded from the iron bars on the other side.

"You're not going to escape that way, punk," O'Malley chortled.

But as the breeze blew into the cabin, thinning the rising butane fumes, Lyon took in a deep breath and bellowed at the top of his lungs, "Thunderfish!"

All of the mercenaries turned to stare in puzzlement at the man, then they looked up as there came the telltale high-pitch whistle of a descending mortar shell.

"Incoming!" Pitman shouted as a thunderous explosion shook the entire base.

Without a word, Schwarz turned to Blancanales and braced himself. Reaching out with his chained hands, the man ripped off the fake mustache glued to his friend's lips, exposing a small lock pick. Immediately, he started working on a manacle.

Suddenly a dozen alarms started clanging and sirens began to howl as another mortar arrived, sounding even louder than the first, closely followed by two more, then a nonstop barrage of high-explosive shells.

Stumbling to the smashed window, Connor could see a thick plume of smoke rising from the direction of the airfield, and a split second later another shell fell from the sky, and there clearly came the terrible sound of a detonating plane, rending metal mixed with the stentorian blast.

Throwing away the cigarette, Sergeant Pitman went for his side arm.

Moving fast, Lyons kicked out with his dry foot to knock the burning cigarette away from the puddle on the floor, just as Schwarz spit out the mouthful of lighter fluid he had been struggling to keep inside. The watery butane splashed over the gun just as the sergeant started to pull the trigger, and he managed to stop just in time. The muzzle-flash would have ignited the damn stuff and set the weapon on fire.

Tossing away the useless weapon, Pitman went for the baton on his belt only to find it gone, along with the mace. Throwing up an arm to protect his face, the sergeant opened his mouth to shout something, and Lyons let him have a long spray right in the mouth. Inhaling in shock, Pitman shuddered as the mace reached his lungs, and he fell aside, convulsing and heaving.

"Sarge," Corporal O'Malley yelled, advancing a step when a knife blade slammed into his throat. Staggering backward, he hit the wall and slid to the floor, red life gushing between his twitching fingers.

Charging around the table, Private Lyons jerked out of the way as Schwarz sent the chair flying, and it crashed directly into the face of Genovese, his broken teeth spraying out to hit the wall.

With a click, the last manacle dropped away and Blancanales charged for the other mercenaries even as Schwarz started unlocking his own chains.

"Son of a bitch," the woman cursed, drawing her weapon to work the slide. But then she recoiled as Lyons gave her a spray of mace in the face. Stumbling blindly, she fired the automatic twice, hitting nothing but coming awfully close to the man. Grimly, Lyons switched targets and sprayed her again directly between the legs, emptying the can. As he had been taught in boot camp, exposed membrane was the same thing all over the human body, top and bottom, front and back.

As the military chemicals soaked through the clothing, the female mercenary twitched as if touched with a red-hot poker, then she did it again with a horrified gasp. Dropping the gun, the woman began to insanely claw at her pants, screaming obscenities.

Diving for the weapon, Blancanales came up shooting, and Connor reeled away with most of his head removed, his weapon discharging harmlessly into the ceiling. Bobbing and weaving, Private Lyons fired twice, the bullets smacking into the floor alongside Blancanales and throwing out coronas of damp splinters. Then the mercenary ducked as Carl Lyons threw the butane-soaked automatic. It missed, but now Blancanales fired directly under the table, hitting the Foxfire mercenary in the knees. Bones and red meat exploded and he dropped, howling. Once the mercenary was in sight, Blancanales fired again, ending his pain forever.

Outside the cabin, the bombardment continued, but the tone of the falling shells changed slightly as they fell inside the perimeter to gently burst into thick clouds of dark smoke.

Snatching a weapon, Lyons flung it forward as hard as he could. The spinning automatic slammed into the head of the wailing woman, and she sighed unconscious to the floor.

Visible through the window, billowing clouds of smoke masked the base, the muzzle-flashes of automatic weapons twinkling like fireflies in a fog. Men were shouting, and Hummers were racing around, crashing into buildings and occasionally each other. Then a massive LAV-25 APC rumbled around a corner, pushing the lighter Hummers out of the way as it headed straight for the front gate.

"I cannot believe that actually worked," Blancanales muttered, going to a water cooler and lifting up the bottle to wash himself clean of the deadly butane. Then he did the same for a crouching Lyons.

"The only way inside this fort was to get captured," Schwarz retorted, taking a thermos off the table and pouring the contents over his head. He had hoped for coffee, but the smell of chicken soup replaced that of butane. Good enough— now he wouldn't ignite, and was protected from the common cold.

"He meant the shelling," Lyons said, going to the table and recovering their personal weapons. The S&W was not his chosen side arm, but he knew it intimately and could trust the ammunition.

"Hey, I'm not just a pretty face," Schwarz retorted, removing a limp noodle from the lapel of his suit.

Hardwiring his laptop to a satellite dish to convert the concave surface into a long-range microphone had been the easy part. That was high school science 101. Rigging the laptop to then run the automortar and start dropping shells on the compound had also not been a problem. The tough part had been laying a fast grid over the place and assigning each one a code phrase for the automortar not to bomb.

"Why Thunderfish?" Lyons asked, stripping off the suit. "You choose the damnedest trigger words."

"Have to," Schwarz said, stepping out of his pants. "Don't want somebody saying them by accident."

"Good point," Blancanales muttered, starting to remove the uniform of O'Malley. The woman was actually a closer fit, but her pants were unwearable by anybody until they had been thoroughly washed, then dry-cleaned, and possibly washed again. Lacking the necessary female anatomy, the man could not even guess how much that must have hurt.

It proved to be lucky that there had been six mercenaries, as the men of Able Team were just barely able to find enough clean clothing for the three of them. But soon the team was dressed in the military green fatigues of Foxfire and armed with M-4 assault rifles. The slim .357 Magnum S&W automatics were tucked into the holsters designed for the Colt .45 hoglegs.

While Lyons and Blancanales checked out the window, Schwarz tucked a battery back into a cell phone and impatiently waited until the screen illuminated before quickly thumbing in a memorized number.

"Kill Thunderfish," Schwarz said. "Repeat, kill Thunderfish." He closed the phone and tucked it away. "Okay, we have five minutes before this building gets vaporized."

Opening the front door, Blancanales leveled his rifle to give cover fire as Lyons charged outside with his own weapon at the ready. The smoke from the shells was thick in the air, and it was clearly mixed with wood smoke from something on fire. The howling sirens painfully buffeted his ears, and there came the steady chatter of small-arms fire mixing with the dull thumps of the exploding smoke bombs.

Looming tall in the murky gloom, the Quonset huts stood in rows like tunnel openings, with people running around them shouting orders or firing weapons. There was a bright flash and a Stinger launched skyward, ripping a huge hole in the camouflage netting over the compound and letting in very unwanted fresh air.

A badly dented Hummer lay sideways in the middle of an intersection, but Lyons found no bodies inside. Taking refuge on the lee side of the military transport, the man sharply whistled twice, and a few seconds later the rest of Able Team arrived, Blancanales hauling the unconscious woman in a fireman's carry across his shoulders.

"Three minutes and counting," Schwarz reminded them, glancing at his wristwatch.

Looking around fast, Blancanales saw a large metal trash bin set between two Quonset huts, and ran over to dump the woman inside and close the lid. Vastly amused, Schwarz started to say something witty, but stopped himself. He didn't like it when the jokes were that easy.

"Good enough. Let's go," Lyons ordered, and started running along the street, checking any road signs. Unfortunately, every one was written in a truncated code that meant nothing to him.

Taking out his cell phone, Lyons thumbed a speed-dial number.

"Yes, Ironman. How can I help you?" Barbara Price asked.

"Give me Bear," he snapped just as somebody cut loose with an M-4 overhead.

There was a pause as the call was traced, and Lyons's vocal pattern was checked against those on record. Less than a minute later, the chief hacker answered.

"We need the internal codes for Foxfire," Lyons stated.

"Thought you might. I'm sending them to you now," Kurtzman confirmed, and a short alphanumeric list appeared on Lyons's tiny monitor. "How soon do you want Santa?"

Just then, there came a pronounced whistling that grew steadily louder. The Quonset hut covering the brig was blown apart, corrugated sheets sailing away like torn autumn leaves.

A heartbeat later the next barrage arrived and the log cabin was blown violently apart, bodies and furniture flying away in a halo of destruction.

"Anytime would be good," Lyons answered, and closed the phone. "Okay, let's find those files."

Now able to find their way, the Stony Man operatives headed directly away from the flaming ruins, passing several Hummers full of armed mercenaries. However, past the next block, the speeding Hummers returned, now traveling in new directions. Some of the drivers were trying to read maps while steering, while others were wearing night-vision goggles and watching the sky for the invaders.

"And these are considered competent mercenaries?" Schwarz asked in scorn, leaping over a fallen telephone pole. "I've seen better organized bar fights."

"I think all of the good mercs got ambushed in Russia," Lyons said, blinking against the smoke. "And these are what's left over. The new recruits and paper-pushers."

"Swell, an entire base full of pencils and boots," Blancanales snorted, juking around a blast crater. "This must have been what the Tet Offensive looked like from the side of the Vietcong."

"I'm surprised they haven't started shooting each other yet," Schwarz added grimly.

A heavy machine gun began to hammer away from a rooftop, and a man cried out in mortal agony.

"You spoke too soon." Blancanales grimaced, tightening his grip on the assault rifle.

Stopping to read a large sign covered with arrows pointing in different directions, Lyons saw a pair of boots sticking out from behind and checked to see a limp body sprawled on the grass. There was a blast crater of a smoke bomb nearby, and blood on his face, but the private was still breathing, one hand clutching the strap of a canvas munitions bag.

While Blancanales checked the mercenary, Lyons yanked open the bag and found it stuffed full of spare clips and grenades.

"He'll live," Blancanales decided, standing erect. "Just as long as he isn't hit by any more shrapnel."

"The shelling should stop any second now," Schwarz whispered, and as if on cue, the shelling stopped.

However the Foxfire defenses continued, machine guns and assault rifles chattering steadily, and more rockets launching as the alarms and sirens blared.

"Come on, headquarters is this way," Lyons stated, slinging the bag over a shoulder.

Crossing a parade ground, Able Team encountered platoons of men dashing around madly, officers shouting for them to defend the gate and protect the wall. Blast craters were everywhere, and spent brass covered the grass like metallic confetti.

Past another intersection, Able Team found the main administration building. A towering pair of World War II howitzers flanked the front steps of a granite building that was draped with a huge section of camouflage netting that was starting to smolder in one section from contact with a searchlight.

There was a full platoon of mercenaries out front, attaching M-60 machine guns to spindle mounts, the linked belts of ammunition dangling from each breech like bands of gold.

Taking cover behind the howitzers, Able Team yanked open the bag and threw unprimed grenades. As the military spheres clattered onto the front steps, the mercenaries dived for cover. Already on the move, Able Team was on them in a heartbeat, the stocks of the M-4 rifles ending their angry cries.

Inside, the team found a middle-aged woman behind a desk, struggling to activate a Samsung Auto-Sentry, the standard 5.56 mm machine gun clearly replaced with a .223 Gatling gun and an oversize ammunition hopper. Okay, that was real trouble.

Whipping a grenade sideways, Lyons bounced it off the back of her head and she collapsed with a sigh. Then the team tore the Auto-Sentry apart with their hands.

"Move your ass, bitch, or I'm leaving without you," a voice crackled from the intercom on her desk.

"Try us instead," Lyons whispered, charging toward the double doors marked with the company logo of Foxfire Inc.

The team crashed through the doors to enter a sumptuous office with elegant furniture and oil paintings on the walls. A row of file cabinets filled an entire wall, and standing behind a mahogany desk that looked oddly familiar to the team, was General Smith. He was wearing a gas mask, body armor, and thumbing rounds into an Atchisson autoshotgun.

"Surrender," Lyons loudly announced, bringing up the M-4 and taking aim.

"Fuck you, feeb," the general snarled, wildly spraying the office. A vase disintegrated and a chair was annihilated, but the weapon was clearly out of his control, and the ceiling got the worst of the yammering assault.

Trying only to wound, Able Team fired in unison, but the general stumbled, and the Atchisson swept across his face, leaving nothing behind.

Snarling a curse, Lyons took a step toward the headless corpse, then turned away. There was nothing that could be done for that kind of damage except to choose cedar or pine. "All right, Politician, guard the door. Gadgets, with me at the files!" he directed, slinging the M-4 over a shoulder.

"There's no need," Schwarz stated, lifting the name plate off the desk. "Look at this."

"Daniel Duvall," Blancanales read slowly, furrowing his brow. "As in Brandon Duvall, superpatriot and billionaire lunatic?"

"So it would appear," Schwarz said, laying it back down reverently. "And we just removed his head."

Going over to the gore-splattered corpse, Lyons checked the wallet, comparing the picture on the driver's license with what he remembered.

"Okay, it's him," Lyons muttered, pressing the fingers of one hand against the screen of his laptop. Later on, he'd have Kurtzman check them against the official version at the NSA, and the local police. But his gut instinct told him it would be redundant. This was Daniel, the only son of one of the most powerful men in America.

Trained to turn disasters into victory, Lyons got the plastic liner out of the wastebasket, and wrapped it around the neck stump to not leave a blood trail, then slung the corpse over a shoulder. It would be much better to make Duvall think that his son had been kidnapped rather than killed. It left them more room for maneuvering.

Just then, a booming voice spoke from the sky. "This is the FBI. Come out with your hands raised."

"The cavalry is here," Schwarz said, resting the rifle on a hip. "Time to go, brothers."

"Okay, this is your specialty," Lyons said, forcing himself to ignore the horrid warmth of the limp body. "Where did he hide the exit?"

Slowly looking over the office, Blancanales said nothing for a few minutes, while multiple helicopters flew by overhead and the gunfire soon decreased into silence.

"Not trying to rush you or anything, pal," Schwarz said softly, going to check the hallway outside the office. "But pretty soon the real boys in blue are going to arrive, and they are much better shots than these groundpounders." There was nobody in sight yet, and the man closed the door, then locked it with an old-fashioned brass key.

Concentrating, Blancanales gave no sign he heard the man. The fireplace was too dirty, and the file cabinets too awkward to move regularly. The bookcases were far too obvious, and there were a lot of rugs, but the hardwood flooring would be ridiculously easy to scratch….

"Rosario…" Lyons gently urged, shifting the corpse on his shoulder.

"There," Blancanales said, going over to a chair piled high with books and papers. The rest of the office was spotlessly clean, so why was this one chair a mess? The only possible answer he could think of was to make sure that nobody ever sat in it and blocked the way out.

Shoving the chair aside, Blancanales trod over the books to check the blank wall, running his finger along the furled wood until finding a knothole set just above head level. Pressing it, he stepped aside quickly. With a sigh of compressed air, a section of the wall slid aside to reveal a steel door with a combination lock.

Reaching for his laptop, Schwarz spit a curse, and Lyons went to kneel in front of the door, working the dial with fingertip pressure. A long minute passed with the sounds of helicopters coming ever closer, when the former policeman finally stood and worked the handle to easily pull open the heavy portal. Beyond was another file cabinet and a flight of concrete stairs descending into the darkness.

Quickly putting the books and papers back on the chair and setting it exactly on the indentations in the carpeting, Able Team entered the passageway. Schwarz went straight to the file cabinet and started searching for booby traps while Lyons and Blancanales shoved the vault door closed.

As it locked into place, there came the pneumatic sigh of the wall panel sliding back into place, closely followed by the dimly wooden crash as the office door was smashed open by somebody claiming to be the FBI….

CHAPTER ELEVEN

Tarabarov/Yinlong Island

The small airport along the DMZ was busy with cargo planes constantly dropping off machinery and leaving with their holds full of manufactured goods and tons of smoked fish. The demilitarized zone had once been rigidly patrolled by armed troops, dogs and battle tanks. Now it was a rather flimsy wooden fence that children hopped over with complete immunity.

"Next, please," said the airport guard in halting English.

"Sir, I am a Slovak, not an American," Colonel Lindquist answered smoothly in Mandarin.

Although pleased to hear any barbarian speaking properly, the guard merely shrugged in response, naturally assuming that Slovak was some part of North America he had simply never heard about before. In his personal opinion, there were Highland Chinese and Lowland Chinese, then everybody else in the world, and he really didn't give a damn about even the Lowlanders, much less barbarians from the other side of the world.

Raging fast and furious, the Ussuri River flowed through the rugged Amur Mountains as if trying to escape into the nearby Sea of Japan. Located in the middle of the river, directly between the hotly contested borders of Russia and China, was Tarabarov Island. The Soviet Union had won complete control of the island decades ago, and built massive fortifications there in preparation for a Chinese resurgence. Instead, the Chinese built fortifications along the opposite bank of the Ussuri River, and the bitter enemies simply sat and stared at each for many years.

Slowly illegal trade developed between the armed guards. First they exchanged small food items to help break the boredom of the long hours, then jokes and forbidden bottles of liquor brewed in the mountains by the local farmers. It was fiery stuff, almost a test of manhood, but it made the long cold nights, and the grim, dour-faced whores, much more bearable.

Unlike the famous Berlin Wall, these armies were Communists, and the soldiers felt little animosity toward each other. If they were ordered into battle, then they would fight and kill, but if not, well, that was okay, too. Soon, in spite of countless regulations, lines of communication were opened across the water, and then when the Soviet Union collapsed, open trade flourished between the encampments. Goods and services flowed legally back and forth to the benefit of all.

In a historic gesture of friendship, Russia gave China all of Tarabarov Island, and half the smaller Bolshoi Ussuriysky Island located directly between Tarabarov and the mainland. The rest they kept primarily a small military outpost that had grown into a prosperous fishing community. The monumental gift was considered a good sign by everybody, and for a thousand miles along the Russia-China border, the island of Tarabarov was considered a beacon of hope for new friendship between the ancient enemies.

"So what are you delivering?" the guard asked, checking the manifest attached to his clipboard.

"Just some welding tanks," Lindquist answered, waving a hand forward.

Dutifully, the ground crew rolled the wooden crate into position. Everybody flinched slightly as the X-ray machine loudly buzzed, and there appeared on the monitor an image of the thermobaric bomb, surrounded by conduits and heat exchangers.

"Odd-looking equipment," the guard muttered with a frown.

"That, sir, is the new Mark 17 duel heat exchange unit." Colonel Lindquist beamed proudly, eagerly launching into a speech. "The top of the Omega Line for acetylene welding units. At less than half the cost of regular—"

"Yes, yes, thank you, very impressive. Move along. Next," the guard said quickly, indicating the next person in line, clearly thankful that the deluge of sales pitch had been escaped so quickly.

Trying his best not to smile, Lindquist helped wheel the heavy crate along the smooth pavement, pausing briefly in front of a chemical sensor. Since he was not carrying any illegal drugs or high explosives, no alarms sounded, and after a moment the clerk operating the scanner waved him by.

Pushing the crate along a line of similar crates waiting for pickup, the colonel randomly chose a spot and dropped the wooden container into place, then strolled across the open tarmac back to the waiting Cessna plane. Unlike most of his equipment, the aircraft was not formerly from the Soviet Union. The Cessna had been stolen by gunpoint from a small airfield on the Black Sea conveniently located near the ruins of Istanbul. When the CNN news crew arrived to cover the disaster, Colonel Lindquist shot them in the head and took the plane, dropping the bodies out the side when it was safely far away from land.

"Well?" the Slovakian soldier asked from the pilot chair, his hands minutely adjusting the fuel to the idling engines.

"Civilians," the colonel replied, as if that was enough of an explanation. "Let's go."

Powering up the engines, the soldier requested clearance from the lighthouse that served as a tower for the crude airport. When it was received, he sent the Cessna into the sky. Lindquist coldly watched the island dwindle as it fell behind, observing the old SAM batteries and rusty machine-gun emplacements designed to protect the crumbling forts from enemy attack.

"'What fools these mortals be,'" Lindquist quoted with a chuckle as he pulled out the radio-controlled detonator, flipped back the safety and waited until the arming light was glowing a bright red before pushing the button.

WITH A DULL THUMP, the lid of the packing crate blew off, releasing a snowstorm of foam packing peanuts and excelsior stuffing. Several of the Chinese workers in the yard looked up at the unexpected noise, and one rushed over to a telephone booth to call in the fire squad just in case. However, it was already too late.

In a rush of fire and smoke, the four Soviet Union jet-assisted-take-off—JATO—units roared into life. Designed to assist massively overburdened planes to achieve flight under combat conditions, the JATO units easily lifted the heavy decahedron out of the crate and sent it soaring skyward, arching slightly on a preprogrammed flight path until the bomb was directly over the center of Tarabarov Island.

In a stentorian flash, the sky ignited over the island and a blast of destruction expanded like a tidal wave from the sun. Airplanes crumpled, roofs collapsed and cars buckled. Glancing upward in horror, people inhaled to scream and the superheated air seared their lungs, stealing their last words in a grotesque rictus of pain. Their hair caught fire, eyes popped and clothing burned as Hell descend from above. Then the physical shock wave pulped the writhing torches mercifully against the ground even as the ocean of flame spread across the island, pouring through every door and window, detonating cars and trucks, melting the roads, then setting off the megatons of ammunition and rockets stored in the bunkers in an orgy of destruction.

Unstoppable, the maelstrom flowed across the boiling river to reach the wooden villages, concrete barracks, gas stations, boatyards, hospitals and schools, annihilating everything it touched, purging the promise of peace from the land like cauterizing a wound.

Bratislava, Slovakia

THE REAR TIRES gently squealed as the C-130 Hercules lightly touched down on the private airfield outside of the capital city. Then the front tires touched down and the pilot dropped the airfoils, feathered the propellers and applied the brakes to bring the massive military aircraft to a rocking halt alongside an empty hangar.

"Rock House, this is Airhead," said the blacksuit pilot into a VOX microphone suspended in front of his face like a silver antenna as he throttled down the engines. "The babies are in the crib. Repeat, the babies are in the crib. Time for a nap. Over."

"Understood, Airhead," Barbara Price replied from the ceiling speaker. "Hope they sleep well. Let me know if they have any bad dreams. This is Lady Money for Rock House, over and out."

"Ten-four, Rock House. Over and out," the pilot confirmed, throttling down the engines to a full stop. "Okay, boys, drop your socks and grab your lederhosen. It's party time!"

"Why are all pilots so bloody weird?" McCarter grumbled, rising from the navigator seat on the flight deck.

"Must be from all the wild sex we have while you grunts are out on patrol," Nathan "Cary" Carrington replied with a ferocious grin.

"But there's nobody here except you…" McCarter started, then raised a hand. "No, don't tell me. It's better that way."

Pulling out a clipboard, the blacksuit gave a knowing wink, then started checking on fuel and oil consumption, getting ready for the next leg of the mission. Wherever that might be. Until further notice, Cary was staying with the team, primarily to safeguard the Hercules, but the blacksuit was more than ready to lend a hand in combat should the need arise. Hanging on the wall behind the pilot was one of the new Barrett 6.8 mm assault rifles, a Nighthunter scope on top, the canvas strap heavy with spare clips.

Clambering down the steel stairs to the main deck of the colossal airplane, McCarter found the rest of Phoenix Force already out of the wall-mounted jumpseats and checking their personal weapons. The clicks and clacks made the Hercules seem as if it was infested with robotic crickets for a few minutes.

"Don't take anything big—this is going to be a soft recon," McCarter directed, sliding a civilian windbreaker over his military fatigues. His Army boots would go unnoticed as a lot of people outside of the cities wore the exact same thing. Before the Soviet Union went broke, the Russian soldiers often traded military supplies for goods and services, and a decent pair of boots got a man a week of hot food at an inn or a night in the bed of a willing sex partner. Both participants considered that a good deal in every way.

"Small arms it is, yes sir," Hawkins replied, tossing a satchel charge of C-4 high explosive into the back of a Hummer.

"Subtle is our middle name, sir," Encizo agreed, adding a MANPAD rocket launcher and a bag of grenades.

Oddly, the ammunition retrieved from the Balaklava submarine base had yielded no information. The brass had serial numbers from the production lots, but it was too old, from the early days of the Cold War, long before there were computer records, and so there were no records of where it was stored or sent. However, the wrapper from the beef stick had come from a private farm located just outside of Bratislava. The snack was not sold in the city, but from a stand alongside the road in front of the farm. It wasn't much of a lead, but it was pretty solid, and better than nothing.

After they finished storing their weapons, it took Phoenix Force a few minutes to release all of the safety straps holding their Hummer tightly into place, and then a few more to check the black vehicle over for any damage incurred during transit. But soon enough, the team climbed on board and rolled down the rear ramp and into the starry Slovakian night. Behind them, the loading ramp cycled shut and closed with a dull boom, then locked firmly into place.

Dominating the entire eastern horizon, Bratislava glowed like a magical fairy land, the ancient spires and modern skyscrapers mixing to make it seem like something from a fable.

"Beautiful land," Hawkins said honestly. "Kind of reminds me of Austin."

"Now, I thought you were a Houston boy," James asked, trying to hide a smile.

"Sir, from the panhandle to Galveston Bay, it's all Texas," Hawkins drawled proudly, tipping an imaginary ten-gallon hat.

"Wait until you see Montreal," Manning shot back, shifting gears. "Now, that's a city."

"So where is the cathedral?" Encizo inquired, removing the tape from the handle of a stun grenade.

"Pardon?" Manning asked, turning onto an access road.

Encizo tucked the charge into a pocket of his windbreaker. "Technically, you cannot be a city without a cathedral."

"Who made that rule?"

"I think it was the cathedral builders' union."

"Ah, mystery solved." Manning chuckled, proceeding alongside a major highway until reaching an access ramp.

Accelerating to merge, the man was surprised to find little traffic at this hour of the night. Bratislava was a well-known hot spot of nightclubs and brothels, but outside the city limits there was nothing but ruins and farmland, with the ebony black of night descended like the lid on an iron pot.

"Okay, where is the first known Soviet Union missile base located?" McCarter asked, checking the clip in his Walther P-38 automatic, then easing the clip back into the handle.

"About fifty miles due south of here," Encizo said, checking the PDA in his hand. "Just take the—I'm not sure how to pronounce the name of the town. Grericadink? No, Gammera? Gor—"

Suddenly the radio crackled into life. "—cade! Cas—" Then it went silent.

It took a full second for the team to piece the two parts of words together into "Cascade," the emergency recall code.

"Firebird to Airhead," McCarter said quickly into his throat mike. "Ten-one, 10-9! Repeat, 10-1, 10-9!" But there was no reply, only static.

"Get hard, people, we're going back," McCarter commanded even as Manning twisted the wheel sharply to send the Hummer across the traffic lanes and crashing through a new wooden safety barrier.

The Hummer jolted from the impact, and went flying for several yards before slamming into the grassy median. Fighting inertia, Manning twisted the wheel against the slope of the ground to stop them from rolling over. The tires spun madly in the dewy grass, then found purchase and the Hummer rapidly accelerated uphill to smash through the other safety barrier to the sound of splintering wood.

A BMW truck hauling logs had to veer wildly to avoid hitting the speeding Hummer, but then the team was past the truck, pulling out their weapons and clicking off safeties. Carrington was a joker, almost as bad as Schwarz, but he would never give the recall signal unless there was real trouble. But how could anything have happened so soon? They had only landed fifteen minutes ago.

"The sons of bitches must have had the private airfields watched," Hawkins snarled, cradling his MP-5 subgun. "Then they waited for us to leave, and hit the plane to see what they could find."

"Sure as hell hope not," McCarter said truthfully as the Hummer raced pell-mell back onto the access road. The dust from the earlier passage had not yet settled. "Because if that's the case then Cary—"

As there came the sound of machine-gun fire, the man stopped talking. Looming ahead of the team was the Hercules. The loading ramp was down once more, bright lights spilling out onto the tarmac, showing a still body missing most of a head. McCarter felt a surge of adrenaline at the sight, then realized the body was wearing a gillie suit, the black-and-gray camouflage patterns perfect for night maneuvers. It wasn't Carrington, but one of the invaders.

"Hold on!" Manning snarled, shifting gears as the Hummer hit the ramp. The jolt threatened to throw the men free, but they hung on tight as the military vehicle jounced back up and into the cargo hold of the Hercules.

There were a dozen black motorcycles parked in the middle of the cargo hold and a group of armed people ransacking the wall lockers. Manning took in everything with a single glance. Everybody in sight was in a camouflage gillie suit, was Chinese, wearing body armor and carrying a silenced assault rifle.

"It's the bleeding Red Star," McCarter snarled, bracing himself.

"Bleeding is right." Slamming on the brakes and twisting the wheel, Manning sent the speeding Hummer skidding sideways across the cargo hold, knocking aside the motorcycles and heading directly for the invaders. Only one of them managed to fire off a burst, and another screamed, then the plane rocked from the brutal impact as the military vehicle ruthlessly crushed the invaders against the interior bulkhead set under the flight deck.

A cursing Manning was still fighting the Hummer to a halt while the rest of the team scrambled from their seats and opened fire on the Red Star agents on the catwalk overhead. The concentrated hail of 9 mm rounds tore their vulnerable legs apart, and the Chinese operatives dropped screaming obscenities.

Charging up the stairs, McCarter shot the first two men in the forehead to stop their cries, and shot the third man in through the wrist, sending his Norinco .50 pistol sailing away to clatter loudly on the deck below.

"Wait!" the man shouted in excellent English. "We can share the Russia weapon."

"Not after Milan," McCarter whispered, and fired twice more, then turned to check on the door to the flight deck.

One of the main hardpoints on a Hercules, the door was still closed, but it had clearly been shot a dozen times with soft lead rounds, and then with something else as there were five big holes punched through the metal, offering a peephole glimpse inside. Nothing seemed to be moving.

Hawkins was already there, jiggling the handle. "Cary!" he shouted. "It's Hawk, open the door." But there was only a thick silence. "Airhead, it's Texas." Nothing, not a sound.

Pushing the other men aside, James slapped a shaped charge on the lock, stabbed in a timing pencil and snapped it off at the lowest mark. They barely had a chance to get clear before the C-4 loudly detonated and the door slammed aside.

Inside, Carrington was slumped over the steering yoke, the hand mike dangling by his side, the cord still dripping blood from a hideous wound in his neck, the white bones in his spine clearly visible. Over on the navigator side, a section of the controls was glowing cherry-red and acrid smoke rose from the melting computer. Instantly, the men of Phoenix Force understood what had happened. When the plane had been breached, Carrington had first destroyed the mission data files before calling for help.

"He would have made a damn good member of the team," Hawkins said, giving his highest compliment.

"He was," McCarter corrected, throwing the dead man a salute. The rest of Phoenix Force did the same, holding the salute for longer than usual as they gave a final goodbye to a fellow soldier.

A siren warbled outside, and Encizo wiped the blood off a window to squint into the distance.

"Looks like everybody is coming to the party," he said succinctly. "Police, fire department, ambulance and a couple of Hummers that could be NATO."

"ETA?" McCarter demanded, flipping some switches on the gore-streaked controls.

"Five minutes, maybe less."

"Okay, everybody grab an away bag," McCarter ordered, pressing a button hard. It locked into place, and began to hum softly. "We have two minutes to get clear before the self-destruct charges blow. Go, go, go!"

Ninety seconds later, the Hummer backed hastily out of the Hercules and wheeled back to charge into the nearby woods.

"Ten seconds," James called, checking his watch. "Nine… eight…"

Yanking the cord from a satchel charge, Hawkins tossed it behind the Hummer and ducked. Instantly, Manning swerved to try to put some trees between the vehicle and the explosive charge.

Seconds later, the Hercules thunderously detonated, the flash banishing the night for hundreds of yards. A split second later, the satchel charge erupted, throwing out a halo of loose dirt and broken branches, completely masking any trace of the Hummer's frantic passage through the dark forest.

"Firebird to Rock House, we lost Airhead," McCarter said into his throat mike, a hand on the transceiver changing the frequency. "Repeat, we lost Airhead. Will continue picnic, but require new piggyback at new location. Over."

"This is Lady Money, Firebird," Price said. "Please confirm that last transmission. Airhead has been lost?"

"Ten-four, Rock House. Airhead is gone. He had a dream about a Dragon."

There was a brief pause. "Understood, Firebird. We'll send Able Baker to Bridge City, and wait for your coordinates. Over."

"Over and out," McCarter answered grimly, and killed the microphone. "All right, this changes nothing. The Farm will have a replacement Hercules waiting for us in Prague. But for right now, we still have a lot of abandoned Soviet missile bases to check."

"ETA, fifty minutes, David," Manning said, shifting gears again and crashing through a wall of hedges to emerge onto the berm alongside an empty highway.

As the Hummer rolled onto the smooth pavement, there came a secondary explosion from the burning Hercules, just as a NATO helicopter swung overhead, flying in that direction.

"Hopefully that's the last we see of the Red Star," James growled, brushing some loose dirt from his curly hair.

"Hopefully not," Hawkins countered, releasing the primer cord from his fist. It sailed away on the wind and vanished into the night.

Concentrating on driving through the dense forest, Manning said nothing, but his expression clearly stated that he would also like to meet more of the Chinese operatives—through the crosshairs of his Barrett .50 sniper rifle.

CHAPTER TWELVE

Saris Castle, Slovakia

"Easy now," Professor Karlov whispered, reaching inside the complex innards of the Russian thermobaric bomb, her slim fingers twisting a path through the array of pipes, conduits and wiring.

The stick of high-explosive TNT was easy to locate, as expected. She removed the detonator, then continued onward. The TNT was only a diversion for the unwary. An enemy would expect to find a booby trap of some kind, so the Russian scientists gave them one right up front. The real traps were far more subtle and infinitely more complex. A ground wire for a device that had no possible need to be grounded. A thermocouple wrapped in insulation, thus making itself useless. An optical feed connected to an electrical plug. Unless you knew this weapon, and the mind-set of the people behind it, trying to defuse this monster would have been impossible.

But that was all for show. It had been exactly as she surmised originally. The only reason to have so many traps inside a weapon was to keep anybody from getting a good look. She had figured out how the weapon operated in the first hour of exploration. It was quite simple, really, and amazingly clever. Now she was stalling, knowing that when the bomb was cracked, she would die.

Encountering a proximity sensor set amid a maze of pipes, Karlov deftly killed the device and removed it very carefully, not allowing the sensor to touch anything on the way out, just in case it was also pressure sensitive. Easing the sensor out of the decahedron, Karlov tossed it away to land in a plastic bucket full of sand. That action caused a frantic stirring of boots on the other side of the locked door, and she hid a smile.

Just wait, boys, there's a lot more to come.

Massaging her hands to help restore circulation, Karlov took a sip of black coffee from a plastic tumbler resting on a wicker coaster. The wicker absorbed any excess moisture that might have formed on the tumbler and prevented it from accidentally reaching the bomb. Her clothing had all been replaced with surgical garb, old and musty-smelling but absolutely static free. That was something every hacker learned to guard against hard and fast. A single spark would erase a dozen of the integrated circuits and trigger an automatic detonation. Easy did not equate with simple. She could build a T-bomb now from scratch, but could she disassemble this one? A single mistake of any kind and—well, at least she would never know about the failure unless there really was a Heaven. That frightened her a little, until realizing that if there was a Heaven, then her jailers went straight to Hell. That thought cheered her immeasurably. Plus, if she went, so did all of them, in spite of their elaborate precautions.

The workshop was located at the top level of a medieval tower, the floor and walls lined with sandbags, huge plastic barrels of water situated in every corner. There were several video cameras set at different angles in the room, each recording everything she did, every move she made. Her pockets were full of chemical warming pads to help her stay warm, and the kerosene heater located just outside the room was steadily blowing warm, dry air under the door. There was no open flame in the room, not even an exposed electrical outlet. She honestly did not think that any of these precautions would help in the least if the T-bomb detonated, but the woman understood the vital psychological necessity of trying. Her captors were mad dogs, but not fools.

However, neither were the Russians. There was a small cellular unit in the bomb designed to relay telemetry back to Mystery Mountain. Unfortunately, there was nobody left alive there at the moment, but that still gave her a tiny window of opportunity. Closing her eyes to pretend she was concentrating on something difficult, Karlov removed her watch and attached a few wires, activated a subprotocol and accessed the Internet, the tiny plasma screen of her watch serving as a crude monitor. It was difficult to see, but a lot better than nothing.

"How is it going?" a voice asked from one of the video cameras.

"Quiet, fool. You made me drop a tool," Karlov snapped ferociously, rattling a screwdriver against a metallic strut. "Leave me alone, if you wish to live!" That brought only silence. Good.

For a harrowing moment the woman thought her plan would be exposed when the phone went online, but the sound of the Internet greeting screen was lost in the gentle rush of the kerosene heaters.

However, even with the miniature monitor, Karlov was at a loss on whom to contact for help. These people were very well financed and might easily control the police, or even be a part of the Slovakian military. The Czech Republic would come to her rescue, but only after days of debate, and by then her bones would be gnawed on by the wild dogs in the hills. She needed to contact somebody smart, hard and fast. MI-5 in the United Kingdom came immediately to mind, but since she had no idea how to contact them or the American CIA, that only left the underworld. Unfortunately, she did not know any criminals aside from street peddlers who sold pirated copies of American and French movies on DVD. Hardly the criminal masterminds needed to accomplish her goal.

Biting a lip, Karlov made a fast decision and began a global search for the richest alleged criminal in the world. Rich would mean they were powerful, and alleged would mean they were smart. The perfect combination. And who would not be interested in purchasing the ultimate weapon so cheaply?

The cost was a single human female, delivered safely out of captivity, Karlov rattled off in her mind. Come on, boys, the price is right. Who wants to rule the world?

Almost immediately, the astonished scientist began to get encoded inquiries from sources claiming to be the Mafia, the Yakuza, somebody called S2 in Brazil, the Fifteen Families and a dozen others. It was almost as if the criminals of the world had been eagerly waiting for just such an announcement.

Ponca, Arkansas

THE ATMOSPHERE of the subterranean computer room was automatically adjusted to always be at exactly thirty-three degrees, and a sonic filtration system removed all allergens and dust mites. To many visitors, the air tasted flat and metallic, lifeless. But Greg Russell considered it immensely refreshing. Although not at the moment.

"Repeat that, please," Brandon Duvall demanded, stepping closer to the humming computer. As he cleared the doorway, a double sheet of Lexan plastic slid into place behind, hermetically sealing off the room from the outside world.

"Destroyed," Russell repeated, straightening his turtle-necked sweater. "The entire Foxfire compound is gone. What wasn't blown up in the barrage—"

Duvall furrowed his brow. "The *what?*"

"Barrage, sir. The base was hammered with mortar shells before the FBI came over the walls and arrested everybody." The hacker paused. "Well, anybody still alive."

"That's quite enough," Duvall rumbled, holding up a restraining palm. "Just tell me where my son is being detained, and I'll have a dozen lawyers there in an hour."

Swiveling his chair back and forth for a moment, Russell struggled to find some way to tell the man. "Sir, I…that's what I wanted to tell you in person. You see…"

"Oh, hell, they put him in Guantanamo?" Duvall frowned, reaching for the telephone on the wall. "I'll have to call in some big favors from Washington on this."

"Dead, sir," Russell blurted, not knowing what else to do. Computers he understood, not people. "He's MIA, missing in action, presumed dead, but after so many big explosions…"

Looking as if he had just been kicked in the stomach, the billionaire said nothing for a few minutes as his whole world crumbled around the man with those simple words.

"Are you sure?" Duvall asked in an unaccustomed soft voice, his empty hands flexing uselessly at his side.

"No, sir, there will be no way to know for certain until…" Russell paused again, unwilling to say the word.

"Autopsy," Duvall supplied, sagging slightly. "Until after the autopsy of the unidentified corpses."

Just then, a spinning envelope appeared on the computer monitor and a chime softly sounded.

"Is it about my son?" Duvall asked hopefully, clutching the back of the hacker's chair.

"No, sir, this is from…" Russell frowned when he read the source of the transmission. Saris Castle? How was that possible?

"From whom?" Duvall demanded. "Open it."

With no other choice, the hacker opened the e-mail, and both men read the contents with growing astonishment.

"Is this possible?" Duvall growled, his heart quickening at the thought of revenge. The people behind the death of the Foxfire team had a captive who would sell the technical details of the thermobaric bomb in exchange for her freedom?

"It could be a scam," Russell hedged, trying to find some way to deflect the billionaire from his real employers. But with the man standing only inches away, that was proving impossible.

"Then again, it might be true," he added hesitantly.

For a few precious moments Duvall debated the possibility of such divine intervention. Anything too good to be true was almost always a trick. Should he…could he…? Then a roaring sound filled his mind and cool reason abandoned the man as his grief flared into the absolute need for vengeance. My world is dead, so must end the world.

"Buy it," the billionaire commanded, leaning closer to the glowing monitor, the harsh light making his face seem drained of any trace of humanity. "Buy the weapon at any price!"

Reluctantly, Russell started typing an encoded reply to the castle, and also sending a duplicate to General Novostk at Podbanske Missile Base. Whatever happened next was now in the hands of the general and his band of freedom fighters. God help us all.

Stony Man Farm

"WHAT DO YOU MEAN they used JATO units?" Kurtzman demanded, looking up from his console.

"That's what the Japanese spy satellite recorded," Delahunt replied. "Just before the island was destroyed, there briefly came the definite pattern of JATO units igniting, but from the cargo storage area, not a landing strip."

"Clever," Kurtzman growled, rubbing his hands along the top of the wheel for his chair. The thieves smuggled a T-bomb in as some sort of machinery, a fuel pump or welding equipment, something like that, and then launched the bomb skyward once the operators were a safe distance away. The JATO units could help shove a B-2 heavy bomber off the ground, so launching a T-bomb would be ridiculously easy. A sky attack from the ground. How were they going to stop any of those?

On the three wall monitors, the nations of the world were seething with military action, armies massing along borders, warships in transit, squadrons of jetfighters crisscrossing the skies, hunter-killer satellites assuming combat positions. Every missile base that was known to exist was ratcheting up to launch status. The news of the stolen superweapon was out, and everybody was preparing to be attacked by both friend and foe. Israel and Hamas were already fighting, as were India and Pakistan, plus Chile and Argentina. So far the combat was just border skirmishes, brief sorties by ground troops, but soon the big guns would come out, and after that, the nuclear weapons.

"Okay, how can we stop these new types of attacks?" Kurtzman demanded. "There must be some way to detect the T-bombs before they are in position. Chemical sniffers. X-rays. Something!"

Delahunt looked at the man directly. "It cannot be done," she stated, the simple words seeming to fill the cold room.

"I refuse to accept that," Kurtzman snapped in reply. "We just have to think of something. If the bombs cannot be detected, how about the JATO units? Those are solid blocks of propellant and—"

"And hermetically sealed until ignited," Wethers declared roughly, removing his pipe to jab it forward. "Aaron, it can't be done. The bombs are invisible to conventional sensors. These people could smuggle hundreds of them into America, and we would have no idea until major cities began exploding into flames."

"I agree," Tokaido added grimly. "It can't be done. Maybe, just maybe we could figure something out if we knew how the blasted bombs worked, what they used as fuel, or a power source. But without that, no, it is flat out impossible."

Furiously, Kurtzman cracked his knuckles, trying to think of something, anything, that could be done. But deep down inside, the computer genius knew that his team was correct. To stop the bombs, they had to find them first, and there was no way to locate one until it detonated. This was a nightmare, with no way out.

Just then, Tokaido jerked his head toward his console and frowned. "Alert," he said in a controlled tone. "Somebody is talking about the T-bombs over the Internet."

"After Istanbul, a million people are," Delahunt retorted.

"Not describing them as a decahedron," Tokaido snapped, his hands flashing across the keyboard.

"But nobody knows that except—"

"The thieves and the Russian scientists who invented the weapons," Wethers finished, tucking his pipe back into place once more. "Good God, could this be real?"

"Are there any pictures?" Kurtzman demanded suspiciously, starting a global trace.

Working steadily, Tokaido frowned. "No, but the bombs are being accurately described as to size, weight and color, exactly as the Pentagon theoretical danger team guessed." The man paused, his eyes going wide. "This is a damn auction. The schematics and structural blueprints for building a thermobaric bomb are being offered for sale!"

"Not the bombs themselves?" Kurtzman asked. "Okay, double the top bid. Triple it! If we can't get a hold of the bombs, then we must have those plans."

"I'm trying to gain access, but so many groups are bidding for the weapons, the server is almost crashing," Tokaido stated, bending over the console. "The seller is rejecting most people just to stay online. Goddamn it, a firewall just went up."

"On it," Delahunt stated. "And…we're through!"

"That was fast," Kurtzman noted, then saw the reason why. The firewall was Soviet military ICE, intrusion counter-measures, but old stuff that the team had encountered years before and already found the back door. "Okay, what's the top bid?"

"It is…freedom."

"Come again?"

"The seller is not asking for money. They're—correction, she is a prisoner of the terrorist group controlling the bombs, and she wants to be rescued."

"She?"

"Confirmed, it is a woman. Calls herself Professor Tanya Karlov of Prague University. Get her out alive and in exchange you get the plans to make the bombs."

"Checking," Delahunt said. "Yes, there is a Tanya Karlov who teaches at the university, and according to the Prague police department she just went missing two days ago, after terrorists raided the dormitory, killing students and staff."

So the deal was legitimate? "Agree to her terms," Kurtzman snapped. "We'll send in both field teams and a hundred blacksuits if necessary."

"Too late," Tokaido interrupted, removing his hands from the keyboard. "The auction is already over. Karlov just sealed a deal with somebody in Arkansas."

Leaning back in his chair, Wethers arched an eyebrow at the pronouncement. Arkansas? It couldn't be Foxfire. Their base was in ruins, and most of the mercenaries were under arrest. So who did that leave with the money and manpower to stage a rescue mission halfway around the world?

"Duvall. It's got to be Duvall," Kurtzman stated, making a sour face as if he had just swallowed decaffeinated coffee.

"Brandon Duvall. We always suspected he was the money behind Foxfire, but could never prove it. Guess now we know for sure."

"Isn't that the lunatic with his own White House?" Delahunt asked, focusing on her monitor. "Yes, I can see it now. An exact duplicate. At least, above the ground."

"Akira, Hunt, crash his computers," Kurtzman directed. "Erase those plans. Or better yet, replace them with fake plans. Karlov must have sent him something in advance to prove what she had."

"She sent him everything, all of it," Tokaido said in disbelief. "I only caught the tail end, but it's enough to convince me she had the real goods."

"Okay, I just cut his landlines, and have moved his communications satellite," Wethers said around his pipe. "Now there is no way for him to reach those files except for a hard intrusion. He'd have to physically rip out the CPU."

"And if he did, then the bastard could send the plans over the Internet using a cell phone," Kurtzman growled. "Akira, block the Net! Carmen, block all cell phone transmissions and have Price send in Able Team immediately. Those plans must be destroyed at any cost."

Nodding assent, Wethers switched to a preestablished secure line and started sending an encoded message to Schwarz on his laptop. For the present, the team was still under radio silence, and there was no other way to contact them without endangering their lives. Even a silently vibrating cell phone in the middle of a firefight could distract a soldier at exactly the wrong moment and result in his death.

"Akira, any chance Duvall said who was coming to rescue Karlov?" Kurtzman asked while a submonitor began to scroll with the biography of the self-made billionaire. In spite of his French last name, Duvall claimed Slovakian ancestry. Suddenly a lot of things began to make sense.

"Yes, Duvall said they would call themselves Foxfire..." The man blinked. "But they've all been arrested. He has no intention of staging a rescue."

"If Duvall has the plans, why should he?" Delahunt countered.

"Which means we can send in Phoenix Force to do the job for him." Kurtzman picked up a receiver built into his console.

"Aaron, the man is crazy, but he seems to be fiercely loyal to America," Delahunt offered hesitantly. "Maybe he intends to give the T-bombs to the Pentagon."

"First and foremost, Duvall is a grieving father whose only son was just slain by the FBI," Kurtzman corrected grimly, pressing a button. "So we must operate on the belief that all he wants at the moment is revenge." There came a subtle click, followed by a familiar voice. "Barb? Aaron here, we have a problem in Arkansas..."

CHAPTER THIRTEEN

Podbanske Base, Slovakia

The huge truck sat in the middle of a snowy field dotted with blue winter flowers. There were a few patches of bare ground, yet clusters of long icicles dangled from the tall pine trees like Christmas decorations. A huge column of steam suddenly rose from the nearby hills, the hot water geyser rising over a hundred feet before abruptly stopping and crashing back down to the bare stones.

Taking that as their cue, and leaving the diesel engine running, the soldiers scrambled from the cab and efficiently dragged off the heavy sheet of canvas covering the rear of the military vehicle. Exposed was a single huge rocket moored to the framework, the aft exhaust vectors radiating faint waves of heat from the warming units.

Five hundred miles deep underground, General Novostk stood in the command room of the old Soviet base watching the video feed. He stood stiffly at attention, with both hands clasped behind his back. At times like these, it was important to appear confident. Especially when you were not.

"Clear the area," General Novostk commanded, and the men in the field hurried away to climb into a battered Red Army truck.

The vehicle had been pieced together from a dozen other trucks and worked fine. It just resembled something experimented upon by the fictional Dr. Victor van Frankenstein.

One of the soldiers jokingly referred to the truck as Adam, although nobody else was sure why. The creature in the movies had never been given a proper name.

"Launch zone clear," a soldier reported crisply as the truck quickly drove away.

"Link up," Novostk directed.

"We're hot, sir."

"Then get her hard."

The soldier pressed a single green button on the master control board.

On the screen, there came the soft pneumatic hiss as steel pitons shot out of the truck to anchor it firmly to the ground, then each wheel individually locked. Next came the thumping of hydraulic pumps building pressure, and then heavy clamps disengaged. Slowly, almost majestically, the framework on the back of the truck elevated, cycling the nose of the missile upward until it was perfectly vertical. Then there came a fast series of hard clunks as everything locked permanently into place.

This was the point of no return. The general felt like saying something dramatic, or important sounding, but he had never been a man for unnecessary speeches. Odd that such an urge to come now. "Launch," he said simply, feeling his heart quicken.

"Starting primary sequence now," the soldier confirmed, flipping a row of switches to follow the procedure exactly as described in the manual.

Wisps of steam came from the vents on the missile as the internal warming unit started working, preparing the massive machine for its fiery assent.

"We are at eighty...ninety...we are hot. Repeat, we are hot," the soldier called formally, sweat on his brow. "Primary ignition in four...three...two...one....*ignition!*"

Instantly winter disappeared from the mountain pasture as a wash of roiling flame thundered from the base of the missile, vaporizing the snow and flowers alike. Protected by a thick slab of asbestos, the truck tires held the necessary few seconds for pressure to build, and then the SS-25 lifted almost lazily off the ground, increasing in speed every second. Then the main boosters kicked in and the view of the missile truck vanished in a deafening cloud of smoke and flame.

"Switching to Adam now," another soldier announced, turning a heavy dial.

There was a crackle of static, then the monitor cleared into a distant view of the missile leaving the partially melted truck behind, and then the ICBM was gone.

"Give me an aerial view," General Novostk demanded, trying to keep the tension out of his tone.

"The trees are in the way, sir."

"Then switch to radar."

Sluggishly, the old flat screen came alive with a pinging noise and the missile appeared on the grid as an elongated blob streaking skyward.

"Tracking on course," a third soldier reported, both hands working the antiquated controls. "First stage is separating and...second stage has engaged. Our bird is already at sub-orbital height and turning into the target vector."

Suddenly the screen went blank.

"The bird is out of range, sir."

So soon? That was a pleasant surprise. As much as Novostk hated the Russians, he had to admire their mechanical expertise. "Switch to satellite," the general ordered smugly, and the screen came back with a much sharper view of the speeding missile just as the second stage broke off to tumble away and the third stage accelerated with unbelievable speed.

"Range?"

"Five hundred miles and counting."

"Range to target?"

"Seven hundred miles and falling."

"How soon until it reaches their radar umbrella?"

"Any second now, sir."

"Overlay, please," Novostk commanded.

A ceiling projector was turned on and the radar grid was shown on top of a wall map of eastern Europe. The SS-25 was flying at maximum speed, slightly more than Mach Two, and was dead on target. The inertial guidance system was working perfectly. Personally, the general had no idea why everybody had switched to satellite tracking systems, which were vulnerable to enemy interference. The SS-25 had no radio receivers to be hacked or jammed. Its guidance system could not be scrambled or redirected. Once locked on course, the ICBM was self-contained and fully independent. Like a bullet from a gun. Simply pull the trigger and wait for the results.

"Target has our bird on radar. SAM batteries have engaged, and MiGs have been launched. The rockets will reach our bird in…two minutes."

"How soon before our bird reaches attack level?"

"Roughly…two minutes," the soldier replied, struggling to keep the shock from his words. "It's a dead heat now, sir."

Nobody spoke in the command room of the underground fortress as the antimissiles streaked skyward and the massive ICBM dived down toward the earth, their combined relative speeds beyond the calculation of the old Soviet computers.

Then, at one minute, fifty-five seconds, there appeared a huge cloud on the screen that spread across the target zone, obliterating any possible view.

"We did it, sir," the soldier said in amazement. "Our bird exploded just before the rockets could reach it. Mystery Mountain is completely destroyed—the whole damn valley is burning."

Neatly removing anybody trying to salvage the data files, the general noted smugly to himself. The superweapon belonged to Slovakia now. Soon China and the so-called Western powers would reap nuclear vengeance upon Russia, burning the hated invaders from the face of the Earth. His people would remain safe in the base, waiting out the riots and starvation and chaos. Eventually they would emerge and build a new Slovakia—master of the world!

"Get the missile crews moving, I want the remaining T-bombs installed immediately," Novostk said, watching the fiery destruction of the once mighty Russian base. "And get me an update on our little Czech teacher. How close is she to cracking her bomb open?"

A soldier at the communications panel covered the microphone before answering. "Sergeant Melori says that the professor claims to be trying her best, but he thinks she is deliberately stalling."

"Such a pity," the general snorted. "I dislike torture, but there seems to be no choice. Have the sergeant try more primitive measures of inducement." He frowned. "But do not harm her eyes or hands—those she will need to continue the work." Turning, the general left the room. "Everything else is superfluous."

Ponca, Arkansas

AFTER ARRANGING WITH Price for a blacksuit to drop off a replacement van in Dogpatch, Able Team rearmed themselves and drove directly to the billionaire's private estate.

Unfortunately the files the team recovered merely confirmed the belief that Duvall owned Foxfire completely and that he had been the man behind the plan to steal the thermobaric bomb. They had the names of the people involved: Lindquist, Hannigan, Johansen, Barrowman, Kessler and James "Jimmy" Jones, but since they were all dead that really did not help any. There were some coded references to a General Nova as logistic and tactical support overseas, but Kurtzman could not find any military officer with that specific name, and expanding the search to similar names yielded too many people. Hopefully, Phoenix Force would get some hard intel after extracting the kidnapped Czech professor.

The one useful bit of information was the exact location of the hydroelectric dam that powered the Duvall estate, along with the names of the Foxfire mercs stationed there and what weapons they carried to defend the power generators.

"Any second now," Lyons whispered into his throat mike, slipping on a gas mask.

Doing the same, Schwarz gave no reply. His face was grim. Whether or not it had been the billionaire's intent, it was unnerving for the soldier to plan a strike on the symbol of America.

"Did you know that Robert E. Lee took the White House once during the Civil War?" Blancanales said in an effort to break the psychological chains that he also felt. "Lincoln chased him out again, of course, but then it was seized again by Cortez in the Spanish American war."

"Say what?" Schwarz demanded, his eyes scornful through the lenses of his mask.

Blancanales shrugged. "Or maybe that was David Letterman in the Battle of the Network Stars."

Unable to stop himself, Schwarz broke into a guffaw, and even Lyons had to briefly smile, the awful weight of aiming a weapon at the White House gone from his limbs. This was not the home of the President, just some lunatic's duplicate, nothing more. On second thought, it was more like a mirror image of the White House as this building stood for the corruption of power, not the lofty ideal that all men are created equal.

Suddenly the lights died in the rolling garden around the White House, and the fountain stopped splashing, then the building itself went dark in sections.

"Go!" Lyons commanded, erupting from the shrubbery and charging across the open lawn.

The weight of their body armor slowed the three men slightly, but they were still making good speed when the stars winked out overhead and the silence of the night was shattered by the mind-numbing reports of a dozen Blofor 40 mm cannons firing on full-auto from the six massive C-130 Hercules planes gliding across the black sky. One of the planes was sweeping the lawn ahead of the sprinting team, the non-stop barrage of antipersonnel rounds chewing up the manicured grass and prematurely detonating the score of hidden land mines. The other five planes concentrated on the White House itself, the maelstrom of shells softly smacking into the concrete building and gently exploding into thick smoke. In only seconds, the structure was lost in the swirling mixture of chemical smoke, white sleep gas and bright yellow tear gas.

Reaching the fountain, the team was buffeted by gunfire from a host of Samsung Auto-Sentries hidden in the rosebushes. Diving behind the casement of the fountain, they threw flares into the bushes and ducked. A few seconds later a Hercules chewed a path of destruction through the flowers, annihilating the robotic machines and detonating several more land mines.

Now openly standing, Able Team fired their own weapons. Schwarz and Blancanales sent 40 mm slugs of depleted uranium into the front door, while Lyons raked the upper stories with the Atchisson. The 12-gauge smashed open the windows and let in the thick clouds of dark smoke. Almost instantly, there came the sound of men cursing and coughing.

Reloading on the run, Able Team crashed into the foyer of the White House, triggering a hail of rubber bullets into a gang of men waving their guns while trying to wipe their eyes clear. The stun bullets slammed them in the stomach, forcing the defenders to breathe deeply, and they dropped, twitching, into unconsciousness.

Switching to infrared, Lyons swept the grand staircase while Schwarz and Blancanales checked the main hallway for any more guards. There were a host of people hacking and coughing everywhere, but all of them seemed to be maids and secretaries. Nobody carried a weapon. This is why the team hadn't simply ordered the wing of Hercules aircraft to blow the house open with a rocket attack; the place was rife with civilians, or at the very least, noncombatants.

Ignoring the grand staircase as too obvious a trap, Able Team went to the elevators and pressed the call button. As the doors opened, they checked the control panel. There was a basement listed, and then another floor that needed a key to be reached. That would be where the computers were, and the most likely location of Duvall.

Just then, the emergency lights flicked on and deadly illumination flooded the smoky atmosphere. There came the sound of running and some muffled curses from the smoky realm of the East Wing. Dropping flat onto the floor, Able Team waited for a visual ID on the runners, then cut loose with their rubber bullets. The armed guards grunted horribly at the violent impacts on their shins and knees. As they fell, the team raked the floor with more stun bullets, ripping off the protective gas masks and slamming several of the guards along the smooth terrazzo like runaway logs to smack into the marble walls and go terribly still.

Stepping into view, a woman appeared holding a towel to her face and brandishing a weapon. Caught in the middle of reloading the Atchisson, Lyons almost pulled his .357 Magnum Colt Python when he saw that she was merely carrying a survivalist flashlight, the kind without batteries that you had to pump to keep the light going. Coughing and crying at the same time, she seemed unaware that the lens was broken, and kept blithely pumping away.

"Tough lady," Schwarz commented over his throat mike as the woman stumbled by only inches away. Her stockings were ripped, and one shoe was missing, a toe ring glittering in the glow of the emergency lights like a lost star.

"Must be part Italian," Blancanales replied, putting a round into the belly of a guard struggling to reach a fire alarm. Smacking into the wall, he dropped limply. The soldier grunted in satisfaction. Just because the switch looked like a fire alarm did not mean that it was. What better place to hide the controls to activate the anti-intruder system? They could flood the building with gas that worked on skin contact, or electrify the floors to knock out everybody and let the guards wearing insulated boots sort out the bodies later.

Pressing the button for the top level, Lyons got his arm out of the way just before the doors closed. Impatiently, the team waited a few seconds for the lift to ascend, then forced the doors open and fumbled along the inside of the shaft until finding the emergency ladder. Now the similarities between the two buildings would work against Duvall, as Hal Brognola had given them the full details of the White House floor plans. Although the team would have to watch out for changes and new additions.

Lyons slung the Atchisson over a shoulder and took the lead down the ladder. Jamming the doors open with a steel wedge, Schwarz was next, and Blancanales followed last, slapping a shaped charge of C-4 to the overhead lintel.

The team neared the basement level as a rush of men appeared in the open doorway and started shooting down at them. Instantly, Blancanales slapped the radio detonator on his belt, and the C-4 charge detonated, sending the guards hurtling back into the corridor in an assortment of ragged pieces.

"Sure hope one of them wasn't Duvall," Schwarz muttered, lowering his Barrett assault rifle. "I wanted to thank him myself for all of this."

"Stand in line," Blancanales growled, resetting the detonator and slapping another charge to one of the big iron bolts set into the concrete wall supporting the ladder.

Reaching the end of the ladder, Lyons looked around the fake bottom of the shaft, and soon found a hidden trip. Carefully stepping out onto the support beams, he got out of the way to allow Schwarz to get to work with his laptop.

Knowing what to expect next, Lyons aimed the Atchisson at the open door of the shaft, briefly wishing that they could close the damn thing. But then the cage would be able to descend, and the team did not carry enough explosives to stop that without also killing themselves. A few seconds later there was a clatter and something small and round rolled out of the open doorway and into the shaft. His finger already on the trigger, Lyons cut loose with a full spray of 12-gauge cartridges, blowing the object back into the corridor. Two seconds later, the grenade violently exploded, and men died, their last breath reduced to an inarticulate scream of pain.

With a dull clunk, the trip disengaged, and Schwarz barely had time to grab the ladder before the false bottom of the elevator shaft slid into the walls exposing an additional twenty feet. Checking the darkness with their Nighthunter goggles, the team saw nothing dangerous, so they switched to UV and now clearly saw a spiderweb of scintillating laser beams crisscrossing the shaft, two of them only inches from actually touching the ladder.

Hugging their weapons tightly to prevent any accidental contact with the beams, the men of Able Team proceeded slowly through the maze until reaching the last two beams, then they each jumped off to land in a crouch at the bottom of the shaft alongside an impressive array of Claymore antipersonnel mines.

Unexpectedly, something fell from above, clattering and clanging all the way down, bouncing off the walls and ladder as the elevator doors started to close. The wedge had come loose.

Dropping flat, the men covered their ears and opened their mouths to reduce the compression damage. A split second later the wedge touched a beam and four of the Claymore mines violently exploded. The combined blast was deafening, and the concussion brutally slammed the men against the concrete floor as a hellstorm of double-aught steel buckshot hissed up the shaft.

Their ears were still ringing from the noise as they scrambled to reach the exit doors and to release the locking bar. High overhead, the barrage of steel pellets nosily tore the elevator cage apart, and loose wreckage started falling toward the waiting lasers.

Bracing himself against a braided cable, Lyons forced the bar clear by sheer brute strength, and the others yanked them wide. Hastily scrambling through, the team dived away from the open doorway when the wreckage reached the beams and all of the remaining Claymore mines detonated in a staggering volley of pyrotechnic destruction.

The blast lifted the team off their feet and sent them hurtling along the corridor to painfully crash into the wall at the end. For a few moments they rode out the roiling concussion, and as it gradually faded away, quickly took stock of their condition.

"Any damage?" Lyons demanded into his throat mike, feeling his arms and ribs for possible breaks. He ached from head to foot, but there was no telltale spreading warmth of a major wound.

"My goggles are dead," Schwarz cursed, yanking off the Nighthunter visor and tossing it away.

"Detonator," Blancanales added, dropping the device.

"Say again?" Lyons asked with a scowl, touching his earbud. The men repeated what they had said, and Lyons realized he was only hearing them with one ear; the bud in the other was silent. All communication with his team would be one way now.

Standing erect, the team dimly heard a thumping noise and then saw a steel gate raggedly descend from the ceiling, forcing its way along badly deformed guides. The blast that had nearly taken their lives had also blown them safely past the automatic barriers. As it reached the floor, the gate began to crackle with electricity, and then an oily gas hissed out from the bars to fill the other side. The paint on the walls bubbled from the touch of the corrosive fumes.

Backing away quickly, the Stony Man operatives raced along the corridor, with Lyons checking a compass to keep them on course, Schwarz checking an EM scanner for any proximity sensors and Blancanales watching intently for any laser beams.

At an unexpected intersection, the team paused and looked down each branch. They all seemed the same.

"We're off the map," Lyons stated, tucking away the compass.

"Well, there's something big and magnetic down this way," Schwarz said hesitantly, jerking a thumb to the right.

"However, there are thermal prints of somebody walking this way," Blancanales said, indicating the left corridor.

"Anything to the right?"

"No."

"Left it is," Lyons declared, starting that way.

A gentle curve took them out of sight of the intersection and brought into view a large door. It was thickly insulated, not armored, and there was a biometric palm reader set into the wall alongside. Clearly, this was their goal.

"Don't touch that reader," Blancanales warned. "There's no thermal residue of it ever having been touched."

Lyons grunted. Another damn trap.

"There is also no lock on the door," Schwarz countered, studying the smooth expanse of burnished steel. Even the hinges were hidden, and there wasn't even any clearance for him to slide a probe through to see the other side. "I guess we have to blast."

"First, let's try knocking politely," Lyons decided, dropping the partially used drum from the Atchisson and working the action to jack out a live cartridge. Reaching into a pouch on his web belt, the man extracted a single black-and-red-striped cartridge and thumbed it into the weapon, then took aim and fired.

The breaching charge slammed into the middle of the door with the force of a dozen sledgehammers, denting the metal inward and popping the internal lock. Swinging open, the door slammed aside another Samsung Auto-Sentry, crashing the machine flat against the concrete wall. Crackling with sparks, the robotic device fired a single round into the ceiling and then went still.

Warily the team entered the room with their weapons at the ready. There was an orthopedic chair set in front of a double keyboard, and an array of monitors. But all of the screens were dark. Sticking out of a microserver was an open CD burner, the tray extended like the hand of a beggar, and just as empty.

Filling the rest of the room was a massive array of blade servers that composed a Cray Supercomputer. But the complex machine was dead silent, the all-pervading hum missing. Nearby was an intercom with an alphanumeric pad and a wireless controller.

Off to the side was located the all-but-mandatory pot of black coffee, and a tentative sniff under their masks brought the richly delicious aroma of Jamaican Blue, the most expensive coffee in the world.

"Nothing but the best, eh?" Blancanales asked rhetorically, touching the pot. It was room temperature.

That was when the men got a sinking feeling as they noticed how warm the air was. Even a desktop PC ran better when the room was chilly, and a Cray needed to be constantly cooled by liquid nitrogen to operate at peak efficiency.

Pushing up his gas mask, Schwarz bent over the keyboard and breathed heavily. But there were too many fresh prints for him to analyze what was the last thing done by the unknown hacker. Plugging the USB cord of the laptop into a serial port, Schwarz tried to access the central data processor of the Cray, and only got a prompt sign.

"It's dead," he announced, removing the cord. "My best guess is that they burned something onto a CD, then erased the hard drive of the Cray. Well, the CPU, anyway."

"So nobody could trace the data to its origin." Lyons scowled. "Any chance of a reboot?"

"Not without spending hours installing new software first, and then I'd have to check for ICE, false dumps and all sorts of shit. We could build a Cray faster."

"How about a hot link to the Cray at the Farm?"

"Same thing, and the danger of the two supercomputers battling each other for supremacy is too big a chance to risk."

"Okay, this Cray is dead. That makes the big question, what did they burn on a CD?" Blancanales wondered out loud. "It had to be the technical plans for the T-bomb. Nothing else makes sense."

"Sounds about right," Schwarz muttered in annoyance, looking around the room. "But what puzzles me is how they got past us in the hallway."

"Maybe they didn't," Lyons said, and twirled the thermostat on the control board all the way to minus 20 degrees.

There came a dull thumping in the walls, and then freezing-cold air flushed from the vents, wafting over the servers of the dead supercomputer.

Switching to infrared on his goggles, Lyons waited a few minutes for the temperature to drop, then checked over the room and immediately saw a row of glowing red footprints on the floor leading to a black section of the wall.

"That's a trap," Blancanales stated, pointing a finger. "Those are boot prints, and no hacker alive would wear those bent over a keyboard all day. Aaron and his people wear sneakers or loafers. Hell, sometimes Carmen goes barefoot."

"Unfortunately, there are no other prints," Lyons stated, walking among the servers to check between the units.

Reaching for his throat mike, Lyons grimaced at the memory of the broken earbud, then glanced briefly at the intercom before dismissing it completely. Even if it was not rigged with anti-intruder devices like those at the Farm, it would be just about as far away from a secure line of communications as humanly possible.

"Call in it," Lyons commanded.

"Tinker to Rock House," Schwarz subvocalized into his throat mike. "It's midnight at the oasis. Repeat, midnight at the oasis." But there was no answer, not even the crackle of background static.

"Crap, we're too deep underground," the man swore, "and there's probably shielding in the walls, maybe even a Faraday Cage to stop EM signals from reaching the computer."

The flow of cold air slowed as the vent gurgled and a thick pinkish fluid began to pump into the room. Able Team recoiled as even through their Delta Force gas masks there was a strong smell of gasoline.

Moving fast, Schwarz reached for the thermostat and stopped himself just in time from changing the setting. The first time would activate the trap, but the second time would set it off.

Just then there came the soft thud of locking bolts slamming out of the jamb and lintel of the gaping doorway. If the door had still been in place, the team would have been sealed inside, unable to blast their way free without setting off the thick fumes of the jellied gasoline.

Sloshing through the icy gasoline, Able Team raced back into the corridor and headed for the intersection once more.

"Two choices left, and which is the escape route is any-body's guess," Blancanales said, unscrewing the cap on his canteen and liberally pouring the contents over his sodden combat boots.

"Both could be death traps," Lyons stated, doing the same to his own boots. The smell of the gasoline was growing strong again as the liquid flowed out of the computer room and into the corridor. They had to leave, and fast.

"Shit, the gate," Schwarz cursed, tossing aside his empty canteen.

Down the main corridor, the gate was no longer hissing out poison gas, but the metal bars still crackled with electricity. The moment the gasoline reached those, the whole place would go up in a fireball.

"Which branch had the strong magnetic read?" Lyons demanded, stepping back slightly.

"This one!" Schwarz answered, jerking a thumb. "But it could just be another trap."

"Okay, then we split up," Lyons commanded. "You two take the left, I'll go right."

"No, wait a second," Blancanales ordered. "This place is a maze of traps and deadfalls, all of them well hidden, except for this one corridor, which pulses with magnetism."

"Which means what?" Schwarz demanded impatiently. Then he smiled. "Which means that is the escape route. The pulse is not the bait in a trap, but a beacon to show Duvall the way out in case he was confused or wounded."

"The pulse still there?" Lyons demanded brusquely, the puddle of gasoline creeping into view around the curve in the corridor.

Schwarz checked his compass. "No, it's gone."

"Which means we missed Duvall by only a few moments," Blancanales added grimly.

"Then move with a purpose, people!" Lyons ordered, starting along the corridor at a full run.

Filled with a sense of impending disaster, the men of Able Team double-timed it along the long corridor, Lyons and Blancanales watching intently for laser beams, while Schwarz kept an eye open for old-fashioned trip wire. If the metal was the right temperature, it would be invisible to both infrared and ultraviolet.

Flickering in the darkness in front of them, there appeared a bright red dot that began to move upward, then arched slightly until starting down again, accompanied with the occasional spray of bright orange sparks.

"Somebody is using a welding torch!" Lyons cursed into his throat mike.

"Yeah, but sealing us out or trying to get in?" Blancanales asked, then remembered that Carl could not hear him over the radio anymore.

"Doesn't matter," Schwarz said out loud. "Either way is trouble."

With no choice, Lyons cracked open a chemical stick and flung it ahead of the team. It hit the floor and rolled, casting a weird blue nimbus until reaching a riveted steel wall. There was a submarine hatch set into the barrier, the wheel lock set in the middle of the veined oval. The glowing red light was now clearly coming from a welding torch moving along the other side of the airtight hatch, welding it permanently closed.

"The colder that weld gets, the stronger it is," Blancanales stated, swinging up his M-203 assault rifle.

"On my mark," Schwarz added, doing the same with his Barrett assault rifle. "One...two...mark!"

Still running at full speed, the two men fired in unison, the double thump of their 40 mm grenade launchers almost sounding like the beat of a human heart. Then the Stony Man operatives dived to the floor a split second before the high-explosive shells hit the wall on either side of the hatchway and detonated. The combined blast shook the whole expanse of the wall, rivets popping out like machine-gun fire and ricocheting wildly off the walls, floor and ceiling. Schwarz gave a snort as something shot through his hair, painfully yanking off his gas mask. A rivet had narrowly missed punching a hole in his forehead by a hair. Literally.

A muffled scream came from the other side of the wall, and the red dot of the welding torch vanished, then a section of wall near the floor began to slowly turn orange, then yellow as the dropped torch began to eat its way through the new location. Then the flame winked out.

Rushing forward, Lyons slapped a wad of C-4 onto the spot, then quickly stabbed a timing pencil into the melting high explosive and snapped it off at the lowest mark. The team got clear and the C-4 exploded, blowing through the weakened section of the wall. There immediately followed a secondary blast as the welding tanks ruptured, and more of the riveted plates dented outward as men screamed into oblivion.

Examining the weakened barrier, Blancanales chose a section with the most number of rivets missing and carefully arranged two wads of C-4, and added two more from Schwarz.

"That's all we got," Schwarz reminded grimly. "So don't screw the pooch."

"Have I ever?" Blancanales answered, inserting radio detonators and reaching for his belt only to find air.

"No comment," Schwarz said with a straight face, lifting his detonator and setting it to the other man's frequency. Any team member could set off the explosives of another man, just in case of a situation like this, or worse, if they were being tortured and the only recourse was the sweet mercy of a swift death.

Scrambling away once more, the men covered their ears and opened their mouths, and Schwarz bit the button. The entire wall seemed to jump from the stentorian force of the shaped charges. More rivets burst loose, and this time a small section of the barrier came free to land on the floor in a ringing crash.

Instantly the three men fired their weapons into the opening, the muzzle-flashes strobing in the darkness. But there came no answering cries of pain. Cracking another light stick, Lyons tossed it through the sagging gap in the battered wall, then warily proceeded to step through the irregular opening, the deadly barrel of the Atchisson leading the way.

On the other side of the dented wall were the bedraggled bodies of several men lying on the littered floor, the tattered condition of their uniforms showing that they had been wearing Level One body armor, the material woefully inadequate to the task of withstanding the fiery blast of the welding tanks. One man was reduced to only a welding mask and gloves, connected together with a charred skeleton, the rest of him minced into hamburger and blown away from the hellish detonation.

Being careful not to step in front of the light stick and make himself a silhouette, Lyons scanned the darkness ahead, but even under magnification he could not see very far. The blackness was near absolute. As Blancanales and Schwarz came through the wall, Lyons cracked a few more sticks and threw them as far as he could. They bounced along the floor and finally came to rest, the blue light slowly growing until Lyons could now dimly see a U.S. Army Hummer parked nearby.

However, his elation was soon eclipsed by the fact that all of the tires were flat, and a thick, reddish fluid was dribbling from underneath the vehicle as if it had been gut shot.

"Shrapnel damage," Schwarz muttered hatefully, cracking another stick and heaving it inside the Hummer. As the light grew, a headless body became discernible behind the wheel.

Rushing forward, Blancanales checked the hands before anything else, then cursed. "It's not Duvall," he reported. "This man has got lots of calluses, and all in the right places for a soldier, trigger finger, edge of palm and the like."

"The man had his own private army," Schwarz muttered, checking the bloody pockets of another corpse. "So why did he need Foxfire?"

"Deniability," Lyons answered, patting down another body for the computer disk. The flesh was still warm, but he forced himself to ignore that. "Rich men always think they can weasel out of jail time, as if having money makes them beyond the law."

"There's often more justice found in fifty cents' worth of hot lead than in a million dollars' worth of judges and lawyers," Blancanales said in a singsong voice that meant he was quoting somebody.

"Amen to that, brother," Schwarz said, wiping his sticky hands clean on a pants leg. "All right, there's nothing here. Any sign of the disk?"

"Unfortunately, no," Lyons asked, taking the radio from the belt holster of a dead man. It was a Kenwood 400 megahertz portable radio, code locked and useless. With an alphanumeric keypad, the combination possibilities reached into the millions. Impossible to solve in the field even by Schwarz and his laptop.

Turning the volume to its lowest setting, Lyons stuffed the military transponder into a pocket to monitor any traffic. Even if he could not understand what was being said, a trained ear could tell a lot just from the tones of voices in a conversation.

"Same here," Blancanales said in disgust, fingering some of the loose wiring dangling from the smashed front of the complex radio set into the dashboard column.

Unexpectedly, there came the smell of gasoline once more, and the man frantically looked over the Hummer. But the fuel tanks and spare gas can strapped to the rear were undamaged; there was only transmission fluid on the floor underneath.

"Time to go," Blancanales announced when a pair of headlights speared through the darkness and there came the sound of a revving engine. It was another Hummer.

"A backup squad," Lyons said in grim satisfaction. "Take 'em alive."

Moving behind the broken Hummer, the Stony Man operatives quickly changed magazines in their weapons and crouched low, waiting for the other men to get into range.

However, the Hummer slammed on the brakes and fishtailed widely, executing a fast circle, and then charging off again back up the tunnel. Instantly the Stony Man team opened fire, then Lyons paused as he heard something sliding along the floor. A split second later a U.S. Army satchel charge was illuminated by the blue glow of the chemical sticks. Cold adrenaline flooded the man at the sight, and he exploded into action.

Dropping the heavy Atchisson, the former policeman made for the satchel charge, expecting violent disintegration at every passing second. Grabbing the canvas shoulder strap, he raced back to the iron wall and flung it as hard as possible through the ragged opening. Then without pausing, Lyons sprinted away from the breach and headed up the tunnel, running for his life along the wall. The fact that he had been able to get it through the breach was tantamount to a miracle. Or a colossal blunder. Clearly the person in the Hummer had been more interested in making sure they were not personally hurt by the explosion than in neutralizing the enemy. That was the sort of mistake a rank beginner made....

In a flash of comprehension, Lyons knew that it must have been Brandon Duvall himself in the speeding vehicle. The disk had only been yards away. But there was nothing he could do about that at the moment. Right now, everything depended upon how far away from the already weakened wall that his team could possibly get in the scant few seconds remaining to them before—

The entire universe seemed to violently explode into flame, pain and chaos, and Lyons was slammed off the ground and sent helplessly flying into the stygian darkness....

CHAPTER FOURTEEN

International Waters, South China Sea

The torrential rainstorm was over as fast as it had arrived, and now the surface of the vast and limitless ocean was smooth and calm. There were no islands in sight, and not a cloud in the sky, just the deep blue of the water merging to the lighter blue of the heavens until a man was not really sure where one ended and the other began. For the moment the ocean with its many moods was serenely at peace.

Aside from the goddamn Chinese war fleet, the captain mentally cursed, minutely adjusting the focus on the computerized monocular.

Standing at the port-side window on the bridge of *Admiral Kuznetsov,* Captain Yuri Alexander studiously watched the Chinese ships moving less than a mile away. Ever since the incident at Mystery Mountain, the two nations had been preparing, almost eagerly, for direct conflict, and when the two task forces passed within a thousand miles of each other, they had both immediately changed course to steam in closer, almost at combat range. Just in case.

The captain snorted. But then, as the old saying goes, the bottom of the ocean was filled with fools who had never said the words, "just in case." All that was needed was a reason to open fire. Personally, the naval officer was only afraid that some damn fool would give them one and start a war that surely would end in the mutual destruction of both countries.

The Chinese fleet was almost a mirror image of his own. They had a single aircraft carrier, *Varyag,* two hulking destroyers, *Kee Lung* and *Ma Kong,* and at least one escort submarine, name and type unknown. Meanwhile, the Russians had the much larger carrier *Kuznetsov,* the two corvettes *Soobrazitelay* and *Boiky,* and a Delta II class nuclear attack submarine, the infamous *Novomoshovsk.*

Sweeping the aft deck of the enemy carrier, Captain Alexander knew that the Chinese ships were older than the sleek new Russian vessels, but they were spotlessly clean and, according to the Kremlin, the Chinese vessels were equipped with the very latest electronics, communications and target acquisition systems. Their 20 mm CIWS antirocket guns were every bit as good as the Russian 30 mm CIWS ARG. If the task forces were head-to-head in direct combat, the results would be spectacular and feed the fish of the South Pacific for a hundred miles. It would be a bloodbath.

"Radar! Any movement by the Chinese?" the captain bellowed across the bridge.

There was an intercom only inches away from the man, and a hand mike clipped to the ceiling, but the captain liked to keep his throat in shape in case all of the technology failed and he needed to stride the deck shouting orders while cannons thundered to the left and guns boomed to the right.

"Nothing suspicious, sir," the sailor reported crisply, his full attention glued to the glowing screen. "Their carrier hauled a couple of their SU-33 Flanker jet fighters onto the deck a few minutes ago, but they're not ready to launch."

Just preparing in case the word comes down, Captain Alexander noted privately, taking his command chair. Or the balloon goes up, and we fire first. Briefly he wondered where the balloon analogy came from. The American Civil War or was it French?

"Sir, we have a blip coming our way!" the sailor announced, a little louder than he meant to.

"From the Chinese?" the captain asked, lurching back out of the chair and returning to the window.

"No, sir, it's a civilian aircraft. A Cessna. No weapons—they're not even built to carry them."

"Good. Satcom, tell them to steer clear of the two fleets," Captain Alexander ordered, staying at the window.

"I think they've already been so informed, skipper," the boson replied, touching his earphones. "They're flying smack down the middle of the alley, maintaining equal distance between both formations."

"Personally, I would have gone around," the sailor at the helm said, one hand resting with artificial casualness on the computerized joystick. "But perhaps they're low on fuel."

Suddenly the tiny plane dipped down to the water, almost touching the waves, and something bright yellow fell out the side hatch. Instantly, the Cessna swung back up into the sky and noticeably increased speed.

"Did they just dump their garbage?" Captain Alexander demanded, arching an eyebrow.

"No way to tell, sir," replied the sailor at the radar console. "I can't see that low."

"Any movement on sonar?" the captain asked, his heart quickening slightly. It would be just like the sneaky Chinese to hire a civilian plane to drop a torpedo into the water to try to get a first strike on the bigger, more heavily armored Russian vessels.

"Nothing hot in the soup," the sailor answered, her eyes half closed as she concentrated on the nonstop pinging in her headphones. To others, it was just noise, but to her it was a detailed picture of the world below. "Aside from some dolphins, our Delta III and that underwater Chinese junk."

Everybody chuckled at the insult, and the brief moment of tension faded away.

"They might be drug smugglers who got frightened when they saw the fleets, sir," the lieutenant at the navigation table suggested. "We could send up a couple of Helix gunships to pursue and force them down." He smiled. "A little show of force for our squinty friends."

"A pleasant enough idea, but a waste of fuel," Captain Alexander decided, taking down the monocular again. "Let them go. And have the galley send up somebody to refill the samovar! How is a man to think without caffeine in his blood, eh?"

"Right away, sir." A sailor smiled, but then the man blinked in surprise as the tiny bobbing object in the water suddenly exploded into flame. What the fuck?

As the tattered remains of the inflatable raft blew away, a white sphere rose above the turbulent water sitting on top of four thick columns of scintillating fire.

"Those are JATO units," the sailor at the radar announced, confusion in his voice. "I can't tell what it is they're supporting, some sort of ball, or sphere... No, those sides are flat, almost like a—"

"Decahedron!" Captain Alexander gasped, dropping the monocular. It was a thermobaric bomb. "Red alert! Aft guns, fire at that sphere. Forward battery, launch everything at that cursed plane. Helm, full speed to starboard. Sonar, tell the Novomoskovsk to crash dive. Security, seal the fleet for an NBC attack. I want these boats airtight in thirty seconds!"

Instantly everybody surged into action, relaying the commands and operating the shipboard controls with lightning speed. The big 100 mm cannons on the corvettes roared into operation, and a flurry of Gauntlet missiles rushed skyward.

But a split second later the lofting T-bomb reached operational height and detonated, the volcanic shockwave reaching out to engulf both fleets in a maelstrom of fiery destruction.

Less than a heartbeat later, a spiraling swarm of Russian and Chinese missiles slammed into the Cessna from a dozen different directions, the overlapping explosions completely obliterating the unarmed aircraft and the two Slovakian terrorists inside. When the tiny pieces of charred wreckage sprinkled down to the choppy waves, there was nobody left above the surface to witness the event.

However, deep below the boiling surface, the two nuclear submarines were now circling each other on a definitive hunt-and-kill pattern, the grim captains impatiently waiting for the skyfire to die away so that they could radio the high command for permission to unleash their nuclear arsenal.

Saris Castle, Slovakia

TWENTY SOLDIERS SAT around the big wooden table, noisily eating canned stew out of tin mess plates. The table was covered with sliced loaves of bread, bowls of apples, bottles of water and a large wheel of peppered goat cheese. Automatic rifles hung from the back of every chair, and a stone wall rack designed for sixteenth-century pikes now carried a wide assortment of Soviet weaponry, pistols, grenades, shotguns and even a bulky rocket launcher.

An open stone fireplace crackled with a large fire that sent welcome waves of warmth, and perched precariously on a board set between two chairs, a television blared with a soccer match between Denmark and Spain.

"That should have been Slovakia," a bearded soldier said around a mouthful of bread. "We are much better footballers than those stupid Spanish clowns."

"Ever see American football?" a skinny soldier asked, sipping a cup of steaming tea.

Outside the narrow windows designed to fire arrows down at invaders, snowy mountains rose and fell like waves on a stormy sea, and a bitterly cold wind blew against the double panes of insulated glass.

The bearded man cut off a chunk of the cheese as if it was a cake. "No. Why?"

"It is a much more interesting game. More violent, anyway. They use hands and feet, and break each other's bones on a regular basis."

"Now that sounds like fun," another soldier muttered, pushing away his plate and starting to pick his teeth clean with a thumbnail. "Rugby is okay, but with all the mud, I can never keep track of which team a player is on!"

The men all laughed at that, then paused as the picture on the television crackled and bizarrely changed into a scene of two naked women having wild sex.

"What in the world...?" one of the men began, then guffawed loudly. "The dish must have shifted and we're picking up a signal from Germany."

On the screen a leather whip cracked and the blonde begged for mercy from the statuesque redhead. It was given, but with conditions.

"How do you know this is German?" a dour-faced private asked, staring intently at the incredible display of flesh.

The other man shrugged. "Who else would be so decadent?"

"Right, there are no lesbians in Slovakia," another man chided. "Only German women do that."

The whip cracked several more times, the noise almost palpable in the crowded room.

"And some French," the man sniffed.

"Never been to Prague, have you?" a short private added with a knowing wink. "You wouldn't believe the stories I could tell."

"You're right," the bald man retorted, intently watching the screen. "We wouldn't believe them."

There was the loud crash in the fireplace of a log breaking in two. None of the soldiers paid the event any attention until it happened again just a second later, and something came out of the blazing hearth to roll across the makeshift dining room and stop directly in front of the old television. The Slovakians had less than a moment to register the presence of the grenade before both of the military spheres cut loose. The combined explosion of C-4 and willie peter filled the room to overflowing, chunks of men and furniture blowing out the tiny window slits and ripping apart through the oak door like a demonic shotgun blast.

The noise echoed throughout the entire castle, and a fire alarm began to dully ring.

STANDING AT AN ANGLE on the sloped roof of the ancient keep, Phoenix Force held tightly on to nylon ropes firmly anchored to the grooved stones. In the distance, a C-130 Hercules banked into the clouds, and their abandoned parachutes fluttered away on the icy wind to vanish into the snowy mountains.

"The room is clear," James reported, reeling in the miniature video camera hanging off the roof and suspended just outside the window of the ward room. "Everybody is dead."

"Not everybody," Hawkins answered over his throat mike, glancing down at the courtyard. Armed men were running around waving their hands and scrambling into various vehicles. None of the old Soviet trucks was armed, the same with the multitread "mudders," which were basically just a tank without a cannon and room for cargo. However, several of the BRDM amphibious scout cars were equipped with 12.7 mm heavy machine guns, and those could be real trouble. Especially if these renegade Slovakian soldiers knew how to shoot.

"Big Ben to Rock House," McCarter said, touching the transceiver on his belt. "Thanks for the diversion. Going silent. Will radio again when we have rabbit stew."

"Confirm," Price replied crisply. "Good hunting. Rock House over and out." With that, the radio went silent.

"Once more into the breach, dear friends." Encizo eased his grip on the rope and let his boots slide along the roof until he dropped off the edge.

The rest of Phoenix Force followed suit and, rappelling down the side of the castle, the men were immediately buffeted by the strong winds. Unable to descend on a straight course, the team scrambled along the rough stonework, their combat boots barely able to find purchase on the mossy blocks. Hawkins almost lost his grip when he accidentally disturbed a nest of falcons tucked deep into a crack, tufts of asbestos insulation puffing out. Cinching the rope tighter around his waist, he ignored the squawking birds and kept going.

Each man was equipped with a piton gun on his belt, but firing one of the steel pegs into the stonework would be easily heard inside the castle, even over the growing alarm. Hanging outside like this, the team would be easy pickings for anybody with a rifle. They had to get inside, fast and silent. End of discussion.

Walking around the exterior of the keep, Phoenix Force headed for the outer wall of the castle. That offered easy access to the tower, and the stonework would give them some protection from snipers. Not much, but every little bit helped in a blitzkrieg.

The sound of revving engines could be dimly heard coming from the courtyard by the time McCarter was at the end of his rope and dropped the last few feet to land in a crouch on top of the wide wall. Swinging around his MP-5 subgun, he crouched low and started forward at a full run, the silenced muzzle of the deadly weapon constantly sweeping for targets.

The castellated stonework gave him brief glimpses of the courtyard below, and he frowned. Some of the soldiers were yanking the canvas cover off a large truck to reveal a 20 mm antiaircraft cannon. The rounds probably could not penetrate the ancient granite of the castle, but the shrapnel would chew the team into bloody hamburger.

Never slowing for a moment, McCarter sharply whistled and pointed to the right.

Stopping, Manning pulled a fat plastic tube from his backpack. Removing the arming pin, he extended the tube to its full length, then he openly stood, sweeping the vehicles in the courtyard below, searching for the cannon.

Shouting loudly in a foreign language, a soldier pointed up at the man on the wall, and several of the Slovakians began working the arming bolts on their AK-47 assault rifles.

Rapidly adjusting for wind and range, Manning placed the crosshairs on the 20 mm cannon and pressed the red button on top of the tube.

Smoke and flame vomited from both ends of the LAW rocket launcher, and as soon the 66 mm projectile was clear, Manning tossed away the useless tube and started running again. A few seconds later there came a thunderous blast from the courtyard, and chunks of the destroyed cannon actually rose high enough to be seen over the wall before tumbling back down again out of sight.

The wall ended at the tower, the structure rising an additional ten stories above the walkway. The door of the tower was made of thick oak beams bound by iron straps wider than a hand. A formidable barrier for the Middle Ages, but not even a hindrance for the twenty-first-century warriors.

Slamming small wads of C-4 onto the lock and both hinges, McCarter backed away and used the radio detonator on his belt. The blast boomed louder than artillery, and the door broke apart, sending out a death cloud of splinters and bent iron nails. James grunted as something punched into his stomach, but he did not fall. Reaching down, the man found the disfigured lock embedded between the ceramic plates of his body armor, the iron compressed badly out of shape. Striking the thing with the folded stock of his MP-5, James got it free and kicked the lock aside. Damn, that had been close.

Sweeping into the tower, McCarter and Hawkins took the point, one man advancing while the other kept him covered, then they switched, and did it again. The rest of the team covered their six, listening intently for the sounds of boots on the old stone stairs.

Reaching the top of the stairwell, McCarter was already starting to suspect the truth. The hallway was empty, aside from a wooden table and a chair tucked neatly underneath. The kerosene lantern in the wall niche was cold and dark.

Going to the middle door, McCarter listened for any movement on the other side, then tried the wrought-iron handle. It was unlocked.

Boldly stepping inside, the man cursed at the sight of the empty room. There was nothing but a bare wooden table covered with an assortment of tools and a pile of curved white metal plates.

"These are interlocking pyramids," Encizo growled, picking one up for a closer inspection. "It's the shell of a T-bomb."

"Which means either Professor Karlov finished her work or they caught her broadcast," Hawkins muttered, glancing around for any bloodstains on the floor.

"Either way, her usefulness to them is over now," James added in a graveyard voice.

Just then, the ghostly sound of a scream could be heard, the anguished cry echoing slightly.

Kneeling on the floor, Manning moved aside some old rags to uncover a drainage pipe. The cry came again, softer this time, followed by hard laughter.

"Where does this lead?" the man demanded, his guts tightening. The old rags were actually a set of antique surgical garb. They had been sliced into pieces and were dotted with red blood. The soldiers had stripped the professor naked before taking her away. That was an old interrogation technique to break the prisoner's spirit before... Well, the possibilities were endless, and none of them bode well for the Czech scientist.

Checking a PDA, McCarter worked the miniature controls with his thumbs to access the historical floorplans. The Slovakians may have done some modifications to the castle, but shifting medieval plumbing was a bigger job than they would have undertaken.

"The pipe goes directly to...the dungeon." The man snarled, tucking the PDA away again. "Double time. We must have Karlov alive."

Surging into action, Phoenix Force raced from the workshop, and charged back down the stairs. Almost immediately, they encountered a group of Slovakians heading up the stairs at a full run. Everybody went for their weapons. But expecting trouble, Phoenix Force got off the first salvo, and the Slovakians tumbled away, torn into pieces from the concentrated hail of 9 mm hardball ammo.

Passing the open doorway leading to the walkway on top of the wall, Encizo paused to slap a Claymore mine alongside the opening, stretched out a trip wire and yanked the arming pin.

Nearing the main courtyard, McCarter lifted a closed fist and the rest of the team stopped, straining to hear anything. Soft voices were whispering to each other, but unfortunately none of the team spoke Slovakian.

Using an elbow, James nudged Hawkins, but the man could only shrug. He knew some Russian, and it was similar to the local mountain dialect, but not enough for him to guess the details of the conversation.

Taking out a grenade, McCarter checked to make sure the tape was securely in place around the arming lever, then lofted the military sphere over the railing. It landed with a clatter, and startled men cursed and snarled, several of them firing weapons for no sane reason.

Pointing their subguns over the railing, the Stony Man operatives opened fire, cutting down the soldiers from above. The renegades jerked about like mad puppets and died on the spot.

Continuing along the stairs to the ground level, McCarter served as the anchor while Hawkins took the point. He moved through the oozing corpses fast and low, ready for anything. Then he dived forward as the hand of a dead man slowly began to open, revealing a clenched grenade. Wrapping both of his hands around the other man's fist, Hawkins squeezed tight, feeling the arming lever click back into position.

"Live apple," Hawkins reported.

Hurrying closer, Manning searched the dead man for the pin, but it was not to be found anywhere.

"Use the pin from one of our grenades," Encizo said, closely watching the exit door. From the other side, he could hear troops running around, the loud crackle of the burning antiaircraft truck. One wrong move on the part of the team, and a hundred armed men would come pouring in. Or simply open fire with the machine gun on the scout car.

"Can't. It won't fit," Hawkins answered, the knuckles on his hands white. "This is a pineapple from World War II."

Going to another corpse, McCarter found another ancient grenade and quickly unscrewed the top to pour out the contents of black powder. Manufactured by the millions, the grenades had been made as fast and as cheaply as possible. Yanking out the magnesium primer from the exposed bottom, he cast it away, then pulled the pin and tossed it over. Manning made the catch and slid it neatly into the hole of the live grenade.

As it clicked into place, Hawkins exhaled deeply and released his grip. "That was fun," he muttered, flexing some fingers. Just then, there came a loud snap as the top of the disassembled pineapple across the room tried to ignite the primer and explode.

"Calvin, Rafe, make a jack-in-the-box," McCarter ordered, starting down the stairs once more. "Everybody else, with me."

As the three men descended rapidly into the bowels of the castle, James and Encizo shifted the corpses to make a pile in front of the exit door, then took all of their grenades and yanked out the pins before stuffing them under the bottom body. If the other Slovakian troops forced their way into the tower, the first wave would be annihilated, and give Phoenix Force a much needed warning that trouble was on the way. On impulse, Encizo added a modern-day Claymore.

"Just in case." He smiled.

Already heading after the others, James nodded in approval. There were few problems in life that could not be solved with the adroit application of high explosives.

Reaching the bottom level of the tower, McCarter swung around his Nighthunter goggles, and clicked on the UV light attached under the barrel of the MP-5. The ultraviolet light was invisible to the naked eye, but through the goggles the dungeon was clearly illuminated, although everything was in shades of black and white.

The dungeon was of classic design, an iron gate blocking access to the stairs, and beyond that wooden doors lined a long corridor. Almost immediately, the men saw more strips of cloth on the cold stone floor, panties this time, and a pair of slippers.

No urging was needed for the team to spread out fast and check every cell door, listening for any sign of activity. Halfway down the corridor, McCarter abruptly stopped at the sound of flesh smacking flesh, punctuated by soft grunts.

Snapping his fingers for the attention of the team, Mc-Carter then pointed at the door and splayed his open hand indicating five men were inside, then he moved his thumb sideways across his throat.

Nodding in comprehension, the team got ready as Mc-Carter got a tiny spray can of WD-40 from his web belt, and squirted some on the hinges before gently pushing on the door.

Silently it swung aside.

CHAPTER FIFTEEN

Little Rock, Arkansas

Hissing steam from under the hood and leaking oil, the Hummer lumbered out of the mouth of the tunnel and started sluggishly moving along the muddy black bank of the Arkansas River.

"Everybody out!" Brandon Duvall commanded, hopping to the ground. "We can make better time on foot than in this pile of horse crap."

"Where to, sir?" a guard asked, hefting an M-203. The bandolier across his body armor was full of 40 mm shells for the grenade launcher, but the ammo pouch on his web belt normally used for magazines for the M-16 was ripped and empty. However, riding in a shoulder holster was a Glock 18 with two spare clips of 32 rounds.

Behind him, the last few remaining members of the house security staff stood ready, one of them armed with a Neostad shotgun, and the other with an X-218 electric Gatling gun. These were the so-called Holy Trio, the personal bodyguards for the Southern billionaire.

"There," Duvall stated, pointing downriver.

In the valley below the hillock, the old Southern town of Little Rock covered quite a lot of land, but none of the stores or office buildings was more than a few stories tall. Dominating the downtown, however, were two sparkling skyscrapers that rose above the city like a pair of glass hands praying to Heaven.

"Brilliant." Russell grinned, slinging a slim laptop computer over a shoulder. "Let's go change the world."

Touching the Glock, the chief bodyguard asked Duvall a silent question, but the billionaire shook his head. For the moment he still needed the hacker. However, afterward…

SEVERAL MINUTES LATER, a second Hummer noisily thumped out of the tunnel, the four flat tires making a hellishly loud racket on the concrete floor. The men of Able Team were riding inside, with Blancanales at the wheel, and Schwarz quickly wrapping a sling around the broken arm of Lyons. His brief stint of parachute training for the Farm had saved his life, teaching the former policeman to tuck and roll and ride out the shock wave of the explosion. Unfortunately he had slammed into the wall, and awoke minutes later as Schwarz snapped his dislocated left arm back into place. However, the right was broken in at least two places. The military painkillers had numbed the arm, and the sling kept it out of the way, but Lyons was reduced to only using his left arm until further notice.

"Whack me," Lyons grunted. "Do it, Gadgets, I gotta stay sharp."

Frowning, Schwarz started to raise an objection, then reluctantly agreed and injected the man with a NATO "Hot Shot." Almost instantly, new strength flowed into Lyons and his heart began pounding savagely in his chest.

"If you start having a nose bleed, then bite down on this," Schwarz said, tucking a capsule into the shirt pocket of the man. "Then go lay down, because you will hit the floor about ten seconds later and faster than a starlet on audition night."

Lyons buttoned the pocket closed.

Just then, another Hummer came into view along the river bank.

"Found 'em!" Blancanales announced, downshifting the rumbling transmission, the gears horribly grinding.

Readying their weapons, the team scanned the area. Birds chirped merrily in some willow trees and a fat rabbit thumped the ground to warn others of his kind about the invaders. But aside from the wildlife, there was nobody else in sight.

Leaving their Hummer, the team approached the abandoned vehicle, wary of more traps. However, it proved to be clean, and five sets of footprints led away from the water and into a nearby forest. Three pairs of combat boots, one pair of shoes and another of sneakers. Those had to be the bodyguards, Duvall, and his pet hacker.

"If they're on foot, then they can't be very far away," Lyons said, stepping carefully from the vehicle. He felt preternaturally strong and also light as a feather. His right arm throbbed, but there was no pain, only a mild discomfort. Lifting the Atchisson, he paused, then merely slung it over a shoulder, and clumsily drew the Colt Python with his left hand, working the slide by pulling it against his belt.

"How about that?" Blancanales asked, pointing with his assault rifle.

Across the river was the city of Little Rock, and at the bottom of the hill was a boathouse, bearing the private seal of Duvall.

"Think the forest is a feint?" Schwarz asked, hefting the Barrett. "What else is in the area?"

"Lots of things," Lyons replied in annoyance. "It all depends on what the madman plans to do now."

"Escape would be logical, but I don't read him as a runner."

"The son of a bitch owns most of the state. He could be anywhere."

"Talk walking," Lyons directed, advancing into the trees.

But as the shadows enveloped the team, there came the thunderous roar of a powerful engine, and an airboat full of men came streaking out of the bushes, missing Blancanales by only inches.

As the airboat skimmed across the ground, the men inside unleashed a barrage of hot lead at the team. Schwarz raised his Barrett and a shotgun blast slammed him aside, the flurry of 6.8 mm rounds stitching across the treetops to no effect whatsoever.

Hit in the sling, Lyons ignored the bleeding wound in his numb arm, and slowly raised the Python, held his breath and fired a fast five times. Clutching their throats, two of the bodyguards fell out of the airboat just as it reached the river. They fell into the murky water, as the craft zoomed across the surface, and then back on to dry land and plowed through a decorative hedge to disappear into downtown Little Rock.

Saris Castle, Slovakia

INSIDE THE CELL of the dungeon, a naked blond woman was bent over a table, her mouth stuffed full of dirty rags. A bearded man in a military uniform stood behind her with his pants around his ankles, thrusting between her bruised legs. Four other men stood around the table, laughing and smoking cigarettes, AK-47 assault rifles resting on their shoulders.

"Hey," McCarter whispered.

As the soldiers turned in surprise, Phoenix Force opened fire, their silenced weapons chugging steadily. The 9 mm rounds slammed the renegades up against the stone wall, red life pumping from the gaping wounds.

Pulling himself free from the woman, the rapist tried to grab the automatic pistol in his fallen pants. Ruthlessly, Mc-

Carter shot the man twice in the face, the hollowpoint 9 mm bone-shredders cutting off his shriek of pain and plowing out the back of his head in a grisly explosion.

Looking up from the table, the woman scowled at the newcomers, then stared in disbelief as McCarter shrugged off his backpack and yanked out a military jacket.

"We will not hurt you," he said.

Breathing heavily, the woman gave no indication that she understood as James knelt and gently eased the dirty rags from her mouth.

Hawking loudly, she spit hard to clear her throat. "Are you...are you from Arkansas?" Professor Karlov asked in perfect English, the words mumbled slightly from a split lip.

Knowing a lie would be the fastest way to earn her cooperation, McCarter nodded. "Yes, ma'am, we were sent by Mr. Duvall to get you out of here."

"Thank God," the professor whispered, a ragged sob catching in her throat, then she went limp.

"Damn, she's out cold," James reported, checking the pulse in her throat.

Fuming impatiently, McCarter debated rousing the woman with drugs or letting her rest while they tried to get out of the castle. Lifting his goggles to talk to her directly, McCarter saw that her skin was covered with red welts from a recent beating with a whip or possibly a leather belt. Suddenly, McCarter was sorry that he had killed the other men so fast.

"Let her sleep," he directed. "James, get her dressed and into that spare body armor."

Pulling a knife, Encizo started cutting the ropes around her wrists, while James began on her ankles. Standing in the open doorway, Manning intently watched for any movements on the stairs, while Hawkins went to check the rest of the cells.

As the bonds were removed, McCarter could see the bruises on her face, and that several teeth were missing. The men were impressed. The Slovakians held her body captive, but she had never surrendered.

"One tough lady," McCarter noted, preparing a syringe of antibiotics and painkillers, and injecting it directly into her neck.

"Bastards," James corrected, his face flushing with barely repressed anger.

When they were finished, the men put bandages on the welts, dressed the unconscious woman in a military jumpsuit and sneakers, then laced on some lightweight body armor. Sliding on a woolen ski mask, the professor now appeared to just be another member of the team, a far less important target to the Slovakian renegades than an escaping prisoner who knew all of their secrets.

Suddenly there came some soft chugs from outside the cell, and everybody brought up their weapons, McCarter and James stepping in front of Karlov as protection. The team relaxed as Hawkins stepped into view.

"Five more of these assholes were sleeping in another cell down the corridor," he said, a thin trail of smoke coming from the silencer on the machine gun. "Don't think they'll wake up anytime soon."

"Any other prisoners?" McCarter asked.

The man hesitated. "Not live ones, no."

The brief pause told the rest of the team more than they wanted to know.

"All right, let's get moving," McCarter directed. "Hawk and I are on point. Gary, carry the professor. Calvin and Rafe—"

"David," Hawkins interrupted. "I've already checked cell nineteen. It's been filled with cement."

That stopped the Briton cold. According to the floor plans that Kurtzman had unearthed, cell nineteen was located over sewer drains for the castle, which in turn led to the Black Tree River. Hidden in the bushes along the southern bank, Jack Grimaldi would be waiting for them in a hovercraft, ready to whisk the team back to the Hercules parked safely twenty miles away.

"Filled?"

"To the ceiling."

"Are you sure?" Encizo asked hopefully. "UV light can cast weird shadows, make a seventeen, or an eighteen, look like another number."

The Texan shook his head. "Sorry, but I checked with my halogen flashlight. Our escape route has been blocked by several tons of cement. I guess these boys knew about the chink in their defenses, and fixed it a long time ago. Years, maybe, but definitely long before the attack on Mystery Mountain."

"No choice, then," McCarter stated, removing the silencer from his weapon. The acoustic device only reduced the muzzle pressure by a few pounds, but in a fight, that could make all the difference. "Wake her up, Cal."

Way ahead of the man, James already had extracted a NATO Hot Shot from his small medical kit. The disposable syringe contained a combination of stimulants guaranteed to get a wounded soldier back on his feet for a few vital minutes, before collapsing unconscious for days.

Injecting the professor in the arm, James tossed away the syringe and rolled up the ski mask just as she sharply inhaled, her eyes snapping open.

"Professor Karlov," McCarter said, then shouted, "Ines Karlov!"

"Yes! What? Huh?" The pale woman was a little groggy, exhausted from her ordeal, but clarity was returning with every beat of her heart. "Why...are we still here? Is there trouble?" Her cheeks flushed with color.

Now, that was more like it. "Yes, ma'am," McCarter stated. "Our escape route has become compromised, and now we have to smash our way out."

"With me as your human shield." She did not say it as a question.

"No, Professor, these men would happily shoot you dead. Once you cracked the secret of the thermobaric bomb, you became a liability instead of an asset." The man handed her his MP-5. "But we need you wide awake and running."

Awkwardly, she took the weapon, testing the weight in her hands. The team took that as a good sign. Obviously she knew something about guns.

"I was trained on a Kalashnikov," Karlov said, offering the weapon back to the man. "Give me one from the dead guards. I can help fight." The missing teeth slurred her words slightly, and the mixture of painkillers and the Hot Shot were giving her a rollercoaster of a headache, but the tough little Czech was grimly determined to do her part. These strangers had saved her life. Honor demanded that she do nothing less for them.

"Five men armed with MP-5 machine guns, and the sixth carrying an AK-47 makes that person very noticeable," McCarter countered, pushing the weapon back. "I'll be using a Kalashnikov."

She understood immediately and blushed slightly, embarrassed that this stranger would assume such a risk. "Then perhaps I should fire only single shots," Karlov suggested, running her hands over the weapon to memorize the location of the arming bolt and selector switch.

"To make it appear that you're low on ammunition, and thus low priority," Encizo finished. "Subtle. But that's just the sort of thing a trained soldier would notice in a firefight."

"Are these men professionals?" James added, taking her wrist to unnecessarily check her pulse.

She flinched at the contact. "Yes, they were trained by the Communists to fight rebels in the hills. Only they sided with the rebels, and when the Soviets departed—"

"They seized control," McCarter concluded, taking a Kalashnikov off the floor and working the arming bolt to eject a round. Jumping free, it glittered in the air and he caught it in a fist, then inspected the brass. Thankfully, it was new ammunition, with no signs of corrosion.

"What else can you tell us about your rap...about your captors?" Manning asked, pretending the slip was natural. "Who speaks English? Who is in charge? Any idea how close are reinforcements?" Only the last question was important. The man hated manipulating a woman who had just been brutalized, but the team desperately needed to know the location of the main base of the thieves. Millions of lives were on the line, and the numbers were falling.

"I never knew how many of them were stationed here," Karlov said, experimenting with different grips. "A lieutenant commands them. He's very smart, knows electronics and speaks excellent English. His second is a sergeant who...does not seem to be quite sane. Not mad, or insane, just...I don't know, off somehow."

She hugged the MP-5 as if drawing strength from the metal of the weapon. "Don't worry about reinforcements. Their main base is many hours away at some town called Podbanske. A general and a colonel are in charge. I have no names. But that is where they have the rest of the thermobaric units." She gave a weak smile. "They wanted them very far away in case I failed or decided to take my own life."

And them along with her was the unspoken corollary, McCarter noted. It was a smart move, but not smart enough. "Is there a Podbanske on the list?" he asked urgently, retrieving additional clips from the dead men on the floor. Thankfully, the cold was helping to hold down the smell.

"Checking," Encizo muttered, running a search on his PDA. "Yes. There is a Podbanske Base two hundred miles to the south-southwest of here." Then he frowned. "Christ, it's an ICBM hardsite! If any of those are still active, these people could destroy every major capital in the world."

"And the bastards have been doing a pretty damn good job already," Hawkins stated angrily from the doorway. The noises from the courtyard were getting dimmer. Any second now, somebody would try to open the door to the tower and start the festivities.

"How do you know such a thing?" Karlov asked. "The location of abandoned Soviet missile bases is a state secret. Who...who are you?" There was real fear in her eyes now, and a finger slipped through the guard to rest on the trigger of her borrowed weapon.

Resting the wooden stock of the assault rifle on a hip, McCarter started to answer when there came some garbled speech from the encoded Kenwood radio, closely followed by a fast series of explosions from the floor above.

A fine rain of dust sprinkled down from the stone rafters of the shaking dungeon as the men of Phoenix Force surged into action. Moving as a unit, the team kept Karlov in their midst as they scrambled up the stairs. She stumbled once and dropped her weapon. But James caught the professor by the elbow and Hawkins returned the machine gun. She seemed confused by the events but nodded a curt thanks and did her best to keep up with the much larger men.

Reaching the first floor, the team found the hot air thick with swirling clouds of acrid smoke. Wreckage and bodies were scattered everywhere, and daylight streamed in through an irregular hole in the wall roughly the size of a door.

Tossing a stun grenade outside, McCarter waited until it exploded, then took the point, sweeping through the ruined doorway with his stolen AK-47 on full auto. The rest of the team was close behind, shooting at anything that moved.

Blinded by the magnesium flash of the stun grenade, the first couple of soldiers the team encountered offered little resistance and were easily neutralized. Throwing around the last of the stun grenades, Phoenix Force then added some smoke canisters and finally high-explosive antipersonnel charges. They had a hundred feet to cross against overwhelming odds and a blitzkrieg charge was their only chance of success.

As explosions rocked the courtyard, Karlov jerked at the slap of every blast, but she never stopped moving. Men wildly screamed as a truck detonated, and a burning tire came rolling out of the smoke. Frantically, she dived for cover and landed hard, the MP-5 skittering away out of sight. Cursing at the loss, she looked around and found an arm holding an AK-47. Prying open the stiff fingers, she retrieved the bloody weapon and began firing short, controlled bursts into the swirling cloud banks.

Snatching away the weapon, Hawkins shoved his MP-5 into her hands. "Hold on tighter," he snarled, emptying the Kalashnikov into a group of men coming out of a doorway. Then he dropped the assault rifle and drew his Beretta 93-R. Swinging down the forward grip of the machine pistol, Hawkins sprayed an entire clip of 9 mm Parabellum rounds at the group. Two of the soldiers dropped, their lives flowing red onto the stonework ground, but the rest managed to get behind cover, and shot back long streams of bullets, the white flashes of tracer rounds brightening the thick smoke.

"HEAT rounds," Manning cursed, beating out a small fire on his body armor.

Moving fast, Karlov ripped the bloody jacket off a corpse and used the damp garment to help the man extinguish the flames.

"Thanks," Manning said, then shoved the woman down.

Even as she fell, something moved through her hair and Manning was slammed backward from a flurry of 7.62 mm rounds. He staggered but did not fall, and fired back with his MP-5, the spray of hardball 9 mm rounds sending the renegade soldier tumbling into eternity.

Fanning his weapon across the scout car, McCarter killed the two men in the front seat, then he rushed forward to jerk open the door and yank out their twitching bodies. Getting behind the wheel, the man swore at the sight of no key in the ignition. Reaching under the dashboard, McCarter ripped out a handful of wiring and tried to hot-wire the vehicle, thankful this was an old model. Modern-day military vehicles could not be hot-wired, just in case they did fall into the hands of the enemy.

Taking cover behind the wreckage of the truck carrying the antiaircraft cannon, Manning covered Encizo while he reloaded, then James did the same for Hawkins, and everybody switched.

"Die, pigs!" Karlov snarled, stepping out into the open and firing her weapon from the hip.

Hawkins grabbed the woman around the waist and bodily threw her into the backseat of the scout car. Sputtering with rage, the professor hit the floor hard, losing her weapon once more, and suddenly she was surrounded by men again, pressing down on her from every direction. A spike of terror bubbled into her throat and she cut loose with a raw scream.

High on the wall, a Slovakian soldier wearing the shoulder tabs of a sergeant called out something in a foreign language at the feminine cry, and pointed a smoking Rex .357 Magnum revolver at the Soviet vehicle. Now all of the other soldiers scattered amid the wreckage and debris turned their attention to the scout car just as Encizo got the 12.7 mm machine gun into operation.

Spitting flame, the stuttering weapon chewed a bloody path of destruction around the courtyard, the big rounds hitting men and machines with triphammer force. Assault rifles broke into pieces before flying away, men crumpled over, windshields shattered, truck tires exploded and rock chips sprayed out from the wall. The sergeant threw back his head, blood gushing from a tattered throat, and lurched forward to plummet down into the courtyard. He landed with a crunching smack reminiscent of a dropped egg, and moved no more.

Just then the engine of the scout car roared into life, loudly backfired and died. Muttering curses, McCarter frantically worked the throttle and gas pedal, trying to find the correct balance.

Finishing the belt, Encizo immediately started to reload as the rest of Phoenix Force began mopup work with the MP-5 subguns and pistols.

A huge lieutenant yelled something incoherent as he appeared from a doorway carrying a flamethrower.

Zeroing in on the giant, the Stony Man operatives peppered him with lead, but the lumbering man did not fall, and sent back a writhing column of fiery annihilation. However, the lieutenant clearly had miscalculated the windage and the lambent flames overshot the scout car by several feet.

Once more, the engine came to life, and this time there came a grinding of gears and the scout car shifted into reverse, rapidly jouncing over the dead and the dying.

Grinning in triumph, the lieutenant sprayed the rear of the armored vehicle with the flamethrower, but the spare tire mounted on the bumper deflected the rush of flames just long enough for McCarter to slam the heavy vehicle directly into the big man. With an audible crunch of bones, the lieutenant flew backward to crash into the wall, rupturing the pressurized fuel tanks strapped to his back. Instantly, he was engulfed in flames, but the insane soldier stubbornly refused to die and somehow rose once more, reaching out with his burning hands for the hated enemy in the scout car.

Mercifully, Hawkins aimed his Beretta 93-R at the human torch, but Karlov slapped the weapon aside, the burst of 9 mm rounds missing the Slovakian by inches.

Climbing onto the bumper, the lieutenant began crawling into the car, only his teeth and eyes showing through the flames and smoke.

Furious over her actions, Hawkins started to shove her away, then changed his mind and handed her the gun. "You're better than them," he stated. "End this."

Defiantly, Karlov glared back, then nodded, and raised the gun to empty the entire clip into the chest of the walking corpse. Hammered off the car, the lieutenant fell to the ground, and impossibly tried once more to rise, before easing down to the cold stones as if falling asleep and went still.

Suddenly there came the sound of running boots along the wall, and a mob of soldiers appeared, slapping magazines into the AK-47 assault rifles. Two of the men carried Soviet RPG launchers across their backs.

"Brace yourself!" McCarter bellowed, and the scout car raced forward heading directly for the locked gate.

The soldiers on the wall sent hot lead down into the courtyard, and the men of Phoenix Force fired back, except for Encizo. Focusing his attention on the massive wooden locking bar holding the ancient gate closed, Encizo held down the trigger, riding the bucking machine gun into a tight grouping. The 12.7 mm rounds punched into the wood, sending out a maelstrom of splinters.

Hunching over the steering wheel, McCarter wasn't sure they were going to make it when the locking bar cracked apart and the scout car slammed into the gate. Steel and wood battled for supremacy for an interminable microsecond, then the gate nosily slammed aside and the scout car exploded out of the castle.

Twisting the wheel with both hands, McCarter just managed to miss a concrete tank trap set prominently in front of the gate, as the side mirror shattered from an incoming round. Fishtailing the armored vehicle, the man wildly maneuvered past several more of the squat traps before finally reaching the open road. Shifting gears, McCarter poured on the gas, and the engine roared eagerly in response, quickly leaving the ancient Slovakian castle behind in their dusty wake.

"They'll come after us," Karlov said, the empty Beretta held tight in her hands.

"Sure as hell hope so," Hawkins answered, passing her a clip of ammunition.

Not exactly sure what that meant, the professor reloaded the weapon and hunkered down in the seat, her mind whirling with the nightmarish images of combat.

A half hour later they reached the rendezvous point. The Hercules was sitting in the middle of a field, only the dim outline of the aircraft visible from the pinpoint running lights along the fuselage.

"Sky King this is Big Ben," McCarter said into his throat mike. "We're home for the holidays and have gifts. Repeat, we have a gift."

"Roger, Big Ben," Jack Grimaldi replied over the radio as the rear hatch began to cycle down to the ground. "Does the gift need wrapping? Over." Grimaldi was the chief pilot for the Farm and had personally delivered the replacement Hercules from a NATO base located outside of Prague.

"Negative, Sky King, gift is bent but not broken. Over and out," McCarter answered as the scout car jounced onto the ramp and struggled to make the steep incline.

With a surge of power it reached the main deck, and McCarter slammed on the brakes just in time to prevent repeating the earlier tactic.

With the brakes squealing in protest, the Soviet vehicle veered sharply to the left, but finally came to a full halt only inches away from the ladder to the flight deck.

Almost instantly, the ramp began to close and the huge engines revved into life.

"Alert, radar says we have guests coming," Grimaldi announced over the PA system on the landing. "I need somebody in the crapper."

Immediately, Hawkins and Manning rushed into the compartment below the ladder, peeling off in opposite directions. The middle section was the head, the lavatory for the plane. However, on either side were situated the exposed Bofors 40 mm nose cannons, often referred to as the "crappers" in crude military humor. The mighty Hercules was airtight, but the head was not, and the whole section always reeked slightly after every use.

The plane was starting to turn around as the rest of Phoenix Force rearmed from the wall cabinets and rushed to the gun ports. Only moments later, there appeared the bouncing headlights for six vehicles, size and configuration unknown.

"We're locked and loaded, Sky King," Hawkins growled over the PA system. "Just say the word."

Suddenly bright flashes of light appeared from the onrushing vehicles, and there came the sound of small-caliber rounds ricocheting off the hull. Then something large boomed, throwing out a gout of flame for yards, and a shell whistled past the airplane.

"Now would be good, guys," Grimaldi yelled calmly.

Without any preamble, the two Bofors cannons roared into operation, the streams of 40 mm shells sweeping across the racing Soviet vehicles. The night came alive with nonstop explosions as if it was raining grenades onto a minefield. Men shrieked as their lives were torn away by hot steel, and the cannon was briefly silhouetted as the stacks of ammunition in the transport ignited, the detonation spreading outward like a hellflower to engulf three other trucks full of soldiers.

Standing ready at the gun ports, the men of Phoenix Force saw the enemy convoy literally blasted off the road, the burning wrecks sent tumbling through the air to crash into the weeds. Not fully satisfied, Hawkins and Manning spent another minute shooting the mounds of fiery metal into twisted scrap, the high-explosive 40 mm shells spreading the debris for hundreds of feet.

"Again!" Professor Karlov yelled, wiping the bloody drool off her jaw. "Shoot them again."

Hearing the pain in her voice, Hawkins and Manning dutifully did as she requested, and kept firing into the night until the hoppers ran out of brass.

"That enough?" McCarter asked.

"Never be enough," the woman muttered, lowering the Beretta. "But it'll do for now." With an obvious effort of will, she forced her fingers apart, and the machine pistol fell to the deck with a clatter. "How soon can we leave this stinking valley?"

"Just as soon as you give us a destination," McCarter answered.

Confused, Karlov looked at the Briton for a long moment. Her personal goal was Prague, or London, or Timbuktu, anywhere in the world far away from here. But they should know that from the deal she had cut with the rich American, Duvall. Which logically meant that...

"CIA?" she asked.

"Something like that," McCarter answered. "Now, tell us where the rest of these sons of bitches are hiding so that we can end this tonight."

"No," Karlov replied. "Unless I can accompany you to watch them die."

McCarter frowned.

"That is the deal," Karlov snapped. "Or are you going to try to force the information? They failed. I told them nothing. Nothing! Not even when I was..." She paused to glare at the band of armed men. "Can you do worse to me than them? Can you?"

"You stay in the plane," McCarter countered, half expecting such a request. "Lives would be lost with a civilian running around during a battle. You stay in the plane, and listen over the radio. That's the deal. Take it or leave it."

Slowly Professor Karlov nodded. "Podbanske," she said, feeling a rush of power. "General Novostk and his troops are at Podbanske Missile Base in the eastern Tatra Mountains."

CHAPTER SIXTEEN

Without a pause, Able Team charged into the Arkansas River.

As the cold water rose to their chests, the men raised their weapons high overhead to try to keep them dry. The sealed ammunition would be fine, but if any floating debris got into the firing mechanism the guns might jam at a critical moment. That was a risk they could not take.

As always, Lyons was in the lead, but now with Schwarz keeping a firm grip on the man's good arm to not get lost in the dark. Without his Nighthunter visor, the river was pitch-black, the shore only dimly visible because of the bright city lights on the other side of the decorative hedge. It was a classic case of the blond leading the blind, but Schwarz kept the joke to himself.

"Rock House, this is the Senator," Blancanales said into his throat mike, wobbling slightly as his combat boots slipped on a submerged rock. "Elvis has left the building. Repeat, Elvis has left the building."

"Confirmed, Senator," Price replied crisply. "Do you need evac?"

"Negative, Rock House, we are in hot pursuit," Schwarz answered, feeling a glass bottle of some kind shatter underfoot. "But we need transport ASAP."

"Roger that, Tinker. Help is on the way. Code reference, A.H. Repeat, A.H. Do you copy?"

"Confirmed, Rock House. Code A.H., Tinker out."

Grimly clutching the Atchisson in his fist, Lyons grunted at the exchange but said nothing, concentrating on putting one boot ahead of the other and not falling over. At first, the cold helped clear some of the fog from his mind, but now it was starting to steal the strength from his legs. He had to get out of the river fast or risk getting swept away into the night.

"Rock House, this is Senator again," Blancanales added, glancing at Lyons. The man's right arm dangled limply at his side, blood trickling from the graze on his shoulder, but he still kept moving, unswayable and unstoppable. "Thought you should know that Jungle Cat has lost his ears. He can send but not receive."

There was a pause. "Copy that, Senator. Leave the mike on, and we will monitor all conversations. Ten-twenty-three?"

"Ten-four," Blancanales replied, and switched the transceiver to the new setting.

Sloshing onto the opposite shore, Able Team stomped the mud off their boots, then started toward the break in the hedges when there appeared flashing lights from the other side and a police car rolled into view.

"Hold it right there!" a voice boomed, accompanied by the telltale click-clack of a pump-action shotgun being jacked.

"Drop those weapons," a woman added, stepping from the vehicle with an enormous pistol in her grip. "And place your hands on your heads."

"Homeland Security," Lyons growled, standing perfectly still. "Identification code Archimedes Hammer."

Flanking the man, Blancanales and Schwarz did nothing, waiting to see if the street cops had received the message yet from the governor, or if they would have to take them down. Every passing second put Duvall farther away.

"Show your badges," the woman demanded.

"Don't have any of those," Blancanales replied, slowly easing a hand into his gillie suit to produce an identification booklet and flipping it open. "But we do have our shields."

"Sorry, sir, I had to ask," the first officer said, lowering the shotgun. "The mayor only contacted the chief a few minutes ago." Civilians called the metal emblem on a police officer his badge; only fellow cops called it a shield.

"What's going on, sir?" the woman said, holstering her Desert Eagle automatic. "Some kind of terrorist attack?"

"Pretty much," Lyons answered, walking toward the police car. "Terrorists have kidnapped Brandon Duvall, and escaped in an airboat."

"Who is it, sir?" the woman demanded. "Those al Qaeda assholes or Hamas?"

"American Nazi Party," Blancanales lied, hoping to hit a nerve.

It worked, and both of the cops grimaced. "Great day in the morning," the man whispered. "Arkansas Nazis?"

"What do you boys need?" the woman demanded, hitching up her gun belt. "We'll be happy to ride along and lend a hand. I'm Ardell and that's Harlan."

"Never hurts to have a cop along to confirm that a suspect, ahem, resisted arrest," Harlan said, giving a knowing wink.

"And we got a grenade launcher in the trunk," Ardell added. "They only issue us smoke canisters and some tear gas, but I do believe a couple of HE shells might have been accidentally stored in there somewhere, too."

"What we need most is intel," Schwarz said, opening the door for his wounded friend. "Have there been any sightings of the airboat downtown?"

Grunting slightly, Lyons slid into the passenger seat. For once, the former Los Angeles cop had no objection to the freewheeling style of law enforcement in the Deep South. This time it was working in their favor.

"You bet," Ardell drawled. "The goddamn thing streaked halfway across town causing a dozen accidents before crashing through the display window of KRPQ."

"Anybody hurt?" Blancanales asked, going behind the wheel and starting the engine. The big V-8 roared into life sounding louder than a B-1 bomber.

"A couple of folks walking on the sidewalk," Harlan answered, getting into the rear. Nobody had to tell him that from this point on, Homeland was in charge, not the police. "We think a janitor was also killed by the thing before it crashed into the reception desk."

"Then the Nazis took everybody hostage," Ardell added grimly, resting the shotgun between her legs. "No accurate numbers yet, but they should be in the vicinity of thirty civilians, and maybe two night watchman."

Which meant that Duvall now had human shields. "Is KRPQ a radio or a television station?" Schwarz demanded, joining the cops on the rear seat.

"Radio," Harlan replied. "Biggest in the state. On a clear night, I understand that folks can hear it all the way out in New Orleans."

"That far away?" Blancanales growled, shifting gears to back away from the river, then turned toward the city.

"Sure. Clear as a bell, too."

Easing the Atchisson to the floor mat, Lyons bit back a curse. With coverage like that, the goddamn radio station would have over a million potential listeners, even at this time of night. If Duvall broadcast the plans for the T-bombs over the radio there would be no way to stop the spread of the information until it reached the wrong people, and then an entirely new type of war would sweep across the world.

"Must still be using repeater towers," Schwarz concluded as the police car hit a pothole. "Probably connected to the station with landlines buried deep underground. This is 1930s technology."

"Works fine," Ardell replied, slightly insulted.

"Have they broadcast anything yet?" Schwarz demanded, snapping open his laptop.

"How would we know?" Ardell asked.

"Nothing has gone out yet," Schwarz replied, touching his earbud.

"We're trying to cut the power," Harlan replied, tilting slightly as the police car raced around a sharp turn. "But that's not an easy thing to do, even in an emergency."

"Leaving us caught between a Rock and a hard place," Schwarz said with particular emphasis.

"Is there any way to stop a broadcast?" Lyons asked, relaxing slightly as the vehicle reached pavement and started rapidly accelerating. There were other cars and trucks on the road, but they hurriedly got out of the way of the screaming police car.

"Sure," Schwarz replied grimly. "We could have the Air Force bomb every tower. But that would take hours."

"How about blowing up the station?" Blancanales asked, veering around a truck full of sheep heading to market.

"You can't do that," Harlan said, hunching his shoulders. "That building is in downtown Little Rock."

"We'd prefer not to," Lyons said honestly, pulling out a med kit to once again start repairs on his arm. The river had washed away most of the blood, but now he was worried about an infection from the dirty water.

Just then a downtown building went dark, leaving a black gap in the twinkling skyline.

"That's the station," Harlan gasped.

"Okay, they're off the air now," Schwarz stated. "That buys us some time."

"Unless they have a backup generator."

"Do they?" Lyons grunted, injecting himself with a second NATO Hot Shot. Almost immediately, the pain faded away again, but his ears began to ring slightly and his heart began wildly pounding in his chest as if trying to escape.

"Don't know, but I sure would," Schwarz admitted, flipping open his laptop and starting to type. The plasma screen came alive with a vector graphic of the Little Rock skyline.

Streaking across a bridge, the police car flashed past crowds of people lining the sidewalks. There were police on every corner, setting up road blocks and directing away the civilian traffic.

"Okay, we have some combat room," Blancanales muttered, stomping on the gas. "What's the plan? Charge in through the busted window and—"

"Can't," Ardell interrupted. "Not shouldn't, but can't. The security shutters were closed after they got inside. The whole building is sealed with steel over every door and window. Crime is pretty bad in the Rock at night, and most stores and offices use 'em."

"So why was the display window exposed?" Lyons asked bluntly, flexing his arm to check the new bandage over the graze. It hurt, but seemed fully functional.

The two cops could only shrug in reply. But Lyons knew. Because Duvall owned the station, and probably ordered the staff to raise the shutters while racing through traffic. There was probably no way through the protective barriers without using explosives. Which the team could not use because there could be a hostage on the other side of the closed shutter.

Taking a corner, the dark building was suddenly directly ahead of the car, and Blancanales swerved to the curb and braked to a halt. "All right, tell your captain to get SWAT hot and start pounding the ground-floor shutters with small-caliber rounds," he directed, throwing open the door. "Don't stop until we tell you."

Stepping to the curb, Ardell frowned. "But small arms fire ain't gonna do shit against...oh."

"It's a diversion to cover you, boys." Harlan grinned, closing the door. "The offer is still good. You're both crack shots."

"Then don't shoot us when we come out with Duvall," Schwarz muttered, closing the laptop and exiting the vehicle

"Good luck, Officers," Lyons stated firmly, clearly dismissing the pair.

The police hesitated for only a moment, then snapped a salute and charged off into the night.

"Duvall built that radio station into a fucking fortress," Blancanales growled, working the arming bolt on his assault rifle. "So how do we get inside?"

"Easy. We fly, of course," Schwarz replied, breaking into a run toward the bank on the corner.

However, the team barely got halfway across the street when a dim figure appeared on top of the radio station carrying what appeared to be an old-fashioned bazooka.

"Incoming!" Lyons bellowed, redoubling his speed to get around the corner of the bank.

The other two men followed his lead and they were almost there when the bazooka gave a dull thump and the intersection was suddenly blanketed by flames and screams.

CHAPTER SEVENTEEN

Podbanske Base, Slovakia

Moving low and fast, Phoenix Force swam through the turgid water of the river that would allow them access to the missile base. Their insulated diving suits helped to keep them mobile, but the bitter cold of the nearly frozen water seeped in through every tiny opening, and it felt as if they were being stabbed with knives. Fortunately their Navy SEAL rebreathers actually warmed the air before the team breathed it. Apparently, Price had considered the possibility of a mountain base, and had included the rebreathers with the replacement Hercules. Mack Bolan himself had once joked that aside from the bullets in his gun, the next most important piece of equipment at the Farm was the mind of Barbara Price.

Kurtzman and Wethers had proposed using the underground river as their insertion point into the Podbanske Base. Little more than a deep creek, the river was so small that it was not even on a lot of maps, yet it was listed as deep enough to support aquatic research. During the winter months, when ice blocked a lot of the nearby tributaries and the excess water merged into the river, it was a secret doorway that was only usable for a few weeks.

The stygian blackness of the underground river was nearly absolute, and Phoenix Force could only navigate by the chemical glow sticks in their gloves. Oddly, there were plenty of fish swimming in the water, but the pale creatures were nearly translucent and completely without eyes, giving them an unearthly appearance.

Silvery plant life clung to the rocky bottom of the icy river, and the poor things visibly shrank whenever one of the team members got too close. However, McCarter figured that was actually working in their favor. Twice so far they had found bald patches where the delicate plants were dead, and the team had wisely skirted along the banks of the river to keep as far away as possible from whatever the Slovakians had buried at those locations. There was no active sonar registering on their helmet sensors, so it had to be a passive sonar, and those were easily fooled. Every member of the team wore a squealer, a small device that broadcast the sound of a school of fish swimming along, to cover their own movements. If the passive sonar was from the Cold War, they were completely safe. However, if the Slovakian general had purchased some brandnew sonar equipment from Milan, then when the team arrived at the base they would be walking into a bloody ambush.

Unfortunately there was no other choice. Podbanske Base was nuke-proof, and when the blast doors closed there was literally no way to gain entrance in less than a month of hard work with drills and thermite lances. The underground river was more than the sole possible access; it was also their only hope. If this avenue failed, then the President would be forced to authorize NATO to nuke the entire valley, in spite of the fact that there were fishing villages and farms nearby. To save a billion lives, a thousand innocent people might have to die. It was the cold equation in their brutal war against global terrorism. But the team would do everything in its power to prevent that dire event from happening, including risking their own lives to save people they had never met or would ever know. That, too, was part of a soldier's burden.

Suddenly the river widened into a basin, and the team went to the walls once more, rising slowly, weapons in hand. Long ago, the Navy SEALs had invented a handgun that could fire underwater, the Heckler & Koch P-11. The range of the steel darts was pitiful, less than a hundred feet, and even worse in the open air, plus the weapon had to be sent back to the shop to be reloaded by special machinery, so those five darts were all the Stony Man operatives had available. Unfortunately the Soviets had invented a machine gun version and against those the team had no chance at all, but an HK P-11 was better than a knife or a clunky spear gun.

A large shape dominated the basin, and McCarter could soon see that it was a small submersible, likely a last-resort escape option for the base commander. He placed a glove on the hull, but there were no detectable vibrations from an engine. Checking through a visor, he saw that the submersible registered as the same temperature as the water.

Swimming closer, James pointed at the submersible, then flipped his glove over in a question. McCarter nodded assent and the man reached into a shoulder bag to ease out a big block of H-3, the underwater version of C-4. Gently, James attached the block to the rear propellers, then inserted a tumbler and turned the arming dial twice. As soon as the propellers began to turn, the tumbler would activate, and two minutes later the H-3 would blow off the blades and twist the shaft into a corkscrew, beaching the Soviet vessel permanently.

Proceeding to the edge of a natural dock, Hawkins extracted a flexible pipe from his belt and slowly raised it out of the water to look around. The tiny mirrors inverted everything, but that made little difference. The dock was completely dark, and there could be a hundred terrorists waiting there, and he would have no way of knowing.

The rocky basin suddenly shuddered and the submarine moved away from the dock until reaching the end of the moorings chains before slowly coming back to loudly slam into the rock.

Using hand gestures, Manning a question, but the rest of the team indicated they had no idea. Unless...

"Missile launch," McCarter mumbled around his mouthpiece, realizing in horror that they might be too late. His hand touched the transceiver on his belt to inform the Farm, but he knew this far underground the radio would be useless. There was no choice. If the Slovakians were launching missiles, this hard probe had just become a blitzkrieg.

Yanking a stun grenade from a belt pouch, McCarter grabbed hold of the iron rungs sunk into the rock to pull himself out of the water and throw. The grenade hit the dock and rattled along a few feet before erupting into a deafening report and a blinding flash. However, there were no answering cries of shock, so the team hastily crawled out of the water with their P-11 guns at the ready. Something moved to his right, and Encizo instinctively fired, the steel dart whooshing away on a smoky contrail to loudly clang into a bucket that tumbled along the dock making more noise than the stun grenade.

"Well, they know we're here now," Hawkins whispered into his throat mike, while tossing around a couple of glow sticks.

"Right, because that was a silent stun grenade," Manning retorted, doing the same thing.

In the ghostly illumination of the chemical sticks, the team could now see that the dock area was completely empty, without a soul in sight. There was a tunnel lined with wooden doors leading deeper into the mountains, ending at a set of metal double doors. Slapping the release buckle on their chest harness, the men dropped the heavy rebreathers and assumed a combat formation to start running along the tunnel, low and fast.

"This place is exactly like Balaklava," James muttered, holstering the P-11 and swinging around a watertight bag to extract his MP-5 subgun. There was no silencer attached to the end of the barrel this time.

"I guess using one set of blueprints made building their military bases a lot cheaper than ours," Encizo growled, working the bolt on his machine gun.

"Penny wise, pound foolish, eh, David?" Manning asked in a terrible Cockney accent while unlimbering an MP-5. His massive Barrett rifle was slung across his shoulders, a 750-grain round already in the chamber.

"Fucking A, bubba," McCarter replied in a perfect Kentucky twang.

Pausing at the first open door, the men saw that the room was vacant, steam rising from a cup of coffee on a desk, the smell of food lingering in the cold air.

Boldly going to the cup, Hawkins plunged in a finger. "Lukewarm," he reported. "They left only a few minutes ago."

"Double-time," McCarter barked, charging down the corridor.

As the team approached the end of the passageway, they cut loose with a barrage of 9 mm rounds that slammed the double doors aside. Instantly, there came a chattering reply, small-caliber bullets ricocheting off the floor. The men hit the walls and fired back as McCarter tossed through a couple of glow sticks.

Incredibly, one of the sticks was shot while still in the air, and the other was hit after it bounced only once off the floor. Torn to pieces, their glowing liquid contents splashed to paint the walls with eerie illumination.

Pulling out a plastic mirror, Hawkins cursed at the sight of a steep ramp leading to the next level, and attached to the ceiling directly above the landing was a Samsung Auto-Sentry. As Manning fired his MP-5 blindly up the ramp, the

Auto-Sentry shot back, the rain of the spent brass tumbled down to musically hit the slope and spread out like golden offerings to a pagan god.

"Going to be a triple bitch running up stairs covered with loose ammo," James snarled, working the arming lever to free a bent jam from the ejector port.

"I think that was the idea," Encizo said, pulling out an HE grenade. "Luckily, I brought along a broom."

Pulling the pin and flipping off the arming spoon, the man threw the grenade hard against the floor and it bounced up the ramp. Instantly the Auto-Sentry fired at the military sphere, and a deafening explosion filled the area. Using the blast as cover, McCarter and Hawkins also tossed through grenades, both reaching the upper landing. The double detonations cracked the walls, and there came a tremendous metallic crash as something large hit the ramp.

The battered Auto-Sentry tumbled through the open doorway, the machine still firing a stream of .22 rounds. Encizo and James were both hit in the stomach, the soft lead embedded into their body armor like tiny gray flowers. Dropping his MP-5, Manning brought up the Barrett and fired from the hip. The cigar-size bullet slammed through the chattering Auto-Sentry, sending out a spray of electronic circuits, and it promptly stopped working, the servo-motors revving down to silence.

The noise of the destruction was still echoing along the corridor when Phoenix Force reached the second landing. Slowing for a moment, James doubled over to clutch his aching stomach and retch into a waste can, then the man forced himself erect, his face even more grim than before.

"You okay, brother?" Hawkins asked in concern.

"Never better," James snarled, wiping his mouth clean on a sleeve of his wet suit.

"Want a Hot Shot?"

"Rather have a breath mint," James joked, managing a half smile.

However, Hawkins saw the man's face was oddly pale, and knew the former Navy SEAL must have taken some damage from the Auto-Sentry. Changing the rhythm of his running, the Texan matched pace with his friend, and they continued through the underground base side by side.

Reaching an intersection, the team quickly separated, two men taking each branch, the maze of corridors and tunnels serving its designed purpose of slowing invaders. But only minutes later, they reconvened at the control room for the Soviet ICBM arsenal. The door was locked, but a single round from the Barrett fixed that problem, and the men poured into the room.

The curved room was fronted by a wide bank of controls, topped with a row of small windows, each looking down into a missile silo. Bizarrely, each launch tube contained an old Soviet Union ICBM, dozens of umbilical lines still attached to the aging hulls.

"These things are dead," McCarter snarled, trying to work some of the controls on the panels. "There's no fuel, no power, no...these missiles couldn't launch if you shoved a space shuttle up their arse."

"Then what the hell did we feel shake the base?" Hawkins wondered, looking around. "Could there be a second launch facility?" From his tone, it was clear that the man did really think such a thing was possible.

"Not according to this," Encizo stated, brushing the dust off a chart showing the complex array of pipes to feed liquid oxygen and liquid hydrogen to the huge missiles. "These tanks are marked primary and secondary. Not Fuel Station 1 or anything like that."

Studying the chart, McCarter traced the feeder lines back to the storage tanks, then followed those back to the— "Garage!" he bellowed furiously, and took off at a full sprint.

Charging along the corridors, the team found recent signs of habitation by the thieves, open bedrolls, laundry drying in machines, kerosene heaters blazing away in ward rooms. Clearly the Slovakians were planning on coming back to the base, yet they had left the dock area in haste.

"Somehow they must have heard that we broke out the professor, and changed their plans," Manning snarled, cradling the MP-5 close to his chest. "With any luck, they're running for the hills."

"Or driving," McCarter snapped back.

That dire possibility put fresh energy into the men and they stopped talking, saving every breath for running. Long before the team reached the garage, the Stony Man operatives felt the bitter cold and feared the worst.

As expected, the door was locked, so they used some of the remaining plastic explosive to blow off the hinges, the explosion oddly flamboyant with sparkles from the added aluminum dioxide dust.

Inside was a sandbag nest with two Auto-Sentries, but the machines stood dark and impotent, the computerized targeting systems not activated, the ammunition hoppers not attached to the .22 machine guns.

"They left in a bloody big hurry," McCarter drawled, using the barrel of his MP-5 to shove over one of the robotic killers.

"And there's why," Hawkins snarled, advancing a step.

In the middle of the garage was a double row of SS-25 missile trucks. The colossal fourteen-wheel vehicles were surrounded by loose tools, stepladders, welding equipment and portable laptop computers. The nose cones of each missile had been removed, the nuclear warheads removed and the interior machinery fully exposed, loose wiring dangling free.

Directly ahead of the fleet was a huge door, the truncated slab of lead, steel and cadmium cycled aside to show the wintry exterior of the Tatra Mountains. A pristine blanket of white snow covered the ground, and there were numerous tire marks heading off in different directions.

"That noise we heard was the blast door cycling up," McCarter realized angrily. "They're going to use these solid-state missiles to launch the T-bombs."

"What kind of a prep time is required?" Manning demanded, checking his watch.

"Once a truck is in position, ten minutes, maybe less."

Nowhere near long enough to have the Farm send in a wing of NATO jets and nuke the entire valley, McCarter realized. Win or lose, the team would have to handle this on its own.

"Well, we can't chase 'em on foot," Encizo growled. "Anything else here?"

"Just the other trucks," Hawkins said in a surge on excitement, slinging the MP-5 over a shoulder and climbing into a cab. It took a few times to get the big engines to turn over, then it caught with a throaty roar.

"Five trucks outside," James announced returning from the exit. "So everybody grab a set of wheels."

"How's the fuel?" Encizo demanded, heading for a truck.

"Half tank," Hawkins yelled out the window, already rumbling toward the exit.

"Same here," Manning added, climbing into another cab. The view was limited as the SS-25 missile extended over the cab for a good twenty feet, The interior smelled musty with age, a loose spring was stabbing his butt and the labels were in Cyrillic, but there was a single big red button on the dashboard that either fired the missile or started the engine. He pressed it hard and a second later the diesel sputtered to life, black fumes blowing out of the side exhaust pipes.

"Don't use the radios—they might be able to hear us," McCarter instructed, climbing into the cab and pushing aside some yellowed copies of *Pravda* announcing Stalin's birthday twenty years ago. The throttle was sticky, but the engine started immediately, and he ground the gears until finding forward.

"Should we try to capture a T-bomb?" James yelled out the window.

"Negative. Kill these people on sight!" McCarter bellowed, gunning the engine to try to get the temperature up fast. You could push a cold gasoline engine, but diesels needed to be warm to really pour on the speed.

Rapidly accelerating, the huge trucks lumbered out of the Soviet missile base and rumbled into the snowy forest, each Stony Man operative following a different set of tire tracks until they vanished from sight.

CHAPTER EIGHTEEN

Downtown Little Rock

Seeing the flash of light in the windshield of the cars parked along the curb, the men of Able Team braced themselves for the coming shock wave. A split second later, a terrible wind slammed them off the ground and sent them tumbling along the sidewalk, smashing into parking meters, mailboxes and storefronts.

As the force wave dissipated, the three Stony Man operatives rose stiffly, each man checking for broken bones. Some equipment had been lost, but their Level Five body armor had saved their lives once more, along with their basic training in boot camp on how to tuck and roll.

"Mother of God," Blancanales whispered, looking back at the rampaging destruction of the intersection. The side streets were still covered with debris and pools of crackling flames. Bodies lay everywhere, amid burning cars and endless piles of sparkling glass. The police barricades and the yellow warning tape were long gone, only a scattering of clothing and guns to mark that they had ever existed.

"That wasn't big enough for a T-bomb," Schwarz said with a dry mouth. "Must have been a Fay bomb."

The garbled word puzzled Lyons for a moment until he realized that the man must have actually said a FAE bomb, the fuel-air-explosive charges used by the U.S. Marines. Just for a trembling moment of time, Lyons felt a touch of true fear. Then he shrugged it off and concentrated on the task at hand. Find Duvall, get the plans, blow off his head and not necessarily in that order.

Staggering out from behind a pile of bodies appeared a bedraggled Ardell. Most of her uniform was still burning, her hair gone, and her face only a blistered ruin. Blindly she was dragging the body of Harlan, his chest blown open wide to expose his smoking organs.

"I got ya, buddy," she gurgled, rivulets of red blood trickling down what had once been her face. "I got ya, pal."

Then she suddenly collapsed and went still, her torment ended forever.

A dull thumping noise sounded again, farther away this time, and a monstrous light billowed from the other side of the bank, closely followed by a deafening shattering of glass and a thousand voices screaming in agony.

"The son of a bitch is bombing the city!" Blancanales raged, taking a step forward, then coming to an abrupt halt. There was nothing the soldier could do to help the civilians, aside from making damn sure no more of them died.

"We end this bastard now!" Schwarz cursed in uncharacteristic rage.

"Agreed," Lyons growled. "Let's go."

As the men started running along the street, in the distance they heard a hundred fire alarms clanging steadily and the howl of a tornado siren, the device activated by the brief maelstrom of the airborne detonation.

Briefly, Blancanales touched his throat mike, then let go. There was no need to put in a call for help. Soon enough everybody in the state, and then the nation, would know about the disaster, and help would start pouring in from the National Guard, the Red Cross and maybe even FEMA.

Angling into an alleyway, Lyons put his back to the wall and cupped his hands. But Blancanales did the same thing, and Schwarz stepped into the cupped hands of his friend and reached upward to grab the bottom rung of a fire escape. Kicking a few times, the man got the rusty metal into motion and with a deafening squeal it slid down to street level, accompanied by a rain of corroded steel.

Scrambling up the zigzagging iron, the men reached the roof and skirted around some brick chimneys to look down upon the roof of KRPQ. The city to the west and north of the building was in flames, and the team took aim, waiting for a target.

Walking around a huge air conditioner unit came a man in a black-and-gray urban-camouflage gillie suit. He was holding what appeared to be an old-style bazooka, and was whistling a happy tune as he removed a cylindrical round from a bulging canvas bag hanging at his side. Going to the east side of the building, he loaded in the charge and started locking down the rear port when Able Team opened fire.

The combined noise of the military weapons was nearly lost in the cacophony swelling from the burning city below, but the killer jerked madly from the incoming rounds and tumbled over the edge of the roof to drop out of sight.

His death scream was still in the air when Lyons grabbed his throat mike. "Jungle Cat to Rock House!" he barked. "We need Little Rock black for sixty. Black in sixty!"

"We were expecting this, Jungle Cat," Price replied crisply. "Black for sixty in four, three, two, one..." At that precise instant, the entire city of Little Rock went dark, every electric light winking out.

Quickly slinging his canvas web belt over a high-voltage power cable, Lyons grabbed on with both hands, ran to the edge of the roof and jumped off the building. Pain took his right arm, and the man held back a cry as the open alleyway flashed below his boots. Just a few seconds more...hold on... you can do it...

"Now, Carl!" Schwarz yelled.

Instantly, Lyons came awake and released the belt. The fall was only a few feet and he hit the roof in a crouch, then quickly stepped aside. Moments later, Schwarz arrived, then Blancanales.

Moving in unison, the three men raced to the brick kiosk and riddled the sheet metal covering the door with hot lead. A strangled cry came from the other side, and the door creaked aside as the bleeding body of another camouflaged bodyguard fell into view.

The electric lights returned across the city, the sirens wailing louder than ever.

Putting an additional round into the man's head just to be sure, Lyons started down the stairs. His every nerve was sharp, and reality seemed crystal-clear, almost preternatural. He knew that was a combination of the drugs and adrenaline. For the moment he was a berserker like the Vikings of yore. A bullet in the heart would kill him, but not stop him for a precious few seconds, and as long as he saw Duvall fall, that would be enough.

Reaching the top floor of the building, the team paused at the sight of three armed men, then continued running when they realized it had been their own reflection in a decorative glass wall. Inside the building was dark, the only illumination coming from a scattering of battery-powered emergency lights set into small niches in the corners of the ceiling. The elongated shadows made everything seem distorted and unnatural.

At the elevator, Blancanales checked the wall chart to see which floor the radio station was on, but cursed when he saw only blank nylon, the floor littered with broken letters. The clever bastards had swiped the board clean.

Yanking out a canteen, Schwarz took a swig then sprayed the board, the water sticking to where the letters had previously been. The studio was on five, the executive offices on this floor, the transmitter and power relays in the basement.

"Studio," Lyon said, gambling everything on the feeling that Duvall would want to be sitting in the control room when he issued a death warrant for civilization. Having a son of his own, the man understood the anguish that must be tearing the billionaire apart. But that was no excuse for wholesale murder; nothing was. A judge and jury might forgive the man, but Lyons was neither, and blood would be the price for Duvall's heinous acts of cowardice.

Running down the stairs, the men cursed as the interior lights came on.

"He got the emergency generator working," Blancanales snarled.

"Just makes it easier to blow off his head," Lyons replied, thumbing individual shells into the Atchisson. Hopefully, his many years of training would pay off in the next few minutes, or else America would pay a terrible price for his failure.

Reaching the fifth level, the team saw a remote-control video camera mounted on top of a soda machine. Aiming and firing in one smooth motion, Lyons shot the fire extinguisher on the opposite wall. The canister dented, then erupted in a wild gush of foam that completely covered the vidcam.

"FBI!" Blancanales shouted, firing another round into the ceiling. "Come out with your hands raised!"

"Homeland Security!" Schwarz added. "Surrender or die!"

A fusillade of rounds answered the men, and they responded in kind, then added some stun grenades. Minus a visor, Schwarz turned to face the wall while Lyons and Blancanales advanced into the booming flash, the cries of the hidden enemies targeting their precise locations. Without remorse, the men of Able Team gunned down the bodyguards as they entered the studio. People bound with duct tape were lashed to chairs in a small lobby, but Lyons and Blancanales ignored them to advance on the studio doors. It was another glass wall, and they saw Schwarz enter the lobby then turn and fire.

His gun partially out of a holster, Russell collapsed back into his chair, lengths of loose duct tape flapping around his wrists like limp tentacles.

"River mud on his sneakers," Schwarz said in explanation, rejoining his teammates.

The glass door to the studio was jammed with loose furniture, desks, chairs and computers piled high as a makeshift barricade. Opening fire, Able Team took out the walls on either side, the avalanche of shattering glass deafeningly loud.

"Stop right there. I have a hostage!" a voice called from behind the control panel. Then Duvall came into view holding a little girl tight to his chest, a Colt automatic pressed tight to her forehead.

Whimpering under the crushing arm, the child wiggled to get free, her eyes wide in terror.

Instantly, Lyons fired.

The 12-gauge stun bags smacked against the cinder-block wall behind the billionaire to bounce off and slamming him hard in the back. Stumbling forward, Duvall dropped the child, and Blancanales and Schwarz opened fire, the 5.56 mm rounds and 6.8 mm rounds taking away his life in hammering fury.

Sweeping the controls with a fast gaze, Lyons cursed at the sight of the power meters, the needles quivering near maximum. The goddamn station was already broadcasting! Every second counted, so he opened fire, the next two stun bags from the Atchisson merely denting on the control board, then the fléchette rounds kicked in and the controls disintegrated under the barrage.

"Did we stop it?" Blancanales asked over a shoulder, placing his weapon aside to pick up the crying child. She fought against his touch, then succumbed in whimpering terror.

"Did we?" Lyons asked, feeling the rush of battle starting to leave, his arms becoming incredibly heavy.

"I don't know yet," Schwarz muttered, sliding into a chair and flipping some switches. That was when the damaged board exploded into electrical sparks and the man was thrown out of the chair with the terrible reek of roasting meat.

Podbanske Base, Slovakia

IT WAS NEARLY NOON and the sun was directly over the rugged Tatra Mountains, the light reflecting off the numerous frozen waterfalls and millions of icicles dangling off the evergreen trees and wild laurel bushes. To a frowning McCarter, the land looked like a Christmas postcard, but felt like the ninth level of Hell. The bitter cold was seeping down into his bones to make every old combat injury throb with newfound pain.

Ponderously, the massive Soviet Union missile truck rolled through the beautiful snowy forest, following the tire tracks of the other vehicle. The vehicles were identical in size, so McCarter tried to stay in the tracks of the first truck, the compressed snow giving him excellent traction and, hopefully, slightly better speed.

However, the armored truck designed to launch a thermonuclear ICBM was anything but fast. In excruciating increments, the speedometer ponderously crawled to fifty kilometers per hour, and the man mentally translated that into miles per hour. Bloody hell, he fumed, my old Robin Reliant could do better than this Cold War relic!

Arching around an escarpment of solid granite, McCarter frantically looked around the old cab to try to find anything he could pitch out the window to try to lighten the vehicle. But there was nothing in sight but the ancient newspaper and some ossified cigarette butts. There might be something in the rear of the truck that he could heave, spare tires, extra asbestos shielding, but that would mean he'd have to stop first, which would make him lose valuable seconds.

Desperately, McCarter considered launching the missile, but it would take too long, and lacking a nose cone meant there was also no navigation system. The missile could go anywhere, including right back down on him or the White House or Windsor Castle, so that ploy was completely out of the question.

The sylvan landscape was a pristine white around the creeping death machine, almost painfully beautiful, with the only sign of humans the double row of tire tracks in the glistening snow. There was no road through the dense Slovakian forest, and the trail endlessly snaked around boulders and copses of pine trees, dipping down into icy creeks and streams.

The cab was intensely cold, but McCarter knew that turning on the heater would put a drain on the engine. So he hunkered down, concentrating on mentally willing the huge machine to move faster. Then the inside of the windshield began to fog from his breath, so he rolled down both windows and suffered the bitter mountain wind, doubly thankful that he still was wearing the insulated diving suit. Unfortunately, every breath felt like he was inhaling needles, and suddenly he understood the plethora of cigarettes on the floor.

There was a movement in the forest far ahead of McCarter. Squinting through the dirty windshield, he wasn't sure if that was the other truck, and deliberately swerved the vehicle slightly to hit the low branches of a tree to knock some of the snow off. As it fell onto the missile overhead, the breeze blew some onto the windshield and he hit the wipers. Incredibly, they worked, and his view noticeably cleared.

Keeping a gloved hand tight on the steering wheel, McCarter swung up his MP-5 subgun and placed a finger on the trigger. At the moment he was heading to the left, and the motion had been to the far right, just past a small pond and some trees covered with glistening icicles. Come on, ya toffee-nosed bastards, he raged privately. Just show me your fat arse one more time….

Incredibly, there came the telltale sound of an engine, and a puff of black exhaust appeared above the trees to instantly vanish. It was them.

Savagely turning the wheel, McCarter charged directly for the pond, the colossal weight of the truck cracking the ice louder than a gunshot. Thick blue water rose over the bumper, a trickle leaking in through the door seal and moving the cigarette butts. Holding the course, McCarter prayed that the pond wasn't deep enough to choke the engine. Come on, just a few yards more. Then the water withdrew as the hood began to rise again, and he was back on the snow. The desperate maneuver had just saved him a hundred feet of distance, but it wasn't quite enough.

The trees were starting to thin, and soon McCarter would be in open country. That would make this a fair race, which meant that he would lose and millions would die. That was unacceptable. Time to kick over the table.

Slamming on the brakes, McCarter fought the massive truck to a ragged halt, hit the autolaunch controls and scrambled out of the cab. He hit the snow running, and charged into the bushes, knocking away a host of icicles.

Behind him, McCarter could hear the pneumatic jacks anchoring the truck, and then the hydraulic pumps activating to slowly raise the missile skyward. Breathing through his nose, McCarter tried to hear past the mechanical noises and was rewarded with the telltale sound of a truck door slamming, closely followed by the hard pats of somebody running over the compacted snow of the tire tracks. The Slovakians had heard the sound of the pumps, and sent somebody to see what was happening.

Crouching low in the bushes, McCarter swung up his MP-5 and waited. Seconds later a man came running into view. He was wearing a military parka and carrying a Samopal assault rifle wrapped in rags to keep the firing mechanism warm. A bulging ammunition pouch hung at his side, along with a hand radio and there was a bandolier across his chest of 30 mm shells.

Raising the MP-5, the Stony Man operative tracked the motion of the enemy soldier to get the rhythm of his steps, then fired a single round. A black hole appeared in the back of the parka, and red blood sprayed out from the front as the man jerked, then fell flat into the snow. Dashing forward, McCarter grabbed the Samopal and checked the load in the 30 mm grenade launcher. High-explosive antipersonnel. Perfect.

Now moving relatively silently along the compacted snow, McCarter strained to hear the engine of the first truck, but the hydraulic thumping of his vehicle filled the forest. Never slowing for an instant, McCarter mentally gauged the wind, angled the stolen weapon over the tree and fired. The 30 mm shell was still in the air when he got a second round into the breach and fired again slightly more to the right, then once more.

The first explosion rocked the forest, knocking loose tons of snow from the trees and bushes and suddenly exposing the enemy vehicle.

Launching another grenade, McCarter tried for the cab, but the shell glanced off the SS-25 ICBM and exploded harmlessly in midair. Thumbing in a fresh round, he aimed for the double row of tires, when somebody leaned out of the cab and cut loose with a Samopal on full auto. The hot lead slapped into the snow all around McCarter, and something tugged on his shoulder, but the man never slowed or tried to take cover. Instead, he raised both of his weapons and cut loose, bracing the bucking guns against each other to try to steady his aim. The 7.62 mm rounds threw sparks off the armored side of the missile truck, but the hardball 9 mm Parabellum rounds buried into the military tires. Unfortunately, none of them went flat as the resilient material proved itself completely bulletproof.

Understanding what McCarter was trying to do, the man in the cab slammed the door shut, then leaned out the window to aim the Samopal with both hands. Diving forward, McCarter felt something hard slap him in the back and then in the chest as he came up still in motion. Damn, the man was a good shot.

Releasing the MP-5, McCarter let it drop by the strap and he answered with the grenade launcher. The shell slammed into the side of the truck, seriously denting the metal but not exploding as the range had been too short for the explosive charge in the warhead to arm. However, the tactic served its purpose, and the Slovakian ducked back inside, only to reappear a few seconds later holding a second Samopal, and firing both of them in the exact same manner as McCarter had earlier.

A swarm of hot lead hummed past the running man, and McCarter emptied the Samopal in reply, then drew the HK P-11 and started pulling the trigger. The 7 mm steel darts whooshed away in a tight spiral to slam into the military tires and out the other side, the packs of fuel still propelling them constantly onward. McCarter put all of the darts into the rear tire, and it finally came off the rim in tattered shreds. The truck shook slightly and veered, slamming into an outcropping of rocks. Caught by surprise, the soldier in the window vehemently cursed as his Samopal went sailing.

Tossing aside the spent weapon, McCarter charged full speed at the truck while throwing a grenade. It hit the side mirror and bounced into the cab—only to come right back out of the driver's side window and explode harmlessly into the scraggly bushes.

Just then there came a thundering roar from the other side of some trees and roiling flame exploded into being as the headless SS-25 launched into the air—destination unknown.

Ignoring the launch, McCarter concentrated on putting all of his strength into running after the escaping truck, and threw his last grenade as high as he could. As the ICBM streaked upward, the grenade lofted high, buffeted by the hurricane-force exhaust, and came down directly in front of the lumbering transport.

Instantly, the driver veered off to the side, but it was too late. The thermite grenade detonated into a staggering fireball underneath the truck that engulfed half a dozen tires, setting them ablaze.

Trying to recover control of the truck, the driver plowed through some bushes, heading for a frozen creek. But the burning tires began to peel off the rims, and the vehicle began to slow as it started to tilt. Steering away from the tilt to compensate, the driver got the truck upright once more, then slammed on the brakes and fought the vehicle to a complete stop. But then there came the sound of the pneumatic pumps anchoring the truck motionless as a prelude to a launch.

Slapping a fresh clip into the MP-5, McCarter fired a short burst at the passenger's side window, then dived behind the truck and sent a much longer volley at the driver's side. As the door started to open, the trick worked and the lead hammered it completely aside, exposing the driver. He was a small man, thin, almost skeletal, with a bushy mustache and a scar across his craggy features. It was Iron Ivan, the leader of the Slovakian renegades, Brigadier General Ivan Novostk.

Going for a kill, McCarter put the rest of the clip into the old man's chest, blowing off chunks of the thick parka and exposing the Dragonskin body armor underneath.

Moving with astonishing speed, Novostk drew a massive Rex .357 Magnum revolver and shot back twice.

The brutal recoil of the big-bore hand cannon should have been impossible for such an elderly man to control, but apparently Novostk knew how to handle it and McCarter was slammed in the chest by the booming Magnum rounds. He fell over backward, landing on his wounded arm, but the man immediately rolled to the side. A split second later, the snowy ground erupted from the arrival of two more .357 Magnum bone-shredders exactly where he had just been.

Loudly, the hydraulic pumps began cycling the SS-25 missile upward, the rear wheels locking into place, an asbestos shield extending from the chassis.

Clawing at his web belt, McCarter got his Browning Hi-Power out of its watertight holster and jacked the slide just as Novostk fired again, missing this time, and then the two men fired in unison. Breath exploded out of McCarter as he doubled over from the belly shot, but as the man forced himself to rise once more, he saw the general sliding down the cab, his left eye now only a gaping hole.

Stumbling away from the truck, McCarter heard the mechanical locks engage as the SS-25 became fully upright. Searching desperately in the snow, McCarter finally saw the dropped Samopal and dived upon the weapon just as the fiery exhaust of the ICBM began thundering from the bottom vectors. Praying there was a shell in the grenade launcher, the man aimed at the asbestos shield and squeezed the trigger. The range was ridiculously short, but just enough to arm the warhead, and the 30 mm shell blew the shield off the truck. The hellish wash of the missile flowed unimpeded across the pneumatic anchors, and they visibly bent under the volcanic outpouring. As the truck tilted once more, the missile listed off balance and began to topple over. Immediately the internal guidance system tried to correct and the ICBM lurched in the opposite direction to slam into the truck and crack apart, the third and second stage coming free as the first stage streaked skyward.

In stentorian majesty the other two sections of the crippled missile slammed into the ground and rolled away from each other, their own internal systems scrambled beyond endurance.

The second stage careened into the trees, the engine unexpectedly roaring into operation, the wash setting the bushes on fire and coating the frozen trees. Knowing what was coming next, McCarter dived for cover as the frozen sap violently exploded, sending out a deafening cloud of wood chips and splinters.

The first stage slammed into the Soviet truck, flattening the body of the dead general into a horrid pulp. The nose cone broke free with the sound of tortured metal and the gleaming white decahedron of the T-bomb rolled into view, trailing a wild tangle of sparking wires. It came to a halt less than fifty feet from McCarter, then several of the pyramids began to glow a bright orange as the primary detonation sequence was triggered early.

Rushing to the decahedron, McCarter slapped a fresh clip into the Browning and started emptying the 9 mm automatic into the humming device, gambling that the trick to kill a nuclear weapon also worked on thermobaric bombs.

EPILOGUE

Oval Office, White House

"So, where did the wild SS-25 go?" the President asked, leaning forward in his chair to rest both elbows on the desk.

"A cornfield in Iowa," Hal Brognola replied.

The President frowned. "It actually made it that far into America without being shot down?"

"Sadly, yes."

"Anybody hurt in Iowa?"

"Just a cow named Annabelle."

"What in hell was a cow doing in the middle of a cornfield?"

"Stealing some corn."

"More proof that crime does not pay," the President said with a wan smile. "What about the other missiles?"

"All of them were destroyed on the ground or captured intact."

"Intact? Impressive, very impressive," the President said, then stopped talking as there was a knock on the door and a steward entered with a tray of sandwiches and coffee.

"And what about your people?" the President continued, lacing his long fingers together. The coffee smelled excellent, and it had been many hours since his last hurried meal with his wife and daughters, but you could not ask life-and-death questions while stuffing your face without appearing to be a complete jackass. His grandmother had taught him that truism.

"At the moment, every member of both teams is in the hospital recovering from his wounds, except for one," Brognola reported. "The man has the luck of a Mississippi river gambler."

"The man who was electrocuted in Arkansas survived?"

"Sir, he has been zapped so many times, I think it makes him stronger."

"About that," the President continued. "Unless I read your report incorrectly, we failed in Arkansas."

"The death toll from the FAE bombs was staggering, yes, sir," Brognola said with a heartfelt sigh. "And a copy of the plan was broadcast over the radio. However, the Stony Man team had already been flooding the Internet with fake plans, so it was just one set of schematics mixed among hundreds of bullshit versions."

"Hundreds?"

"Hundreds, with more coming. Bear is still pumping out nonsense versions of the T-bomb, and will keep doing so for about a month." He smiled. "Some of them are pretty far out there. One is a combination of a Betamax and a fire extinguisher, while another is just an ordinary air conditioner turned inside-out. Nobody sane would try more than one, or two, of these damned things before figuring out they're all useless."

"But what if somebody does decide to try to build every version?" the President asked with a frown. "Eventually, they'll find the real plans, and we'll be right back where we started."

"No, sir. Every set of plans generated by us includes a tracer circuit. Long before they finish any bomb, the FBI arrives to arrest them…then lets them go."

"Because the plans are nonsense," the President finished, the tension flowing from his face. "Reverse psychology, eh? Clever. Very clever. The nation could have used you in the Cold War, Hal."

Sitting back in the chair, Brognola said nothing, his face a study in neutrality.

"Ah, of course." The President grinned. "Never mind."

"Speaking of which," Brognola said, reaching into a pocket and extracting a computer disk. "These are the real plans."

He laid it on the desk, and the President picked up the shiny CD as if it were radioactive. There had been so many innocent lives lost over the superweapon, from Istanbul to Little Rock, but now he could return a copy of the disk to the Russian ambassador to let the other nation diplomatically know that America was now similarly armed, and the balance of power was restored.

Opening a drawer, the President dropped the disk inside, then sealed it tight with a twist of his thumb on the biometric lock. The doctrine of mutually assured destruction had kept humanity alive for decades, and hopefully it would continue to do so for many more. However, it was good to know that if the doctrine ever failed, and the blood hit the fan, the nation would survive because there was always Stony Man.

The Executioner®

Don Pendleton's

THREAT FACTOR

Warlords threaten to turn Somalia into a battle zone...

A Somali pirate attack raises a red flag when the stolen cargo is Russian tanks and ammunition— enough to start a civil war. Called in to seek and destroy the weapons, Mack Bolan knows the only way to head off future bloodshed is to cause some deadly mayhem of his own!

GOLD EAGLE®

Available September wherever books are sold.

TAKE 'EM FREE

2 action-packed
novels plus a
mystery bonus

NO RISK
NO OBLIGATION TO BUY

JAMES AXLER

DEATH LANDS

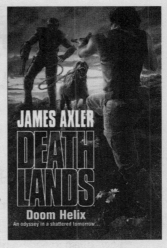

Doom Helix

A new battle for Deathlands has begun...

The Deathlands feudal system may be hell on earth but it must be protected from invaders from Shadow Earth, a parallel world stripped clean of its resources by the ruling conglomerate and its white coats. Ryan and his band had a near-fatal encounter with them once before and now these superhuman predators are back, ready to topple the hellscape's baronies one by one.

Available September wherever books are sold.